RHUGER'S CRIDHE

ORC MATCHED BOOK 1.5

CARLOTTA HUGHES

WWW.AUTHORCARLOTTAHUGHES.COM

First Edition
ISBN: 978-0-9893799-6-0 [EBOOK]
ISBN: 978-0-9893799-7-7 [PRINT]

www.authorcarlottahughes.com

For Connor.

May the Morrigan's Wings
Guide you swiftly on your journey,
Cloak you from your enemies,
And carry you safely home.

TABLE OF CONTENTS

CONTENT INFORMATION

Content Awareness:

Please note that there are aspects of the story that may be upsetting to some. Rhuger's Cridhe has darker themes than Rhuger's Pearl. It is my responsibility as an author to be transparent with my readers so that they have a comfortable experience.

Chapters in the Table of Contents with an **asterisk*** are chapters that contain *explicit* sensitive content. For a full list of what chapters include what kind of sensitive content, please jump to the Content Awareness section at the back of the book. Please also note that I'm including *mentions* of sensitive content besides *explicit* scenes and they will be marked in the Content Awareness section, accordingly. A full list also exists on my website: *www.authorcarlottahughes.com.*

Positivity Awareness:

Fat body rep, anxiety rep, depression rep, healing trauma, ADHD rep, ASD rep

Autism & Neurodivergent Representation:

Amelia is a character who is autistic and has other neurodivergent experiences. I wanted to have a female main character who is autistic and neurodivergent because of the lack of representation in the romance genre. I am Self-Diagnosed with ASD and neurodivergent. Amelia's experiences are based on my own experiences and mental framework. These experiences do not reflect those of the entire spectrum of ASD and should **NEVER** be used to invalidate another person's lived experiences.

If you have questions regarding the validity of Self-Diagnosis for ASD, I highly suggest you read this paper by the University of Washington's Autism Center *https://tinyurl.com/yc7ukwjz*. Wherein they support self-diagnosis of autism as, most commonly, accurate.

A Note On Orckin Culture:

Because of the decline in the orckin species, their once broad and varied culture was significantly affected. Oral traditions and education were altered or eradicated to keep the wanted narrative. This occurred rather easily, as the orckin industry revolves around trades, and not all orckin are taught to read and write. Thus, some of their traditions passed from common knowledge entirely or were only mentioned in old tales.

This includes alternate forms of life paths for both males and females and gender identity outside of the binary. As the series progresses and humans and orckin find their cridhe mates with one another, the pressures of species propagation significantly ease, allowing for traditions, genders, and philosophies that were stifled to resurface. Especially with humans reintroducing similar concepts with their mates.

It is important to note that while it is not *required* for females in the orckin culture to produce orclings; it is an expectation by their society and often seen as an honor. Not all the five clans approach this in the same way, and often manipulation is used. Which, of course, is not completely informed consent. Consent is a big factor in this series, and occasionally a point of conflict, as they reestablish rules of conduct within their culture.

Overall, as the orckin revive their lost culture, there will be outdated modes of thinking, harsh punishments, misunderstandings, heavy conflict, and compromises.

Teanga Dhubh or Black Tongue, the primary orckin language, is loosely based on Scots Gaelic. A pronunciation guide and index exist at the back of the book. You can find voice clips on my website courtesy of *https://learngaelic.scot/*

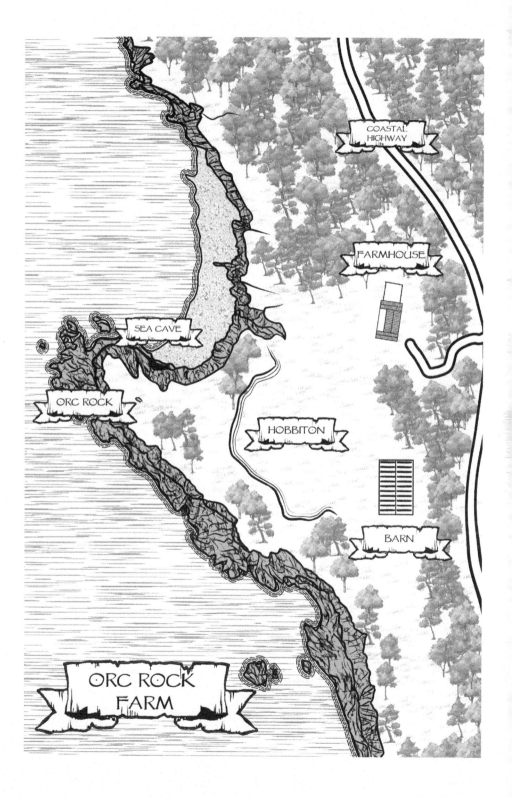

CARLOTTA HUGHES

CHAPTER 01*

AMELIA

"RHUGER!" A bellow reverberated from outside moments before the door to our home tree exploded. All the lovely water flowers my mate had painstakingly carved into it were now reduced to raining splinters.

Rhuger sat up and put himself between me and the door, taking all the wood chunks that would have hit me. The wood bounced off of him, only leaving scrapes. Huge, stomping footfalls echoed in our house. A familiar looming form blocked the light that filled the doorway as I blinked in confusion past Rhuger's tattooed shoulder.

"Grandpa?!" I asked, completely bewildered. My grandfather stomped into the room and pulled out a sword, pointing it at Rhuger with a ferocious scowl. He caught my glare and looked at me with what looked like chagrin as I made sure Rhuger and I were covered and not bare-ass naked to the world. But then he caught Rhuger's gaze as he looked over his shoulder at his Rìgh and the scowl returned.

"Not now, my little chestnut. Grandpa's gotta tan this Oc'Turin hide. Then we can have a pleasant chat over some tea about mating without Grandpa's blessing and-" My grandfather took a deep breath just then. He froze. Gaze darting to me. Or more accurately... at where my stomach was under the bedding.

Tears gathered in my grandfather's eyes, and he sobbed. Dropping his sword, he snatched his hands over his heart like he'd been shot.

"Grandpa...?" I asked, scared that my massive orc grandfather, who could bluster with the best storms, was blubbering and crying big Studio Ghibli tears right in front of me.

"I-I'm going to be a..." He took a deep, fortifying breath. "*GREAT*-grandpa!" The word was strangled at the end as he began bawling with his hands over his face like he was about to die and...

Wait.

WAIT A MINUTE.

"Did you just say..." I began just as Rhuger's head whipped to me, eyes wide and tearing up as well. His gaze searched for something in mine, but I was clueless.

"Rìgh Thorn, are you sure...?" Rhuger rasped, swallowing hard, his voice hoarse on a throat gone dry.

"Smell her yourself, you Oc'Turin *bastard!*" My grandfather wailed as guards came rushing in.

Rhuger clutched me to him, shoving his nose against my neck, and breathed deep. I could tell he smelled *something* because he froze and his grip changed from frantic to something that went beyond tender. His hand slid up through my tangled hair to cup the back of my head.

Pulling away from me, he was openly weeping. He cradled my face in his hands and kissed me so sweetly I forgot anyone else was there for a moment. The captain of the guard, Ophir, coughed, and I pulled away.

Grandpa Thorn was still bawling uncontrollably into Ophir's cape, while another guard I hadn't met yet patted his shoulder. Both *guards* were crying.

"Did I miss something?" I asked anxiously, gaze skittering from male to male as I clutched the blanket to my chest.

"You bear my child, pearl," Rhuger replied, his silver eyes glowing like hazy autumn moons in all that black as he gave me the most heartbreaking smile. Rhuger's whisper carried and my Grandpa Thorn began howling anew.

I looked at Rhuger, confused. He kissed me gently again, lips tasting of his salty tears before he bent to my waist and placed kisses on my stomach through the blanket. He began speaking low in Teagna Dhubh; the words rolling out of him in a lilting song as he laid his head on my stomach and caressed the chubby softness there.

Super sweet, but I was incapable of appreciating it at the moment what with my brain trying to process that one night of terrific sex had resulted in immediate pregnancy. I *was* close to when my cycle was supposed to start, but it was still kind of early. Did that mean that my orckin ancestry made it so I was fertile early because of all the orgasms Rhuger had given me the last few days? And *how* exactly could they fucking *smell* it?! But then I remembered that orckin were capable of smelling hormonal shifts including pregnancy. I was just confused over how *immediate* this all was.

"What's all the fuss up here?" I heard my great-grandmother Ruksala's voice carry over all the manly weeping and I heaved a sigh of relief. If anyone could tell me what was going on without falling apart like a Nature Valley granola bar, it would be her.

"Grammy Ruksala?" I called, my voice unsteady.

"Child? What's all this?" She whacked the sobbing guard I didn't know with her walking staff before being led in by Rorich. The poor guy's eyes went wide and even he sniffed as his lip quivered and tears threatened. "What is my giant son bawling like an orcling who got refused a toy for?"

"Mama..." Grandpa Thorn choked and sniffed down at his own mother, who was easily two feet shorter than him and had to crane her neck all the way back to scowl at him. "This Oc'Turin bastard went and... and..."

"And what? Made your granddaughter happy? Yes, I know. And? I set them up together, you overbearing nag." Grammy Ruksala wasn't having any of Grandpa's shit. I snorted. Grandpa looked utterly betrayed. I... wasn't all that surprised at Grammy Ruksala's admonition. Looking back on my first day in Baile Coille, it was pretty obvious.

"So what is all the crying for?" She demanded, looking at me.

"I guess I'm pregnant... I think...? They just smelled me." I explained, lost, patting Rhuger's head where it rested on my tummy. Trying to comfort him, even in my confusion. "Why are they all crying? Is it bad?"

"Bad?!" Rhuger shot up from where he'd been crooning to my belly to cup my face in his hands just as my grandfather began hollering in outrage in the background. "You carry my child. This is *beyond* joy, my pearl. In less than a day, you've made me the happiest orc alive. You've taken me for your mate and now you carry our orcling."

"Well, you guys are all sobbing like I'm gonna die!" I shouted, stressed. "Am I gonna die, Grammy?" I leaned past my mate to get my great-grandmother's honest opinion. From what I'd gleaned, orckin pregnancies seemed tricky.

"Outside of the usual risks with pregnancy? Och, no." She scoffed. "Few females mean fewer pregnancies. That's why these oversized orclings are making such a fuss. It's humans that breed so quickly and take orc seed like fertile soil takes rain."

"Really?" I asked, intrigued. I mean, it made some sense. But then the question of why Grandma Ruth and Grandpa Thorn only had one kid and my mother only having me smacked me upside the head.

"Humans don't really need the luibh gaoil, or numerous orgasms, to promote fertility, as female orckin do. And your cycles occur more often than ours." Grammy Ruksala explained. "The gate along the border with the Oc'Turin clan isn't the only one. And your grandfather wasn't the first orc to pass through it. Just as you're not the only human to come to us. Well, mostly human."

Her gap-toothed smile was warm as she tottered over and patted my cheek.

"I'm very proud of you, girl. You do your family and your clan great honor. And if my son wasn't so caught up on controlling your life here, he'd welcome his new grandson." The glare she shot my grandfather was pure venom and distaste. Like he'd shamed her and their ancestors and she was giving him the stink eye. Grandpa Thorn hung his head and came over, kissing the top of my head before grasping Rhuger's forearm.

"Welcome to my family, Rhuger Oc'Turin." He said gruffly.

"I thank you for your warm welcome, Rìgh Thorn Oc'Dellor."

"Wait... Rhuger Oc'Turin is your full name?" I asked, blindsided by this fresh development. "Like, your family name is the same as the clan name?"

Rhuger nodded, uncertainty in his expression as his eyes got that shuttered look to them. Then I looked at Grandpa Thorn who winced. Then at the guards who just shuffled their feet awkwardly. Did *everyone* but me know? I couldn't remember a single time where someone said Rhuger's full name. Just Rhuger, Fògradh, or...

Oc'Turin.

I went cold and an icy well opened up in my belly. I'd thought they meant that he was an outsider and called him by his clan's name to mock him. It hadn't dawned on me that maybe it was an honorific. That *maybe* it was *actually his name.*

"Your mate's an exiled prince from a rival clan, my girl." Grammie Ruksala cackled at my shocked face. "And you? You're a princess. Didn't my son tell you?" She turned to Grandpa Thorn and made a 'come here' gesture with her hand. "Cough it up, son. You lost the bet."

I jerked as that nugget of information hit me like a ton of bricks. A *princess.* I was a fucking orckin *princess.* What, in the love of every romance book trope to ever exist, *was this shit.*

"What the absolute fuck, Grammie," I said, angry. Everyone went still and quiet with surprise. "NONE of you thought to tell me who I was sooner? Who Rhuger was? And what *bet* are you talking about?"

"You didn't know?" Rhuger asked me, surprise and uncertainty warring in his tone.

"No." I looked up at my grandfather, who suddenly looked contrite. No *wonder* he'd made it seem like Rhuger wasn't an option for me. He was not just an exile, but a *royal* exile from an enemy clan.

"What did you think a Rìgh was, girl?" Grammie Ruksala clucked with a frown. "Your grandfather and I had a little bet whether you two would get together before Rìgh Orok came back. He thought you wouldn't, and he'd have to name Rhuger your mate himself. Fool."

"That's the last time I'm betting with you, mother." Grandpa Thorn said, handing over a small pouch. Grammie Ruksala grinned her gap-toothed smile and tucked the bag into one of the many pockets in her pumpkin orange cardigan.

Wait. Grandpa Thorn would have *actually* named Rhuger as my mate? I thought he *hated* him. He just threatened to *kill him* just a few minutes ago! I felt the edges of my psyche begin to snap and crisp in my rush to process everything. Process all of the possibilities and outcomes that could have happened against what had just been revealed. Nothing made sense, and yet... *it did.*

The crown of flowers during the Welcome Feast, that my neamhnaid skin meant I came from the *royal* line,

"I thought a Rìgh was a lord. Not a king." I said, my words falling flat into the silence. That icy well in my belly sapped all the joy from me and wrenched my guts that my family *bet* on my relationship with Rhuger.

And it suddenly became clear *why* no one else thought to say anything. Why everyone already thought that I *knew* who I was and who Rhuger was. They all thought my grandfather had *told* me.

And it made a wicked sort of sense why Rhuger had kept trying to push me away like he wasn't worthy. He was an *exile*. From a *rival clan*. And he was *their prince*. No wonder he kept acting like he wasn't worthy.

"Grandpa..." I growled at him, to everyone's shock, including my own. I didn't know I could sound like that. "Why didn't you tell me?"

"I wanted you to be happy, chestnut. I wanted you to grow and heal and I didn't want you to be burdened by this." He murmured, gesturing helplessly.

"So instead of treating me like a person, you decided what I could know. You decided not to trust me." Grasping the blanket from the bed, I wrapped it around me, standing tall and getting up in his face. "You decided that my fate was worth *betting* on and you *bet against me*. I've survived worse than the truth, survived pain you couldn't imagine. I fled *thousands* of miles from the man who thought he could control me and make me miserable. If you truly loved me and wanted me to be happy, you would have told me. Instead, you were *just like him.*"

The words snapped into the air, bitter and harsh, and I saw as each word landed. My grandfather aged years right before my eyes. I hated that it hurt him. I hated that he'd tried to control me and lied to me.

"Chestnut..." He swallowed.

"Out." My arm shook as I thrust my arm at the door. "All of you."

"You were hurting so badly already. I didn't want you to hurt more, chestnut..."

"OUT!" I screamed. No one moved.

So I whirled around, threw one of Rhuger's tunics on over my head, and drug my leggings on, letting the blanket fall. It wasn't long before I'd shoved my feet into boots and laced them.

"Amelia," Rhuger murmured. "Where are you going?"

"Since no one is leaving and giving me the space I need. *I'm* leaving. I need some *fucking* air." With that, I stood and walked straight for the door. Ophir stepped into my path and I jabbed him right in the face. His nose crunched beneath my knuckles, blood gushing out of his nostrils as he staggered back and out of my way. My grandfather grabbed my wrist, and I snapped my hand around against the weak hold of his thumb, breaking his grip and glaring him down, to his utter shock.

"Everyone is so certain I'm fragile. That I'll break. That I'm precious and dainty and weak. No one's bothered to find out what I'm capable of." It's like he forgot he was the one who began training me in martial arts as a child. "You thought I would stop learning how to fight at your *tricks*? You *left*. And learning how to fight was all I had left of you, Grandpa. You have no idea who I am."

I heard Rhuger buckling his kilt on behind us in the deafening quiet.

"Where do you think you're going?" I asked him over my shoulder, tone sharp enough to cut.

"With you." He said simply, looking up at me from under his lashes where he had his head bent to attach his belt and weapons. "I will give you the space you need, but I will not leave you."

"You didn't tell me who you were," I stated.

"I thought you knew and chose me despite it."

That truth hung heavy between us.

"I can take care of myself, you know," I murmured, throat suddenly tight.

I would have chosen him had I known who he was. Nothing had ever felt so right as being with him. It just sat wrong in my chest that I made a choice that big without all the facts. Like no one trusted me, but they expected me to trust them.

"I don't doubt it. You are my mate. Where you go, I go." He said simply with a shrug that was way too casual for how shuttered his gaze was. And as I'd learned in my short time with him, I saw it for what it was.

He was afraid.

Afraid I'd reject him now that I knew the truth.

Something tore in my chest at that. I couldn't reject him, just as I couldn't stop the sun from rising. I just needed a gotdamn minute to process.

I did the only thing I could think of. I held out my hand.

The relief on his face was palpable, though he hid it well from the others. With quick strides, he prowled to my side in a matter of heartbeats. Rhuger slid his hand into mine and laced our fingers before inclining his head towards the door.

So I turned and led him by the hand outside into the morning sunlight. As my feet hit the loamy earth at the base of our home tree, I ran. Feet pounding a rhythm on the flagstone path. Rhuger's grip on my hand did not falter as he followed me into the deserted forest on the outskirts of Baile Coille.

CHAPTER 02*

AMELIA

We ran at a good clip for a while. I was out of shape though, despite all of the nocrys training, so I came to a halt in a clearing. Rhuger had barely broken a sweat, and here I was sucking in air like a bellows, practically pouring sweat. Sun glinted on him through the leaves of the trees overhead and turned where it touched the lines of his face and arms to a golden glow. Damn orc skin had the best built-in highlighter a makeup fanatic could ask for. It wasn't fair.

But then again, mine had a pearlescent sheen to the peachy greyness of my skin that marked me not only as part orckin but part of a royal line. A line I had no idea meant that I was *literally* a fucking princess. I was internally screaming into the void as my thoughts started tumbling around like rocks in a dryer.

"I would have told you, had I known you didn't know who I was." Rhuger rasped, swallowing hard. Still obviously torn up about what had just happened back at our home tree.

In response, I bent over to brace myself on my knees, holding up a finger in silent supplication for him to wait a minute before I ducked my head. It took a few moments to get enough air in my lungs to where my blood wasn't begging for it. When I stood up, I ran my fingers through my hair, forgetting, at the moment, that I now had claws and hadn't retracted them. It had been something I'd been seriously keeping in mind so I didn't accidentally hurt anyone. Instead, I nicked my own pointed ear and hissed.

Rhuger was suddenly super close.

"Amelia, what happened? Let me see." He demanded, so I tilted my head and showed him my bleeding ear tip.

"I forgot I have claws now," I muttered, irritated. "I'll be okay just-"

My words cut off as he bent down and gently wrapped the tip of my pointed ear in his long black tongue, and sucked on it. The pain immediately lessened.

"What are you doing?" I asked, bewildered a flush rising in my cheeks. He let me bat him away with my hands. I reached up and the tip of my ear wasn't stinging so badly, or bleeding anymore. I looked up into his shuttered gaze and I realized for the thousandth time how handsome my mate was.

"Our saliva can stop bleeding and stave off infection." He grumbled, shuffling his feet.

"Oh, that's neat. I wish mine did." I said, marveling.

"You might. Do you wish to try?" He reached out a forearm and a claw, looking all the world like he'd lay his arm open to give me the opportunity to see if I had super-healing spit.

"No! I don't want you to hurt yourself. It's not that important, okay?" Rhuger nodded and dropped his hands. Looking like a lost little boy.

"I believe you, Rhuger," I told him, sighing and looking into his silver gaze. "I believe you thought I knew. And that you would have told me if you'd known I didn't."

His stiff nod was a relief, and I realized he was waiting so rigidly because he thought I would reject him now that I knew the truth.

"I won't reject what we have, okay?" Walking up to him, I grasped his hand in mine and looked him dead in the eyes, so he knew I meant it. "What I feel for you is the truest thing in my life right now and it's the same for you, I think. I would have chosen you even had I known who you were. That kind of thing doesn't matter to me. What matters is that you're by my side and seek to make me happy, just like I do for you."

Rhuger's body shuddered before he let loose a breath I hadn't realized he'd been holding. A few tears slipped down his cheeks and, without thinking, I reached up and brushed them away for him. Claws safely retracted this time.

"You're my mate and the father of our child. You treat me amazingly well and are loving and kind. I don't know what I did right to end up your mate, but I wouldn't choose anyone else over you— ever." I murmured into the space between us.

Rhuger enveloped me in a crushing embrace, his body trembling in pent-up emotion. Had he really thought I'd leave him? That I'd give up everything we could have together over a misunderstanding?

I sighed and held him close, rubbing soothing paths up and down his back with my hands. It took a few minutes, but eventually the quiet sobs that were wracking him ceased and he pulled away, brusquely shoving the tears off his face. Raising my hand, I cupped his jaw and gave him a gentle smile. I was about to say something when my stomach let out an outrageous, gurgling growl.

"What the..." I look down at my stomach with wide eyes.

"My mate and my bairn are hungry. What kind of mate would I be if I didn't get you breakfast?" He laughed before kissing me soundly, tasting salty from his tears, and stalked off a way toward a cluster of trees.

When he returned, he carried a variety of fruits and something that looked strangely like celery. He sat me down on a nearby rock and prepared the food for me with a small, sharp boot knife. Rhuger cut up one of the oddly shaped fruit, almost like a starfruit but bumpy, and began holding pieces of it up to my mouth.

"You could just hand me the fruit." I chided, trying not to smile.

"I could. But where would the fun be in that?" He asked with a wicked grin and a renewed mischievous sparkle in his eye. "This way I can touch your lips as I feed you and tempt you to suck on my fingers as you sucked on my cock last night."

I blushed but refused to back down. So the next bit of fruit he fed me, I took it and his finger in my mouth and sucked on his finger *hard*, flickering my tongue against the sensitive pad of his fingertip. His rumbling growl of pleasure had my toes curling. But instead of continuing to tease me, his gaze grew pensive. This time, he handed me a piece of fruit and I popped it into my mouth.

"I didn't expect everyone's reaction to be like that," I mumbled around a mouthful of the crisp fruit as he continued cutting up the fruit, popping pieces into his own mouth too. "Honestly, I knew there was a *chance* I'd get pregnant after last night. I just didn't realize it would be so immediate. I thought we'd have some time."

"You've never been with child before?" His question was asked gently, and it warmed my heart he was so considerate of my feelings.

"No. Not that I'm aware of, anyway. I took birth control but ran out before coming through the gate." I shrugged. "It's not like I'd been with my ex-husband after the uh... Incident... So there was really no reason to keep taking it once I left."

"Birth control?" He asked as he cut me another slice of another fruit that looked like a cross between an apple and a strawberry and handed it to me.

"It's medicine to keep unwanted pregnancies from happening," I explained, taking the sliver from his fingers. I nibbled on the fruit and a heady flavor reminiscent of bananas and cinnamon exploded on my tongue.

"You took it to keep from mothering a child with your ex-husband." The statement fell from his lips, thoughtful. "You do not mind mothering a bairn with me, though?"

"You're a wonderful male. You're my mate. I think you'll make a fantastic father if you're as good to our children as you are to me." The easy praise made this seven-foot orc dip his head in a bright green blush, a small smile tugging at the corners of his mouth.

"I would do anything for our children. Just as I would do anything for you." The simple sincerity of his words made my heart flutter and ache.

He'd been without love, praise, and acceptance for so long, that he treated even the smallest compliments I gave him like treasures. I decided right then and there that I would love on him *so hard* and never let him forget how I felt about him. How amazing he was and how much I appreciated him. He deserved nothing less.

"Just one of the many reasons I love you." I smiled, then sobered as a thought hit me. "I am worried about being pregnant here. Not being entirely orckin, I'm anxious about how our child will develop. Pregnancies are scary times for any woman. I'm just afraid of complications and how they'll be treated here."

"Is Earth better equipped to handle pregnancies?" He asked,

thoughtful.

"Medically, I'd have to say yes. You mentioned the Oc'Veltas can travel to the stars. So I'd assume they have medical advancements too. But they haven't shared them. Humans can fly to the stars, too. And our medical advancements are impressive. They could be better, of course. It's nuanced and a little complicated, but overall, Earth would be better equipped to help with any pregnancy complications." I shrugged at him, feeling a little helpless at trying to explain.

"I think I understand, at least a little." He said as he ate some of the fruit, voice quiet and eyes shuttered once more. "I wish the Geata was fixed. So we could ensure you got the best care for our bairn."

Feeling for him and having seen enough of that look for one day, I knelt down next to him and tackled him to the ground. Surprised, he laughed and set the fruit and knife aside. He rolled so I lay on my back in the grasses, staring up at the cloudless sky, the hazy impressions of two of the moons lighting a big part of the heavens.

Rhuger's smile for me was genuine and soft. Full of contentment I had never seen in him before. Here I lay on my back in the grass looking all the world like a chubby little hobbit, with the orckin equivalent of a Balrog warlord staring down at me with so much tenderness. It had struck me before, how different we were in that regard. Witnessing his martial prowess at the Mating Tournament cemented that he was high-octane and loved the thrill of battle. While I was decent at martial arts and knife tricks, it was all for the dopamine hit from doing a good job.

I was so tired of being strong and I'd become tough to survive my ex-husband. Rhuger made me feel safe. And I'd begun to let go of that stranglehold I had on my need to be constantly on guard.

"Am I too soft for you?" I whispered the question as I lay there, looking up at where Rhuger was propped up on his side, one hand curved around my soft waist.

"How do you mean?" His silver eyes focused on me, brow furrowing.

"Well, you're a warrior. And, though you're exiled, you're still a prince. You still have so much opportunity stretched before you." I began, letting the words slip past my lips. The worries I'd held so close to my chest that I hadn't realized had existed until now unraveled as I spoke. "I know some martial arts. I can fight, but not to the degree you can."

"Okay." He murmured, waiting for me to continue.

"Are you sure I'm a good match for you? I'm worried I won't be able to keep up. That I'll fall behind." It was an old wound. I'd always strive to keep up with my peers and yet still fell to the wayside. Either too far ahead or too far behind. Too much or not enough, just like Adam had hounded into me.

"I don't need you to keep up with me," Rhuger replied, tone soft and sure. "You give me what I need."

"What's that?" I asked, voice shaking as I tried not to sob.

"A safe place to rest. Somewhere I can let my guard down. Where I can bury myself in softness and forget the rest of the world exists for a little while." Rhuger murmured as he laced his fingers with mine. "You won't fall behind. You can't. Because I'll always come home to you. You are my home. And I'll always take you with me."

Maybe it was from being emotionally neglected by romantic partners. Maybe it was because this was all new to me and I had trouble regulating my emotions. Hell, *maybe* it was because of all the baby hormones that were being dumped into my system so suddenly after having insta-baby-sex. Regardless, my feelings were running rampant and I felt like I would burst from them.

So I distracted myself.

I looked down the powerful column of my mate's throat with its whirling black tattoos to his torque. A wicked thought entered my mind and I grasped it as if it were a tie. I tugged Rhuger down to me so we were nearly nose to nose. His reaction was immediate, shifting from relaxed guard to dominant predator in the blink of an eye.

"Naughty little pearl." Rhuger's voice dropped into a deep, rolling rumble that crackled with desire. "Don't you know that if you grasp a male's torque or his belt, like that..." His mouth curved into a sinful smirk. "...you're bound to find yourself in all sorts of trouble..."

"Oh?" I asked, voice gone high and breathy in the face of such masculine power pinning me amongst the wildflowers.

"Oh, yes." He murmured, drawing out the s-sound around his sharp teeth. "A male can't be held responsible for what he does to such a bold female. It's as clear a signal as any that she's ready to mate. Immediately."

I didn't hesitate and tugged on his torque again. This time, he rolled on top of me, pinning me to the ground with his weight. I squirmed beneath him as he ground his hips between my legs. Grasping my wrists, he held them above my head with one hand, his other trailing along my jaw, my throat, the ties at the front of *his* shirt...

"I like it that you're wearing my tunic..." Rhuger growled, teeth flashing as his pupils blew out his silver irises until his eyes looked like glittering pits. "... That you willingly wear what's mine, wear my scent..." He slipped a clawed hand up under the tunic to gently scrape against the underside of my breast. My breath came light and fast, desire burning like a beacon as I could feel the hard length of him pressed against my pussy. I couldn't help the soft moan that escaped me as I realized I'd completely soaked my leggings already.

"That's because I'm yours, my Rìgh," I whispered, squeezing

my thighs around his hips to punctuate my point. "Just as you are mine."

I admit, I was a thirsty ass bitch, who could only think about stuffing as much of his cock inside of me as I could get as fast as I could get it.

Pulling my shirt up to my armpits, I exposed my breasts for him and he growled as he claimed my mouth. Rhuger's hand slipped from my breast to curve over my soft tummy, as if cradling the child growing there, before drifting down to slip his fingers under the waistband of my pants. Releasing my wrists and my mouth, he leaned back on his knees, tugging my pants from me. I eagerly lifted my hips so he could tug them down, and he made a sound of approval as his gaze trailed along my exposed skin.

Gods, he couldn't get my clothes off of me fast enough. I wasn't even willing to wait for him to take off his kilt and planned to lift the swiftly tenting leather and spread myself wide for him so he could rut me in the sunshine. But he had to get my pants off first and my boots were getting in the way. I whined at the idea of being completely naked while he was still clothed, kilt lifted so he could fuck me into the ground beneath us, the wild woman he claimed. Needing it to become our immediate reality with a vicious desire.

A branch cracked somewhere within the treeline, and Rhuger froze above me. He took a deep breath and then was off of me like a shot. I sat up, pulling my shirt down and my pants up. Rhuger was standing in front of me, swords already drawn, staring off in the direction of the sound.

In the next breath, I lunged for his knives and palmed them. If we were about to be attacked, I wasn't about to let my mate face it alone. I wasn't about to let my child come to harm without fighting with every ounce of blood in my veins, either.

As I got to my feet and readied my weapons, I saw a good dozen orcs stalk from between the trees and out into the tall grasses and wildflowers. I felt the blood drain from my face. One orc was the giant womb-splitter who had hunted me when I first arrived on Talam. The one who would have killed me if Rhuger hadn't spirited me away.

"Give us the female and you can leave unharmed, Fògradh." A short orc bristling with knives called.

"Do you really expect me to let you just *take* my mate?" Rhuger's voice was low, even, and it bit like sharp steel.

"Our orders are to take her alive. You? Not so much." The short orc shrugged like it wasn't a big deal.

"Who are they?" I whispered behind Rhuger. He didn't move.

"And what does Rìgh Orok of the Oc'Turin want with Leanabh Banrigh Amelia of the Oc'Dellor?" Rhuger asked.

"That's not our business. Or yours." The orc replied with a sleazy grin that spoke of what Orok wanted from me. I felt panic flare and flap against my vision, darkening the edges like black wings. Suffocating and horrible.

I'd been mated. I'd even gotten pregnant. All before the date and time Rìgh Orok was slated to come for me, just like I was supposed to. I should have been safe, should have been free from the cruel future everyone had painted for me if I became Rìgh Orok's mate.

But it looked like Rìgh Orok couldn't care less if I had a mate or not. Was pregnant with another male's child. Come hell or high water, it seemed he was determined to take me as his mate for whatever nefarious purposes he had.

"Then come and take her from me," Rhuger growled, head dipping to his chest, arms spread wide, with his blades held high. Rhuger was, without a doubt, the stuff romance novels were made of. If we weren't in mortal danger, I would have *severely* appreciated his words and how gotdamned hot he looked.

The short orc glowered and made a curt gesture to the orcs at the far ends of their line. I felt my heart skitter in my chest and my palms slick as a sick cold fear settled in my gut. The four orcs that left the line and stalked towards us were jacked, like bodybuilders. My mouth went dry. If they were Oc'Turin and trained in war just like Rhuger was... We wouldn't stand an ice cube's chance in hell.

My mate, my cridhe, stepped forward to meet them. I stayed where I was in a defensive crouch, knives at the ready. And I made the hardest decision of my life.

Whatever was about to happen? Whatever the outcome of the battle we were facing. I was going to survive it all for our child.

And then I was going to take my revenge.

RHUGER

Such a brave female, my mate. She'd gone for my knives the moment she'd registered the situation. Pride swelled in my chest for her valor and willingness to fight with me against our enemies. She was truly a descendant of the Iolaire'lasair warriors and would have done them proud.

I knew the orcs before me. All twelve of them. I'd trained with them my whole life, and I'd give them credit. They were good.

But I was better.

Their leader gestured and four of the orcs peeled off from the edges of their line. I stepped forward and hoped Amelia stayed where she was. The last thing I wanted was for one of them to get close enough to hurt her or take her captive. Especially now that our bairn grew in her belly.

They were built like most of the Oc'Turin. As if their hulking muscles were carved of green stone. One swung his sword in feinting arcs as they approached on confident feet. Another held a whip and the remaining two orcs gripped axes. They were smirking and laughing, completely unafraid of the threat I posed. A distant part of me yearned for my longsword and my bow. I'd make quick work of them if I had them. But my short swords would do. I'd fought more warriors with less, after all.

It was time I showed them what a war Rìgh's son, trained in both the Oc'Turin and Oc'Dellor fighting styles, could do. Taking a deep breath, I loosened my limbs, rolled up onto the balls of my feet, and kept them all within my sight. They separated, splitting apart to form a half-circle in front of me, just out of reach. They were smart not to circle me completely and let my mate be at their unprotected backs with those knives in her hand. Though I doubted they saw her as much of a threat. Fools.

The orc with the sword advanced quickly, swinging his sword up in a lethal underhand arc from its position in the Boar's Tooth guard position. With a flick of my wrist, I deflected his upcoming sword, his blade shed against mine for a moment, sparks flying. His sword tip sunk into the ground at my feet and I flew into action.

Pushing against his sword with my own, I vaulted up and spun. My free sword flashed a deadly arc in the fading light. I saw his eyes widen, the reflection of my sword in his eyes, as my blade sunk into his exposed neck. The steel slid like a hot knife through butter down into his chest, to sprout from between two of his ribs at his side.

I rolled over his falling body and ripped my sword free. It split his chest and neck open in a spout of blood and flesh. The three other orcs paused for a moment at how quickly and efficiently I'd felled their ally. It was all the advantage I needed.

Before the two axe wielders could recover, I rushed them. One blocked my downward stroke, the other wasn't so quick, and my sword severed his wrist where it gripped an axe. He shrieked as he fell back, dropping his other axe and clutching his wrist as it gushed blood. A swift reversal of my swing sliced a second smile into his neck and he fell lifeless into the grass.

The orc who'd withstood my initial attack pressed forward, wielding both axes with deadly proficiency. I kept him at bay, swiping his axe blows aside with my blades as I faded and he pursued. This one was a true warrior. Every movement was effective and meant to conserve energy.

As he brought down his axe, I feinted and spun, his swing exposing his back and side. Just as I was about to lunge forward and impale him with my sword, the whip snatched my wrist. I snarled in the direction of the male wielding the whip as I attempted to jerk my wrist free. It gave the axe wielder enough time to recover, turn, and press an attack.

With one hand incapacitated, blocking two blows at once quickly became difficult. The axe-wielder brought both axes down at once to break my guard. I met his weapons with my blade. We stood there for a moment, all of his weight and strength pressing down into my block, my other arm still trapped by the whip and the tension the other orc was keeping on it.

This wouldn't do, playing games with these lesser warriors. I had a mate and orcling to protect. I grinned at the orc with the axes, startling him, then snapped a front kick straight between his legs. He grunted, shoulders hunching. His press eased, and I pushed him to the side. He spun to evade me and my arcing slash that should have taken his head. But that damned whip-wielder had tugged at just the right moment and pulled me off my balance.

As the axe-wielder attempted to recover, I sliced through the whip. It really wasn't the best weapon against a sword, especially ones as sharp as mine. He quickly dropped the handle with its unraveling braided thong and unsheathed punching blades.

So. He could handle distance and close-quarter combat, but not middle ground? Interesting and foolish.

I slid into one of Uther's stances with my right sword poised over my shoulder to guard my back, the fore sword held near my hip, blade angled to my right foot. It was a stance they'd likely seen in battles against the Oc'Dellor, but not one they'd trained for. They hesitated and readied themselves. Clearly not expecting me to bother learning fighting techniques from a clan they thought inferior to themselves. Projecting their own ignorance onto me. It was about to be their downfall.

The Oc'Turin's approach to battle was more centered on power and endurance. The Oc'Dellor was focused on evasion and tactical advantage. Uther had run me through the wringer the first year I'd been with the Oc'Dellor. Most of their moves involved footwork and a core six-pointed star pattern that every move utilized. Fiercely glad I'd put myself at Uther's mercy, I was about to put all of his training to good use.

The short orc in charge barked orders and two more of his warriors peeled off from the woods to join in the fun. A third raised a bow and notched an arrow. I barked a laugh of delight. Finally, they were taking me seriously.

The length of the severed whip slipped from my wrist, and as it fell, both orcs I'd been fighting rushed me. I spun and caught the axe with my left sword as I rotated my right shoulder and swept an arc out behind me as I moved, keeping the punching blades at bay. I could hear the twang of the bow and the whistling of the arrow. Dropping to my knees, I spun again as the arrow flew past overhead and shoved my right blade up under the axe-wielder's guard and into his gut.

Blood showered the grasses in a red rain as his axes fell to the earth.

The male with the punching blades rushed me. I spun on my knees with the dying axe-wielder, letting him go to skewer himself on his ally's blades. Before I could recover, a mace hissed past my ear from behind me and grazed my shoulder. I cried out and reversed my blades in my hands, sliding them backward against my sides. With a thrust, I sank them home into the groin and belly of the orc behind me who had attacked me with the mace.

Another twang of a bowstring heralded another arrow released, and I barely dodged it as I jumped to my feet. It sliced my cheek as it passed. My skin was already knitting the fresh wound back together as I knocked the next arrow aside with my sword. The archer was getting on my nerves, and I was afraid a misplaced shot would hurt Amelia.

So I shoved one of my blades into a corpse, picked up a fallen axe, and flung it at the archer. I didn't bother to watch it land. I just ripped my sword free and charged the orc with the punching blades. The sounds of the axe sinking home in the archer's skull and the body as it collapsed in a heap on the ground were a song singing in my blood.

Five of the twelve orcs had fallen, bleeding out and watering the earth in a matter of minutes. And I was about to take out a sixth. I was bred for war and born to worship my cridhe. No one and nothing would alter that.

A few sword strokes later, the severed arms holding the punching blades plopped onto the ground. Followed by his head and his slumping corpse. As I turned, other soldiers approached. Including the massive orckin who I recognized from the day Amelia had come through the Geata. The one who had threatened to fuck her until she died.

Baring my teeth at him, I barely registered as others charged me. Absently, I blocked their blows and slaughtered them as if I were slicing fruit for my cridhe. They were inconsequential compared to the massive brute before me. *He'd* threatened my precious pearl. And he was going to die for it.

The giant male had a kilt on this time, but not much else. He grinned at me, missing teeth giving him a smile of broken daggers. The bastard taunted me with his knowing grin, puffing his chest out and baring his throat as if I weren't a threat to him. I knew what he was doing, knew it was affecting me, but I couldn't find it in me to care. All I knew was that I would kill him for what he put my mate through.

One fighter with twin maces was becoming an annoying distraction because he was actually proficient enough with them to be a problem. Gritting my teeth, I cast my gaze about and almost froze. More fighters were stepping out from beneath the trees and out onto the field. I'd fought against worse odds. But never with my cridhe and my bairn's lives hanging in the balance.

"Enough!" barked the giant orc in a deep, thunderous voice. He stomped forward, knocking his fellow soldiers out of the way.

My opponent locked my swords amongst the flanges of their maces just long enough to bide some time. I ripped my blades free, chipping the steel, and sliced open his belly with the jagged edges. But his ploy had worked. As I turned to face the monstrous orc to kill him for his transgressions against my cridhe, he reached down and grasped me by the throat.

I slashed at his arms with my blades, but he barely winced. Just slapped them free from my hands. Then he lifted me up into the air without even a whisper of effort. And squeezed his gigantic fingers around my throat. I couldn't get him to let go. I kicked him in the groin and attempted to break his thumb with both hands. I tried everything. Nothing worked. He was made of different stuff, just as I was. But if he kept squeezing, I would not make it out of this encounter alive.

A knife whistled past my face and sank home into my opponent's left eye. He howled, spraying blood all over my face and the grasses below us. He dropped me and ripped the knife from his eye, ripping the orb out with it. I coughed around my bruised windpipe on my hands and knees, trying to draw in air.

He roared and stalked over to Amelia, who'd thrown the knife. She was frozen in fear, eyes wide and hands trembling as they held the remaining knife. The mountainous male barked a growl and backhanded her. She dropped to the ground like a stone and I felt my heart tear.

"NO!" I roared and charged. My vision had gone red. I'd carve that orc up and serve him to my mate like a feast. I'd chain him and torture him for weeks before I allowed him to die!

But my sprint was cut short as the short orc side-stepped toward me. As I passed him, he brought the hilt of his sword down on the back of my skull. I saw sparks and then nothing as I fell into oblivion.

CHAPTER 03[*]

AMELIA

"*RHUGER!*" I screamed my mate's name as the world spun around me. The womb-splitter had backhanded me with hardly any effort put into the blow. He'd stunned me enough that the world spiraled around me. But not enough to knock me out.

Not enough to keep me from hearing Rhuger scream and run for me. Not enough for me not to witness as the leader whacked my mate on the back of the head, crumpling him to the ground. I wanted to rage, to fight, but all I could do was throw up in the grass and close my eyes against the world.

The womb-splitter bent down and snatched me by the hair and lifted me so I was barely on my knees. I grimaced at the pain and at having my hair pulled by anyone but my mate. The short orc approached, parting the tall grasses and wildflowers like an oily smear in an otherwise idyllic setting. He swam in and out of focus as he leaned down to look me in the eye.

"Well, hello there Leanabh Banrigh." The leader, barely over five feet tall, grinned. "Our Rìgh wishes to rescue you from the clutches of the Oc'Dellor and the Fògradh."

"What kind of bullshit is that?" I mumbled, vision still blurry. "Gaslighting me and my family. Fuck you. I was perfectly safe and happy with *my* clan and *my* mate carrying *our* child."

The short orc scowled down at me. Seemed he didn't like my answer.

"I wouldn't speak like that to the Rìgh if I were you." Came his low, hard reply.

"Not my Rìgh," I muttered, longing to lie down but knowing it was dangerous to do so with a concussion.

Rhuger was my Rìgh as he held my heart. My grandfather was my Rìgh because he was the head of my clan and family. Rìgh Orok wasn't even a titmouse fart in my mind. He was so far removed from my world as to be insignificant. Of course, until he insisted on shoving his entitled ass into my life. Now he was a problem, and one I was going to have to face alone.

"Oh, he will be." The dark, lecherous grin he gave me then made my skin crawl. "Take her to the Rìgh, and bring the Fògradh."

The panic that bubbled in my chest, such a normal thing for me, ceased immediately. No. I would not panic this time. I would not let fear win. Everything inside my chest went ice cold, hard, and vicious. I'd survived hell at the hands of my ex-husband. I'd survived on a completely different planet and even found my place in this new world.

I could survive this, too.

The womb-splitter, who thankfully was wearing a kilt, let go of my hair and grasped me by the back of my neck. I grunted as he lifted me to my feet and moved us toward where Rhuger lay prone in the grass. My heart thundered in my chest as we drew close. Blood seeped from a gash on the back of his head, but it wasn't as bad as I thought it'd be.

Womb-splitter kept his grasp on my neck as he bent and snagged one of Rhuger's wrists. He stood and jerked, nearly popping his shoulder out of the socket. A strangled cry burst from my lips as I tried, and failed, to look back to see if Rhuger was okay. Womb-splitter dragged my mate behind us even as he pushed me forward toward whatever horrid fate awaited us.

It was a short walk through the forest to a great fissure in the Fàinne Sleagh that ringed Baile Coille. More of those trailing, dangling vines with the flowers that bloomed on the underside of their leaves obscured the crack in the rock I knew was there. Those vines didn't grow anywhere else but at the entrances to Baile Coille.

There was a larger group of Oc'Turin orckin who'd been waiting in the trees while Rhuger annihilated the first group of fighters. They'd come through at the short orc's call, stripping their fallen of their weapons and dragging their corpses with us. Leaving nothing but blood stains behind in the grass.

One of the unburdened Oc'Turin males held aside the vines so we could pass through. Stepping into the crevasse wasn't comfortable. Womb-splitter had to walk sideways in order to fit and his grip on the back of my neck often tightened to the point of pain as he pushed me ahead of him and dragged my mate behind us.

The walls were covered in those multi-colored ferns, but no light reached us from above. It was a dark sort of twilight, and I often stumbled over the rocks and bones that littered the ground. What the hell lived in these fissures that left bones behind? Unable to satisfy my own morbid curiosity by looking up, I focused on my breathing and kept on my feet so the bastard holding my neck didn't accidentally snap it.

It was one thing to drag corpses behind you like the orcs that followed us did. But I could hear Rhuger's labored breathing through his crushed windpipe. I could only hope Rhuger would survive getting dragged over the sharp stones and bones that littered the ground. I had to bite the inside of my cheek to keep from crying at the thought of how shredded his back would be once we got where we were going. Of infection and fever.

Curling my lip, I swore to all the gods I'd been raised honoring that I would get my revenge on them for what they had done, were doing, and would do to my cridhe.

There was chittering from above and I fought down my panic. Some animal hindbrain of mine told me to stay quiet, move quietly, and let my captors bring down the wrath of whatever lurked above us. Whatever happened, I would survive it too.

But nothing did. The suns were setting by the time we'd reached the other side of the fissure in the great Fàinne Sleagh. We were well past the hanging vines on the far side, deep into the dense treeline when the orckin started chatting.

"So easy." Womb-splitter barked a laugh from behind me. "You know, female. The Rìgh wants you as his mate. A Fògradh of bad breeding isn't good enough for a Leanabh Banrigh."

"I don't even know what that is." I bit out between gritted teeth.

"Your grandfather never told you? Ha!" He thought it was the funniest thing in the world and jerked my neck as he reared back to bellow his humor to the canopy and the rising moons. I'd forgotten what the term meant, I'd only learned it that morning, but now I remembered. When he'd ceased laughing, he bent low so he could whisper in my ear, "It means 'princess' in Common."

Gods, his breath was downright *foul*. I gagged but couldn't escape the miasma that emanated from his mouth each time he breathed.

"Rìgh Orok promised to share you with me." His dark lecherous chuckle was bad enough, but then he ran his black bumpy tongue along the side of my face and that went *beyond* disgusting.

I said nothing as he pulled away, breathing through my mouth so as not to smell the leftover *skink* from his saliva. I wasn't stupid enough to bitch him out, though I longed to with every fiber of my being. It didn't take a genius to recognize he could split me in half even without his dong. And no amount of tear-down was worth that.

Twilight was over when we arrived at a little camp. There was one larger tent, surrounded by a few dozen smaller tents, fires, cook pots, and sleeping nocrys. Torchlight flickered and scattered shadows against the trees as we stepped into the clearing. Heads turned and silence fell as Womb-splitter's heavy footfalls heralded our arrival.

There was a full contingent of soldiers staring at me as I was forced to walk toward the larger tent. A banner with fangs on it in green and silver flapped from the top of it. I was going to meet the bastard who wouldn't take no for an answer. Immediately.

Womb-splitter pushed me through the tent flaps and shoved me to the ground, finally releasing my neck. I got to my hands and knees, rubbing and cracking my sore neck. Staring at a pair of sturdy boots with shin guards, I looked up to see Rìgh Orok seated in a surprisingly plain chair.

His piercing yellow eyes devoured me and it felt like a bunch of banana slugs as it slithered over me. Flicking his gaze behind me, he motioned to Womb-splitter who dropped something. Painfully, I turned my head and saw Rhuger lying on the ground, unconscious. My heart wrenched at seeing how dirty and banged up he was. At the blood that was leaking out from under him. Unable to help myself, I bared my teeth at Womb-splitter who laughed.

"You smell of Rhuger." Came Rìgh Orok's dark voice filled with amusement and a hint of a whine. Like a blood-sucking mosquito. I looked up at him, teeth still bared. "And his spawn."

"Rhuger's my mate." I hissed through my gritted teeth.

"Not anymore." Rìgh Orok's eyebrows shot up as he tapped a rhythm with his claws against the arm of his chair. A slight smirk quirked one side of the mouth I longed to shred. Then he said the one thing that made me wish I wasn't pregnant. "Your child will be raised as mine."

Fuck that noise.

Fuck that noise *so damn hard.*

The kid was mine and Rhuger's and no psycho was going to lay a *finger* on our child. I growled deep in my throat. A sudden, vicious sound that had Rìgh Orok grinning like a madman.

"Still have that *spunk* I see. I'll break you of it yet." His dark laugh made me flinch.

Panic threatened to bubble up inside me again. And once more, I quenched it. Knowing that I would survive whatever happened. I said nothing, gave him nothing but my defiance and my bared blunt teeth. Would he start his lifelong torture of me tonight? Or would he wait to do it publicly? I was a bargaining chip, a power play, but I wasn't sure yet what his angle was.

"Don't you worry your little Neamhnaid head. You're safe tonight. It wouldn't do to harm my mate-to-be before we got home tomorrow." It was like he'd read my mind. His gaze was predatory, victorious, even. Then it shifted into something flat and hard. "If you try to escape, I'll kill Rhuger in front of you and then give you to Ergit to play with."

I looked at him in utter confusion.

"Ergit is my right hand." Rìgh Orok waved a hand behind me and I turned my aching neck to see Womb-splitter grinning at me with rotten teeth and a gaping hole where his left eye had been. He reached down and fondled himself through his kilt, and I grimaced, closing my eyes. I turned back to Rìgh Orok, the surprisingly less vile of the two.

My head was swimming, and I couldn't mask anymore. Couldn't keep a blank look on my face. So I stared up at Rìgh Orok with unveiled disgust and hatred. He did not like this.

With a snarl, he swung and punched me right in my temple. I blissfully blacked out. My last fading thought was hoping Rìgh Orok kept his word about me being 'safe'.

And keeping Rhuger alive if I *behaved.*

Screams woke me up. Groaning, I opened my blurry eyes. I was lying on something soft, but my face screamed in pain from where Rìgh Orok had decked me. It'd been a long time since I'd been hit in the head like that and I'd forgotten how much it hurt. I could see an open tent flap and the fires flickering beyond it.

There were more screams and the clash of steel. Some high, piercing sounds like metal screeching against stone made me wince. A dark form darted in front of the tent flap and froze. It was enormous and had six legs.

I distantly registered that I was staring at a dorcha'aon, and I was unable to move, barely conscious. I fought to stay silent, hardly daring to breathe. The massive six-eyed head swung to look at me, anyway as if it knew precisely where I was.

FUCK! I was an easy meal. Every self-preservation-fueled

hindbrain instinct was screaming at me to get up. To run. To find shelter or a weapon.

But instead of charging into the tent to devour me as I imagined, it dropped something from its serrated maw. It was Womb-splitters left arm. My eyes widened as I stared at it. It'd been the arm he'd grasped my neck with.

Well, I sure as shit was awake *now*.

Looking up into the six eyes of the dorcha'aon, I went cold. It was the same one that I'd run into with Inassa the day we went flower-picking for the tournament. It lowered its head slightly in acknowledgment, as if it remembered me. Then he swiveled his enormous head, baring his fangs in a wicked snarl before lunging off after more prey.

I lie there, staring at Womb-splitter's arm until the screaming died down and the fires burned low. Even when the camp went fully silent, the remaining fighters finally finished cleaning up, I lay there staring at the severed arm.

And wondered why the hell that dorcha'aon had spared me twice. Had torn the arm off of the orckin who'd hurt me. I only hoped he'd let Rhuger live.

I woke the next morning to the sounds of orckin packing up camp. My head ached abominably and my mouth felt like I'd tried gargling a fistful of cotton balls. Able to move, I reached up and tenderly touched my throbbing cheek. I hissed but kept pressing, checking that no bones were broken.

Thankfully, there weren't any broken bones, and the swelling had gone down from where Rìgh Orok had decked me. I took it slowly, sitting up on the cot they had placed me on so as not to aggravate my headache further. Getting hit in the head twice and your neck clutched like a vise was bound to cause anyone a pounding skull.

When I finally got to my feet, I went outside, squinting against the early morning sunlight. My eyes finally adjusted, and I paused, shocked. The entire, well-ordered camp I'd walked into last night was a shredded ruin.

Tents were split and torn, splashed with blood and bits of flesh. The cook pots and fires were a mess, but re-erected by the survivors to make breakfast. Banners and poles were snapped and trampled in the mud. There was a dark, mounded pile of bodies and parts to one end of the camp. Reins tied to the nearby trees, the nocrys didn't have a mark on them.

Frowning, I looked for Rhuger. I was afraid for him, but strangely, not. If that truly was the nocrys who'd shifted in front of me, he'd already had a chance to kill my mate and hadn't. So for him to kill my mate now made little sense to me. Eyes scanning the camp, I finally spotted where Rhuger was tied up against a post, close to where the nocrys were.

He may have been beaten, but he was awake and in one piece. That was all I could hope for right now. As if he'd heard my thoughts, Rhuger's head turned unerringly to where I stood in the entrance to the tent I'd slept in. One of the few that hadn't been destroyed. The relief on his face mirrored mine.

I made to step out of the tent to go to him, to check on him and talk to him. But a looming shadow stepped into my path. I jerked back, thinking it was Womb-splitter, but another orckin stared down at me.

"Stay in the tent." Came his gruff demand.

I flicked my gaze between my cridhe and my new guard. He took a half step forward and I quickly backed up into the tent, stomach growling. The orc snorted and stalked off, returning moments later with a bowl of some sort of porridge with chunks of fatty meat in it. He shoved the bowl into my hands and closed the tent flap behind him as he left.

Well. At least it wasn't Womb-splitter guarding me. At least Rhuger was alive. And at least they were feeding me. But then I realized why. I was a pregnant female.

My hunger fled me as the thought hit me that they probably wouldn't feed Rhuger. Wouldn't let me share my food with him, either. Tears slipped free to plop into the porridge. I didn't want to eat it if it meant Rhuger went hungry. But I shoveled it down, anyway.

I had a baby to think about.

CHAPTER 04*

AMELIA

I was later kicked out of the tent while two remaining soldiers packed it up. I wasn't allowed near Rhuger, so instead, we stole glances at one another when we could. Getting as close to my mate as my new guard would allow, I noticed Rhuger didn't look as bad off as he had the night before. He wasn't bleeding a lot, his skin already knitting together in pink bands from where he'd been dragged along behind Ergit.

In a rush, it hit me. Rhuger healed faster than other orckin. Glancing around as surreptitiously as I could, I noticed that a lot of the orckin who'd survived the dorcha'aon attack were seriously wounded, with deep gashes that were roughly patched up in field dressings. Some limped, and some had their arms strapped to their chests. There was barely an orckin around that wasn't wounded.

Other than Rhuger and I.

My mind whirled with the implications of my mate healing so quickly. Of his prowess in battle and how he had endured his past. How that dorcha'aon had seen *something* between Rhuger and me that day when he had shifted to ask me what I was. Evidently, he had deemed that particular *something* worth protecting.

Still thinking at a thousand miles an hour, I obediently followed my new guard as he led me to the nocrys. Some were saddled and ready to carry what soldiers were left. The rest had wagons or travois strapped to their harnesses. The wagons were loaded with goods and equipment. While the travois were loaded with the dead.

Rhuger was tied to the back of a wagon, a lead chain that led from his neck to his bound wrists. His hands were completely bound in leather, so he couldn't use his claws to get free of his shackles. He looked tired, his back a torn wreck. I choked back tears at the state the love of my life was in. How were we supposed to get out of this mess? Freedom almost seemed hopeless.

Until I looked into Rhuger's eyes. They were bright and sharp as freshly honed steel under his dark brows. His expression was solid, determined, undimmed by our predicament. I swallowed my tears and gave him a slight nod. If he could face this with such bravery, then so could I.

We approached Rìgh Orok who stood watching me with his arms crossed over his armor. His sickly yellow eyes were full of bitter rage. Evidently, I wasn't the only one to recognize that no one had been left unscathed from the dorcha'aon, except Rhuger and I. Even Rìgh Orok had claw marks down his left arm.

I fervently wished he'd get an infection and die a slow death. And I also hoped that the dorcha'aon was alive and well somewhere. Grateful to him for the mercy he showed us.

As I stopped in front of Rìgh Orok, my new guard stepped to the side and handed his Rìgh a length of rope. I swallowed hard as he roughly grabbed my hands and knotted the rope around my forearms and wrists tightly. Able to keep from flinching, I just stared ahead at nothing as Rìgh Orok snatched me up and set me on top of his nocrys.

My bound wrists were tied to the pommel of the saddle. I didn't need to be told that if I fell off or attempted to flee, I'd be dragged along. Rìgh Orok vaulted up behind me and I fought to keep my face neutral. When all the orckin had mounted their nocrys, he made a whooping call in Teanga Dhubh that I didn't understand and spurred his nocrys forward.

As we passed the line of nocrys pulling travois piled with the dead, I saw one pulling a lone body. It was Womb-splitter. Ergit.

Time seemed to slow down as I took in the damage done to the body. His arm had been torn from its socket, a shredded patch of skin showing where the dorcha'aon's teeth had gone to the bone to get the leverage necessary to accomplish such a feat. From his hip down to his knee, the dorcha'aon had practically flayed the flesh from bone, left to flap against the side of the travois. But it was the state of his torso and face that got me.

His torso looked as if the dorcha'aon had dug down into it as a dog does into dirt or sand. What was left of his guts was piled atop him. But his face, his skull, was concave. The dorcha'aon had taken one massive bite out of his face and taken everything but his remaining eyeball, his ears, and the back of his skull with it.

Bile rose in the back of my throat, and I fought to swallow it. What had made the dorcha'aon mutilate his body so badly compared to the others? Then it hit me. Other than Rìgh Orok, the only orckin from our abduction to touch me, to harm me, had been Womb-splitter. My blood turned to ice in my veins. What on Talam could it possibly want with me? Why would it go to such lengths to protect and avenge me? To spare me and my mate?

Too many questions whirled in my thoughts as my head pounded a wicked staccato. Turning away from Womb-splitter, I swallowed hard. My mind and my guts weren't cooperating, especially with the residual headache from the concussion. I didn't want to heave all over the back of the nocrys's head while we rode. Didn't want to show any weakness to Rìgh Orok, who gripped me around my waist so hard I felt bruises forming.

So I did the only thing I could at the moment. I dissociated and withdrew into myself. Let the world around me fade to gray as I stared ahead with a blank expression on my face.

Hours later, we reached the edge of the forest. The towering trees and wild undergrowth grew sparser, with more tracts of moss, ferns, and grass between them. I remembered a little about the Oc'Turin clan from Hisouk. He'd been teaching me more than just Teanga Dhubh, stating that, as the Rìgh's granddaughter, I should know at least a little about the politics I found myself a part of. I was immensely grateful to him for it.

If it wasn't for Hisouk and Rhuger, I'd be clueless about the fact the Oc'Turin lived in stone buildings with grass roofs to hide them amongst the hills and plains of the steppes. That they venerated a deity of war and that their training was akin to worship. How females were treated as weaker, second-class citizens. How power was the highest virtue one could strive for within the clan. And how their numbers had been dwindling the fastest of every clan.

It didn't take a genius to figure out why.

We rode over countless grassy hills and plains. Rough rocky sections jutted up from the grasses like jagged teeth that wound their way south towards hazy, distant mountains. The rest of the scenery was nothing but a sea of grass and the occasional stubby, wind-swept tree. There were birds, small burrowing creatures, insects, and a herd of some sort of scruffy, lowing animals in the distance that looked like bison. But more like how some 13th-century monk would paint a bison after having it described to him by a traveler.

There was enough monotony to the scenery that it reminded me of the drive I'd made just a few weeks ago across America. Of the countless miles along Interstate 40 with little to nothing around but dirt, rock, and scraggly plants. Of how I'd zoned out and processed as I'd escaped a fate that would have killed me.

Had it only been a few weeks ago? Felt more like a decade at this point.

Around midday, what appeared to be an odd rock formation seemed to rise out of the plains. As we drew nearer, I realized it was a massive statue of some sort. The thing was gargantuan. As tall as a skyscraper and carved from one large block of stone. It was half submerged in the soil, and depicted a kneeling warrior with his stone sword thrust into the earth. It wore a helm and armor, its face grave and forbidding. The finer details were lost on me, though. All I could think about was if it was that tall kneeling, how big it must be if it were fully standing.

Then I noticed what lie around the statue's knees. There was a little stone hut nearly hidden in the side of a hillock and covered with a turf roof. Smoke rose from a chimney and I could smell something cooking. Stacked stones lie in groups, spreading out from where the statue knelt.

I recognized them for what they were. Cairns. When the earth was too rocky to dig a grave and the land too dry to burn a pyre without risk of a wildfire, a body was placed on the soil, and stones stacked over it. Serving both as a tomb and a grave marker.

There were several tall stones in a pattern around the statue, similar to standing stones on Earth, like Stone Henge. They were tall by our standards, but didn't even reach a quarter of the way up the statue's thigh.

"What *is* that?" I whispered. The first thing I'd said all day. Rìgh Orok grunted behind me and adjusted his hold around my waist. Thankfully, he hadn't grown a boner the entire ride and his arm had slackened when he realized I would not bolt. I'd still have bruises, but at least he hadn't kept a hard grip on me.

"That is Carrachan Neach-gleidhidh." He explained gruffly. "A fallen giant from ancient times. It's where we bury our dead who died in battle."

"It doesn't look like it's fallen. It looks like it's keeping vigil." I murmured, the winds sweeping the low, rocky grasslands, snatching my words from my lips. The hairs rose on my body as I stared at it.

I knew little, but this I knew was true. This watching statue wasn't dead. It was very much alive.

Like the gàrradh, Ruksala's gaze, Hiskouk's tea reading, or the Craobh na Beatha. Some old magic that lingered on this planet lived in that statue. It was both fitting and jarring to have such a monument keep watch over the souls of the Oc'Turin dead.

"We'll break here!" Rìgh Orok shouted back down the line. "Unload the bodies and lay them out for the priest."

The line of nocrys and soldiers halted. As everyone dismounted, a tall, willowy male exited the stone hut and glided over to us. Rìgh Orok left to speak with him and my new bodyguard came over to monitor me.

"I have to pee," I told him. He just grunted and led me around the back of the hillock where the hut was. There was a stone outhouse, and I was strangely relieved to find one. I'd been afraid I'd have to pee in the grass with all the world able to get a good gander at my fat ass.

My bodyguard even had his back turned and stayed that way as I entered the outhouse, did my business, and exited it. Wordlessly, I stopped at his side and he nodded down to me. We returned to where the soldiers were laying out the dead along the ever-widening spiral at the kneeling form of the stone giant.

The priest stopped at each corpse, or what was left of them, and said a small prayer in a low tone and language I hadn't heard yet. But when he arrived at Womb-splitter's corpse, the priest paled. Rìgh Orok demanded the priest say the last rites, pointing savagely at his fallen friend. But the priest shook his head and said something in that other language that wasn't Teanga Dhubh or Common. Rìgh Orok stiffened, roared, and walked away. The priest avoided Womb-splitter's corpse like the plague.

What the hell was that all about?

Once the dead were laid out and the priest got to work, we loaded back up and turned west toward the setting suns. Rìgh Orok's grip was cruel again, and I fought not to wince. I hadn't had time to see my mate during our break, but I could almost feel him and his calm strength whispering to me with the wind. Steeling my nerves and buoying my spirit from somewhere at the back of the line.

We will survive.

The mantra repeated in my head as Rìgh Orok's claws pressed into my belly and the nocrys under us prowled the vast grasslands of the Oc'Turin territory toward their capital.

CHAPTER 05*

AMELIA

We arrived at the capital of the Oc'Turin clan at sundown. I wasn't sure what I expected. Small sparse huts and poverty, most likely. Instead, it was a bustling little city that was embedded on either side of a deep gorge. There were small waterfalls that splashed down established stone waterways between the terraced layers of buildings, carved from the rock after thousands of years of erosion, to the broad river far below. Mist from the falls drifted through the air, catching fire in the light of the setting suns. A hauntingly beautiful scene that reminded me of Rivendell.

The broad streets were cobbled in the same grey stone as everything else in winding switchbacks up and down the gorge. Carved railings followed the outer edges of the avenues, their weather-worn scale-etched surfaces standing as a measure of safety for the inhabitants. Sunstone braziers were set high overhead on stone pillars like street lamps, the posts carved to look like winding serpents.

Possibly the same type of serpent Rhuger had hunted and shingled our home tree with back in Baile Coille. It made sense that a clan that valued power would use a great wyrm as a symbol and motif for the city. I'd just imagined everything to appear far cruder than it did. But then, maybe this place was like similar to my marriage with my ex-husband. Seemingly lovely at first, with the monstrous aspects not rearing their head until you were already caught in the snare. Until it was too late.

As we made our way through the city, there were multiple bridges that crossed the span of the gorge at different heights. Their pillars plummeted down deep into the swiftly moving waters below. Even the bridge pillars were carved, resembling giant orckin holding the bridges upon their shoulders.

The homes and buildings were cut into the sides of the gorge in orderly, terraced levels. The higher the terrace, the larger and more elaborate the building was and carved with extravagant detail. All the roofs were made of grassy turf. Some of them even acted as small gardens for the homes on the terraces above. Stone rain chains dangled from the gutters, catching the moisture from the falls to be collected and used by the city's residents. And despite everything being made of stone, there were hardly any straight hard lines in sight. Everything was curved to mimic serpents or the river below. A marvel of stone and turf and curved architecture that spoke of unparalleled craftsmanship and skill.

But it was what loomed before the massive waterfall at the mouth of the river that really blew my mind. The gorge narrowed nearer to the falls. Straddling this narrower stretch was an enormous stone building that was built straight into the rock on either side of the falls, which fell in a powerful torrent behind it. It was imposing in its construction as it arched over the chasm beneath it. The top of the building was mostly flat, glaringly out of place amongst the curves of the city, with turrets interspersed along the parapets. The rest of the building's architecture, though, favored the powerful, sinuous nature of the city's theme.

High above the building, the mouth of the waterfall was literally the stone-carved head of a massive horned and fanged serpent. The enormous cousin to the smaller serpents carved elsewhere in the city. Water gushed out of the stone serpent's mouth to plunge into the riverbed below in a deafening roar. It was an imposing sight, but one that didn't inspire fear in me like it probably should have. Instead, I had a similar tingle of awareness to when I'd looked upon the stone giant on the steppes. As if the lifeblood of the river had imbued the stone wyrm-head with a type of sentience over the long life of the city. And like with the stone giant, it was hard to tear my gaze away.

The more I looked at the details before us, the more I saw how the city reflected the serpentine aesthetic. Serpents and fangs were carved on every spare blank space. Even the enormous woven green and silver banners that hung from the bridges had that same herald of silver fangs on a green field as the flag that had waved over Rìgh Orok's tent the night before. I didn't need to be an expert in textiles to appreciate how glorious the banners were, even from so far away. There was far more talent here amongst the Oc'Turin than just the art of war. Though that talent didn't lack one iota in expressing power just the same.

"Welcome to Clach-tholl." Rìgh Orok said behind me, his fingers finally easing from around my waist. "And that keep at the head of the river is Cìp Carragh. Your new home."

I said nothing, still staring ahead, lost to the gray haze of dissociation. Still absorbing what I was seeing without actually *seeing* it. None of this felt real to me. More like I was standing in a hologram of a movie. Where I was *in* it, but not a *part* of it.

As we wound our way down the cobbled avenues toward the keep, orckin came out of the houses and onto the roof gardens to cheer for their returned Rìgh and his *liberated* mate-to-be. They threw stalks of twirling grass to spiral their way lazily to the cobbles at our feet. Their own version of a flower-petal welcome. The sounds became deafening and I felt darkness closing in on the edges of my vision.

It wasn't until the end of the line, when the last wagon rolled into view, that the cheers turned into booing. It seemed they remembered Rhuger, and not fondly. I dared a glance over my shoulder and saw people throwing food waste down where Rhuger must have been. Clenching my jaw, I refused to let anything show on my face. Instead, I turned forward again and inwardly raged at my mate's humiliation, not caring if Rìgh Orok could smell it on me.

Rhuger didn't deserve to be treated that way.

Eventually, we made it to the keep. We rode in through a double iron and stone gate to a bailey devoid of gardens that had flourished within the bailey at Daingneach under Hisouk's care. Only a small patch of greenery existed near stables for the nocrys to shit on. The rest of the bailey was dedicated to warcraft. Training grounds of all kinds and a smithy ate up any free space available. It was a cold, hard place made more so by the din of the waterfall. Thankfully, the sentries closed the gates behind us, blocking out the crowds who had followed us to pelt their exiled prince with whatever they had on hand.

I wanted to *burn them all alive.*

Instead, I sunk my claws into the palms of my hands. Allowing the pain to center and steady me so I could keep the blank look on my face. My scent was one out of hundreds in the bailey and no one seemed happy to be there. So I might have been physically out of place with my pale grey neamhnaid skin and chubby body, but my expression and scent fit right in.

I couldn't very well exact revenge for my cridhe surrounded by warriors in the stone cage of the bailey. No matter how much my claws itched to rip out Rìgh Orok's throat. That would have to wait, *I* would have to wait. So I swore to bide my time, glean what I could, free Rhuger, and make them all *pay*.

All the martial drills were called to a halt, every soldier lined up in exacting rows to greet their returned Rìgh. I felt countless eyes on me as Rìgh Orok dismounted and held out a hand to me. I turned my head to look at his scarred palm, then up into his banana slug yellow eyes. Tugging at my restraints, I silently reminded him I wasn't able to play the princess, so he could 'sweep me off my feet' if my hands were bound to the pommel of his nocrys.

A flash of irritation flickered in his gaze and was gone. With quick, efficient moves, he sliced the ropes free from my wrists and pommel. They slid away from my arms, revealing chaffed and bloody flesh from the rough cordage and long ride. Without asking, he picked me up around the waist and set me down on my feet. If it wasn't for the riding lessons Sigg had given me, I would have face-planted in front of everyone, including my gods and theirs. But, I managed to keep my feet. I stood tall, my vertebrae popping as I reminded my body what it was like to be in any position other than saddle-bound.

And *still*, I could feel hundreds of male eyes on me. Devouring my shape and smell and pearly skin like starved beasts. I refused to look at them, refused to grant them power over me. Instead, I looked ahead to the stone steps that led up to the entrance to the keep. The stone serpent's maw spewed forth the river overhead, looming like a death threat.

I only felt their gazes leave me when Rhuger was dragged forward.

"Take him to the dungeons. I'll deal with him when I'm good and *ready*." Rìgh Orok snapped at the males hauling my mate towards us. Heading past us to an entrance in the cliff that must have led to where the dungeons were. When Rhuger got close enough that I could see him better, I froze.

The state my mate was in tore the breath from my lungs and drained the blood from my face. They'd taken his boots. Left him to walk all those miles on the rocky ground of the plains barefoot. Bloody footprints left a damning stain on the cobbles in his wake. Flicking my gaze up from his limping feet, I noticed that they'd shorn his lovely, silky hair. Cut it so short, that only a few inches stuck out in uneven tufts.

And that's when I noticed everything else. They'd beaten him. More than once on our journey. Some wounds looked almost healed while others were fresh. A couple of his fingers were sticking out in unnatural directions. His nose was broken and his lip was split, his brow swollen over his left eye. Rhuger kept one arm tucked close to his side as if his ribs were broken.

But the worst part was the long, raw lash strokes I saw peeking over his shoulders. And when he turned, his back was an absolute *travesty*. Someone had *whipped* him as if they'd meant to kill him, not just punish him. The lesser marks were mostly healed. But the larger ones, the deeper ones that could have only been made by the vicious bladed lashes of a cat-o'-nine-tails, were sluggishly knitting back together before my eyes. I could see the white notches of his vertebrae and I almost fainted as understanding dawned.

If he hadn't possessed his insane healing ability, he would have died miles ago. That he'd survived this entire journey and not fallen, just to have his corpse dragged behind us, was an outright miracle. A miracle that was about to be further tested in the bowels of the Oc'Turin dungeons.

Rage was an icy red mist that invaded every atom within me. Obliterating anything and everything else down to my very soul. Whoever had done this. Whoever had had the *gall*, the absolute *audacity*, to mutilate my cridhe like this was going to *pay*. No matter what happened, I was going to leave those motherfuckers with *meat mops for hands.*

By the grace of whatever higher power was looking out for me, I managed to keep my expression neutral. I caught my cridhe's gaze. His eyes were hazed with pain, but still sharp and clear and alert upon me. Raking over me to make sure *I* was okay and taking stock of what he found. When he saw how my forearms and wrists were chaffed and bloody, that my face and neck were swollen and bruised, I swear I saw his silver eyes flash red.

But my wounds were *nothing* compared to his. I couldn't even feel them past the roaring in my head that matched the wrath of the waterfall behind me. I couldn't even blink in the face of how they had brutalized him.

My soul ached and bled and tore at seeing my other half so hurt. There was *nothing* I could do for him right now. And it *ate me alive inside.*

A soft whisper of understanding passed between us in the mere moment we had as he was dragged within touching distance. No matter what, I was his cridhe, and he was mine. No matter what we faced, we'd do all we could to survive. And if the gods lacked mercy, and we died at the hands of these power-hungry wretches...

It was worth it all. For our souls to overcome unfathomable odds to touch across the vastness of the universe. To know what it meant to be whole. To be *home*. Even for a moment.

But between one heartbeat and the next, my beloved's onyx and silver gaze passed and that moment was gone.

CARLOTTA HUGHES

CHAPTER 06*

AMELIA

I don't remember much after Rhuger was led toward the gaping maw in the wrought stone in the cliff face. Toward the dungeons and whatever cruel torture they had planned for him. All I remember was passing through the keep doors and into the darkness beyond. There was an older sour-mouthed female in a grey dress that took my arm and steered me away.

We walked through hall after hall, up and down stairs, through passageways, and along walkways. Likely some meandering path meant to confuse the shit out of me so I couldn't escape. What they failed to realize was that there were a *bunch* of open windows and archways on both sides of the keep. I was able to keep track of where we were by the unique rocks that jutted out past the waterfall on one side and the city on the other. I had a very good internal mental map, courtesy of being neurodivergent. Yay.

After a while, the old female seemed to grow tired of her own game and led me into a room on the far side of the keep. It was a private bathing room. Gorgeously appointed for someone feminine with looping swathes of cloth to soften all the stone, flowers in carved stone vases, and a lovely pool full of hot water. Flower petals were strewn everywhere and great embroidered cushions offered plenty of seating. Or places to fuck.

But beneath all the soft colors and pretty flowers were more of those serpents carved into the rough stone. Even at the back of the bathing pool, there was a relief sculpture of a gorgeous, surprisingly curvy, female orckin wrapped sensually by a powerful, sinuous horned serpent. The fact Sharn explained that there were few curvy females and that *I* was a curvy *part* orckin female, made me a little uneasy. Why would orckin carve an attribute they rarely saw in their own kind?

Unless... It was a depiction of a female like me. Human *and* orckin. Being dominated by the symbol of the Oc'Turin. The concept slithered into my bones and left me feeling queasy.

"Strip." The old female ordered as a group of scantily clad females entered the bathing room from a side door.

Some were tall and willowy like Sharn, others were broader like Manira, and a few were shorter and smaller built. Not unlike Grammie Ruksala. Not wanting the old sourpuss to have a reason to hurt me, I started to strip. Within moments, many pairs of hands were on me, helping me take my clothes off. Before I knew it, I was standing there naked amongst a throng of gawking females in wispy slips.

I wanted to scowl at them. Tell them they were being rude and making me uncomfortable. Instead, I just continued to stare ahead at nothing while taking in what I could.

Glancing down, I noted the bruises and scratches over my belly. As if Rìgh Orok was incapable of handling anything soft. As if he'd been thinking of clawing out my baby. It was a good thing Rhuger hadn't seen these. He would have gone nuclear.

Looking back up, it was as if the females didn't even notice the scratches and bruises, the bloody scrapes, or the raw flesh of my forearms. Instead, they bustled close to me, encircling me with lots of giggling and bouncing boobs. If they weren't taller than me so I was getting an eyeful, they were short enough to shove their face between my breasts. One actually fake stumbled and did. The older female pulled her aside and chastised her, but the short female wasn't even listening. Too far gone in bliss to care.

Well... That was new. Were they high?

The gaggle of giggling females dragged me towards the pool and down into it. There was a little stone bench in the center of the pool that they insisted I sit on. Their slips turned see-through the second they got wet and I had the distinct impression things were about to get far more intimate than I was okay with.

Not that I'd never been attracted to women. I had. But Rhuger was my mate. For me, whenever I'd been in a romantic relationship, no one else had existed on a romantic or sexual level. That state of being was now permanent because I'd found my cridhe. My *home*. No one did or ever would exist in that capacity for me ever again.

A couple of the females combed out the tangles in my hair with soft brushes and combs. Others got loofas and soaps and pretty scented bath things to rub, scrub, and rubba-dub me into a shiny rosy glow. Once my hair was washed and oiled, my skin scrubbed, and my shoulders and arms massaged, a drop-dead *gorgeous* female came toward me in the water.

She was stocky but built like a brick house. Her hair was wavy black and glossy as it spilled over her shoulders. Her eyes were a deep sunset pink, such a strange color to see in someone's gaze. Where the slip she wore didn't cover, her skin shone in the glowing light of the sunstone lanterns. It was that rare dark black with a pink sheen to it, making her look like a goddess of twilight and bedroom whispers.

Gliding up to me, she looked at me coyly from under her lashes before sliding her perfectly manicured hands down the tops of my thighs. She gently grasped my knees and spread my legs wide. Before I could close them, she slid between them and pressed herself up against me with a soft gasp.

Hot *damn*.

If I hadn't been taken with absolutely *no* desire for anyone else, I would have truly let her do whatever the hell she wanted to me. But nothing sparked within me at her touch. I didn't feel threatened by her actions as I would have if she had been a male. I just had an uncomfortable feeling in my gut and a visceral need for this to *stop*.

Because *no one* should ever touch me like this except Rhuger. My *mate*. My *cridhe*.

So when she leaned in to kiss me, a heated look of desire in her eyes, I leaned back and shook my head no. She tried again, and once again, I shook my head no. This time more firmly with a scowl.

Too much had happened for me to be capable of opening my mouth, let alone speak. I'd been within my mind for far too long. Masking the best I could through the horrors of the last day and a half. I only hoped she understood and stopped.

"She's not for the likes of you! She's for the Rìgh. Don't sully her before he's got his chance to bed her." The old female snapped and the gorgeous stocky female between my thighs ducked her head in a pout and thankfully backed off.

I sighed in relief through my nose.

If Sharn was here, she'd die in perfect sapphic bliss, surrounded by horny females that wanted to pleasure each other like bonobos. Which a few of them were doing, as their task of cleaning me was now complete. One female was even seated at the edge of the pool underneath the relief sculpture, her head flung back against the stone and her hand on the back of another female's head as she feasted on her. Moaning loudly and throwing her legs over the female's shoulders.

Well, at least someone was enjoying themselves.

I stood and turned from the orgy that was just beginning in the pool behind me. There were a few females that didn't participate. Instead, they helped me dry off and get dressed in some sorry excuse of a dress. Not unlike the one I'd worn at the Mating Tournament. Only this one was a deep emerald. With *sparkles*.

Joy. I got to glitter.

But really, this dress was worse than the one from the Mating Tournament and it had nothing to do with the glitter. There was a front panel and a back panel that connected at the shoulders by thin chains. Both sides had *deep* v-necklines that plummeted down to just above my belly button before continuing down to the floor in a single swathe of fabric. It left absolutely *nothing* to the imagination and I had the distinct feeling that this dress was designed for someone more slender than I was. The thing barely covered my nipples, groin, and ass crack.

They slung a belt low around my hips to keep the 'dress' together. It was made of golden, twining serpents that devoured one another. Like an orckin version of the ouroboros. It was pretty, a work of art in and of itself, but I didn't have it in me to care. One attendant knelt and slid jangling bangles onto my ankles and a cold knot formed in my gut. They felt like bells on a pet collar.

I was thankful for how brusque these other females were. Obviously the proper servants instead of the bed servants who were currently screaming their orgasms into the steamy air behind me. I winced as the sound reverberated against the stone and pierced my eardrums.

Gentle fingers applied cosmetics to my face and styled my hair. But I'd already dissociated again. When I came to, I was standing before a set of double doors at the end of a long, stone hallway carved with more twining shapes and decorated with elaborate tapestries. I blinked and noticed that the old female was still with me. She squinted at me like she wasn't sure if I was a simpleton or not, before knocking loudly on the doors.

I could hear the sounds of pleasure on the other side, and my insides turned into cold noodles. What the *fuck* was I supposed to be doing? They'd had females willing to *prime* me to be fertile, so Rìgh Orok could supposedly *breed* me. Even though I was already pregnant. Was I really going to have to follow through with this?

But then I paused at the sound of the male moaning on the other side of the door. It was *not* Rìgh Orok. The other male's cries reached a high, fevered pitch just as another male roared his release.

Ah. *That* was Rìgh Orok.

The doors opened then and a pretty, slender female with high breasts and narrow features stood on the other side. She was dressed like me, but in a shade of silver to accentuate her dusky green skin that glowed with a pearly sheen like mine.

Ah. So Rìgh Orok liked to collect pearls, did he?

I looked past her and saw Rìgh Orok still rolling his hips into the ass of a slender male who kept crying out in ecstasy with his hands fisted in the silver sheets. Rìgh Orok moaned loud and low with his head flung back and his claws sunk into the male's slim hips. His pleasure mate's cock kept spurting cum all over the bedding.

Ew.

Nothing wrong with what they were doing or whatever kinks they were enjoying. I just wanted to puke over seeing Rìgh Orok doing *anything* remotely sexual. If I truly had to bed him, I *definitely* was gonna puke in his face and have no regrets about it.

The other female took my hand and nodded to the older female who left. The doors closed behind us as she led me to two elaborately bedazzled cushions near the massive bed the two males were on. As she did, I looked around, keeping my eyes anywhere but where Rìgh Orok and his pleasure mate were coming down from their orgasms.

The room was definitely masculine in taste. Dark woods mixed with leather and hard stone. But there were surprising touches of lighter, prettier things. Delicate glass bottles, colorful pillows, and other luxuries and comforts. Glancing at the female holding my hand, who must be Orok's official mate, I seriously doubted that they belonged to her.

They most likely belonged to the slender male who had turned his head to look at me. I had to hand it to Rìgh Orok, the male *was* damned pretty. With elegant features, turquoise eyes, and skin like burnished copper, dusted in body glitter to make himself appear to be Neamhnaid. But then he smiled an evil smirk at me and I decided he wasn't all *that* pretty.

Rìgh Orok's mate knelt gracefully on the silver pillow and she tugged at my hand, her head bowed and eyes downcast in submission to her Rìgh. I almost broke my mask, my lip threatening to curl and a bark of a laugh nearly choking me in a dark need to slip past my teeth. Instead, I knelt, not as gracefully as she did, on the emerald cushion. It seemed Rìgh Orok had to keep us color coded to remember who we were.

Gotdamnit, I was too tired and hungry for this shit. I hadn't had food since that morning and I was famished. My body ached, my heart longed for brutal vengeance, and my head demanded I sleep.

"Took you long enough." Rìgh Orok grunted as he pulled free from his pleasure mate.

The male, who I was now going to call Sparkle Cheeks, held his ass cheeks wide and looked up adoringly at his Rìgh in his prone position. Rìgh Orok's cum dripped out of his ass, down his balls, to plop and mingle with his cum on the bedding.

Rìgh Orok smirked and slapped the other male's ass in approval before turning his attention to us. To *me*. An unwilling participant in this.

My eyes were of course drawn to Rìgh Orok's... *Package*. It was... Well, it was *smaller* than Rhuger's, to be sure. But then, Rhuger was also bigger and taller than his brother. So he *seemed* proportionate. Regardless, seeing his swaying dick and balls dripping with cum made me want to puke all over the pretty woven rug beneath the ridiculously decorated pillow I knelt on.

Strangely enough, it was then that I noticed that what I thought were statues were really artfully posed orckin females who sprang to life the moment Rìgh Orok left the bed. They helped clean up the pleasure mate and changed the bedding. Hell, one even came over with a cloth, knelt at the Rìgh's feet, and *wiped off his dick*.

I mean, bless that poor female for being subjected to such a *duty*, but I was grateful.

My mind blanked at the entitled absurdity of it all. I wanted to rage, I truly did. But human kings had done more outlandish things for no apparent reason, so I continued to keep my expression blank and my mouth shut. Rìgh Orok stood staring at me and panting as the female finished. Then he placed his hand on her face and shoved her to the floor with a haughty expression.

It didn't take a genius to realize this prick was a misogynist.

He strode over to stand before me, his cock and balls *way* too close to my face. Gods, if only I could punch him in the dick and survive the aftermath...

He then reached down and snatched my face in his hand, pressing his claws in ever so slightly and wrenching my head back so I was forced to look up into his slimy yellow eyes. His gaze was assessing. Making a dismissive sound, he released my face.

"All females want *good orckin seed* in their bellies. To *swell* with child and carry on our race." He said with a fervent look in his eye.

Pretty sure I could say with confidence on behalf of both orckin *and* human females that was a big '*NO, THANK YOU*'. And now I understood why Rhuger had appreciated the way the Oc'Dellor treated their females. He'd wanted a partner, his cridhe, not a baby-making machine. Somehow, my grandfather had found a balance between treating females like people and promoting promiscuity to do what was possible to keep their race from dying out.

Recognizing that look in Rìgh Orok's eye as a villain about to monologue, I sat still like a good submissive little female and waited for him to give me all I'd need to destroy him.

"I don't give in to the *weak desires* of females. You are here for *our* pleasure at *our* whim." Rìgh Orok said, his arms spread wide like some preacher at a pulpit.

He started blathering on and on, and I quickly tuned him out. Every single point he thought he made like a paragon of insight, was precisely what I'd heard from far too many dudes with a microphone and a podcast. He was just a control freak who hated females, felt his superiority threatened, and sought to create a facade of power and authority.

At least I already had everything I needed to tear him down. All I had to do was kick his ass. Publicly. It was going to be far easier than I'd imagined.

After almost an hour of him preaching his inane evil master

plan at us, his pleasure mate got bored enough to come over and kneel before his Rìgh. He gently turned Rìgh Orok more to the side so we'd be forced to watch him as he sucked his master's cock less than three feet away. Rìgh Orok was pleased, grinning and caressing his pleasure mate, who literally lapped him up like a cat with cream.

Dear *lordt* my eyes.

I dared a glance at the female next to me, but she still sat there absolutely still. As did all the other females who littered the suite as living statues. Nothing more than decoration.

"Look at me, Oc'Dellor." Rìgh Orok snapped, and despite myself, I did. The grin that lit his face was full of condescending entitlement mixed with avid lust. He held his pleasure mate's face between his hands and began to fuck his throat with a panting snarl. Not caring one bit if he hurt his partner. Only focusing on holding eye contact with *me*.

And that's when I realized this sick fuck wasn't getting off on getting sucked off. He was getting off by fucking his pleasure mate's face in front of two females he had no intention of *ever* touching. Denying we'd have any potential physical urges. Like we weren't people to him.

It was the power trip he got off on.

Rìgh Orok roared as he shot his load down poor Sparkle Cheeks' gagging throat. It burst past the seam of the male's mouth to dribble down his chin onto the floor in front of us. All the while, Orok's eyes were still locked with mine.

And I found myself *bored*.

So I cocked an unimpressed eyebrow at him and then looked over at his so-called mate, who sat demurely like this was normal. Her eyes were empty, though. And it was enough to tell me of his cruelty.

His uninspired cruelty.

"You will watch, Oc'Dellor." He growled as he shoved Sparkle Cheeks away. And I saw the adoration in the male's gaze as he swiped at his chin. The poor sap was actually in love with this sick bastard. Actually thought that all of this was what constituted *being* loved. I pitied him.

"My name is Amelia," I replied blandly. The first thing I'd said nearly all day. "And I don't consent to watch this."

He did not like this.

"Your name is whatever I say it is, *female*." He rumbled as he stalked over and backhanded me. "Your consent doesn't matter, either. Now, *you will watch* as I fuck this male and you will dream of all the ways I *won't* take you with my massive cock." He said smugly as he returned to the bed, pulling his pleasure mate along. He threw him onto the bed, flipped him over, and slapped his ass roughly.

It elicited a moan from the slim male before Rìgh Orok slammed his cock home in his ass in one punishing thrust. Sparkle Cheeks cried out and nutted all over the bedding. Well. That was fast.

I swallowed a mouthful of blood and unfocused my eyes as Rìgh Orok grunted like a rutting boar over the smaller male. There was no love or care in what they were doing. There were all kinds of folk with all sorts of proclivities, but there was always a line that shouldn't be crossed. And Rìgh Orok right pissed all over that line and mooned it as he skipped down to hell.

Rìgh Orok was a sociopathic, sadistic misogynist with unresolved mommy and daddy issues. But he wasn't the first male I'd known like him. I would survive this. I'd survived being the orc on the bed, after all.

So instead of focusing on what was happening in front of me, I let memories of Rhuger flood my mind. His deep, rumbling laugh that was like pure velvet. How sweetly he would cup my face before kissing me. How those silver rings of his irises in all that black would somehow smolder hotter than smelted ore when he looked at me with that heavy-lidded gaze of his. I thought of his tenderness, his touch, the way he would moan my name. And how perfectly we fit together, physically, mentally, and emotionally. One soul in two bodies.

"Och. My new little mate smells hungry and jealous." The bastard laughed and flipped his plaything over onto his back before grasping his hips and sinking into him again. Sparkle Cheeks moaned wildly and writhed beneath my captor like it was the best sex of his life. Perhaps it was.

I threw up a little in my mouth.

"Watch me come inside this orc, mate. And know that my seed will never be yours." He growled before picking up his pace, hips snapping so hard against the Sparkle Cheeks' ass that I was sure someone's balls were going to rupture.

This idiot thought I was getting horny off of his shitty porno fantasy? *PPffft*

Whatever.

I decided not to disillusion him. So I pretended he didn't exist again and let my mind drift into my sea of memories of Rhuger. How sweet he tasted. The reverence he'd shown as he held me when we mated for the first time. How easy it was to break his control, just by showing him how much I wanted him. Oh, and how he'd spanked me and ate me out.

Yeah, good times.

I distantly registered that Orok was roaring his release, Sparkle Cheeks wailing his name. But it was far away, and I had my memories of Rhuger holding me close as we fell asleep tangled together to buffer the horror of the situation. He was saving me without even being here.

I loved that orc so fiercely that tears pricked my eyes.

At least things weren't as bad for me physically as I'd feared they would be when Orok abducted me. He couldn't care less about my body, it didn't suit his desires. It was my mind he was trying to break.

Too bad for him I'd been broken and re-broken repeatedly. I had put myself back together more times than I cared to admit. It was like being tortured by the best and then having a complete amateur come in and fumble around. It was both a relief and almost an insult.

I only hoped my cridhe was alive. That I could somehow save him. I just prayed to whoever would listen that Orok continued to be predictable.

CHAPTER 07*

RHUGER

I couldn't tell if it'd been hours or days since they dragged me away from my cridhe and down into the dungeons that I knew so well.

I'd been a captor here before, after all.

Back when my younger brother Orok conspired for the Throne of Fangs. He'd murdered our father in cold blood and pinned the crime on me. Coerced my mate-to-be to become his. Slowly and systematically destroyed everything that was mine. Everything I'd wanted or loved. All because our mother had favored me more.

Because I was the child born of love. A love she'd had with a traveler. One that Orok's father had seethed over until he murdered my mother's love before her eyes. And took her as his own mate.

I couldn't blame her for loving me the way she did. And I couldn't blame her for only seeing Orok as the product of the murder of her love and subsequent internment. I also couldn't blame her for getting fed up with the abuse she endured daily at her mate's hands. Jumping from the Serpent's Mouth to her death.

She had been the Banrigh in her own right. As I was her eldest son, I should have taken over the Throne of Fangs when Orok's father died. But because of the circumstances of his death, I was blamed, imprisoned, tortured, then exiled.

Only a few stood up for me. And were severely punished for it, my best friend Kholt included. I'd missed him greatly these past years. I hadn't seen him yet, but I fervently wished he was alright. That he'd somehow managed to flourish in the Oc'Turin court.

When I wasn't hanging from chains against the back wall of a cell, I was whipped or beaten. The jailers, along with the warriors and elite, had learned a long time ago that I healed abnormally fast. That something in my parentage, some old magic, still lingered. They hated me for it. So they took every chance they got to inflict as much damage as they could. But they refrained from organ damage and dismemberment, thankfully.

It'd been at least a few hours since a jailer had come in to lay into me. The lashes from the whip were almost done healing. But healing came at a cost. Each time I healed, it sapped my strength. I would grow weaker and weaker until I couldn't hold up my head. As it was, I was having trouble standing as I faded in and out of consciousness.

The sound of keys jangling cut through the quiet dark followed by a lock sliding open, and the squealing of hinges. It took immense effort to keep my body from falling into a trembling fit in the face of the heralds of my next beating. I lifted my head as a torch swung into the choking black of my cell. Blinking against the light, I couldn't get my eyes to focus beyond the flames to see who had come to beat me next.

But there was a hissing intake of breath, as if in shock. They set the torch into a bracket on the wall and suddenly a face I knew almost as well as my own swam into my vision. I had to be hallucinating. I hadn't realized it'd gotten this bad so quickly.

"What in the darkness between the stars did they do to you?" Came a rasping voice that had acted like a guiding light in my mind whenever I'd found myself in a dark state. The words were a familiar curse I hadn't heard since before my exile. I blinked and frowned, fighting to focus. The sharp planes, flattened mouth, scowling expression, and scarred throat made my pulse quicken in recognition.

Kholt.

It truly was Kholt.

I was so happy to see him. And I was torn between the joy of reuniting with my best friend and the knowledge that my cridhe was in the clutches of my mortal enemy. Unable to stop myself, a tear slid from my swollen eye to drip off of my chin onto the stone floor. The only tear of mine to ever fall in this cursed place.

"Kholt," I said his name, my voice dry and my lips cracked. He moved then, striding quickly to my side.

"I'm here, brother." Kholt rasped and lifted a water skein to my mouth.

I gulped it down greedily, my body needing fuel and water to heal. Things my jailers had denied me to prolong my punishment. When the skein was empty, he tossed it aside and broke open a hand pie he had brought with him.

"Eat it slowly." He commanded, and I obeyed. He hand-fed it to me in pieces. It was warm and delicious, filled with meat and vegetables. I nearly sobbed. "It's all right."

So strange to have him comfort me after all the times I'd comforted him. Once I'd swallowed the last of the hand pie, I took a deep breath. My ribs were already knitting back together. Even that small amount of food and water did wonders for the worst of my wounds.

"Where's Amelia?" I growled and pulled on the shackles overhead.

"In the throne room." He said, face a determined mask that I read like the back of my hand. He knew she was my mate. Knew she carried my bairn. And was ready to do whatever it took to make sure we got out of here alive. I didn't deserve him. "Someone owed me a favor. So I called it in. Swapped with them to be the one to come get you."

"Is she hurt?" I asked as he lifted a key and undid the shackles.

Still too weak to stand on my own, Kholt caught me and held me upright. My shoulder joints screamed in agony after bearing my weight for so long, my arms a riot of pins and needles I couldn't hope to move yet. I grunted as he ducked down to haul one of my limp arms over his shoulders. He was a good handspan taller than me, built for speed, and as strong as a buabhall, one of the large fluffy beasts that roamed the grasslands in herds. But thankfully he didn't offer to carry me.

"Distant," was all he said, and I growled deep in my throat. I knew what it meant when she was distant. And I swore to shred my brother's corpse for putting her in that state.

As I staggered alongside Kholt out of the dungeons, I noticed what was left of my jailers and grinned. Kholt just handed me another hand pie as I snatched a water skin off the table by the door. I ate and drank as much as I could as we walked toward the keep. Forcing myself to keep it down even as my guts roiled at having so much food and water shoved into them after so long without. I had to be strong for my cridhe as she was being strong for me.

AMELIA

After a sleepless night of watching Rìgh Orok fuck Sparkle

Cheeks, I was about ready to go postal. If I *ever* had to see that much cum come from any other male than my cridhe, I'd be knocking male dick in the dirt. How his other female mate, her name was Sagra I'd discovered, dealt with this shit for years, I had no clue.

Unable to sleep, change, or eat in a cold stone keep made me cranky. For gods' sake, I was *pregnant,* and I was *hungry.* Instead of getting a hot breakfast, or hell, even a cold one, Sagra and I were ushered down to the throne room. To get the great *honor* of being Rìgh Orok's arm candy.

We were given little stools to perch on that matched our sorry excuses for dresses. Not unlike the cushions in Rìgh Orok's room. Sagra perched daintily on hers. Mine? Well, my ass nearly enveloped the little thing. I probably looked like I had a stick up my ass.

Unable to get comfortable, I followed Sagra's lead and leaned against the throne. It helped ease the ache in my ass somewhat. It would have been nicer if the throne wasn't *literally* made of giant fangs. Probably from those massive serpents that the Oc'Turin were obsessed with.

Rìgh Orok entered the bustling throne room and everyone bowed low as he swaggered up the steps in a fine tunic and trousers. A crown of smaller fangs and gold perched upon his head. With a flourish, he sat. As one, the orckin in the room stood straight once more. No seating for any of these orcs.

"Welcome, my clansmen!" He called, loud and clear and slightly whiny. "Today is a fortunate day! I have saved Leanabh Banrigh Amelia Oc'Dellor from the clutches of my traitorous brother!"

Bullshit! I ached to screech it until everyone's ears bled. Instead, I kept my trap shut as the males within the throne room whooped and hollered at their Rìgh's 'victory'.

"She has agreed to be my mate!"

Lies!

More cheering and excitement from the males in the audience. The females mostly held blank expressions like Sagra and I. Guess you had to in order to survive the dastardly Oc'Turin court.

"And she now bears my orcling!"

Mufukka WHAT did you just say?!

Now the crowd went *wild*. Their Rìgh, in one fell swoop, had saved a princess, defeated his brother, earned the love of the princess, and got her with child. What a crock of shit.

Oh. I was going to kill him.

Maybe it was the rush of baby hormones. Maybe it was the lack of sleep mixed in with being hangry or hell, being held hostage by a misogynistic, sadistic sociopath. All I knew was I was one mouse fart away from committing *murder*.

Rìgh Orok raised his hands with a grin on his face. Oh, he was reveling in the power he wielded at this moment. And I was internally champing at the bit to knock him down a peg or two publicly.

"Now, we will bring forth the traitor who killed my father and sought to steal the Throne of Fangs from me! The one who abducted a princess in order to plant his foul seed within her! My brother!" Rìgh Orok nearly spat with the force of his words as they flew from his mouth in bitter resentment.

A small contingent of guards ushered in a shambling, broken-looking form. My heart nearly stopped in my chest as I saw what they'd done to him. Saw the bruises, gashes, burns, and whip marks that were sluggishly healing. It took everything I had not to let out a broken wail at what they had done to my cridhe.

But as Rhuger's gaze locked with mine from across the room, I could see that deadly surety in his eyes still. They hadn't broken him.

Not completely.

I was so far removed from what was happening around me, that my eyes and my expression must have continued to register as completely blank. Because Rhuger's brows furrowed as he searched my gaze. A heartbroken flicker as if he hadn't found me still in here, lying in wait, surviving. One of the guards kicked him in the back of the knees and sent him to the hard stone floor. I roared into the void in my mind as he struggled to sit back on his haunches.

"Well, brother? What do you think of my new mate?" Rìgh Orok asked as he cupped his hand around my throat, tilting my head up at a painful angle, showing everyone the bruises Womb-splitter left me with, making everyone assume he'd done it. "So lovely and so lusty."

"She's *my* mate," Rhuger growled into the quiet of the crowded throne room. "*Not yours.*"

I couldn't help but slip my gaze to the side where Rìgh Orok was panting against the side of my face, watching Rhuger kneeling on the floor with hungry eyes. I swear he must have had a raging boner by the lusty gleam in his eye. What a sick fucking bastard. His breath stank and I nearly gagged as he ran his disgusting tongue up the side of my face. Did Rìgh Orok get that habit from Womb-splitter, or was it the other way around?

Rude.

If all males here acted like this, no wonder Rhuger up and left this shit-hole.

I could see the sudden wild-eyed fear in Rhuger's expression from across the room when I didn't react. Here I sat, his mate with his child growing in her belly, at the feet of his enemy and brother. Looking for all the world, a placid, dead-eyed doll. Like I'd been thoroughly broken.

I tried to reach for him, heart to heart, soul to soul. To let him know without words that I wasn't broken. Just a hunter biding her time. Playing pretend to encourage an opening in her prey's defenses. But I wasn't sure if it worked.

"Kneel before me, Oc'Dellor. Show your false mate how I like to be sucked." He growled into the quiet. Rhuger began hissing, teeth bared, and the guards yanked him roughly, shoving him to the floor. One of them stomped a booted foot against the side of his head so he'd be forced to watch from the rough stone pavers of the throne room.

Something snapped inside me. The mouse fart that was going to break this asshole's neck.

This fucker wanted to mess with me? That was one thing. But he'd hurt my mate. Repeatedly.

They all gone learn today.

So I got to my knees at Rìgh Orok's feet, like the blank obedient doll they all assumed I was. My gaze cast to the floor, to Rìgh Orok's boots. And that's when I saw it. My chance.

Heh. *Chance.* Like my name.

So I put on the lusty goddess mask I'd dazzled men with in the past, and began wrapping my arms around his leg, using my upper arms to plump up my boobs. I licked my lips and, like every orc I'd encountered so far, Rìgh Orok found it utterly fascinating. Even though he refused all females, my tongue seemed to be the ticket.

Pink tongues, go figure.

As I slid my whole body up his leg, I palmed what I needed from his boot. I crawled between his legs over his kilt, sliding up his thigh with breathy cries, my breasts squishing against one leg. While he was distracted, I brought up my arm that I had hidden behind his calf. My salvation was hidden against a wrist he'd bound so tightly during my abduction that I'd have scars for the rest of my life.

Moaning softly, I kept his gaze locked on my face, my mouth, as I flicked my tongue out and around, showing off what I could do with it. I reached for his belt, and tugged at the buckle, making a show of wanting Rìgh Orok's cock in my mouth.

Orok's breathing hitched, despite himself. Rhuger roared behind me, face plastered to the stone floor, heartbreak in his voice. Orok groaned in erotic victory, in satisfaction over breaking his brother, in breaking *me*. And that was the green light I needed.

I jerked my arm in a sharp, quick jab toward Orok's groin.

The bright flash of steel in my fist made his eyes widen in fear as the small honed boot knife I'd palmed parted his leggings and flesh like a hot knife. Blood gushed from the severed arteries, splashing my arms, chest, and throat with its coppery tang. My fist met his groin, and the knife hit the bone of his pelvis.

I'm pretty sure I severed part of his junk. *Good riddance to rancid garbage.*

Orok began screaming, high-pitched like nails down a chalkboard. With a sneer, I ripped the knife out of his groin and slammed it home into the side of his neck. His mouth snapped shut, screaming cut off, yellow eyes bulging as he made a choking sound. Blood bubbled out from between his lips. He tried to grasp at me, at the knife stuck in his neck, with feeble, weakening hands.

I stood between his bloody legs, hand still firmly gripping the boot knife in his neck. With a satisfying wrench of my arm, I pulled the knife free and tore open part of his throat. His hands scrabbled at his neck in vain as his smiling throat spurted blood like a geyser.

No one in the throne room moved. Not even the guards behind the throne.

"My name is Amelia Chance Oc'Dellor. Great-grandaughter to Fear a Chì Ruksala Oc'Dellor. Granddaughter to Rìgh Thorn Oc'Dellor and Ruth Dellor. Daughter to Sheila Dellor and Austin Chance. Mate to your rightful Rìgh, Rhuger Oc'Turin. And mother to a child of the Oc'Dellor and the Oc'Turin clans. I refuse your touch, you sick bastard. And the only cock I'll be sucking is my mate's."

Now, it was a gamble whether Rìgh Orok had the same healing abilities as his brother or if he'd bleed out quickly. I glanced down at his belt and stacked the odds in my favor. With a cold finality, I ripped his sword free from his belt. Spinning with his sword in hand to get the momentum I needed, I screamed my vengeance as I swung my arm out in a perfect arc.

The sharp, honed blade sliced through fingers, muscle, tendon, and bone with a sickening, squelching thunk. The blade bit deep into the ivory back of the throne, the jarring jolt shuddering up my arm. I watched as Rìgh Orok's mouth twitched and his rancid yellow eyes dulled to the cloudy haze of death.

The silence that followed was so thick it could have been cut with a crumbly Dorito chip.

The only sounds were my harsh breathing and the slow *drip-drip* of Rìgh Orok's blood as it fell from his new sword necklace. After a moment of shocked silence, the hiss of sliding fabric slithered through the room as Orok's bloody body slumped down against the back of the throne. Without a head.

The stump of his neck shot spray after weakening spray of blood. Blood splattered me and everything close by. Sagra stumbled back off of her stool and away from the throne, covered in the lifeblood of her abusive mate. Orok's body hunched forward, and I side-stepped as it fell out of the throne to flop lifelessly on the stone dais below. Blood pooled out from the wounds I'd inflicted to drip down the steps in a macabre cascade. Orok bled out quicker than I'd imagined he would.

I turned to look at his head where it sat on the broad blade of his sword where it'd severed it from his spine. Orok's last expression was one of slack-jawed surprise. The crown of gold and fangs now sat at a crooked, jaunty angle on his snarled ears. I smiled, covered in his gore.

Gripping the crown and head by the hair in one fist, I yanked the blade free with the other. Turning, most likely looking like Carrie hanging out at the Red Wedding, I gazed out over the throne room. I lifted the severed head of their unhinged Rìgh into the air.

A heartbroken wail shattered the silence. It was Sparkle Cheeks, Orok's paramour. They dragged him away, screaming his pain in a haunting promise.

I didn't feel sorry in the slightest.

Looking down at the guards holding my mate, I bared my blunt teeth, and they nearly fell over themselves to get away from what was mine. Rhuger pushed off of the floor and sat back on his heels with his chin held high, nobility and power radiating from him in equal measure. His face was a cultivated, blank mask.

But his eyes *burned* with pride.

In the pause between heartbeats, I saw the pattern that lay before me. My mind laid all the pieces into place. All the bits of information I'd absorbed and gleaned these past few weeks and how they wove together. And I saw the path I needed to take to finish the pattern, to pull it all together.

It was a game of power, of change, whether any of us knew it or not. It started when I left my ex-husband. When Grandma Ruth showed me the Geata and told me about my heritage. Ever since I'd arrived on Talam, and met Rhuger, I'd disrupted, altered, and reformed the power structures wherever I went. I was a catalyst for change to people who desperately needed it.

So I would do what I was evidently pretty damned good at.

Shake some shit up.

I slowly came back into myself from where I'd been hiding in my mind. Let Rhuger watch as I became fully aware and alert. The relief that flickered in his gaze warmed me down to my very toes in their ridiculous slippers.

I let my hips sway as I stepped over Orok's corpse and descended the stairs of the dais. I held Orok's sword down at my side and his head and crown out in front of me. Stepping in his swiftly cooling blood, I left crimson footprints behind me as I sashayed toward my mate. A vengeful echo of Rhuger's bloody footprints when we arrived at the keep.

Coming to a halt before my mate, I lifted my chin and pushed my shoulders back. A victorious, bloody valkyrie gazing down upon her kneeling mate. "I have brought you the head of your enemy who sought to take your throne, your mate, and your child from you." I held up his brother's head. Orok's tongue flopped out like a slimy leech.

"You honor me greatly, mate." Rhuger's grin was wicked as he completely disregarded the head and crown, instead taking my blood-splattered attire from my bangle-clad ankles up my thick bare legs to where the wisps of gold-speckled emerald fabric covered the apex of my thighs before barely spanning my breasts. All held in place by that golden snake belt and a few flimsy chains.

"Is my lusty goddess still hungry for her mate?" He asked clearly, quietly, head tilting like a predator. His silver irises glinted like moons in the black skies of his eyes from under his brows. I knew what he was asking.

"Yes, Rìgh Rhuger," I said into the quiet. Granting him his title without giving two fucks if his people agreed. I was a peer, recognizing a peer. These peons could go get ganked for all I cared.

I knew what this meant, to agree with what he was asking. For his claim upon me and upon the throne of the Oc'Turin to hold any water, he'd have to prove it. To the entire clan.

By publicly fucking me.

It was all a power play. And I was the centerpiece, the extension of his will in Orok's death. It was the only way forward toward the best outcome. So I'd do it. To save my mate, my cridhe, my clan, and my child.

Rhuger got to his feet then, in one smooth, powerful motion that made my thighs squeeze together. Stepping slowly and purposefully closer, he leaned his head down to sniff me. His lip curled as a dark growl rumbled from his throat to skim across my skin like another pair of hands.

"The bastard didn't even bother to touch you. Too busy fucking his pleasure mate, then?" His clawed finger hooked under my chin and tilted my face up to his.

"He thought he could break me with such uninspired cruelty," I murmured into the space between us, letting him see how I felt, how blessedly boring Orok had been.

"Fool." Rhuger spat. His rage at what I'd had to face caused his body to shudder. To hide it, he paced around me. "You're made of far stronger mettle than he was. Brave. As wicked and sharp as you are soft and lovely."

The heated twinkle in his eyes as he passed in front of me, fingers trailing along my blood-soaked stomach, told me precisely how much he liked that about me. Rhuger took Orok's head and crown from my hand and tossed them aside like trash. The crown bounced and rolled away between the feet of our audience. Then he took the sword from my other hand and wordlessly held it out, hilt up, eyes still riveted on me. Someone rushed forward and took the sword from him, his arm dropping to his side.

Then he prowled behind me and pulled me roughly back against his chest making my breathing hitch. Rhuger laced the fingers of our left hands together. Then his right hand gripped my hair and gave a light jerk backward, so I was looking up into his eyes. My breath caught and my heart hammed as heat pooled at my core.

It felt *good*.

"You killed him for me?" Rhuger asked into the quiet of the throne room. His lips were mere inches away from mine. His breath fluttered my hair and warmed my face.

"Yes, my mate," I murmured, my voice carrying clearly in the silence.

"You refused his touch? His demand that you pleasure him?"

"Yes, of course, my love."

"You denied his claim to my child?" He guided our entwined hands to rest against my soft belly.

"Without hesitation, my Righ." The heat in Rhuger's gaze was enough to cause my desire to pound hard between my thighs.

"And you chose me as your mate, an exile, without knowing who I was? And when you found out, you remained true?" He asked, his voice asking like there was no doubt. But his eyes on mine held fear. He was afraid I'd disappear again. Like after everything we'd been through together, it would just be a dream. Like mist in the dawn.

Adorable *idiot*.

"Of course, I remained true to you," I said, raising my hand up to cup his cheek. The flutter of his eyelashes was the only sign of his relief.

"And will you now allow me to take you in the ways of the

Oc'Turin?" The wicked smile that split his mouth as he spoke had heat rushing to my face.

"You can take me any way, anywhere, any time you wish, Rìgh Rhuger Oc'Turin." I declared. "But I *do not* share, nor *will I* be shared."

My declaration was a line drawn in the sands of time. The precedence that could change the course of the future.

"Then get on your knees, pearl. Show these Oc'Turin how my lovely human Oc'Dellor princess sucks her mate's cock." His eyes were heavy-lidded with lust as he released his grip on my hair.

"Do you... do you still want her...?" I whispered as I moved against him, giving myself the opportunity to ask before we went farther. Sagra was here, now mateless and likely willing to take Rhuger back if he wished. "Your mate-to-be?"

"No." He replied without hesitation, voice pitched low so only I could hear it. "She went to him willingly. You are and always will be above any other in my life." His words tasted of truth and mirrored what lay in my heart. Whatever residual anxiety I had over our bond fled.

I turned in his grasp and, without being asked, knew kissing was off the table for now. This was a power play. Tenderness would have to wait until we were alone. So I'd play Rhuger's lusty goddess.

I looked up at my mate from under my lashes. Let the lust for him I'd kept shuttered in my mind these past days loose. I bit my lip and lifted my chin as my hands rose to my neck, then trailed down to my breasts, where I grasped them and fondled them for him. He grew still, his gaze burning like a brand as I left finger trails in the blood of his brother that still painted my body. Gliding my hands down the soft curves of my belly, I grasped the serpentine belt and snapped the thin chains holding it together.

Rhuger's lashes flickered and his breathing hitched

imperceptibly when I broke the chain. That small display of strength made him hungry to do such things for himself. I reached up and snapped the small decorative chains that held the swathes of cloth together over my shoulders. The chains fell as the blood-soaked cloth fluttered down to pool at my feet. All I wore now were the bangles around my ankles.

His gaze raked over me, pausing briefly over the bruises and scratches on my stomach Orok had left on me that the dress had hidden. I saw him stiffen. Saw the fury build in him like a volcano ready to erupt. But he couldn't afford to lose control. Not here, not now.

"Rìgh mo cridhe," I murmured. Rhuger's gaze snapped up to meet mine, and I gave him a saucy wink before licking my lips. Distracting him and keeping him here with me. Centered. Focused.

Catching his attention with my fingers, his gaze fell from my mouth to my hands. His eyes were hungry as he watched me skim my chest with my fingertips. I teased my breasts, flicked my nipples for him, and arched into my own hands, filling them to overflowing my claws. Rhuger's lashes fluttered against his high cheekbones and I could see a bright green flush rise in them.

Rhuger hadn't expected me to put on a show for him. And oh boy, did he like it. This delightful male was about to get spoiled.

So I ran my fingertips up and down my curves for him, guiding his gaze to wander my body. I could already see his erection tenting the front of his kilt. I licked my lips at him again, thinking of how damned *delicious* he was. Biting my lip, Rhuger's breathing hitched, gaze zeroing in on my mouth as I reached for him. I ran my hand up and down the hard length of him beneath his leather kilt. The pulsing ache between my thighs grew desperate for him. He could smell the shift as he let out a stuttering groan.

My mate's grin was devilish as he tilted back his head, exposing his throat, his eyes slit and intent upon me, pupils blown out with desire. Most would think it was a show of fearless power. But I saw it for what it was. Surrender. To me.

I let my hands slide up and down his chest before gently dragging the tips of my claws down his stomach to the wicked v-cut into his hips. His cock jumped against the weight of his kilt and I smiled.

"Sweet temptress, do you enjoy toying with your mate?" He growled, his mouth curled up in the corners. Like a cat who'd caught a canary.

"I always want you hungry for me. I enjoy it when you fuck me blind, remember?" Murmuring, I circled him as he'd circled me, brushing my shoulder against his arm as I did.

And then I acted like a skank-ass ho as I circled around him like the sexiest damn stripper pole in existence.

I slid and undulated against Rhuger. Rubbing my hands and breasts and ass against his arms, his nearly healed back. My back to his, I reached up behind me and slid my hand up his neck to cup his throat. Rhuger froze, then shuddered as I dragged my claws across his throat in a soft caress.

His growl was thunderous, chest heaving, hands clenching and releasing by the time I returned to face him. Rhuger's expression was so feral as he struggled to hold himself still, it made my belly quiver.

We needed this. Needed each other and this intimacy after so much pain. Needed to comfort and remind one another of the goodness we shared. That the darkness we'd faced wouldn't taint our future.

So I took the step forward and pressed myself entirely up against him. I tilted my head back and looked him in the eyes. Let the love I had for him show as I smiled up at him. He let out a strangled sound close to a whimper, and I chuckled.

Without breaking eye contact, I slid down the front of him, as closely pressed to him as I could. I could feel his monstrous erection through his kilt as I slid my stomach and breasts past it on my way to my knees.

Settling myself on my heels, bangles jangling in the silence, I knelt before my Rìgh. My mate. The only person I'd ever surrender to.

I dropped my gaze from his beloved face down his beautiful body to eye the buckles on his kilt. Deciding how I was going to get the blasted thing off of him so I could get him in my mouth, I got a wicked little idea. Leaning forward, I teased the leather tongues loose from the buckles with my teeth. It wasn't nearly as difficult as I thought it'd be, so I made quick work of undoing the three buckles on his hip.

But there was a round of approving murmurs coming from the surrounding crowd. I'd honestly forgotten they were there. Freezing up wasn't a part of the plan, but I couldn't help it. I sat there, fighting the need to bolt, to cover myself, to cry.

A large hand rested on my hair. I looked up and Rhuger was gazing lovingly down at me. He slid his fingers through my hair against my scalp. Petting me. Grounding me here in this moment with him.

It was so calming; it soothed away the fear and embarrassment. I'd set myself on this path. I could face it, do it. Taking a deep breath, I kissed his palm to let him know I was good to continue.

"Such a good lass." He whispered into the space between us. The heat that'd been building between my thighs throbbed hard, and moisture slicked out and down the insides of my thighs.

CHAPTER 08[*]

RHUGER

I'd been absolutely terrified when I realized Amelia had
withdrawn so far into herself as to be blank, nearly lifeless. No hint of
life or spirit sparked in her uisge-beatha eyes. No whisper of feeling
drifted between us. A connection I'd grown so used to these past
weeks. As if we didn't need to speak to share our feelings. We knew
them as if they were our own. But that connection had gone quiet, and I
realized how echoingly empty I was without it.

She sat perched on an impossibly small footstool on Orok's left,
while Sagra sat on his right. A sparkling emerald mockery of a dress
barely covered her from the hungry gaze of the horde. And my
conniving brother sat there between these two neamhnaid females as if
he owned them. Proud, and relaxed, his eyes burning with an insatiable
hunger to control everyone before him, no matter the cost.

I spared a quick glance at Sagra. It had been years since I'd seen
her when she'd broken off our official mating bond. A special
engagement for Oc'Turin royalty forged by political ties, not emotional
ones. Which was reinforced by Sagra's neamhnaid skin, the symbol of
her heritage as one of the last of her line. The ceremony had been held,

but I hadn't been the groom. Instead, I'd been locked in the dungeons under the tender care of my jailors.

She looked mostly the same. Still willowy and elegant with narrow features. Dressed in a sparkling silver excuse of a gown to match the one my cridhe wore. But the hollowness to her cheeks and eyes hadn't been there before. Her unflappable obeisance marked her so bent to my brother's hand that she might never recover. Gazing upon her now, the only emotion I felt was pity.

I'd wanted her once, badly. But her betrayal had cut me deep. Her unwillingness to believe me when I'd been accused of murdering Orok's father, had curdled and hollowed out any hope I had for having a mate and orclings. Because we'd been friends long before the idea of a political marriage had been broached. And if one of my closest friends thought so little of me, how could I ever hope to garner the regard of another female?

Despite it all, I'd carved out a place for myself with the Oc'Dellor. Built a home tree. And waited. For *years*. And then I'd found my cridhe. Scrabbling on the floor of the cave within the Croabh na Beatha as the Geata closed behind her. A shaft of buttery afternoon sun cut across her face and set her uisge-beatha eyes glowing. I'd known then that nothing would ever be the same. Just as I knew now that none of the feelings for Sagra that I'd cleaved to for so long existed anymore. And I was okay with that.

My gaze returned to my sweet, curvy, lovely cridhe, and my heart shattered behind my ribs. She was still blank. Staring at me as if she didn't even know me. What had Orok done to her since he'd captured us to make her this way? When the guards shoved me to my knees and ground my face into the stone floor, I roared for her. Hoping she'd hear me, hear my love for her and my pain over our situation, and wake up. Pleading with her to not give up on me. On us.

But she sat there, like a lifeless statue, as my brother touched her, licked her face, and ordered her to her knees. Ordered her to choke on his cock in front of the clan. A public claiming that, by clan law, meant she was fully his. It was far worse torture to watch her rub herself all over my brother than all the punishments the jailers and soldiers had inflicted upon me. It was an agony I'd never known to watch her seduce him, watch her ready herself to show all the clan that she was his by sucking him off.

Orok *knew* it would kill me to have the one person in all the universe that was home to me become his beaten plaything. And I could tell by the vile glint in his eye that he was already hard. And it had nothing to do with my mate crawling up into his lap from the floor and everything to do with me.

Orok possessed a lust that went far deeper than just power. The need to possess me and all that I'd earned had been his lifelong desire. Because I had been our Mother's favorite. Because warcraft came so easily to me, even as a child. Because his father always compared him to me and beat Orok if he found fault in him. And beat me when I tried to protect Orok.

And later, when we'd reached adolescence, it was because I refused to let him into my bed. He was my brother, someone I protected, and some wicked bent in him saw me as more than just his blood kin. I'd thought he'd adored me as younger siblings do their elders. But I'd been so very wrong. I'd already taken male lovers by then so Orok raged at me for refusing him. It hadn't mattered that I'd explained it was because we were kin and had nothing to do with his gender, he refused to acknowledge the truth of it.

Instead, he'd taken all of the soft sweetness in him that I had sought to protect from his father and let it turn vicious and vile. From then on, his sole purpose was to take away anything and everything that was mine. To punish me. To break me. And now, he finally had the means to do it and to do it thoroughly. Amelia had caught his gaze with her flickering pink tongue, and despite my brother's lack of attraction for females, he was enthralled. I struggled against my captors, thrashing in a desperate gambit to break free and drag Amelia away from him.

But then she'd done the one thing no one could have ever expected someone so soft, so kind, to do.

She'd slit my brother open from knee to groin with his own boot knife. Severing the arteries and likely part of his malehood. When he'd screamed, she'd ripped out the knife with a brutal viciousness that set my heart racing and slammed the tiny blade into his neck.

Then she made the declaration that changed everything.

"My name is Amelia Chance Oc'Dellor. Great-granddaughter to Fear a Chì Ruksala Oc'Dellor. Granddaughter to Rìgh Thorn Oc'Dellor and Ruth Dellor. Daughter to Sheila Dellor and Austin Chance. Mate to your rightful Rìgh Rhuger Oc'Turin. And mother to a child of the Oc'Dellor and the Oc'Turin clans. I refuse your touch, you sick bastard. And the only cock I'll be sucking is my mate's."

Then she'd yanked out the knife, tearing open his throat, pulled free his own sword from his waist, spun, and decapitated my brother *in one stroke*.

My mate, my cridhe, keeper of my soul, *annihilated* the source of every evil thing I'd ever endured in a matter of heartbeats. Wiped the stain of Orok from my life and my future as if he were just some simple spilled fion-math. And breathed hope into my veins that we might actually survive all of this to bring our bairn into the world.

I'd thought I loved her before. But those feelings were *nothing* compared to the fierce, vast expanse of love and pride that swelled in my chest for my sweet pearl. She'd done what no one had before her. She'd protected me. Avenged me. Claimed me as her own.

Then she'd jerked Orok's sword free from the throne of fangs.

Grasping his crowned severed head in a bloodied fist, she held it high. She'd bared her blunted teeth at my guards and they'd scrambled to get off of me. When our gazes met, there was an endless moment of understanding. Our connection singing bright and true between us once more. We both knew what this was. The path that was set before us that flowed through all the obstacles and machinations around us like water was all about control. How to manipulate it.

I'd grown up with these ravenous power games. I knew how they worked. But Amelia didn't. All of this would hinge on her willingness to not just take a *step* outside of her comfort zone, but an *entire territory*. Because what was in store wasn't for the weak of heart.

But again, my mate surprised everyone, including me, with her bravery.

She cocked her broad, curved hip, descended the stairs like a Banrigh, and prowled towards me. Her hips swayed in a way that hypnotized me and set my knot flooding with cum. Wearing nothing but some gold jewelry, strips of fabric, and my brother's blood. She could have worn nothing or been dressed for the wintry mountains in Oc'Blyre territory, and my reaction would still be the same.

She came to stand before me as I knelt at her feet. Amelia was the only person I'd ever kneel to. Even the gods did not know the taste of my knees on their sacred ground. But I'd gladly prostrate myself before my cridhe. It was a heady thing to sit at her feet as she stood before me, a vision of power incarnate. Tuly an Iolaire'lasair of old. Bloody, fierce, wielding a sword in one hand and the head and crown of her enemy in the other. *Our* enemy.

There was something so erotic about being at her mercy. But now wasn't the time to explore such things. To see what debauched delights my cridhe could create with me if I submitted to her as she did with me.

Instead, we played the game of power. The push and pull between us as natural and wordless as breathing. So I'd asked, and she'd answered. Ensuring everyone in the throne room bore witness to her words, her fealty, her fertility, and her love for me.

When I told her to get on her knees and show everyone how I liked her to suck my cock, I wasn't sure if she'd do it. Not with everyone watching.

Quietly, she'd asked me if I still desired Sagra. As if she could ever hold a candle to the sun that was my cridhe. Such an insecure and unsure question. Did Amelia still not think that she was the only female for me? That even if she died tomorrow, I'd never be able to take another to my bed? Did she still think of herself as undesirable as her ex-husband made her feel?

I was going to break her of that notion immediately. So I told her as much. The tension seemed to ease from her shoulders, but I knew that seed of doubt still lingered. And I planned to root it out for good.

It was the greatest test of will to hold myself still, to refuse to snatch her to me and devour her, as she touched herself and broke the gold that kept that sorry excuse for a dress on her luscious body. As the fabric fluttered to the ground, still soaked in Orok's blood, I froze at what the dress had concealed.

Deep scratches and dark bruises littered the soft comfort of her belly over where our bairn grew. Rage flooded me in such a furious wave I nearly roared. I nearly vibrated with the combined horror and madness that bathed my vision a bloody red. I'd known about the bruises on her neck from Ergit's fingers and the bruises on her temple and cheek from being hit. But the ones on her stomach...

Whenever I'd seen Orok ride with my mate tied to the pommel of his nocrys, he'd clutched her to him tightly. As if afraid I'd somehow get loose, murder them all and make off with her. I was shaking as I stared at the damage done to my cridhe by my brother. If he hadn't been dead, I would have taken a *long* time tearing him apart.

"Rìgh mo cridhe," Amelia murmured and my gaze snapped up to meet hers. And as she'd done the first time I'd sunk myself inside of her and nearly spent before I'd fully filled her, she distracted me. Brought me back. And I let her.

She licked her lips and ran her perfect little neamhnaid hands over her delectable curves, guiding my gaze where she wanted it. The haze of violence faded away in the face of Amelia's carnal caress. I was in her thrall completely, so I did what I had when she'd caught me masturbating at the thought of her outside of the travelers' cave. I bared my throat to her. Surrendered to her.

And she *rewarded me*. Gods, the way she moved against me, touched me, let me feel her softness all around me as she circled me, had me straining at my mental leash. And when she'd placed her hand around my throat from behind... Dragged her tiny claws against my throat in the most thrilling caress? I barked out a deep growl, so close to pinning her to the ground and rutting her like the animal I was.

Instead, I managed to hold on. Managed to keep that facade up, even as she pressed against me and slid down my body, her stomach and breasts squishing against my erection. I'd centered her as she'd centered me when she remembered we weren't alone. Praised her. And when she was alright to continue, she unbuckled my kilt with her blunt little human teeth to the approval of those watching.

As she undid the last buckle, I grasped the leather and tossed it aside, my cock springing up and curving nearly to my stomach now that it was free of the reinforced leather. Now there was nothing between me and my cridhe. Pre-cum dripped down my cock in a steady stream, dripping thickly to the floor. Evidence of how desperate she made me for her.

She made a little sound in the back of her throat, almost a whimper, her expression turning lusty. I wanted my cock down that tight little throat of hers. I wanted to feed her my cock and have her suckle it until my knot exploded. Wanted to see her *swallow it all* again.

"What are you waiting for, pearl?" I crooned, my voice gone hoarse with my own imaginings. Unable to help myself, I ran my fingers through her soft brown waves, cupping the back of her head and pulling her to me, even as I angled my cock towards that damnable mouth of hers. "Show me again how good you are at swallowing every last drop, like a good lass."

The look she gave me then from under her lashes, those intoxicating uisge-beatha eyes seeing precisely how badly I wanted it. With a tiny smirk, she let me guide her head toward my weeping dick. Pressing her soft lips against my crown, she gave it a light kiss before loosing that devilish pink tongue. She gave my crown a good, long lick, gathering my slick on her tongue with a soft groan.

How her tongue vibrated against me as she lapped at my slit nearly had me seeing stars. She ducked her head, licking along the ribbed underside of my cock from base to crown, not wasting a drop as I'd commanded. Dipping her tongue along the sensitive grooves in my shaft had me hissing in building pleasure as the pressure in my knot began throbbing.

If she didn't take me in her mouth now, I was going to burst all over her.

The thought of my seed splattering all over her perfect breasts and body, leaving her neamhnaid skin decorated with pearls of my own, left me snarling back against my release. She looked up at me from under those long lashes, on her knees before her Rìgh, opened her mouth, and let me feed it to her. I watched as my cock disappeared between those lovely lips inch by devastating inch.

She loved the taste of me, of my seed, and moaned against my cock as she sucked me in greedily. I couldn't help the jerk of my hips and my growl of satisfaction. Amelia's lips reached my knot and my crown hit the back of her throat. Gods, how I wished she could take me completely. But I was too long and too thick for her.

As if she'd read my mind, she looked up at me, her mouth stretched wide around me, its slick hot heat and the feeling of her tongue edging me close to madness. Then she grasped my hips and pressed herself forward, pushing my cock further into her mouth and down that decadent throat. Letting out a ragged moan, my hips jerked and I could feel my knot release a few spurts down into her belly.

Beyond all belief, she took me completely down to the base, her lips pressed firmly against my groin. With gentle suction, she closed the seam of her mouth around my girth and drew herself back, still following my orders. My lashes fluttered against my cheeks as I watched her, already so close to spending.

"That's right, pearl. Don't waste a gods' damned drop." I hissed raggedly, cutting off in a moan as her lips passed over my sensitive knot. I thought I'd been through torture before. Foolish of me to think that my cridhe was incapable of surpassing it all with her mouth. She was shredding every last thread of resolve I had to continue this farce of control the Oc'Turin needed. She reached my crown again and moaned as my seed coated her tongue. Hissing from between my fangs I made my demand. *Do it again.*

With a hum that had my knees threatening to buckle as it set every nerve alight, she did.

Sliding both hands into her hair, I watched her, wild-eyed, as she repeated it several more times. Then she released my hips and clutched at my shaft as she lost herself to my taste. Amelia focused on my crown, flickering her tongue along and underneath my foreskin, down to flutter against my frenulum, and around my head in circles.

Her hands stroked my shaft and my knot, squeezing it to shoot my cum into her mouth where she swallowed it greedily.

"Just like that, Amelia." I groaned. "Suckle it. Fucking suckle my cock. Swallow every drop for me."

She let out a broken moan against my sensitive flesh at my praise as she picked up her pace. Bobbing her head quickly up and down, she somehow kept her lips tight around my shaft, so the luscious pressure from her sucking didn't waver for a moment. Not caring anymore, I moaned my pleasure for the others to hear. Let them know that *all of this* was mine, that *she was mine*.

The building pleasure and pressure at the base of my spine were almost too much to take. I was breathing in rough, growling pants.

"I'm going to come now. Be my good lass and drink it. If you spill a drop, I'll have to punish you." I snarled, hips jerking forward, desperate to meet her. She just closed her eyes and gave herself over to my will.

And that's when I snapped my hips forward until I was deep in her throat. Shattering as pleasure tore me apart from the inside out, I roared her name, eyes riveted on her. She slipped her fingers between her squeezing thighs as my hips rolled, my knot trapped inside her mouth behind her teeth.

After a few bestial moans, as I came down from the great heights she'd taken me to, I could pull out of her mouth. Amelia gasped and took a few deep breaths before looking up at me with swollen lips. She'd palpated my knot enough, released enough of the pressure, that even though my orgasm continued to cause my body to shudder, she'd already swallowed every droplet my knot contained.

"Good lass," I growled, my chest heaving as I watched her squirm with her hand still between her juicy thighs. Knowing she was in such a state had my knot flushing with seed swiftly. I cupped her sweet, rounded face between my hands and ran a thumb over her swollen bottom lip. "Good lasses are to be rewarded. What do you want, pearl?"

"I want your cock inside of me." Breathless, her voice rough from having my cock shoved deep inside her throat, she told me precisely what she wanted me to do to her. Begged me to give her what she craved. "I want your seed in my womb. *Please*, my Rìgh, I want you to fuck me until you ruin me for any cock but *yours* for the rest of my days."

"*That's my princess,*" I breathed in a desperate snarl as I kneeled before her, my large hand cupping the back of her head before I devoured that decadent pink mouth of hers.

My tongue clashed with hers and I didn't care one bit as I tasted myself on her sweet little tongue. My cock throbbed a needy tattoo, impossible to deny or ignore as every instinct, every feral, primal desire demanded I rut my mate until my cum ran down her thighs and she fell asleep in my arms. Sated with her belly full.

So I turned her around and snatched her back against my chest. Clutching her to me hard, as if I were trying to merge with her. Slipping into the passion singing in my blood, I roughly played with her breasts. Palming them and rubbing my hard callouses against my cridhe's sensitive little nipples. Even as I pressed the rock-hard length of my cock against her plush, perfect ass.

CHAPTER 09*

AMELIA

I moaned. *Loud*. It felt so damned *good*.

For whatever reason, my horny meter was off the charts. My skin sang and sizzled wherever he touched. Lines of fire and pleasure slid down to pool in my core and cascade down the insides of my thighs.

He dipped his head to my neck and began licking and sucking all along my neck, shoulder, and jaw. That long, sinuous, black tongue of his, wickedly fluttering against my sensitive flesh. Then he began a rolling litany of Black Tongue, crooning it into my ear as he took the lobe in his sharp teeth and nipped it.

Fuck me, it was so hot. I had no idea what he was saying, and it didn't matter. He could have been reciting a recipe for split pea soup for all I knew. His low voice, rough with lust, was just so damn *sexy* it was like he was trying to fuck me with his voice, too. I shuddered and whimpered in his arms as I ground my ass against his swollen dick.

He was making me lose my gotdamn mind, and I couldn't get enough of him. Couldn't get him close enough to sate me.

Rhuger slipped one hand down my stomach, pausing and rubbing the soft rolls there, cherishing our child growing inside of me, before dipping lower. His thick fingers slid between the crisp curls of my mound, already drenched and dripping from how badly I needed him.

He groaned, cupping my entire sex roughly in his hand. As if claiming it. Loving how it responded to him and him alone.

My inner walls clenched hard with want, causing more of my juices to flow past his fingers and down my thighs. Rhuger chuckled and lifted his hand to my mouth, slipping his fingers past my lips and having me taste my own desire. I drew his fingers into my mouth and sucked on them as if they were his cock. Worshiping the fingers that brought me such ecstasy even as I bucked backward, grinding my ass against him.

"So ready for me already, pearl?" He chuckled in my ear before removing his fingers. I threw my head back over his shoulder, and I watched, completely transfixed, as he raised them to his own mouth and began licking his fingers clean, one by one. Rhuger's eyes rolled back into his head and he groaned like it was the best thing he'd ever tasted.

"Yes!" I cried, breathless and desperate. "I need you *now!*"

He looked down at me then, throat still bared to me, gaze shuttered and whispering of things he'd like to do to me in the dark. I shivered in his arms as he slowly slid one hand from where it had been grasping my hip, to curve up under my breast, between them, up to cup my throat. His fingers and palm slipped around my neck like my favorite necklace as a rumbling growl started low in his chest.

Rhuger, with his massive, powerful hand that could end me with half a thought, oh so gently tilted my head back. He bent his face down to meet mine, looming over me. And even with his beautiful hair a shorn wreck, he was still *devastating*. He was still my god of dark desires, moaned into the shadows, whispered in secret places, and roared beneath the stars.

"Where are your manners, my sweet pearl?" He whispered against my mouth in a low rumble. Teasing me as his lips moved tantalizingly just out of reach. His words fanned my face as we shared air.

"*Please*, Rìgh mo cridhe... I need your touch like I need air to brea-" his sinful, wicked mouth cut off my weak and desperate words. I melted against him.

His kiss started soft, gentle, almost chaste. Full of tenderness and adoration. In a matter of heartbeats, it had changed into the wild hunger I knew so well. Both sides of the same male who was my everything.

No matter how hard he kissed me or how deep he delved his tongue into my throat, his grip around my neck was tenderness incarnate. His other hand as it slid down my hip to curve over my thigh on its way to where I needed him most, wicked and sensual. The different sides of him unleashed upon me at once nearly had me weeping. He was everything I'd ever wanted, craved, and more.

"That's my pearl." Rhuger rumbled, voice cracking slightly as he pulled his mouth from mine. As his fingers slipped into the waiting, throbbing heat that pounded between my thighs. I cried out in ecstasy as he slid his fingers slowly against my clit, down, down until they reached my core. Rhuger was shaking from restraining himself, pressing his face into the side of mine, hiding it within my wavy hair. As if he didn't want them to see how desperate my pleasure made him.

"You've been so good for me." He murmured as he slid his fingers up over my clit again, then down toward my opening, which was quivering in anticipation. He nuzzled my ear as he growled, "You swallowed every drop I shot into that addictive mouth of yours. Did you like how it tasted?"

His breathing hitched as he rubbed his cock between my ass cheeks and up along the small of my back. Rhuger timed his thrusts with how he slid his fingers into me more and more with each pass over my clit. Unable to help myself, I rocked against him, sandwiched between his thick fingers and his weeping cock, his hand still cradling my throat in debauched bliss. I moaned and nodded, trembling and twitching, lost in my desire for him.

"*I need to hear you say it...*" He snarled into the sensitive shell of my ear just as he shoved his three thickest fingers inside of my desperately clutching cunt.

"*YES!*" I wailed into the throne room. The single word echoed off the stone. "Rhuger, you taste so *fucking good!*" I jerked as he shoved his fingers deeper inside of me, the heel of his palm pressing against my clit.

"Do you like to kneel at my feet? To have me dominate you and take you as I want?" He growled, voice gone raspy. Letting me know that he knew I did and loved it just as much. When I didn't immediately answer, Rhuger began finger fucking me in earnest. "Well? *DO YOU?!*"

"Yes... *yes...YES...YES!*" I cried out with each relentless thrust of his fingers inside of me. Panting and skyrocketing toward climax.

Because *fuck me,* I *loved* it when he dominated me. When I could hand over control to him. Give him my trust, my body, my will, and know he'd hold all three in the highest regard. That he'd give me what I needed, what we both needed.

"Come for me then, my beautiful mate, show these miserable wretches what it means to be cridhe. To take *everything* I give and still want *more!*" He snarled into my ear. I shuddered and clamped hard around his fingers, my moan drawing out as the orgasm dragged me so high.

Then I shattered in his arms, throwing my head back against his shoulder, screaming his name. Bucking hard against his massive erection that leaked a steady stream of pre-cum onto my ass down to coat his fingers where they were still pumping in and out of me. The thought of him shoving his cum inside of me with his fingers like that made my toes curl.

After what felt like an eternity of ecstasy, Rhuger finally removed his fingers, and my orgasm waned.

I'd barely taken a breath, my body still spasming from the intensity of my orgasm, when I felt him shift behind me. I glanced over my shoulder, down my back, where he'd pulled me back up onto his lap with my thighs sprawled wide over his hips. This position opened me wide and left me vulnerable and eager to submit.

So similar to how he'd pinned me to the bed like a butterfly our first night together and railed my brains out. The memories overlapped my anticipation, and I ground back against him shamelessly, openly moaning and begging him to take me. To fill me with every inch of him.

"Are you ready for your reward, my love?" Rhuger whispered darkly, his hands shaking as he grasped my hips. His expression was wild, unhinged, and unlike anything I'd ever seen before.

"Rhuger..." I moaned as my body still shuddered from the last orgasm he'd given me. He pressed the head of his massive cock to my core, and I nearly came undone, remembering the feel of his girth inside of me as he edged that line between pain and pleasure.

"Yes, my sweet pearl?" His tone was laced with amusement even as he trembled from his restraint.

"Yes, I'm ready. Fuck me, Rhuger!" I ordered, growling at him over my shoulder, too far gone to do anything but demand what I needed as I propped myself up on my hands, locking my arms and arching my back. His dark chuckle rippled along my skin like another hand, and I shivered.

"So demanding..." He murmured as he slipped his hand from my hip and shifted it up my spine. His long, thick fingers that had just been fucking his cum into me grasped the back of my neck in a caress before he fisted his hand in my hair, jerking my head back. My hiss ended on a moan and my core clasped at the tip of him greedily, kissing him and begging him for what we both so desperately craved. "But what are you to call me when we're like this?"

Fuck, he was going to drive me to madness like this! I couldn't take it. I couldn't play this game anymore. I needed him too badly. So I immediately capitulated, looking him in his fierce silver eyes over my shoulder.

"My Rìgh..." I moaned, doing my best to hold still like the good girl he wanted me to be, instead of pushing back to slide him inside of me as I needed. "My mate... My *cridhe! PLEASE!*"

As the word 'cridhe' fell from my lips in a desperate moan, Rhuger's irises blew out wide, registering what I'd said. It was the first time I'd ever called him my cridhe outside of calling him the king of my heart, and it sent him over the edge. With panting growls, he wrapped his arm around my waist, bracing it against my hips, and thrust *hard*.

I was so tight from my last orgasm that he'd barely made it in to his swollen knot. Then he pulled my hair, tilting my head back farther so he could look into my eyes as he pushed his knot inside of me so slowly. Watching my expression like a hawk as it pressed, demanding entrance, and my body gave, making room. Utterly defenseless against his invasion and loving every second of it. I stretched around him, shaking from the angle and his size, little cries escaping my throat as his gaze bored into mine.

Then his knot slid in with an audible *pop*. He snarled and slammed his hips forward into my ass, ramming home inside of me to the hilt. Hit my sweet spot so hard I saw stars and writhed as I gasped through the pleasure of it. Opening my eyes, tears sliding down my cheeks, I looked into the smoldering gaze of the male I loved.

"*So fucking perfect...*" Rhuger's voice was a thunderous rumble as he bared his teeth briefly, his hips grinding into my ass as if he had no control over them anymore. Sliding his hand around to cup my belly, he hissed. The thought that I was carrying his child seemed to set him loose. "You are the lush, soft, decadent beauty, and I am going to rut you like the *beast I am*."

"*Ah!*" That was all I could utter before he grasped me tight around the waist, pulled out of me until his knot popped free, and slammed into me again.

My mind nearly blanked as he thrust his knot back in, stretching me even as the head of his cock hit that sweet spot. Gods, it felt like his knot was beyond full, beyond anything I'd experienced with him before. *And I wanted more.*

I took a ragged breath and grasped his forearm in my hand, claws digging in. I was completely prone in his arms. He was carrying *all* of my weight in his arms and hips. But it was like I weighed nothing to him as he began a punishing rhythm against my ass, his hips snapping against my jiggling backside as if he were spanking me. Punishing me even as he rewarded me.

Gods, I loved this orc!

Every thought fled me as the head of him and all of his ribbed cock ran over that place that made me so weak. I knew I was moaning, screaming, crying, as he absolutely railed me as if his life depended on it. All the while staring into the glittering black night skies of his eyes with their eclipsed silver rings.

The last time he'd stared into my eyes as we had sex, it was as if he were afraid I'd disappear like some unattainable dream. But now? Now his eyes burned into mine like a brand. Forever marking me as his and his alone. Knowing I was his as surely as he was mine. Tied together as two halves of the same whole from across the universe. Together against all possible, rational, even ridiculous odds.

It was as if he'd finally admitted to himself that what we had could never be broken or lost. That no matter how many lifetimes came and went, we'd still find one another. Come *home* to each other.

I released his forearm and shakily reached up to cup his cheek, crying out with each thrust of his hips. Rhuger's eyes widened for a moment, but he didn't lessen his pace. I let everything I felt for him fill my eyes. My love, my passion, my hope and happiness, the laughter and care, the tenderness, and every unspeakable emotion too complex for words.

"I love you." I panted between thrusts, between cries. Rhuger's brows drew together as he leaned into my hand and closed his eyes. A tear only I could see slipping free.

"And I love you." He rasped through his heaving breathing.

Releasing my hair, he hauled me up against his chest, grasped my chin, and turned my head so he could kiss me. All without faltering his pace. Able to get some leverage in this angle, I reached over us to grasp his shoulder, rising and slamming down to meet him stroke for stroke. He moaned raggedly into my mouth, his teeth scoring my bottom lip.

Releasing my chin, he wrapped me up in his arms and growled into my ear, "I want to mark you. I want to be rough..."

"Yes!" I gasped in ascent. How he would be rougher than he was now, I wasn't sure. But I wanted to find out. "Let go with me, please!"

Then he pressed his face into the crook of my neck with a moan, and he did.

I hadn't realized quite how much he'd held back before. How much restraint he'd shown as if afraid I'd break. Not that he was harder, rougher, or more violent about his movements. More like he stopped separating himself into a seducer, beast, and tender lover. Let them all mingle and become one. Accepted them all as parts of the same whole. Just like we were.

Then I let go too.

And it was as if time had no meaning anymore. Neither did any sense of place. All there was were the two of us frantically, desperately trying to become one soul again, even for a moment. Using the senses we had to reach that pinnacle of connectedness where neither of us knew where one started and the other ended.

I was screaming his name, feeling myself begin to splinter, to unravel, moments before he bit down on where my shoulder and neck joined. I thought it would hurt. I'd expected it to hurt. But instead, it was like drinking concentrated luibh gaoil. Like pure light and bliss singing along each and every nerve until it felt like I was made of starlight.

Blood gushed from between his teeth and I could hear him growl ferociously between swallows of my blood. As if the blood in his mouth was like his teeth in my neck, his cum down my throat. And it was at this moment he'd lost all control.

His hips snapped against my ass. His cock nearly split my pussy in two over and over again in an unhinged rhythm. It was like he couldn't fuck me fast enough or hard enough. My orgasm just kept rolling into the next one and into the one after that, until I was delirious with pleasure and bucking wildly in his arms.

"Rhuger!" I screamed his name again, my body pulling him as

deep inside of me as it could as I came.

"Amelia!" He roared into my bloody neck as he thrust one last time and followed me over the edge, shattering with me into a million stars of glittering pleasure. Stardust returned to where our souls had been born.

CHAPTER 10

AMELIA

When I finally spiraled back into my panting, sweat-slicked body, something burned and itched along the skin of my chest. Rhuger pulled out of me then. The bulge in his shaft, keeping all of his seed inside, was finally soft enough to slide free. A torrent of our juices sluiced down my thighs and onto the floor.

A rumble went through the crowd and it suddenly dawned on me—I'd just had some out-of-this-world, mind-altering sex in front of a bunch of unfamiliar orcs. My face heated.

Someone said something in Black Tongue and Rhuger rumbled a laugh, his hands carefully helping my shaky form off of his lap. I glanced up at him over my shoulder then, embarrassed and riddled with anxiety after what we'd just done, *where* we'd done it. And feeling left out of the conversation with my limited Teanga Dhubh.

"My mate is mostly human. They produce their own slick." He rumbled in Common for my benefit.

I blushed hard at his words. Wishing I had something to cover myself up with. Realizing how vulnerable I'd allowed myself to be in front of so many. And strangely, not feeling any shame about it. I knew there were differences between me and a full orckin female, but I didn't know it'd be discussed in an open forum like this. But I guess the orcs would have questions.

Rhuger saw my embarrassment and gently turned me towards him, seeking to soothe me.

"My mate is sweet and lusty and lovely, I-" His words froze on his lips as his eyes shot to my chest. He paled about three shades lighter. My chin snapped down, and I felt my brows shoot to my hairline.

"What the...?" I reached a shaky hand up to touch the beautiful scrolling design that now covered my chest. It spanned from shoulder to shoulder, seemed to crawl up my neck, and plunged down between my breasts.

Rhuger made a strangled sound. I snapped my head up to look at him, but something caught my eye. The tattoos on his arms now spanned over his pectorals. I realized then that he now had markings in the same place as I did. As I stared, I realized they were the same as mine, too. The lines were bolder, stronger looking, and more masculine. Yet still the same beautiful design.

I placed a shaking hand on his chest, and he jerked as if startled. His eyes locked onto my hand, where it rested over his heart and the black whorls there. Rhuger gasped as he touched my markings, pulling his fingers back quickly, almost as if he'd thought they'd burn him.

"Rhuger?" I asked, voice shaking. His eyes met mine, and he swallowed hard. He laid his hand over mine where it lingered over his heart.

"My cridhe." He murmured thickly.

And that's when the room erupted in shouting and whooping

and a weird mix of cheers and anger. I was so confused by their responses, but I ignored them. They weren't important right now. Rhuger was.

"I thought... I thought there weren't any more cridhe?" I asked in a hushed whisper. As if afraid that if I said the words, they'd come true and the marks would disappear.

"There are now." He growled, hand grasping the nape of my neck and pulling me forward to press his forehead to mine. "You've honored me greatly, pearl. You fill me so full of joy I could burst with it."

I saw the tears dripping from his chin and pulled back to look up into his eyes. The silver of his irises near glowed with the love that suffused his expression. Reaching my hands up, I brushed them away, kissing his cheeks and then his mouth.

"My Rìgh Rhuger." A rumbling voice called in Common. Rhuger and I looked up at a towering hulk of an orc dressed in a high-necked tunic and leather pants, his belt bristling with weapons. He was holding two cloaks, one and each hand, and offered them to us. "In case you and Banrigh Amelia wish to cover yourselves."

Something glinted in this orc's eyes. It was interest—but not in me. In the marks that were on both of us. As if it rekindled some small spark of hope in his hard onyx and teal eyes. Such a startling and pretty color on someone so stoic and grim looking.

"Thank you, brother," Rhuger said, grasping one cloak and flinging it over my shoulders. Rhuger stood in a fluid movement, turned to grasp his kilt, and buckled it on.

The strange orc stood guard, eyes flicking over the crowd that still filled the throne room. A warrior keeping watch for threats. He noticed my gaze and glanced down. I held the cape closed over my nakedness, over the markings, too. His gaze on me was thoughtful, considering. Almost as if I posed the universe's greatest riddle. Rhuger's booted feet stepped in front of us and his teal eyes turned to my mate. My *cridhe*.

"Your cridhe is a fierce little thing." His voice had a raspy quality to it. "Are all humans this way?"

"She is that." Rhuger grinned. "As for other humans, I don't know."

"Some of us are, not all. Humanity is a spectrum just like for the orckin." I said. The male's eyebrows shot up.

"Is it because of your human blood that your mating marks appeared?" He asked me directly, and I shrugged.

"I don't know. Maybe? Humans don't have mating marks back on Earth."

"Are you wishing for a human mate now, Kholt?" Rhuger elbowed the orc good-naturedly before reaching a hand down for me.

"If I could find my cridhe, I wouldn't care if they're orckin or human, male or female or other," Kholt replied, brows furrowing in thought, even as he went back to scanning the crowd with his piercing gaze.

I took Rhuger's large, warm hand in mine and allowed him to tug me upright. He wrapped his arm around my rounded shoulders and kissed the top of my unruly waves. He bent and nuzzled at my neck, where he'd bitten me. It didn't hurt, but a tingle whispered over my body and I had to fight a shiver.

To distract myself, I thought about the new male who was an ally of my cridhe. Kholt sounded like he meant what he said about finding his mate. It seemed so at odds with what I'd seen of the Oc'Turin so far. Perhaps there was hope for this clan still if a lot of them secretly felt this way.

"Perhaps more humans will find their way through now that Amelia has." Rhuger offered. Kholt grunted noncommittally.

"You should probably speak to the clan before you carry off your cridhe." Kholt's sudden, lopsided grin was almost as sexy as my mate's. If we could fix the gate, Kholt would have a gaggle of human women after him in a heartbeat.

Kholt was tall, a little taller than Rhuger, and his skin was a dark grey-green which made his teal eyes all the more startling. He had broad shoulders and was built like a swimmer. He kept his hair cut short, and the slightly longer top curled gently, leaving a few locks to lie carelessly on his forehead.

Kholt had some scars, but nothing too terrible. One did cut almost across his throat just above his torc where the high-necked tunic couldn't completely hide it. I wondered if that added to the raspy quality of his voice. But I knew better than to ask someone about their scars and I didn't want to be rude to someone who clearly cared for my cridhe.

Rhuger's hand squeezed my shoulder, and I realized both males were watching me as I stared openly at Kholt like a dunce.

"Sorry, just thinking," I muttered. "If we could get the gate to work, Kholt would have a fan club."

"A what?" Kholt asked, one thick black eyebrow rising slightly in question.

"A group of people who would fawn over you," I replied and grinned when he blushed, looking away out over the crowd to hide his embarrassment. Aww, the big ole stoic hardass was a bit of a shy smol bean. That was cute. Yep, he'd have a fan club for *sure*.

"What about me?" Rhuger asked, sounding put out. I just looked him up and down and cocked an eyebrow at him.

"Pretty sure I'll need to cut a bitch. You'd have a fan club too, but they can't touch you. You're mine." I told him dryly. Rhuger tipped back his head and laughed. The sound seemed to startle Kholt, almost like he'd never heard Rhuger laugh before.

"Och, that I am." He crooned and nuzzled my neck over my bite mark, making me blush and tingle.

Kholt coughed pointedly, still trying to look like a hardass even with that slight bright green flush on his chiseled cheekbones.

"Right. Time to talk to the horde." Rhuger sighed and turned, leading me toward the dais and the Throne of Fangs.

A bevy of servants was hastily mopping up what was left of the blood, Orok's body was already gone. Along with his head and crown. Kholt kept pace behind me, guarding our backs, and I was insanely grateful.

Rhuger turned and sat down on the newly cleaned throne. His shoulders hid the deep gouge I'd made in the bone from cleaving Orok's head from his much shorter body. As if sensing my hesitation, Rhuger dragged me down to curl into his lap. This was an entirely new feeling, being curled in a male's lap, let alone not having him complain about how heavy I was. Instead, Rhuger settled deeper into the throne and wrapped his arms around me as if getting comfy.

"Let me know if I get too heavy and I'll get up," I whispered. Kholt's eyebrows shot up into his hairline as he moved to stand behind us. Rhuger's expression as he turned his head and slowly blinked at me was a mixture of amusement and exasperation.

"I thought we'd already established that I'm far stronger and have more endurance than one of your human Ma-reens." He said dryly.

"Rhuger, I'm *heavy*." I whisper-snapped.

"Not to me," He replied, looking thoroughly unimpressed.

"Seems I still have to break you of that little habit."

"What habit?" I asked, frowning at him. Sitting in his lap we were eye-to-eye.

"The one where you constantly think you're too much." He replied, cocking an eyebrow. My mouth closed with an audible *clack* as my face flushed. Rhuger dipped his head to meet my gaze after I ducked to hide my shame. "It might be true for some, but not to me. To me, you are absolutely perfect in every way just as you are."

Hot diggity dog. Not again! This orc just knew precisely what to say to make me squirm. And as I did, his gaze grew heavy-lidded and a mischievous grin spread across his devilish mouth. Kholt cleared his throat, reminding us that we weren't alone, and Rhuger and I turned to look out over the crowd.

The throne room had quieted. All eyes now resting on my mate and me. Kholt stood behind us as a guard. The first orckin and warrior to have our backs as we entered this new phase in the Oc'Turin clan's history. It evidently wasn't a small thing either, to have Kholt stand with us, as a lot of the males in the crowd looked at him, and then at us, with grudging respect.

"Today is one that will go down in the ages as one of significant change." Rhuger's voice boomed, carrying throughout the room and commanding attention. "My mate, human and orckin, the mother of my child, and slayer of my enemy has called forth our cridhe marks." There was some murmuring and shuffling of feet at this. "Orok, my brother, is dead. So are his ways. The cridhe marks are proof that change, and fresh blood, are needed to guide the Oc'Turin clan to a new age of prosperity."

More grumbling and some smattering of applause broke the silence. It was clear the room was divided. Rhuger glanced up at me and lifted his chin, granting me permission to speak. I swallowed hard and leaned on my corporate training.

"Change isn't easy," I said, voice carrying in the sudden stillness. "We'll all need to work together, not just as a clan but with other clans as a unified people, in order to survive. There is hope between orckin and humans, to keep our kind alive. If we can get the gates to open, rules of conduct will be established to help humans feel safe. If you want a chance to meet your cridhe, you'll need to embrace these necessary changes and help us create this new world." A considering silence met my words, one that was more respectful than I'd expected. "There are no guarantees. That you will meet your cridhe or that you will find a human willing to mate with you. Regardless, we need everyone to work together on this towards our future as *one* people."

There were more nods now, and a round of applause split the air. Rhuger smiled up at me, proud of my words. I couldn't keep the blush from rising up my neck to heat my cheeks, and I tried not to squirm in his lap and distract him again.

"We will begin by creating a council of Oc'Turin—elected by you—to help us establish a plan to bring forward to all the clans. Beginning with the Oc'Dellor." A chorus of growls met his words. "They differ from the Oc'Turin, yes. But how they treat their females is far better than how we treat ours. I've lived among them for years now, learned their ways, and I've seen with my own eyes how it has benefited their entire clan. We need to learn from them, from my mate's people, if we hope to secure the gate and woo humans to help save our kind."

"Why should we listen to your cridhe?" An orc called from the back. "She's not one of us. Not fully orckin either! Who is she to say what is good for us and what isn't?"

"Because I'm mostly human. If you want help on the other side of the gate to secure it *and* to learn about Earth, it would be in your best interest to listen to me." I replied, trying not to be frustrated that they couldn't grasp the logic of it.

"Why do we need you? We could do it on our own." Another chimed in, glowering. As if needing help from a *female* was abhorrent.

"HAH! I'd like to see you drive a car." I barked, my patience running thin already. It'd been a long few bad days and I was *over it*. "My world differs vastly from yours. You *will* need help to navigate it. And you *will* need my grandmother's permission to access where the gate is located on her land. She is Rìgh Thorn's mate, Banrigh in her own right, and absolutely brilliant. If anyone on Earth can help us make this a reality, it's her."

"Then that means that the gate will be controlled by the Oc'Dellor!" Another shouted.

"No!" Rhuger growled, and those present quieted. "Part of the plan will be to establish an unbiased group to monitor, guard, protect, and operate the gate. It is my opinion that no other group on Talam deserves that honor more than the descendants of the Iolaire'lasair."

Deafening, unrelenting, *blistering* silence met those words. I glanced down at my cridhe, trying not to show my surprise. He'd held the Iolaire'lasair in high regard any time he talked about them. But for a strictly patriarchal people, this was a *hard* sell.

"Seeing that we're hoping orckin find their cridhe amongst humans, it means we can lift old pressures off of the orckin females." I ventured, looking back over the crowd. "Plus, most of the remaining orckin are male. No human, male, female, or other, would feel comfortable coming through the Geata to a pack of hulking, horny orckin males." There was a smattering of laughter at that. "Having an elite female orckin fighting force on both sides of the Geata, with the females drawn from all clans of Talam, sworn to this one duty above all others, will make all the humans feel a lot safer coming here."

There was a thoughtful quiet after I'd spoken. Rhuger

surreptitiously squeezed my thigh in thanks. He was sweet, but he didn't have to thank me for backing him up. It was a brilliant idea, one that solved so many problems with equal parts diplomacy and fairness. It was an opportunity to give the females back control over their own lives, and their destinies. And pride swelled in my chest at the benevolence and foresight my cridhe possessed.

"Are the marks real, or is it a trick?" A younger male voice called.

"Are you... Are you seriously asking that question?" I turned and cocked my head to the side. Finding him in the crowd, I stared at the male in alarm and exasperation. My thoughts were completely thrown off the diplomatic rail, like a bullet train hitting a dump truck. "What, did you think we'd scribbled ourselves in invisible ink that only showed up after ya fucked real good?"

There was an uncomfortable silence where I could hear a few orckin shuffling their feet. Someone coughed quietly. While a few others laughed nervously. I felt Rhuger's eyes on me and I looked at him, where he was disguising his wobbling smile with his hand in a kingly fashion, one eyebrow cocked at me as he tried not to laugh. I wasn't sure if *everyone* could see his shoulders shaking and the humored flush to his cheeks or not, but I thought he looked cute.

Definitely biased.

"What?" I asked him innocently.

Instead of answering me, he coughed into his hand and put a proper Rìgh-ly sort of expression on his face. Putting his hand down, he turned to his... *our*... people. Yeah, that was going to take some getting used to.

Shit, if Rhuger was now Rìgh that made me Banrigh, which meant I was now a *queen* when only a couple of days ago I thought I was just some *lady*. And two *weeks* ago I was just some woman fleeing her abuser across the country with her three cats.

Holy cannoli, what had happened to my life? I glanced over at my cridhe and blinked. Then the only word that mattered whispered through my heart. *EVERYTHING*.

"All of you witnessed the marks appear after we mated before you. There was no trick." Rhuger called out. Then, with noble grace, he stood, carrying me in his arms like I was some dainty princess, and began prowling for the door. Not giving a shit as orckin scrambled to get out of his way. "Now, if you *don't mind*, I've got my cridhe I need rut before I go *mad* with my desire for her."

CHAPTER 11*

AMELIA

The raucous noise of the throne room died as Rhuger carried me down the stone-carved halls of the Oc'Turin keep.

"Where are we going?" I asked, a little breathless. I'd thrown my arms around his neck as he'd nearly started jogging. Orckin in the halls stepped aside as we passed, eyes nearly popping out of their skulls as they noticed Rhuger's cridhe marks. One group of females had downright laughed and openly wept. As if understanding without being told that their entire world was about to change for the better.

"To our rooms," Rhuger rumbled. His gaze was warm, and his lips curled up at the corners. "The mating frenzy's already begun. Can you feel it?"

"Oh, I thought I was just horny." I laughed, and Rhuger laughed with me, shaking his head before kissing me soundly.

"You may be growing our child, but that doesn't stop the marks from demanding we mate. A lot." He grinned and waggled his eyebrows at me, making me giggle. Rhuger's expression softened, and he whispered, "Gods, I love it when you laugh... it sounds like music.

How did I get so lucky?"

My face flushed red in a rush. I looked down, my shoulders tucked up toward my burning ears.

"I wonder that a lot, too," I murmured before ducking my head into the crook of his neck. He chuckled, the rumbling of it humming along my sensitive skin until I wanted to squirm.

"Still so shy, pearl?" He asked, the humor still lingering in his voice.

Then he sidestepped quickly enough that it startled me and I looked around. Rhuger had slipped us into some shadowed alcove. A tapestry hung over the entrance, light barely filtering in. It was some sort of small storage room. There were linens and cleaning supplies, barrels, and crates. The space was cramped and there was hardly any room for us.

Before I could ask him what we were doing in there, he'd set me down on a barrel close to the tapestry-covered doorway. With a desperate speed, he'd grasped my wrists and pinned them over my head against the stone wall. The cape fell away, exposing my naked curves. A thunderous growl ripped through the tiny alcove as he roughly kneed my legs apart and pressed into the space between them.

I trembled as his rumbling growl slid over my skin like another hand. My breathing hitched when he pressed the tented front of his leather kilt against where I needed him most. A small cry escaped my lips, my legs wrapping around his hips on their own.

"I can't wait, pearl." He panted as he loomed over me, silver gaze flickering in the dark. "I can't wait until we get to our rooms. You're too damned soft. A Source blessed *feast* and I'm *hungry...* You smell too fucking good and I... Uhhnnn..."

Rhuger stood there, shuddering in his restraint, waiting for my answer. His chest heaved with his panting breaths. His free hand was roaming up and down my thigh even as his hips twitched against me.

"What do you want, gumby?" I breathed into the charged silence. Nipples pulling taut in the cold.

"I want to rut you in here until the barrel breaks beneath you. Until you scream my name so loud someone comes running to see if I'm *killing* you or *breeding* you." The words rasped from his throat and my pussy flooded in need. "But... as much as I'd like that, I want you to be a good girl for me and not make a sound. I want to see how quiet my cridhe can be for me..."

Moaning softly at the image he'd conjured, I looked up at him and nodded. He just slipped his hand up from my thigh to place a finger over my open mouth. Reminding me I needed to be quiet. Too far gone to argue or even put together a coherent thought. I closed my mouth and nodded.

"Good lass..." He breathed as he reached down and pulled up his kilt, not even bothering to take it off.

Remembering not to moan, I let out a shaking breath instead. Gods, the thought that he couldn't wait, couldn't even be *bothered* to take off his kilt to *fuck me* sent me sky high. I'd never had someone want me so badly before. Never been with anyone whose passion matched my own.

The thrill of it. Of being naked and pinned against some wall in a random nook where we could be found at any second. Of the rushed, blistering need we shared as Rhuger hooked his forearm under my knee and lifted it, opening me wider for him as he partially straddled the barrel to get the angle he wanted. His ragged breathing and how his broad hand so easily pinned my wrists, as if I were some dainty flower of a woman instead of a battleaxe babe.

And how I needed to be good for him and not wail and scream my pleasure, as I so wantonly did whenever he touched me. I'd never been so vocal before, but his hands, his scent, his voice, and his girth just made me forget everything else but us. Made it so I couldn't care less where we were, what time it was, or who was there.

With one hard, ruthless thrust, Rhuger slid inside of me to the hilt. I gasped and arched my back as he let out a low moan. Rushing, he wrapped his arm around my waist and began rutting me as if his life depended on it. Like he'd die if he didn't.

We fucked quick and hard, the need for release obliterating anything else. My breath was coming in great heaving gasps. It was so difficult to keep from crying out at how fucking good he felt. He'd asked me to be good for him. And I wanted to be good.

"I love watching you take me." He growled. "Love watching every inch of you ripple and give. As your pussy swallows my cock just like that pretty little pink mouth of yours."

Gods, his dirty talk was on a whole other level right now. I had to bite my lip so hard it bled to keep from moaning aloud.

"Who knew something so soft and sweet could take such intense pleasure from all the rough mating I'm capable of?" He asked me and I shuddered in his hold. His thrusts didn't lose their speed, but his hips slapped harder against my ass, deeper inside of me as if demanding proof that I loved it.

And oh, I truly *did*.

"If I..." *Thrust.* "Didn't know..." *Thrust.* "Better, I..." Whispering between his thrusts was proving difficult. Both to remember what I was trying to say and to stay as quiet as possible.

"You what?" Rhuger asked and thrust into me *hard*, making me gasp. It took a few more moments and a few more snaps of his hips for me to remember how to speak.

"I'd say you..." *Thrust.* "...wanted me to..." *Thrust.* "Scream!" I bit my bottom lip to keep from making anything more than a tiny squeak as my toes curled. I felt blood coat my tongue, and I couldn't feel the pain.

"And what if I *do*?" He growled, one side of his sinful mouth sliding up in a devious smirk as he increased his pace. "What if I *do* want you to scream? To be a bad girl and disobey me? All so I can show you exactly *how* I want to punish you..."

He released my waist and slid his hand up to cup my throat, to tilt my head up so I couldn't avoid his devouring gaze. Whimpering, I saw the heat there, saw how badly he wanted me to scream. To punish me in ways I knew I'd enjoy. It was a battle of wills as he stared into my soul while he pile-drove me into the wall, the barrel beneath me rocking and splintering from the impact.

He may be the dominant one while I held the power as his submissive, but I was weak when it came to his desires. For they so often mirrored my own. My breathing hitched as I prepared to let go, to scream for him. To find out precisely what a punishment from my cridhe would entail. And how much I'd revel in it.

Someone suddenly tugged open the tapestry covering the doorway. Light streamed in on us and my mind bleated in panic at being caught.

With my face and neck frozen in place by my mate's hand, I could only look from the corner of my eye to see who was there. A young maid stood frozen in the light shining in from behind her. She looked like she was in her early twenties, willowy and lovely, and dressed in a simple smock. Her enormous emerald and obsidian eyes were riveted on us. On our cridhe marks.

My human instincts told me to stop, to hide my body, to be ashamed of being caught.

"What are you looking at, pearl?" Rhuger's rough, panting

growl rent the air and made me shiver. And this guy didn't even *slow down*. Instead, he followed my gaze to the doorway. Even after registering that there was someone watching him pound me like a screen door in a hurricane, he didn't bother stopping. Just looked indolently at the girl and said in a bored voice, "It's occupied."

When the female just continued to stand there and stare, he let out a rough roar deep in his throat, startling her so she dropped the tapestry. I could hear her retreating footsteps as she fled. Shocked, appalled, and frankly impressed at his lack of fucks to give, I just stared at my mate with wide eyes as I panted.

"Where were we..." Rhuger's deep rumble flickered over my skin, lit up my cridhe marks, and I bit back a moan. "You enjoyed getting caught, didn't you, pearl? And don't lie to me. I felt how your tight little cunt clenched around my cock. It felt like you were close to coming. Seems like I'll have to finish what I started."

And with that, he released my wrists, pulled me off of the barrel, spun me around, ripped the cloak off of me, and bent me over the barrel with his fist in my hair.

"Don't worry, pearl. I know what you like. I know how to make you scream for me." He pressed the heel of his hand up against my backside, pushing it up so he could slide himself home. I let out a low moan deep in my throat as he leaned over me and rested his forearm against the wall above where he had me pinned to the barrel. I could feel him there, pressed against my sweet spot as he ground his hips against my ass. Then he bent low over me so I could feel his breath tickling the shell of my ear. "So sweet and good. I'll teach you how to be bad for me."

My eyes rolled back into my head at his words as I throbbed around him *hard*. Hissing, he chuckled and slammed his hips forward. The tip of him hit my sweet spot before sliding past it, the ribbed underside of his cock rubbing over it in tiny aftershocks of pleasure.

Unable to help myself, I started a keening moan.

"That's right, pearl." Rhuger rasped from above as he primally rutted the soul out of me. "Sing for me. Let me hear how much you want it. Let everyone hear who you belong to."

So I did. My moaning turned to screaming as I lost all control and climaxed. My clawed hands left deep gouges in the barrel's wood as I sought to hold onto the world around me while I shattered.

"That's it, that's my bad girl." He ground out between his teeth.

His rhythm faltered as he tried to drag out my orgasm. But with me screaming his name repeatedly so everyone could hear who was mercilessly murdering my pussy in this cramped little storage closet, he couldn't last. He roared my name as he rocked inside me. The hot wash of his cum inside of me made my blood sing.

When we finally came back to ourselves, Rhuger gently slipped free of me with a groan. He helped me off of the barrel and slipped his kilt back into place, before wrapping me back up in the cloak. I was trembling like a newborn fawn and it wasn't because of the cold. Smiling sweetly down at me, he pressed a tender kiss to my lips before scooping me back up into his arms.

He shouldered his way past the tapestry and out into the hall. He froze, and I looked to where his attention lay. The hallway was packed on one side with a blushing, giggling horde of young females. They spotted us and squealed. Their noises reached higher octaves when they saw Rhuger's cridhe marks.

I bit back my apprehension. Most men, or males I'd imagine, would have preened and puffed out their chest at having so much female attention. But when I looked up to gauge his reaction, he seemed almost irritated.

"Are you okay?" I whispered, reaching up to cup his cheek.

Rhuger's gaze snapped down to mine, his wreck of a haircut nearly making him look goofy as some tufts stuck out in all directions. His gaze softened when he registered my worry, and a small smile tugged at the corners of his mouth.

"I'll be fine once we're alone." Rhuger rumbled, pressing his forehead to mine. "This will take some getting used to."

Being here. In the place with so many of his worst memories. He made to pull away, but I wasn't having it. I grabbed him by his green, pointy ears and yanked his face down to mine. I gave him a resounding smack of a kiss. Pulling away enough to look into his eyes, I let him see I understood.

He dove in and gave me a passionate kiss in return. When he released my mouth, I was seeing stars and was breathless. The young females were still giggling, but Rhuger was moving away from them.

"How long will we be doing it like bunnies?" I asked as we stepped out of view of the gaggle of twittering young maids.

"At least a week. Ideally, it's a full triple lunar cycle that we would have to ourselves in our own home." He grinned, then turned pensive. "What's a 'buhn-ee'?"

"Small furry animal, rodent-like, makes a good pet." I rushed through the explanation with more pressing matters at hand. Or I *wish* were in hand... "Can we really leave them like that? The Oc'Turin?"

"No... we'll have to break to start our plan." He explained as he rounded a corner, nearly jogging with me in his arms, his hands occasionally shifting and roaming as I bounced against him. "I trust Kholt to oversee the creation of the Oc'Turin council. Until then, we won't be needed. We are the first cridhe pair in two generations. They will give us space. Just not as much as I'd like."

"If you had it your way, we'd never leave our rooms." I chuckled and noticed how tight his jaw was. How focused he was on getting us to our rooms as quickly as possible. I had the feeling that if we didn't get there soon, we'd traumatize another group of orckin by fucking out in the open in the hallway.

"Exactly." His wicked mouth was so damn smug as it curled around those sharp teeth of his, turning into the most breathtaking grin. Jesus take the wheel. My lady parts were rioting. If I didn't have him inside me soon, I was going to lose my gotdamned mind.

CARLOTTA HUGHES

CHAPTER 12

RHUGER

My old rooms from when I was still with the Oc'Turin had been cleaned and a fire lit in the hearth. Likely, as soon as Orok's head had hit the floor. My rooms had originally been carved straight into the cliffs on the far end of Cìp Carragh away from the front gates. A location not favored by the Oc'Turin elite, but a quiet one. The rooms were simple but held luxuries most of the Oc'Turin weren't likely to get.

The bed had tall posts with drapes to keep the warmth in. With a fireplace large enough for me to step into. The floor was covered in thick rugs, furs, and pillows for lounging. There were a few chairs and a desk. And there were private hot-spring-fed baths in an alcove at the back. Private baths were rare anywhere on Talam, but it'd been something I'd insisted on having made. Having quarters near the falls and the springs that fed it made it possible and I'd thanked the Source more than once for this happenstance.

I didn't much care to bathe in the public baths. Just like the Oc'Dellor, the Oc'Turin baths were hot-spring-fed and had drains. But, unlike the separate baths in Baile Coille, the other Oc'Turin males had a habit of bringing their females into the communal baths to share with their fellows. The water was never clean by the time they were done.

The last thing I wanted was to bathe in the spend of dozens of males.

So I'd paid to have the baths installed. I'd never been happier for such foresight. I didn't want any others looking at my mate as she bathed. As her body glistened in the steamy air and rivulets of water cascaded over her perfect plump curves. That was my pleasure alone.

"Your room looks so comfy." Amelia smiled at me, her uisge-beatha eyes near glowing in the low light.

"There's a bath in the back." My slow smile and the heat in my gaze sent my cridhe's skin to flush that pretty pink.

"You have your own bath?" She breathed, obviously pleased.

"Yes. Yours now too." I chuckled, desire darkening my voice. I couldn't shake the thought of watching her bathe.

"Getting clean sounds wonderful..." Amelia's voice trailed off, and she stole a glance towards the alcove. I set her down on her feet, already aching for her body against mine.

"Then get to it." My amusement increased when I slapped her ass, and she made the cutest squeak, jumping in surprise from the impact. It was a reminder and a promise. Because my cridhe loved for me to spank her and fuck her hard enough to smack her ass with my hips. Pleasure and pain, reward and punishment all in one. *Gods* she was perfect. More than I could have ever hoped or wished for. And here she stood looking at me coyly from over her shoulder, my own, my *cridhe*.

"Scoundrel." She tried not to smile, but the corners of her mouth and her blush couldn't hide from me.

"Och, you knew that already." I couldn't hold back my chuckle, nor keep my kilt from tenting as I thought about spanking her in the baths. About how I'd exact her punishment... for screaming my name wantonly until we'd gathered an audience. Both my good girl and naughty lass. Two sides of an irresistible coin wrapped up in someone so soft, so sweet, and kind. Yet deadly.

Her body was still painted with Orok's dried blood, her thighs still streaked along the insides from our combined desire. I was glad she could bathe and wash off the taint of my brother. I'd miss seeing the dried cum on her thighs. But that was easily fixed.

Amelia clutched the cape tight around her as she strode for the bath. I watched her go and then looked around my old room. So many memories clung to the stone walls. And I was about to spend the next week making a lot more with my Banrigh, my cridhe, my mate. *MINE.* Buried between her thighs where I belonged.

My smile turned into a wicked grin as I tugged off my clothes and tossed them in the corner. I heard her gasp from the other room. I prowled to the opening and found her standing calf-deep in the wide pool that encompassed most of the room. Hot water trickled in from a small waterfall near the ceiling at the back.

My cock stiffened so fast I felt a lightness in my head, my erection curling up towards my navel. Because she stood there, gorgeous curves and soft skin glistening with the water vapor from the rising steam. Her ass was a perfect peach shape that made my mouth water. The soft swells of her hips begged to be gripped. I leaned against the doorway, transfixed, as she waded deeper into the hot water. Soon she was chest-deep and dove under. She resurfaced quickly, her soft wavy brown hair plastered to her head and upper back. Working quickly, she washed off the last of Orok's blood, her hands skimming the pillowy softness of her body in a way that wasn't slow and erotic. Instead, it was second nature, and yet, all the more intimate for her lack of self-censure. Water streamed from her neamhnaid skin in tantalizing rivulets that made me want to lick and suck them from her skin.

I must have made some small noise of need because she whirled in the water, parting the steam. Her eyes caught sight of me and widened, her pupils blowing out in desire as her gaze dipped down to my erect cock. Where it was twitching and leaking slick.

Pushing off the stone doorway with easy, predatory grace, I sauntered over to her. Her throat bobbed as her eyes raked over me again and again. I loved how she looked at me, like she could devour me with her eyes. The little pink tip of her tongue slipped out between her lips to wet them and I growled, hunger rising higher. I stepped into the water and was soon hip-deep, gliding towards her through the steam.

When I reached her, I lifted a hand to slip a few strands of wet hair from her cheek behind her ear. Her uisge-beatha eyes were huge as she stared openly at me. Then I slid my hand down her neck in trailing touches, to where I'd bitten her and marked her as mine. It had healed already and as I brushed it; she shivered and her cridhe marks seemed to pulse and set my heart to racing.

There were few who knew the truth of the mating marks and the bond between a cridhe pair. A knowledge kept quiet by the Rìghs, Banrighs, and Feadhainn a Chìs as the marks faded from our people. I knew the truth about them because my Màthair had told me about them with a wistful smile. As if she'd hoped to have them herself with my father before he'd been killed.

The first marking of a cridhe pair initiated the black tattoo-like designs to bloom over our chests. Not always immediately, but not long after. While all other bite marks could heal, the scars fading with time, this bite mark never would. Each time their mate touched the bite mark or the mating marks, they would come alive. Letting that person feel what they were feeling. Whether it was love, lust, hate, sorrow, or any other emotion that affected the body.

There was a part of me that hungered for her to bite me, too. So I could feel what she did. But her blunt little human teeth wouldn't be able to pierce the hard flesh of my shoulder.

I drew my fingertips across the skin of her chest, feeling the mating marks of my cridhe come to life like thousands of sparkling stars. Was this what it felt like to be a god in the act of creation? To bring life and breath from stardust?

"What are you doing?" Amelia asked me, her gaze going hazy from feeling both her desire and mine. I slid my hand up to grasp her chin, tilting her face where I wanted it.

"You gave up your kisses for the rite. The least I can do is give you what you crave." My voice was guttural, my every instinct screaming for me to turn her around, bend her over in the water, and fuck her until we fell unconscious.

"But I crave all of you." She breathed, chest heaving in the water.

"Then all of me you shall have..." My mouth hovered over hers and she moaned helplessly into the space between us. Snarling, I lunged forward, claiming her mouth. All of my raw hunger took over, and it was like I couldn't pull her to me close enough, breathe her in enough. I reached under the water and grasped her ass, hoisting her up until she wrapped her sweet thighs around my hips, her arms wound tight around my neck.

I couldn't slap her ass under the water, so I settled for grasping the globes of her bottom and kneading them with my fingers. Amelia moaned loudly into my mouth and I devoured it, devoured every sound she made like it was a feast. My cock was trapped between us and that wouldn't sate either of us.

So I moved forward in the water until I could perch her on the lip of an underwater bench at the far back. It ran along most of the wall under the waterfall that poured hot clean water down the rocks next to us. Her thighs fluttered around my waist as I shifted against her.

I moved my mouth from hers and began teasing her earlobe between my teeth.

"Are you going to be my good lass, pearl?" I rasped into her ear. "Are you going to let me taste you? Fuck you? Sate you?"

She moaned.

"Use your words, cridhe." My voice pitched deeper as I nearly purred. I loved hearing her talk dirty. Loved hearing the need in her voice. The need only I could satisfy. I began rubbing my erection up and down her slit, the tip of my cock running over her clit and causing her to gasp.

"I need you to fuck me Rhuger, my cridhe." She shuddered in my arms, her voice wobbling as she pleaded with me. "I'll let you do whatever you want, please."

"Soon..." I chuckled darkly, and I ducked my head down to her throat. "Such a good lass..." I growled against her throat. I licked her pulse with my long black tongue as my hand rose to cup her breast. She moaned and began grinding her hips against mine, desperate to get the tip of me inside of her. I tilted my hips back, out of her reach, and she cried in outrage.

The mating frenzy had her tight in its grip, alright.

Amelia grasped what was left of my hair in her fist, and tugged —hard. My head snapped back, and I hissed down at her in surprise.

"I need you *now*." She snapped, all sweet pleading gone, and I grinned.

"So demanding, my lusty goddess." I crooned, cock sliding against her slit once more.

Her swollen lips shuddered with her breath for a moment before she leaned forward and began laving my neck with that slick, tiny tongue of hers. I tilted my head back and groaned. She began to nip at my throat with her blunted teeth and suck on my flesh, her pretty lips becoming a tight seal as her tongue and mouth worked my shoulder as if it were my cock.

Fuck, it felt so good. It made me want to fuck her in this pool until she was bathed in my seed. The overwhelming need to plant my cock deep inside her had me lifting her legs up over my shoulders. With a sharp tug, I yanked her to the edge of the lip. She cried out, but I leaned down, swallowing her cry with my mouth. Slipping one hand between us, I grasped the shaft of my cock and tilted it forward until it pressed at her entrance.

"Oh yes, *gods yes!*" she breathed into my mouth.

Once I had the angle I needed, I thrust into her in one long, slow stroke, as she was so damned *tight* again. Every time I slid into her she was tight and hungry and felt like *heaven*. She moaned, her hips twitching as her head fell back. Snarling, I wrapped my now free arm around her torso, fisting the hair at the back of her neck in my fingers. My other hand reached under her to span both globes of her ass.

I lifted her up in the water and hugged her tight to my body, cock buried all the way inside of her cunt. Her hands held onto my shoulders, tiny claws sinking in and ratcheting my desire for her up even higher. With a roar, I slipped my cock in and out of her tight cunt. It already clutched at me like she was about to reach her climax. And I wanted more of it.

"So deep... you're so deep!" She cried. Her uisge-beatha eyes sparkling and hazy with pleasure.

"How does it feel, pearl?" I growled. Needing to hear it. Needing to hear her demand more of me. Because *gods*, I wanted to give her *everything*.

"So *fucking* good, don't you dare stop!" She wailed into the surrounding steam.

So I didn't.

A few more strokes had her panting and moaning my name. Her breathing hitched, and she came undone, shattering in my arms as she screamed her pleasure. Her body spasmed around my cock. And despite how badly I wanted to join her in release, she had commanded me not to stop.

And I *needed* to have her scream her pleasure at least once more before I could roar mine.

I set her back on the lip of the underwater bench. Before she could protest, I pulled out of her, pulled her to her feet, spun her around so her back was to my chest, and bent her forward until her hands braced on the wall in front of her. I crowded closer. Her thighs were braced against the wall under the underwater bench, and her back bent with her ass high in the air as she clung to the wall.

She writhed and panted as I entered her so, so slowly. Begging me so sweetly with her foul pink tongue for me to fuck her—fuck her *now* and fuck her *hard*—I couldn't help the dark laugh that broke from my throat. And the ragged gasping moan that tore from her lips as I slid in to the hilt was sweet music to my ears.

Leaning forward, I placed one hand on the wall above her head and gripped her hip with the other. The change in angle was one I knew that made her fall apart, hitting that sweet spot deep inside of her. My grin, like my thoughts, was wicked as I started a painfully slow rhythm. Each stroke in and each stroke out were long and slow so she could feel every ridge along the underside of my cock rub inside of her. And each time I entered her to the hilt, I rolled my hips to give her that extra bit of pressure against her sweet spot.

"Let go, Rhuger. Let go and just rail me, please!" Her hands scrabbled for purchase on the wall. "I need you! I want you to come with me!"

But I did no such thing.

Somehow, I lasted through her orgasm as she came moments later, despite how tightly her cunt clenched my cock, attempting to milk my knot dry. As soon as she stopped spasming from her pleasure, I pulled out and turned around with her in my grasp. I sat down on the bench then, cock spearing up through the water, and turned her around in front of me.

"I want to come with my cock inside of you and your breast in my mouth." I gasped as I pulled her to me and she slid up over my thighs to straddle me, knees on the bench. Sitting up enough, I took her nipple into my mouth. She moaned loudly and her hips jerked in response. So sensitive, my mate.

Such a godsdamned delight.

My sharp teeth teased and nipped at her nipple as I laved her with my tongue. I was so careful not to break her skin between my teeth; I didn't want to hurt her here. Taking my cock in hand between us, I shifted and slid the tip inside of her. She panted and slid down my shaft until she was seated completely on it. Then she grasped my head to her breast, back arched backward, and rocked with me inside of her.

I shifted my mouth to her other nipple and began licking and sucking on it as I thrust upwards to meet her rocking motions. The noises of us joining and parting in the water were so erotic when they joined with the sound of her voice and the sounds of pleasure she made in my ear. Releasing her breast, I rose to speak into her ear.

"You're so fucking perfect, my mate. That's right, cry and moan for me with that sweet voice of yours. Your cunt is so tight, your long legs and round ass so inviting. I don't belong anywhere else but here plowing you until you scream." Growling at her in Black Tongue was a tool in my ever-growing arsenal to make my cridhe come undone. "I will fuck you until you beg me to stop. Until we're both spent. And I'll do it every day until the gods take me. I can't wait to see your belly swell with our child, Amelia. So sexy and lush and fertile. And once you birth our child, I'll fill you with my seed again and again and again until you're pregnant once more."

She loved it when I spoke to her in Teanga Dhubh. She started rocking against me harder and I picked up my pace to meet her thrust for thrust. I kept trying to hold back, to hold off from my release, but that wasn't an option anymore. Because now all I could do was think about taking her when her belly was swollen with our child and filling her with my seed, even though she was already so ripe.

It was enough to bring me right to the edge.

"I want you to come for me, cridhe." She whimpered as my rhythm slipped and my release was within reach. But I wasn't about to spill my seed without seeing her come at least once more. I grasped her wet waves in my fist and dragged her lips to mine. I devoured her mouth. The change in angle was perfect too as she cried into my open mouth each time we parted for breath. I snaked my free hand around her torso and clutched her to me.

Then I lifted my hips and fucked her as hard and fast as I could get my body to move.

Her cries turned into screams and she squirmed and writhed as her orgasm built and built and built. Between one scream and the next, she went rigid and her cunt sucked my cock so deep inside of her I was afraid it would break off. But then she was clenching around my cock in twitches and waves and all I could do was roar my release into her mouth as I splintered into millions of shards of knife-keen pleasure.

CHAPTER 13*

RHUGER

After we'd come back into our bodies, panting hard and languid, I decided it was best for us to actually get clean before taking her to my bed. *Our* bed. The thought that all we had separately, was now *ours* was a warming thought in my chest. I'd given up hope of finding anyone to share my life and world with. To have a female who appreciated all that I was, without needing to change, was a blessing. Having her be my cridhe and the mother of our orcling was a miracle.

Sweet thoughts of my mate cradling our orcling had me smiling softly as I slid free of Amelia and sat her on the bench. She protested a moment before realizing I'd done so to grab some soaps and bathing tools left nearby in a bucket. Taking out a bar of soap that smelled like juicy fruit, like her, I worked up a good lather between my hands before standing in front of her. The bucket bobbed and drifted lazily in the water next to us.

"What are you doing?" My cridhe whispered, voice hoarse from screaming my name.

"Bathing you." I rumbled, a smile still curling the corners of my mouth. Such a foreign thing to me, smiling all the time. But something

I was delighted to get used to.

"You don't need to..." Amelia said, blushing that lovely pink.

"But I want to," I replied. Standing in front of her I held my soapy hands before her in supplication. "May I?"

"Okay." She answered, ducking her head, the delicate tips of her ears so pink they were almost red. *Adorable.* How she seemed so open and wanton with sex, but these small intimacies made her into a shy, blushing maid.

"Look up for me," I murmured, and she did, those intoxicating uisge-beatha eyes glowing.

Gently, I slid my soapy hands into her wet hair with my claws retracted. She hummed and her eyes slid closed as I began massaging her scalp and the base of her skull.

She still had bruises from where Ergit had gripped her neck in his monstrous hand. Not to mention the large one at her temple, the other on her cheek from when she'd been struck first by Ergit, then by Orok. It would take a few days for them to heal, maybe longer, with her human blood. The smile dropped from my face as combed my claws through her hair. I rinsed the soap from the silky strands with water from my cupped palm. She'd been through so much in such a short time. Yet she still looked forward to and sought out the small pearls of joy and love where she could.

Truly, my mate was a marvel.

Taking the soap into my hands again, I lathered a cloth from the bucket and washed her back, her shoulders, her neck... Source deliver me. Every inch of her was lush perfection sprinkled with freckles like the night sky with stars. As I passed the cloth over my bite mark, my knuckle grazed it and she shivered, a blush riding high on her cheeks again. No matter how many times I saw that blush, I'd never grow tired of it. Never grow tired of knowing that I was the reason her heart raced.

I kneed open her thighs and stepped between them. Amelia's breathing hitched in a soft squeak as I stepped into the space between them. Leaning over her, I braced my forearm above her head. A steamy echo of when I'd rutted her in the little storage closet. When that maid had caught us and my cridhe had thrilled at it. At how I'd refused to stop plowing her when, really, I'd been too lust-drunk to care about anything but her. It had nearly driven me to madness, and I'd used my carnal knowledge of her body to make her scream my name until mortar slid from between the stones in the wall.

"Do you have any idea what you do to me, my sweet pearl?" I growled into her ear, trailing kisses down the soft column of her throat. My fingers brushed her wet locks from my path. This kind of tenderness was a carnal ache that felt so damnably good. Slow, steady, building to something wild and wicked. Absolute anticipation with each breath and each heartbeat.

"N-no..." she murmured against my shoulder.

"Then let me show you..." I breathed onto the mark I'd left where her neck and shoulder joined. Amelia shuddered, her perfect little neamhnaid hands grasping around my waist and up my back, drawing me closer.

With a dark chuckle, I opened my mouth and raked my sharp teeth over my mark with a guttural roar. An echo of how I'd marked her before all the Oc'Turin. My cridhe's blood had been so impossibly sweet and salty as it had hit my tongue. The sharp edge of iron in it mirrored the burning in my soul as it was reforged with hers.

I let out a ragged moan, my knot already swollen and my cock pressing against her push curves. My goddess, my Banrigh, was a feast fit for a king. For me and for me alone. Licking my mark on her, I hauled her out of the water and pressed her back against the stone.

Kneeling on the bench while holding her up by her generous ass that overflowed my scarred hands, I moved my kisses to her cridhe marks.

As soon as my lips brushed them, they tingled. I pulled back in surprise, my expression matching my mate's. I didn't hesitate, but pressed my mouth to her chest, kissing and licking and sucking her flesh. Tracing her mating marks with my worshiping lips until a singing started in my blood.

Amelia was trying to wrap her thighs around my waist, but they were too weak from all of our fucking. Taking pity on her, I got off of the bench and set her back down upon it. I lunged forward and claimed her mouth, devouring every soft cry as our different tongues danced together perfectly.

Then I remembered a little wicked notion. Pulling back from my cridhe, she attempted to follow, desperate to keep kissing me. Smiling, I stayed just out of reach until she whimpered.

"Since you were such a bad girl and disobeyed me..." I whispered against her lips. "Now you're going to take your punishment..."

Gazing into the deep pools of her uisge-beatha eyes, I slipped my hand down the soft rolls of her belly. Slid my fingertips between her thighs under the water. I saw the moment she felt me against her aching flesh, watched with wild hunger as her expression shifted, her mouth opening in a lovely pink circle as a breathy moan escaped her.

"*Rhuger!*" Amelia cried.

"That's my princess..." I growled as I worked her with my fingers.

She began grinding shamelessly against my hand, her breaths coming quicker as she climbed towards her release. And just as she got close, I removed my hand and brought the fingers that had just been inside her up to her mouth. I pressed them between her lips so she could taste the remnants of us as she squirmed in protest.

Amelia bit and sucked on them in equal measure, attempting to punish me for keeping her from orgasm even as she glared at me. She didn't know yet that the line between pain and pleasure often blurred for me. Anything she did with her mouth, her claws when we were like this would be erotic tinder on the fire of my need for her.

Pulling my fingers from her mouth, I grasped her jaw and dragged her mouth to mine. My hunger let my resolve to punish her slip. Before I could cave, I grasped her hips and sunk inside of her in one vicious thrust. Amelia threw her head back and screamed as I began a nearly unhinged rhythm.

Again, I drove her to the threshold of climax, and again I refused her. I pulled out of her, nearly spending in the process from the pressure in my knot. Amelia shrieked in outrage and attempted to slide her hand down between her thick thighs to finish the job herself. But I snatched her wrists and pinned them over her head, growling as my gaze bored into hers that sparked with fury and unfulfilled need.

"Not so fast, cridhe." I *tsked* at her. "You still haven't finished receiving your punishment. When you've suffered enough, I'll let you come."

"This is *cruel and unusual punishment!*" She yelled at me as she thrashed against my grip. Her breasts bounced and jiggled with her movements and I found my gaze locking onto her hardened nipples. On all that soft flesh as it rippled with her writhing.

"Not as cruel as you are, my sweet, wicked pearl." The words slipped from deep in my chest, unbidden. Rough and nearly cracking with the emotion of it. For I spoke the truth. I blinked slowly, then skewered her to stillness with my gaze. "Every glance, every movement, every ripple of your body and how it cushions every damned part of mine, every *sound* you make, and each smile you give me is like a cruel knife to the heart. You so carelessly gift someone who's only known *famine*, a *feast* of softness, tenderness, and love. An unusual, painful cruelty in all of its kindness, its sweetness."

Amelia breathed heavily as she registered my words. Her brows furrowed as she opened, then closed her kiss-swollen mouth. Looking for the right thing to say, and failing.

"Give me a pain I understand, Amelia." I rasped, suddenly and irrevocably vulnerable. "This ache inside my body, my soul, is foreign. I don't know how to live with it. Not yet."

"What do you want me to do?" She asked me in a small voice. The goodness in her warring with itself. Easing my pain by inflicting another kind of pain wasn't something she understood. Not yet.

"You can't truly hurt me. You're incapable of it." I swallowed thickly. "But I want you to *try*."

She nodded her agreement before she spoke. "Okay."

I released her wrists and wrapped my arms over hers, down to grip her ass. Again, I lifted her out of the water and pressed her against the rock wall of the bath as she wrapped her long, luscious legs around my hips. My mate slid her arms up around my back, her claws sinking in ever so slightly, testing. I groaned at that small pain. Then I thrust inside of her, burying my cock to the hilt inside of her core.

She wailed and I captured her mouth with mine

With each thrust, the anticipation in me built. Would she do what she said? Would she at least *try* to use her nails and teeth to give me the pleasurable pain I craved from her?

As I attempted to pull away from our kiss, she bit down on my bottom lip, drawing blood. Groaning jaggedly at the spike of sensation that ran from my lip straight to my cock, I felt my body go loose and taut all at once as I started railing her against the unforgiving stone.

Amelia bit my earlobe, raked her teeth across the front of my throat, and sucked hard on every inch of me she could reach even as she met me thrust for thrust.

Edging her along her release had primed her. Each slap of my hips against her ass and thighs wrung a cry from her. Soon she wasn't just crying out, she was near shrieking her pleasure from my cock sliding home inside of her.

"Rhuger!" My name fell from her lips in a wail before she flew into her release. She clenched down on my cock so hard, it hurt and made me groan from the pleasure of it.

Amelia, in the throes of her passion, sank her claws into my back as she screamed. Scoring the flesh and drawing thin lines of blood to run down my newly healed scars to the water below. I hissed, snarling into her ear as the line between pleasure and pain blurred further. She shivered and her pussy clenched around me like a fist as I thrust harder.

"Again," I demanded in a ragged moan, so close to coming. "Carve me with your nails again. Let me feel how badly you want me with those little neamhnaid claws of yours."

She blinked at me for a moment, still riding her orgasm, unsure. But, ever the brave female, she nodded and kissed me. A heartbeat later, her claws raked down my back again, slicing through the healing flesh from her last onslaught. I choked a sobbing moan into her mouth as my rhythm faltered.

Unable to stop moaning and growling like a wild beast, I felt my knot swell to the point of pain, dancing along that line as I slammed into her sweet cunt. I could tell she was close again too, but unlike normal, she was fighting to be present, to give me what I needed from her. Gods, I loved this female with every fiber of my being.

"Uuuhhnn! Amelia... I'm going to come." I told her with a

shaking groan, unable to hold back anymore.

"Come for me, Rhuger." She panted a moment before she clenched her thighs around my hips, locking me to her as she sank her blunt human teeth into the meat of my shoulder. Even as her claws drew lines of burning pleasure down to my ass. Hurtling me over the edge to explode into pure ecstasy in her arms.

I screamed my release to the ceiling of the bath as my knot locked me inside of her. As I felt her blunt teeth pierce the flesh of my shoulder and my blood run down my chest. My scream turned into a roar as she marked me. As her teeth in my neck tightened our cridhe bond until I couldn't tell where I ended and she began.

Her walls clenched and rippled along my cock even as she bucked against my hold. My knot kept her where I needed her as I rode my orgasm, grinding into her as deep as I could get while I released my load of cum deep inside of her womb. Our bodies rolled together, undulating through the shared release that rocked us.

Eventually, shaking, I knelt on the stone bench and held her against me, still sunk deep inside of her. Amelia released my neck from her bite, and I bucked into her hard as I moaned around the harshness in my throat. If I'd had any more cum inside of me, I would have burst again, overflowing her womb to gush out around my cock.

But my knot was soft, and I was spent.

"Are you okay?" My sweet little cridhe asked, as her hands found my face, and held it so she could see me for herself. She froze when she saw.

I was crying. The release had been so good and so needed in that way that it had left huge tracts of tears sliding down my cheeks. I knew my expression must have shown what I felt. Devastation, unsurpassed bliss, shame, and love.

"Oh, gumby." She whispered as she kissed me with such

tenderness I sobbed into her mouth with the perfection of it. The physical pain, pleasure, and release finally matched what I felt inside.

Somehow, her punishment had become mine. Her claws and teeth in my skin were a wretched, soaring freedom. Even as her softness and sweet kisses grounded me in a strange, yet welcome, comforting solace. The openness I'd felt between us in our bond when she'd marked me seemed to drift into slumber, a whisper of what it had been. We were ourselves once more, yet still so strongly connected.

She didn't just give me what I wanted, but what I needed. In equal measures pleasure and pain. A perfect understanding of everything I couldn't say that could only come from a connection like ours. A cridhe bond.

"Let's go cuddle, love." My mate said as she pulled herself from me and led me from the bath to our bed. I followed her like the willingly tamed beast I'd become. "Let me give you what you need."

And I did.

AMELIA

When Rhuger had asked me to hurt him, I'd been torn, conflicted. I didn't want to hurt him because I loved him. But he needed this, and I was the only person who could give it to him. I'd seen how quickly he could heal, so I knew whatever I did wouldn't cause permanent damage. Yet I still found it difficult to do it.

I had to warm up to it. Biting his lip and drawing blood, the taste of his blood so different from mine. Earthy and fragrant with that spice I could always smell on him. I was surprised to find I liked the taste of it. Bit by bit I nipped at him, left hickeys all over every inch of him I could reach, gauging if I was going too far or if I could keep going by his body's reactions.

And he'd loved every moment of it. My pleasure mounted at knowing I could make him feel like this. I hadn't meant to orgasm so soon. I'd wanted him to go first. But I hadn't been able to help it. When I'd come undone, that leash I held on that tiny, vicious part of me dropped, and I sunk my little claws into his back and raked over every delectable inch of it.

He'd nearly come apart at the seams and had begged me to do it again, so I did. And when he'd started unraveling, had actually told me he was coming, I'd followed my instinct. As I clawed at his back one last time, I sunk my teeth into the meat of his shoulder as hard as I could. I was surprised my teeth could pierce his skin, but they did, and that's when the last puzzle piece clicked into place.

Intense pleasure overwhelmed me as Rhuger let out a jagged, broken scream that ended in a reverberating roar. His blood slipped into my mouth and down my throat, lighting me up from the inside out. Even his marks made my flesh tingle where it touched them. It felt as if there was nothing between us now, our connection so open and strong I could feel his pleasure, his pain, and everything in between as if it were my own.

Our shared orgasm had lasted a long while. The both of us grinding and riding it out. When it finally passed, my belly felt so strangely full. And when Rhuger pulled out of me, it became obvious why as cum sluiced down my thighs into the water. How much could this guy cum in one go?

It was when I'd pulled back and seen how my cridhe was crying that I froze. Had I gone too far? Had I hurt him? But, in reading his expression I realized that no, I hadn't. Quite the opposite. I'd given him the release he'd needed. An emotional one, just as intense as the physical one.

"Oh, gumby..." I murmured as I pulled him to me. My big, powerful, capable mate sobbed into my mouth as I kissed him with all the love I had in me. "Let's go cuddle, love. Let me give you what you need."

Then I'd pulled away and got off of his lap. My legs were shaking like crazy, but I managed to lead him out of the bath to our bed. He followed behind me, almost like a lost little boy. It broke my heart, so I did the only thing I could. I'd crawled into bed and held the blankets up for him to slide in with me. Then I'd pulled him close so his head rested on my chest and sang *Fly Me to the Moon*.

Rhuger tangled himself up around me as if he couldn't get close enough. I kissed his forehead and hesitantly rubbed circles on his shoulders, afraid to touch the marks I'd left on him. But to my surprise, they'd already healed. So I relaxed as I crooned to him, rocked him, and showed him how much I cherished him.

"I love you, Rhuger," I murmured against his forehead as I trailed my fingers gently over him. He shuddered then gripped me tighter.

"I love you too, Amelia." He croaked as he buried his face between my breasts.

My mate had been crying on and off as his emotions had sorted themselves out. I understood how it felt after an intense release. Rhuger had given me a few strong ones where I'd cried. But nothing as profound as this, not yet anyway.

I never understood how some women hated to see their men cry or belittled men and boys for crying. How men did it to each other too. Crying was as human as breathing. A means for us to process, release, and move on from emotional times in our lives. It was valid and sacred in its own right. Rhuger would never receive judgment from me for crying. He deserved to be completely himself and accepted as he was. Just like he did for me.

"Do you want me to do that every time we're together?" I

whispered the question as I slid my fingers through his shorn hair. I'd have to cut it for him. But for now, we both needed comfort and rest.

"No," Rhuger mumbled against my chest where he was listening to my heartbeat. "Just sometimes."

"Will you tell me when you need it?" I asked softly. Rhuger nodded and wrapped his arms tighter around my waist. "I need to hear you say it, gumby."

Rhuger peeked up at me with one piercing eye, calling me out on my bullshit without even saying a word. I just smiled down at him and kissed his forehead.

"I promise I'll tell you." He replied, sounding slightly put out and just a teensy bit annoyed.

"Good boy." I teased, and he went absolutely still.

With a growl and a rush of movement. Rhuger had me pinned to the bed.

"You might not want to tease me like that, mate. I might have to put another bairn in you." He growled playfully. I froze, face going red and pussy clenching so more of his cum slid out of me onto the bedding. He smelled it, looked down, and then back up at me. A slow, seductive smile curled his mouth. "Like that, did you, pearl?"

"Maybe," I said, my heart beating madly against my ribcage.

"Well, you can't be squirting out my seed if you want me to breed you." He whispered against my lips as he slid his fingers down to push his cum back inside of me. I whimpered and wriggled beneath him. It didn't matter that I was already pregnant, the concept still made me tremble in anticipation. "Again?"

"If you're ready, yes." I breathed.

"That's my good lass..."

CHAPTER 14*

AMELIA

Days passed filled with love, tenderness, snacks, and fucking each other's brains out. Rhuger discovered he really enjoyed having me on top. And it became a position he liked to return to. He wasn't lazy, on the contrary, he was *very* energetic about it.

"I love watching you move on me." He groaned as I rocked above him. I'd lost count of how many times we'd had sex. Whatever this cridhe frenzy was, it was one hell of a drug. And strangely, we never hurt more than a little soreness. Our bodies healed quickly to counteract any potential injury.

"Mmmmhhh." was all I could manage around my lips, swollen from his kisses. My eyelashes fluttered against my cheeks as my eyes rolled back from how good he felt inside of me.

"And I like that I can take control whenever I want." His silver and black eyes sparked and, between one thrust and the next, he had rolled, pinning me to the bed with his hips. My arms pressed above my head amongst the pillows, both wrists in one broad hand.

My heartbeat ratcheted up into overdrive. He heard it, smelled the change in me, and thrust into me hard until I cried out. My legs were too weak to do anything more than tremble at his sides as he pounded into me with long, hard, slow thrusts.

I was so damn close.

Again.

Not that I was complaining.

Rhuger suddenly stilled above me. Weakly, I panted as I opened my eyes to look up at him.

"So lovely." He whispered as his hand released my wrists to trail his thumb against my trembling bottom lip. I darted my tongue out to taste the salty heat of the tip of his thumb. He groaned deep in his throat.

Something sparked in his gaze once more and his hand dropped to cup my throat. In a flurry of movement, I found myself seated above him again. Rhuger took his time looking at my quivering curves as his fingers flexed softly around my throat.

"Are you going to be a good lass for me?" He rumbled. When I didn't immediately respond he did a figure eight with his hips.

"Yes!" I gasped.

"Good girl. I want you to crawl up here and kneel around my head." He growled, tugging at my waist and thighs. Pulling me up towards his face. "Get up here and let me worship you."

"What?" I asked, balking. Rhuger's words finally registered and I refused to move an inch.

"I want you to ride my face." He said, "Ride my face as if you were riding a nocrys."

"But I'm heavy and you might suffocate!" I told him, shy and alarmed all at once.

"You're not heavy. Not to me." He tilted his head back into the pillows and bared his throat for me, looking down at me from under his lashes. As if silently begging me to be a thigh collar around his neck.

I whimpered at how gotdamned sexy he was. And at how he constantly reminded me that he was powerful enough to toss me around like a ragdoll. Something that I still hadn't gotten used to after a lifetime of being a tall, thick woman whose ex-husband hadn't even attempted to carry her across the threshold.

"But I haven't cleaned up!" I protested. For gods' sake he'd be eating more than just *my* juices if he ate me out now.

"I don't care." Rhuger's brows furrowed.

"But..." I tried to protest again but he reached a hand up to cup my face, his thumb sinking between my swollen lips.

"Did. I. Stutter?" He asked me darkly. His gaze gone sharp and hot all at once.

"No..." I whimpered around his thumb. I succumbed then and sucked on his thumb as if it were his cock.

"Then get up here and let me taste you." He almost snarled. "Let me worry about breathing. I can think of no better way to meet my ancestors than drowning in your sweet honey."

Rhuger grasped my ass and lifted me off of his cock. I made a sound of protest and then one of alarm as he practically dragged me up his body. I was shaking like a newborn colt from all of the exertion of our mating. But his hands were steady and sure as he helped me place my knees on either side of his head.

I looked down at him, face flushed not just from our lovemaking but from embarrassment. His eyes were like brands as his gaze raked my face, down my body to the juncture of my thighs where he'd had his cock planted just moments ago. "Now, sit."

Hovering there, I didn't dare bring my weight down on him. He noticed as I resisted his hands and his gaze grew dark and shuttered from under his brows.

"I SAID SIT." He barked the command.

And as if my legs had a fucking will of their own, my knees gave way and I dropped until his hands caught my hips and ass, a mere breath from his mouth. Smirking in victory, one eyebrow arching in challenge, Rhuger flashed those sharp white teeth of his.

"So you like being told what to do. Don't you, my luscious cridhe?"

"Mmh." I whimpered. He opened his mouth as if to demand I speak, but I beat him to it. "Only by you."

Chest swelling as he took a deep, hitching breath, Rhuger blinked slowly, gaze turning molten. Oh, he liked that a whole lot. That I only enjoyed being told what to do by him. My cridhe.

Gaze focusing on what was right in front of his face, Rhuger fucking *licked his gotdamn lips* at the sight of my dripping pussy. With a grunt, he tucked his arms up under my thighs to lock me into place against him. He nuzzled my inner thigh and planted a swift kiss there before that long black, ridged tongue of his slipped out from between his lips and he pressed his mouth against my mound.

And *fuck*, he didn't care. He really didn't. Not one bit. Just lapped at me and drank our juices down as my thighs shuddered around his head. He groaned against my clit as if our combined desire was the most delicious thing he'd ever tasted.

"Oh, gods!" I cried, grasping onto the headboard so I didn't completely collapse from the intensity of my reaction.

"Are you praying to me, sweet goddess?" Rhuger crooned, cocking an eyebrow up at me from where he was still comfortably nestled between my thighs. I looked down, and he made sure I could see as he licked me from core to clit.

"Yes!" I screamed as his tongue delved deep inside of me. I bucked against his hold.

Rhuger just chuckled and adjusted his grip on my upper thighs, black claws digging into my soft flesh without piercing it. Skirting that thin line of danger that lay between pleasure and pain that he'd introduced me to. His tongue vibrated with his laugh.

I could feel his laughter against my sensitive flesh and all rational thought slipped from my grasp. I couldn't take it anymore and I was done playing nice. Panting, I slammed a hand against the headboard and sunk my fingers into what was left of his dark hair.

"If you want me to ride you, I'll grant you your last wish." I hissed and shuddered, releasing the leash I was keeping on myself. On that small vicious part of me that I constantly held in check. He spread his hands wider across the tops of my thighs as I ground against his mouth. He worked his tongue, lips, teeth, and nose against my slick flesh. I could feel his breath as he took in and released air between each rock of my hips. All the while, his silver gaze was like a brand, watching me move from between my thighs with predatory intent.

I kept his head pressed to my pussy with my fingers fisted into his hair. Moaning his name, I threw my head back, nails scoring the wood of the headboard.

"Yes, gods Rhuger. *Yes!*"

Rhuger's right hand left my thigh. Before I could question it, I heard him moan against my pussy. The wet sounds of him working his cock with his fist pitched my pleasure into something almost painful in its rightness.

With a few flicks of his tongue, I was flung into my orgasm. It hit me so hard that I couldn't take a breath. Just rolled my eyes back in my skull as I rode out the spasming of my release, bucking wildly against Rhuger's face.

I felt the hot spray of his seed against my back as he cried out against my pussy. Felt it drip heavily down my back as I squeezed his skull between my quivering thighs.

Finally able to take a breath, I wept, tears pouring down my face. There was nothing left—he'd claimed every part of me I'd ever been insecure about with fervent desire. My emotions were so big and overwhelming that I felt like I was being hollowed out by them. I released Rhuger's hair and brought my hand shakily up to try to hold back the sobs that barked out from between my lips.

"Amelia. Pearl. Are you alright?" Rhuger asked frantically, chest heaving, his eyes alight with panic as he helped off of him to lie down.

I shook my head against the wave of my sobs.

"Did I hurt you?" He asked, and I saw him pale. I shook my head vigorously again.

"No!" I wailed, reaching for him and pulling him down to me. He hadn't hurt me. Quite the opposite.

I wound my arms tight around his neck and buried my face against his neck as I wailed, unable to hold my feelings back any longer. Shakily, I wrapped my legs around his hips and I held on until he relaxed against me. He kissed my forehead, murmuring sweet Black Tongue in his lilting voice. I clung to him with my shaking body as the emotional release drained away with my tears. Finally, feeling tranquil inside for the first time in ages, I could breathe again and was reduced to hiccups.

Rhuger pulled back and brushed my wet hair from my cheeks along with my tears. He was so serious as he looked down at me. So conflicted.

"Can you tell me what's wrong?" He asked, voice cracking on his whisper.

"It was so good!" I sobbed, surprising him. Emotion threatening to rise up like a tidal wave again.

"Then what's wrong? Why are you crying?" He asked, trying to wipe away the tears that continued to fall.

"I..." I choked, trying to find the words. "I needed that so badly. Needed you, *us*, so badly. It was so good."

My words couldn't encompass the entirety of what was making my heart bleed. I'd never known it could be so damn good between two people like that. That I truly was safe with him, that he accepted all that I was with no judgment. Reveled in our connection as much as I did.

This must have been what it felt like for Rhuger when he'd asked me to mix pain with his pleasure. When he'd broken down afterward. We'd fully claimed one another and everything we'd ever felt shame for without fear.

"This is healing. You are healing." Rhuger whispered, mouth open in soft understanding. As he recognized in me what I'd done for him.

I nodded, and my face broke with more tears. I was healing. From everything, I'd endured. All because of him.

"Och, pearl." He murmured and bent to place his lips firmly on my trembling ones. "I'm so glad. So glad."

He pulled back, and I froze as I realized he was openly crying. Rhuger's gaze was so full of love as he pressed another kiss to my forehead, my mouth, and my wet cheeks. He rolled us until we were on our sides and he tucked me up against him and rested his head against mine.

"So glad." He whispered as we melted against each other.

Some emotional leash snapped for him too as we lay there, crying and comforting one another. This was healing for both of us. Our bond strengthened so it was a constant, comforting hum in the back of my mind. Our broken hearts mending and fusing into one. As they always should have been.

"Chan eil ach na diathan a 'tuigsinn mo ghràdh dhut, oir tha e seachad air glacaidhean bàsmhorachd a-mhàin." He murmured.

"What does that mean?" I asked nasally, now physically and emotionally spent. My nose was stuffed and my head throbbed from all my tears.

"Only the gods understand my love for you, for it is beyond the grasp of mortality alone." Rhuger's voice had grown rough and soft with his exhaustion.

"Do you always say such sappy things when you speak Black Tongue to me?" I asked with a small smile, brushing his remaining tears away with my fingertips.

"Och. Sometimes it's filthy, though." Rhuger chuckled and pulled me tighter as he lifted the blankets up over us. I couldn't help but grin at my roguish cridhe.

We fell asleep tangled up in each other and, for once, there were no nightmares for either of us.

CHAPTER 15

AMELIA

We spent the next week wrapped up in one another, the clan giving us more space than we'd expected. We took breaks to sleep and eat and bathe. And generally, just enjoyed one another's laughter and company. There wasn't any pressing need to leave our rooms, so we didn't. Kholt himself brought us food and drink, claiming he didn't want anyone to poison it.

But it was adorably obvious he wanted to check on his friend. He kept us updated on the state of the newly formed Oc'Turin Council. Kholt would dare thoughtful glances my way. Not in any sort of predatory manner, but in a considering way that had me wondering what was at work behind those teal and onyx eyes. His occasional glances either made Rhuger jealous or he'd just brush it off. It was easy for me to see Kholt was gauging to see if we'd reached a point where we could be dragged away from our bed without Rhuger going into a bloodthirsty rage.

Kholt would leave with instructions from us for any pressing issues, and Rhuger would immediately jump back into bed with me. Claiming he didn't want the scent of another male to cling to my neamhnaid skin. I'd just laugh and grab his ears or torque, yanking him to me for a loving, blistering kiss that would calm him. And I always seemed to be able to calm him with a smile, my laughter, or a kiss. It was the most amazing feeling to be such a balm and safe space for him.

During our long talks, Rhuger admitted to me he and Kholt had been lovers at one point. That it was behind them now and they were strictly friends and brothers in arms. He looked hesitantly at me as if waiting for me to fly into a jealous rage.

But I couldn't find it in me. Not even an iota of it. As far as I was concerned, and I explained as much, I was glad that they had been there for one another when, by the sound of it, their lives had been full of so much pain. How could I possibly begrudge either of them any comfort growing up in a place like this?

My acceptance surprised Rhuger. I explained I could already see that the love they held for one another wasn't romantic anymore. And that their friendship was sacred to me and not something I'd ever want to come between. Which had made my cridhe openly gawk at me and then blush. Uncertain if he should be offended that I wasn't jealous and territorial, or pleased my love for him was so deep and honest.

He settled for both.

Eventually, a hesitant yet sturdy knock rapped on our door. It wasn't Kholt's usual knock, so I looked at Rhuger quizzically. He growled his irritation at the door and sat up in bed. Before Rhuger could get up to answer it, an attendant opened the door wide.

The slender male in nice, clean attire stopped dead in his tracks. His eyes nearly bulged from his skull when he saw me sit up in bed, the sheet clutched to my chest in an attempt at modesty. His eyes were riveted on my chest above the sheet, where the mating marks lay stark against my pearly skin.

A harsh roar cut through the silence and the attendant jerked, tearing his eyes from me to look at his Rìgh.

"That is your Banrìgh you're leering at. Do it again and I'll pluck out your eyes for your insolence." My cridhe's menacing growl left the attendant shaking. "Now what is so important that you had to come here to interrupt our mating frenzy?"

The poor attendant babbled incoherently, absolutely terrified of Rhuger and a moment away from pissing his pants. I laid a gentle hand on my mate's arm and almost immediately, Rhuger's body language softened.

"What is it?" I asked around Rhuger's imposing frame.

"You are requested to join the council." The male swallowed hard, openly sweating and doing everything he could to not look at me directly.

"When are we expected?" I asked.

"As soon as possible, Banrìgh." The attendant said, staring hard at the flagstone floor.

Rhuger stood from the bed, bare ass naked, and stalked to the door. I couldn't help but admire how Rhuger's dump truck ass and back muscles shifted as he walked. It made my mouth water.

The attendant stood stock still, his eyes wide and body language screaming fear. How bad had it been with Orok that he'd fear a ruler quite this much? I'd expected respect, deference, and maybe a little fear. But nothing like this. Or was it because the memory of who and what my cridhe was, was reawakening slowly in the Oc'Turin people?

"If that is all, get out of my sight." Rhuger snarled and slammed the door in the attendant's face.

"You didn't need to scare the male nearly to death, gumby." I admonished gently, this was not the first time he'd gotten so fiercely territorial.

"You are my cridhe. They shouldn't look at you like that," Rhuger growled as he sauntered back to bed. I couldn't help but track his cock as it swung between his powerful thighs as he walked. My heartbeat quickened and the ache to have him inside me again was demanding.

"People are going to ogle our marks. It's not forever, just until everyone realizes it's real." I murmured, my heated gaze sliding up his body to meet the molten silver of his.

Rhuger placed a knee on the edge of the bed and leaned forward, bracing one hand next to my hip, dubiously concealed by the thin sheet. With the other hand, he grasped my jaw in his powerful fingers and tilted my face towards his so we shared breath.

"He was ogling more than your marks, cridhe." Rhuger scowled.

I just rolled my eyes at him.

"Well, he was probably in the crowd watching when you claimed me in the throne room," I replied dryly, unimpressed by his grumpy, overbearing attitude after growing up with Grandpa Thorn to contend with.

Aaaand that was evidently the *wrong* thing to say

"You are staying here." He bit out, clenching his jaw as he released mine.

"Um, excuse you, no. I'm coming. I will dress modestly, but it's important for me to be there, Mr. Overbearing." I snorted as I threw the blankets into his face and stood up. "Really, I'm your mate and your Banrigh, and I'm the only human around. If we're going to make this work and prove that the marks are real, I need to be there. You know this is the truth."

"Just because it's true doesn't mean I have to like it." He glowered as he followed me over to my wardrobe, where I was flipping through a bunch of new dresses and clothes. He yanked out a dress and went to hand it to me.

"No." I laughed at both his scowl and the horrid thing he was trying to get me to wear.

"If you come, you'll need to cover up. Wear this, please." At least he'd said *please*...

"I. Said. No. I'm not wearing that." He was huffing in indignation as I continued to flip through the clothes.

Finally, I found what I was looking for. I yanked out the clothing and placed the items aside. If I was going to be a Banrigh, I was going to dress how I wanted. Thank you very much. No one was going to dictate what I wore, *especially* my mate.

"I thought you liked me telling you what to do." Rhuger bit out. That made me turn and look him dead in the eye as I once again began flipping through the clothes. I raised my brows at him and he looked uncertain suddenly.

"If you'd think past all the baby-making hormones, you'd remember that I do, in fact, *not* like being told what to do. The only time I like *you* telling me what to do is when we're alone and intimate." I said, pursing my lips and returning my attention to the clothes in front of me.

Rhuger just stood there, scowling even harder if that was possible, as I pulled out a folded garment and shook it out. It was a pair of soft leather pants and I immediately bent to yank them on. His scowl softened as he realized I wasn't dismissing our dynamic, but reinforcing its boundaries. A smile played on his lips as I straightened.

"Those used to be mine. When I was young." He murmured.

"I figured." I beamed at him as I pulled the large white shirt over my head. The laces were loose, so my mating marks were visible on my chest. I snagged a purple lady's bolero-looking thing. It was heavily embroidered, and it lacked sleeves. But it had a hood, and it had a corset-type bodice that laced up the front to keep everything modest. Didn't need my boobs bouncing boobily, distracting everyone present when we were supposed to have a serious discussion, after all.

After finishing tying up the laces, I looked in a beaten metal mirror and grinned. I felt a little like a rogue from a fantasy story. I liked it.

Next, I snagged the sword I'd beheaded Orok with and slipped the cleaned blade into a sheath, sliding my belt through the frogs and belting it to my waist. The thing was heavy, but evidently beheading a leader with their own weapon meant the one who did the killing got the enemy's sword as a prize. Rhuger had told me it was a sign of power and prowess. That it would be a symbol of respect.

I hated the damn thing.

It wasn't just because it wasn't something I liked aesthetically —call me a bougie bitch all you want. The thing was ugly, and I'd prefer a prettier sword. It was also because each time I looked at it or thought about it, memories crowded into the front of my mind in crystal clear slow motion. How I'd wrenched it from its sheath at Orok's side. How my hair had whipped around my face as I spun to gain the momentum I needed. And the look in Orok's slimy yellow eyes when he saw Death knocking.

It haunted me.

Despite everything the asshole had done to me and to Rhuger, I'd killed someone in a moment of pride and desperation. I'd gone through the scenario hundreds of times in the past week. Mentally destroying myself over how I could have tried something else. But it all came back to the same thing—Orok would have raped me and abused me and tortured Rhuger and possibly murdered us both.

All for power.

Even the illusion of it.

Regardless of the kill-or-be-killed situation, guilt wracked me. I'd fought in the past but never been an aggressor. Killing Orok had been satisfying for what he'd done to me, but more importantly, what he'd done to Rhuger. I didn't need to know the entire history between them to know Rhuger hadn't deserved to be treated that way. Whether Rhuger told me the entirety of that story or not, was up to him. I respected that.

Eliminating Orok, a source of dark deeds and vile abuse, held an edge of righteous vengeance. One I didn't realize I thirsted for so badly. I wished I'd sought retribution against my ex-husband Adam for what he'd done to me. Orok's blood had cleansed my own hands of the part I'd played in my abuse. Or, more accurately, my lack thereof.

Because when Adam had abused me, I hadn't fought back. I didn't seek vengeance. I didn't want to hurt him because I loved him. His betrayal had frozen me in place. I'd only sought survival and escape.

Orok's death was a dark echo of my mental turmoil. I hated to fight. I hated to be used. It had been a no-win scenario. And I wasn't nearly as destroyed by my loss of innocence as I'd thought. It scared me. I terrified myself at what I would endure and do to survive. To protect those I loved. The lengths I would go to.

I'd been standing there, hand gripping the ugly bone and leather handle of the sword, knuckles white, for a while. My mind was a wreck. Rhuger came up behind me and placed his hand on my fist, where I could feel the bone handle cutting into my flesh.

"Do not let the guilt of what you did to survive devour your thoughts, pearl." He murmured, brushing a lock of hair away from my face as I looked up at him. "A first kill is always tough. You were brave and strong. You saved me."

I nodded stiffly. Because we'd talked about it in the dark hours of the night when I'd woken screaming. Rhuger knew he'd be killed once Orok had played with him enough, broken him enough, and grew bored. Kin or no kin, Orok had been a cruel bastard.

And the gentle surety and love Rhuger emanated whenever he reminded me that I'd saved him, saved his life, bound my aching heart closer to his. Because, over the course of our short time together, we'd saved one another. Both physically and emotionally. Propping one another up as we grew and healed together. A wondrous, beautiful experience that hurt even as it soothed.

Another knock cracked against the door of our rooms, breaking the heavy silence. Rhuger called out and this time, the attendant didn't come in, he just hollered from the other side it was time to go. Rhuger flicked his gaze over my attire and bent to give me a swift kiss. Lips soft and warm and fleeting.

He himself wore his usual leather kilt but with a black shirt. The laces untied to show off the cridhe marks and the gold torc that clasped his powerful throat. The clothes available to him ranged from simple to extravagant, yet he stayed himself—something I deeply admired about him.

He turned to lead the way toward our new responsibilities. I couldn't resist—his ass was so enticing. With a hard, quick, open-handed slap, I smacked Rhuger's perfect ass. He froze mid-step, head snapping to look at me over his shoulder in heated surprise.

"I hate to see you leave, but love to see you go." I grinned.

"Do that again lass and I'll need to fuck you where you stand." His smile was slow and crooked, hooded gaze molten as his eyes raked my form.

"Promise?" I flushed, once again turned on.

"Oh, yes." He whispered before jerking his head forward and stalking towards the door.

We both knew if we continued to play like this, absolutely nothing would get done. Well... *I'd* get done. Repeatedly.

I followed Rhuger out the door, startling the attendant who'd moved to the other side of the hallway just in case. He bowed respectfully, avoiding looking at me, and turned to lead us to the throne room. As we followed the attendant, Rhuger clasped my hand in his, lacing our fingers and giving it a gentle squeeze. An echo of all the times he'd led me through his world since I arrived on Talam, like high school sweethearts.

He knew this would be difficult for me. It was something we'd discussed. Because I wasn't just going to be a princess who could hide occasionally, but a queen meant to lead and rule and provide. It wouldn't be easy, but we'd agreed to find a way for me to navigate this new role while respecting my limitations and boundaries.

I loved him so much for it.

When we arrived at the doors to the throne room, Kholt was there to greet us. He looked haggard and irritated, and it put me on edge. What had made him so aggravated?

Rhuger placed a swift kiss on the top of my head and strode over to Kholt. They conversed quickly, and I gave them what privacy I could by looking around at the lovely carvings in the stone surrounding the doors. It was little wonder my mate had carved all the surfaces of the home tree he'd built in Baile Coille, having grown up with so much of it surrounding him.

Kholt's teal gaze flicked to me over my mate's shoulder and

Rhuger's did the same. Shit. Whatever was stressing Kholt out had something to do with me. Rhuger clapped his friend on the shoulder and turned back toward me, his gaze shuttered. I braced myself for whatever new obstacle was about to hit us.

"Pearl," Rhuger began, voice canted low and gaze steady as he stopped next to me, "There's been a development with the council."

"Okay," I replied, waiting for the news.

"There are two things. The first is that they are questioning your origins, your right to rule, and how you intend to be Banrigh of the Oc'Turin while also being the heir to the Oc'Dellor clan."

"Oh, so seeking to discredit me? That's nothing new." I replied dryly with a self-deprecating half smile. "Trust me, that's something I'm well versed in dealing with. What's the other thing?"

"The council is debating whether the Oc'Turin need a ruler at all. That maybe, the council itself should rule and seek to take over the Craobh na Beatha." He said, mouth a flat angry line. "There are many on and off of the council who don't approve of me being Rìgh."

"Why? That doesn't make any sense."

"It's because, though my mother was the rightful Banrigh, being the daughter of the previous Rìgh, Orok's father had killed mine for the right to wed my mother." Rhuger's tone had gone flat, his gaze shuttered as he remembered ugly things. I reached out and held his hand in mine to remind him he wasn't alone anymore. Rhuger cast me a grateful smile and squeezed my hand.

"Okay, so what's the plan?" I asked. "You realize that this is all bullshit, right?"

"I do." Rhuger nodded. "We'll need to show a unified front of strength and win them to our side. The people know what I'm capable of, though they've seemed to have conveniently forgotten for the moment. They listened to you when you chopped off my brother's head. Perhaps they'll listen to you now."

"Ah."

RHUGER

It was all a steaming pile of nocrys shit. Kholt had kept us up to date on the formation of the Council and their initial meetings. Unsurprisingly, they'd opted to hold secret meetings to scheme me out of my throne for a second time. But what *had* surprised me was how quickly they were willing to discredit Amelia.

They couldn't very well claim she *hadn't* beheaded my brother. There had been far too many witnesses for that. Instead, they sought to challenge her claim. Of being the granddaughter of Rìgh Thorn Oc'Dellor. Of being part human, part orckin who'd come through the Geata long thought broken. Not to mention her complicated position now that she was the heir of one clan and Banrigh of another.

It was simple for them to dismiss *me* almost altogether, as I'd been gone for years. Never mind that I'd held many of our clan's fighting records and was named Duhb'Oidhche by the priest for my near-unstoppable prowess on the battlefield. That I'd brought our clan honor and victory over the years. After all, I'd always been dismissible in the court's eyes.

Duhb'Oidhche. A title that was only given to those considered to be an Orcling of Neit, our revered god of war. Whether Neit blessed the orckin or they truly thought the orckin to be his offspring was always debatable. Regardless, I was the first Duhb'Oidhche in over three generations. *That* was how rare the title was.

But I'd been a junior leader of a scouting party when I'd earned that title. Since then, I'd lost my mother, my position, Sagra, and all that was rightfully mine to my treacherous little brother. I'd become an exile from my clan. So, to some orckin amongst the Oc'Turin, it was all easily forgettable.

Now I stood with my cridhe at my side and our bairn growing in her womb, my brother dead by her hand, and the Throne of Fangs rightfully mine. I'd come too far to let the scheming of lesser orckin take from me any longer. I glanced down at the female who had stumbled into my life mere weeks ago and had irrevocably changed it for the better. Far beyond my wildest hopes and dreams. She smiled up at me and gave my hand a reassuring squeeze before I nodded to Kholt and he opened the doors for us. They swung wide, and we strode out into the throne room to meet the council and our people.

An hour later, I sat on the Throne of Fangs, a smaller chair carved from deep emerald stone in delicate, intricate designs, sat next to it with my cridhe perched upon it. The throne had been my mother's after Orok's father had claimed the Throne of Fangs for himself, despite it being rightfully hers.

There were many things I was planning on changing in the coming months, including the thrones. Amelia and I had spent a lot of time discussing the ins and outs of what lay before us. Not just as Rìgh and Banrigh, but the world we wanted to bring our bairn and all future bairns into. I'd always excelled at strategy and planning. I'd known my cridhe was extremely intelligent, but I'd gained a new appreciation for her insight and ways of seeing the world.

She often described it as a pattern, a web, and that everything was connected through it. She wasn't wrong. I'd often felt and seen it, though not as deeply as she seemed to. I trusted her insight, just as I trusted my gut.

I gazed down at the councilor before me as he waxed poetic about the histories of the clans and how the lines of succession and might were often convoluted. He'd been hedging around what he truly wanted to say, attempting to gain all of our agreement on these outer thoughts, before striking the heart of the matter.

"Clarify this for me, councilor. Is this line of discussion intended to discredit my cridhe's lineage or mine?" I asked. The councilor sputtered at being interrupted.

"Well, both." He said, standing straight and raising his chin in defiance. A slow, calculating smile split my face.

"I see. So you're challenging the word of the Rìgh of *another clan* over the legitimacy of his heir. And, by challenging *my* lineage, you're discrediting my mother, who was, by the way, the legitimate heir and Banrigh of the Oc'Turin. Her position was stolen from her by her second mate, Orok's father." I said. The councilor's mouth pressed into a thin line and he puffed out his chest in indignation over my counter. "Additionally, the right of rule outside of lineage for the Oc'Turin is *power*. Is it not?"

"Och, it is." The counselor bit out.

"And what, pray tell, did my cridhe do?" I asked, leaning forward in the Throne of Fangs to rest my elbows on my knees as I stared dead into this sniveling cnuimh's eyes.

"She... killed Rìgh Orok." He replied.

"She *slaughtered* and *beheaded* the *late* Rìgh Orok." I snapped. "Thus, regardless of her *lineage*, that you are so blatantly questioning, she has won the right to rule through *power*."

A hushed quiet descended upon the room. Looking at where Kholt stood nearby, I could swear he was fighting a smile and a laugh. He knew how I'd been trained. Knew I'd suffered under the tutelage of countless experts to become the Rìgh I was meant to be. The Rìgh I was now.

To be lectured over things I'd learned when I was *five* was asinine.

"Furthermore..." Amelia began, and I turned my head to look at her as I sat straight once more. She sat with regal posture, and pride swelled in my chest over how seamlessly, she was integrating into her role as Banrigh. "You are not only questioning *my* lineage, which I can assure you my grandfather Rìgh Thorn would just *love* to hear your argument, but you are also questioning my *cridhe's*."

The counselor looked at my mate with a patronizing flick of his gaze. The urge to pluck out his eyeballs was so great a growl rumbled in my chest. The councilor flinched and cast his gaze more respectfully on Amelia's booted feet. She reached over and gave my hand a loving pat before she continued. I felt that small touch like a warm blanket on a cold night.

"You realize that not only does he have the right to rule because of his lineage, but he has the most experience, having been trained to actually *become* a Rìgh from a young age. Politics, economics, diplomacy, warcraft, infrastructure... all of these, and more. Are you saying that you, Councilor Mayten, a merchant who sells wool coats, would be far better trained in how to fulfill the role of Rìgh than Rìgh Rhuger?" Bless my cridhe for being so wicked with her tongue.

"Well, I-"

"Have you also forgotten his prowess in battle? What did that priest call you, cridhe..." she said, turning to look me in the eye. Providing me an opportunity to remind them all of what I'd accomplished before becoming an exile.

"Duhb'Oidhche. An Orcling of Neit," I replied. We turned to look at the councilor and the other six who stood to the side. Most were merchants, leaders of minor clans, or educators. "And if the rule of power was what you were intending to challenge, I assure you, only death will find you."

It was obvious they hadn't expected us to work together as a team. They'd likely thought our rule would be like Orok's or his father's. But no. My Banrigh was my equal in all ways, and I would not lessen her for even a moment, for all the power of the clans combined.

CHAPTER 16*

AMELIA

"There is one thing left to deal with," I said, rising to my feet from my throne. "There has been a transgression. One that I, as Banrigh, cannot let go unpunished."

Murmuring began in the throne room as councilors, elites, and common folk all looked between one another at this new development. I stepped forward on the dais and a hush fell over the crowd. I gazed out over them and recognized that I was a mountain, a river, a galaxy. Large and imposing and spectacular. I was female, a creator, and a nurturer. But also, capable of razing their world to ash.

"Many of you think I'm too soft. That despite beheading your previous Rìgh, you believe I am a pawn. A puppet. That, as a female, I'm weak-willed. That our plan to re-instate the Iolaire'lassair is doomed, and that they were just fairytales all along. You believe females are too weak to do what a male can do on the battlefield. I'm here to prove you wrong." I said, voice frigid and dripping with disdain. "Kholt, if you'd be so kind."

I glanced over my shoulder to see Rhuger's stark confusion. I gave him a small smile before turning my gaze back to where Kholt was leading a male before him. His massive, calloused, and scared fist clenched the male's shoulder so hard his knuckles were white. The male stuttered and protested, claiming he'd done nothing wrong.

Meanwhile, two attendants had brought forth a small table and two chairs. An empty bucket sat atop the table, along with a small drawstring bag. Chatter rose as Kholt passed the horde, filled with confusion and speculation. He pulled out the chair facing the dais and plopped the male into it.

The male in question was, what I realized then, average-looking for orckin. Deep sage green skin with several scars. High cheekbones and a strong jaw. He wasn't the buffest, but his eyes held a look to them that was simultaneously sharp and as flat as a shark's. One that told me plenty of what this male was capable of.

"Now, I've come to understand that the Oc'Turin choose violence first, as power is your clan's creed," I stated, looking out over the crowd. "I want to make this clear, what is about to happen is *not* how we anticipate ruling going forward. But if you require violence to understand what we will, and *won't*, put up with... If you need violence to agree with my position as Banrigh, then I will provide you with the righteous judgment you require. It is my proof to you of what I am truly capable of."

A tense silence fell over the crowd. Everyone slowly came to terms with the fact that something horrible was about to happen to the orc seated before me. I descended the steps from the dais and came to a halt behind the empty chair on my side of the table.

"My knives, if you please," I murmured and held out my hand as I gazed out over the crowd.

"As my Banrigh wishes." Kholt rasped and handed me a leather-wrapped bundle. I set the knives down on my side of the table with deliberate care. The male looked at it, unsettled, but held his head high.

"Is it true..." I began as I slowly took off my pretty bolero and handed it off to an attendant. I could have worn a dress for this. But I didn't want fashion to get in the way of what I was about to do. "That while on our journey to Clach-tholl after being kidnapped, you beat my cridhe bloody and shattered three fingers in his sword hand?"

I rolled up my sleeves very carefully, not looking this horrible male in the eye. Not letting on to that dark little vicious piece of me that had gotten me through so much. That piece of me that had ignited under my skin the moment I saw how badly beaten, whipped, and broken they'd left my cridhe.

"What of it? I was under orders." The male scoffed. "It's not like the... Rìgh... couldn't take it, what with how fast he heals up."

I paused, fury so bright and icy in my veins I wouldn't have been surprised if my boot prints left frost in my wake as I strode forward and gently flipped open the leather-wrapped package. It was my set of knives, forged by Conn Oc'Ain at the behest of my grandfather. Finally finished and brought with a messenger after we'd sent word to him about what had happened here.

They were gorgeous, my knives. With a wicked curve to them, not unlike that of a falchion. The edges were sharp as freshly chipped obsidian and the spines serrated. Each one was engraved to look like a feather. The hilts were made of the same lovely purple wood that my grandfather's bookshelves in his study were made of. And each came with its own sheath.

One by one, I removed the knives from their sheaths and laid them along one side of the table. With each knife I set down, I spoke into the utter silence in the throne room.

"One of you whipped my cridhe from just outside of the Fàinne Sleagh in Oc'Dellor territory, all the way to the front gates of Cìp

Carragh." The soft thud of the knife against the wooden table made the man pay attention. "With a cat-o-nine-tails tipped in sharpened stone chips."

"One of you stole my cridhe's boots, so he was forced to walk barefoot the entire way here to approach his home and rightful place with bloodied footprints." The second knife I set down made him flinch. The third knife I held up to the light, inspecting its immaculate craftsmanship for all to see.

"And *you* beat my mate every chance you got on our journey here," I murmured, words clear and low and soft as I finally looked this rabid piece of filth in his cold, dead, eyes. "You thought you could touch my *mate*. My *cridhe*. And come away from it unscathed? He might be used to being treated this way by his own clan. But hear me now when I say that if any of you..." At this I looked around the throne room, gaze sweeping the crowd from under my drawn brows. "... dares to harm my cridhe, I will come for you. And I will do to you what I'm going to do to these three."

The male eyes went wide and a cold sweat broke out on his skin as he finally realized he'd fucked around and was about to find out. He licked his lips and let out a watery chuckle as he shook in his chair. "And what is a fat female like you going to do to me with that little paring knife, eh?"

No one laughed with him.

"Kholt, be a dear and hold his hand steady for me, would you?" I asked softly as I sat down, knife held casually in my hand.

"What are you going to do with that?" The male barked, trying to rip his hand free from Kholt,

"I'm going to make it so you harm no one again with your wretched, cowardly, pathetic claws." I bit out every word like a wolf crunching bone. "I'm going to leave you with meat mops for hands."

At first, the male was confused. But realization dawned on him quickly. Suddenly horrified, he panicked and tried to back away from the table, but Kholt didn't let go and forcibly held the male down. Then he attempted to go for one of the two remaining knives, and I grinned.

I lunged. My knife bit through flesh and tendon and bone with a satisfying *thunk*. The male screamed and Kholt held the male's free arm behind his back as he grabbed the wrist of the hand I'd just impaled to the table like a decrepit moth with broken wings.

Ripping my blade free, I sat down at the table. Kholt repositioned the male's hand and I got to work. Oh, so carefully, I sliced into his middle finger, the flesh parting like a hot knife through butter. It was faster work than I'd thought as I flayed the flesh from each of his finger bones. And he bled a lot more than I'd expected.

I couldn't have him bleeding out before I'd finished even *one* hand. Which was what the small bag was for. In it was a powder made from some plant that Kholt assured me would stop the bleeding. With each flayed digit, I'd reach into the bag and sprinkle a little powder over his raw flesh.

The male screamed almost as much when the powder touched him as my knife. But I tuned his screams out as I methodically and meticulously removed each bone from every finger and dropped the bones into the waiting bucket.

When the first hand was done, I looked down at the long strips of powder-covered flesh that spread out from his wrist. They lay in a coagulated puddle of blood and powder in wild disarray. By now, the orc had blacked out twice, only to be punched awake by Kholt. The throne room was as quiet as a tomb as I waved at Kholt and he wrangled the male's other hand into place.

"No... no, no, *no*, *NO!*" the orc sobbed as I raised my knife to his whole hand. "I'll do *anything*, PLEASE!"

I paused and looked up at his wretched face.

"You should have thought of that before you beat my cridhe." I rasped. "You should have that of that before you beat and tortured the females you were supposed to protect."

Because he'd been an abusive son of a bitch to any female he could get his claws on. Kholt had told me *all* about this male. About each of the males and their crimes. None of them were worth pardoning.

His face went pale, hope died in his eyes as he realized that there would be no mercy from me. His screams rang off of the stone as I got to work on his other hand, dropping bone after flayed bone into the bucket.

It was a few hours before I'd gone through all three males. The ones who beat him and whipped him lost their hands. The one who stole Rhuger's boots lost his feet.

I'd become rather expert at flaying flesh from bone by the end of the process. This whole thing was going to cost me in the long run. I knew it had stripped some of my innocence from me that day. But I had been far kinder to them than they had been to the Oc'Turin females and those under their charge.

Regardless, a price had to be paid for their deeds. Taking their lives would have been too good of a punishment. Too easy. And I wasn't about to put my cridhe through deciding their sentence. And executing it. He'd been through enough already.

One time Kholt had stopped by our rooms, Rhuger had been dead asleep and we'd been unable to rouse him. So I'd asked Kholt if he knew who had hurt my mate on our journey to the Oc'Turin city of

Clach-tholl. He did.

Kholt told me about how he'd already dispatched the guards who had tortured him in the dungeons when he went to retrieve Rhuger at Orok's behest. We agreed it had been too quick and painless of a punishment. I asked Kholt about the males who had hurt Rhuger on our journey. Who they were and how vicious they were. His answers left me trembling with rage.

So we'd concocted this plan. To punish those who had harmed the male we loved, to prove to all present that a female *could*, in fact, be as ruthless as a male, and cement my power and right as Banrigh. It was cold, clean vengeance made bloody and brutal by my hands.

Now I stood from my chair. My leather pants, shirt, and boots were soaked in blood that still dripped thickly from the tabletop. Blood covered my face and chest in splatters, right over my cridhe marks. Kholt directed two guards to drag away the last of the males who sobbed the entire way.

I handed my knives to Kholt, and he took them reverently. The vile sins of the orcs who hurt Rhuger bloodied each one. Made clean by the retribution I wrought from the mangled wrecks of their hands and feet.

Then I turned and grasped the handle of the bucket. It wasn't as heavy as I'd expected it to be as it dangled from my blood-caked hand. I looked up at the dais and saw my cridhe sitting on the Throne of Fangs with a forbidding cast to his features.

I vaguely wondered what he saw, what he thought when he looked at me now. Standing before him, bathed in the blood of his enemies, holding a bucket of their bones to offer him as tribute. This was the part of me he'd never seen. The part that I'd kept a choke hold on my entire life. So I could be good and fit the mold others had made for me.

Because I'd always known what I was capable of. I hadn't hesitated when my knife parted flesh from bone or when the screams and pleas of the males echoed around me. I hadn't hesitated or flinched from this task because, if our roles had been reversed, neither would Rhuger.

We were two halves of the same coin. Dark and light with our edges blurred.

I strode toward my Rìgh, my mate, my cridhe, with my head held high. As I mounted the steps to the dais, I lifted the bucket and held it so he could see my work. Then I set it down at his feet. Turning to go to my chair, an attendant stepped forward. She was a slim thing, malnourished, and a few years younger than me, with pale green skin that sported several bruises and golden eyes with bags under them from lack of rest.

But despite her state, her gaze was sharp and focused. She bowed to me with deep respect etched into her body language. Nodding to her, she held out a towel, and I took it from her. She stepped back and away, melting back into the crowd of attendants that waited off to the side.

I didn't know who she was, but I'd have to find out. That same knowing I'd had many times now since Rhuger and I stepped on the path of power that the Source had laid before us, niggled at the back of my mind. Knowing her golden eyes would haunt me until I figured out where she fit into all of this.

"Counselors. Anything you wish to say to me?" I asked as I wiped splattered blood from my cheek with the towel.

"No, our Banrigh." The lead counselor said before dropping into a low bow, the rest of them following suit.

"*Never* take my kindness and compassion as weakness *ever* again." The words fell from my mouth like molten slag. "We will reconvene to discuss the plans for all orckin people tomorrow."

The seven of them scrambled to agree with my announcement. I looked at my cridhe. His gaze still held a mixture of warmth and a shuttered emotion I couldn't identify. With a wink, he turned to look out at the crowd still gathered in the throne room.

RHUGER

What my mate, my love, my *cridhe* had just done for me, the cruelty that I knew would haunt her, was a gift of loyalty I'd never thought possible. I watched for hours as she flayed the hands and feet of those who had tortured me on our journey here. She'd done it with such meticulous care and focus, even as they struggled against Kholt's grip. And Kholt, he knew about this, had planned this with my mate.

The friend who'd freed me and protected me more times than I could count, and the moon goddess I was lucky enough to call mine who had saved my battered heart and shattered soul, working together for *me*. Emotion welled up and choked me, tears threatening to spill over this act of love, devotion, and loyalty from two people I cared most for.

Kholt glanced up at me then, his teal and onyx gaze steady, that blankness he'd had there for so long, finally rolling back. Exposing the friend and male I once knew to the world again. As if this act he was helping Amelia with was easing away that survivor's mask. And then I realized why. He was witnessing the true nature of a cridhe bond up close, seeing what lengths Amelia would go to for me, and realizing he might one day find such a bond with his own cridhe.

I swore then and there that I would do all that I could to help him find his. Of everyone I knew, he'd been through the worst, and deserved his cridhe the most.

Looking down at the back of my cridhe's head, where it was bent over her bloody, wretched work, something in my chest ached. I'd waited years for someone to even appreciate me as a person, as a male. And now I had someone that loved me unconditionally. Someone who gave me all the support I could ever need. Who sought my approval and protection while providing the same for me. She was both the sweet, innocent, gentle beauty who cared more than she should, but also a force of nature, powerful and fierce. She was everything I'd always craved. The Banrigh of not just our people, but my heart.

She then stood as Kholt had two guards drag out the sobbing wreck of an orc who had whipped me bloody. Turning to face me, she grabbed the bucket of flayed bones in her fist and her gaze found mine. They were alight with fierce determination even as her face, chest, and pants were splattered and drenched in the gore of those who'd hurt me.

Most would have only looked at the surface and seen her cruelty. But I saw it for what it was. That small, vicious, ruthless part of herself that had kept her alive through all the abuse she'd endured. The part of her that wouldn't allow what had happened to her, to happen to anyone else she loved, especially me. The awe and wonder I felt at that moment that not only did she exist, but that she was *mine* for the rest of our lives hit me deep, resonating endlessly within my very being.

When she'd strode for the dais, bucket in hand and head held high. When she'd proffered me the bucket of bones as a gift. And when she'd kicked out the councilors, all I could think about was pulling her on top of me so she straddled my thighs and thrusting up into her sweet cunt on this throne of fangs and corruption. To cleanse it with her siren's cries as she came screaming my name as I knotted her, filling her with my seed.

It was an image I couldn't get out of my head. And one that I longed to turn into reality. Not now, but perhaps...

I realized everyone was looking at me. With a wrench, I jerked back my slavering need to rut my mate and remembered why we were there. Even as my cock strained against the leather of my kilt, slick soaking into it. I offered my cridhe a saucy wink before looking out over the horde.

"People of Oc'Turin." My voice rang out clearly as I took in my clan's horrified yet blank faces. "It is not our plan to rule with fear, as my brother did. But with justice, compassion, and honor. Take what you've seen today to heart. Because though we will move forward with benevolence, *never* forget that we are only kind because we have made ourselves so."

CHAPTER 17*

RHUGER

After cementing our right to rule the Oc'Turin, we returned to our rooms. There was a heavy silence as we walked through the halls. No one followed us, and the halls were blessedly empty. I knew Amelia was an emotional wreck inside, though her mask was firmly in place. I could smell it.

When we reached our rooms, the posted guard opened the doors and then closed them behind us as we retired within. Amelia dashed to the privy, tucked in the back near the baths without waiting to remove her sword or boots. Sounds of her retching, coughing, and sobbing met my ears, and my heart bled for her. I paused only long enough to remove my weapons before I followed her into the small room.

She was on her knees in front of the privy, hurling up the contents of her stomach. I knew this wasn't from our bairn growing inside her as I bent down and gently gathered her hair into my fist, so it wouldn't be in her way. Rubbing circles between her shoulder blades, I murmured to her in Teanga Dubh. Mindless words of comfort.

She retched again, and it pulled at memories of when I'd first brutalized someone. First killed someone. There had been no one there to hold back my hair or ensure I was okay. But I took comfort knowing that had my cridhe been here on Talam then, she would have.

"I-I…" Amelia stuttered as she sat back against the wall, her blood-stained hands over her mouth as tears poured from her eyes. I released her hair and pulled the lever that rinsed the privy.

"Shh, cridhe. I'm here." I murmured, kneeling before her and rubbing her leg. Waiting for her to come to terms with the fact that what she had done was torture. I wished I could drag her to me and kiss all the memories away.

But I knew from experience that wasn't how it worked. Each time I did something cruel, either through force, coercion, or rage, it took a little from me. It didn't matter if it was justice, it still left a mark.

"I maimed them," Amelia murmured shakily. "They won't be able to do anything anymore…" Her eyes were enormous in her head as she stared sightlessly ahead. "*I did that.*"

"You did," I said, taking one of her small hands in mine. Blood still crusted her nails, and I grabbed a cloth from a basket and wet it in the sink before I began to softly scrub the blood from her hands. "You also meted out justice for what they'd done to me. You cemented both of our places as Rìgh and Banrigh. Also, you gave the people a healthy dose of fear, to hold us over until we can show them what true power is."

"True power…?" She muttered, sightless gaze swinging to me, her bottom lip trembling.

"Cruelty and fear are easy tools to showcase one's power and garner loyalty," I said as I finished cleaning her hand. I bent down to kiss her palm in benediction before I picked up her other hand to clean it, too. "That is the easy way to power. It is far more difficult to garner loyalty through compassion, fairness, and justice. For the people to see the true power in it. It takes a powerful ruler to instill loyalty in a people like mine through service."

There was a thoughtful silence as I gently scrubbed the caked blood from her nail beds.

"You mean like my Grandpa Thorn." She murmured.

"Yes, like Rìgh Thorn," I replied as I kissed the palm of her freshly cleaned hand.

"Why are you so good to me?" she asked, her voice raw with pain. "I'm not a good person."

The question hit me straight to the heart. My gaze met hers, agonized and sorrowful, and I reached up to cup her face with my hand. I wiped away her tears with my thumb. We were both struggling to learn our worth, but she was at a disadvantage because she had only just learned that cridhe mates existed, let alone come to understand precisely what that meant.

"You are my cridhe," I whispered. "Your joy is mine. Your pain is my pain. I know your ex-husband was a wretched, selfish, cruel man who could not see the value in you as a person. I know he instilled this thought that you don't deserve to be treated like you should. You are my life's greatest gift and a source of joy I didn't think was possible. You are my heart and you've taken all of me, accepted all of me, without hesitation. Even when you saw me slaughter Orok's men. You didn't shy away from me, didn't look at me with disgust."

"I see you Rhuger, and I am not afraid." The words slipped from her trembling lips, but her gaze was steady, full of a knowing I was still learning to comprehend.

"I see you Amelia, and I am undone," I replied, voice gone hoarse. "You are all I ever craved and more. How could I not repay all the love and kindness you've shown me in kind?"

"I'm not a good person, Rhuger." My cridhe insisted. "I knowingly and deliberately hurt those males."

"But Amelia, you *are* a good person, despite what you did today. And even in the midst of what you did? You made sure they didn't bleed out. You made sure your cuts were clean. Those were small kindnesses, regardless of whether you think so." I stated, voice sure.

"That's a cold consolation, gumby." She murmured.

"You saved my life," I declared and Amelia, my heart, looked up at me with those damnably addictive uisge-beatha eyes of hers, swimming with tears. "If they had found me wanting in power or lineage as a leader, they would have put me to death."

Amelia went utterly still. Not even breath escaped her lips as she looked up at me in total shock, the blood draining from her face. Turning her as pale as a specter.

"What kind of *backward, uncouth, abhorrent* line of thinking is that?! Why would they *do* that?!" she cried in indignation.

"I was exiled because I *let* Orok take the throne. He had my hands tied in more ways than one when he did it, so I couldn't challenge him outright in a duel. I was exiled and shamed instead of killed. He thought it a much more fitting end." I explained, watching the heartbreak in her lovely round face. "I think it confused your grandfather. Knowing my clan's ways, yet there I was, one of the most ruthless warriors of our lifetime, a shamed and exiled prince, content to submit to his rule and his clan's ways. To earn the right to build a little home tree for a mate that he didn't seem to care about obtaining amongst the females of the clan."

"Is that why he was so grumpy about us being anywhere near one another in his presence?" she asked me.

"Quite likely. Though I also think it's because he was a little jealous of all the time I got to spend with the lovely granddaughter he'd missed so much." I smiled as I pushed back her hair from her face. She took my hand and rested her cheek against my palm, sighing at my touch.

"We have to face the council tomorrow." She whispered.

"We do."

"We need a game plan, don't we?" Her eyes were still closed as she asked.

"Yes, but nothing like today. We've established our position and right to rule. Now comes all the dealing and compromising. And we have to get them on our side regarding the Clan Meet." I explained as she looked up at me with so much trust and determination.

"Alright, let's get planning." She said and held her hand out to me. I stood and helped her to her feet, planting a swift kiss on her forehead and caressing her stomach where our bairn grew.

"Brave female," I whispered, and she smiled up at me before we headed toward our desks.

The next few hours were grueling as we plotted our presentation for the newly elected council. Amelia and I were both literate, she in her English and me in Black Tongue, Common, and several other small dialects. But her English writing wasn't the same as Common. The letter system was completely different. So, working around this, we used symbols and pictograms to represent ideas on bits of paper that Amelia moved around as we worked.

Kholt stopped by later in the evening as we were mentally exhausted. He brought us dinner himself, once again claiming that he wanted to ensure no one poisoned our food. Thoughtful and appreciated. But I knew it was a ruse to check on us.

While my cridhe and I ate, we explained our plan to Kholt, hoping for his insight. I'd grown up in the Oc'Turin court and was trained to rule it. But I'd also been gone for years and was behind on the current schemes and plots within Cìp Carragh.

Thankfully, they were the usual schemes. Jockeying for position and power either within the court or the ranks of soldiers. Accumulation of wealth to an extreme excess even by ruining other businesses. Anything and everything that could be considered a gain in power.

Even the Council's formation had been full of such schemes. Which was why a wool trader had led it and not a politician. In terms of power, Mayten the merchant outclassed most of his peers. Which was good for us, because they all hated him for it. It was a tool in our arsenal in case he became a problem.

I didn't care if I used less-than-noble tactics to keep our positions. Amelia's display had bought us time before someone else attempted to test the waters of power again. But we needed to act quickly to implement our ideas, to show them all a better way.

I just hoped their sense of reason wouldn't force me to far more horrifying means to get the people's acceptance. Glancing at my cridhe as she rubbed at her forehead with the heel of her wrist, and seeing how she smiled and thanked Kholt as he brought her a cup of water, made me pause. Despite beheading Orok, despite her removing the bones from the hands and feet of those three males, she was charming. She charmed just about everyone who came into contact with her. Her manners and her openness drew people in. And her small kindnesses were like drops of rain on the parched earth of our people.

Perhaps we had been going about this the wrong way. The way they expected us to, instead of the way we were. Everyone loved a wonderful hero's tale. The triumph over dark and unjust power, the charm and wit they possessed, and how they gained the respect and support of those they met along the way. The sacrifices they made and lovers won.

Everyone loved a wonderful hero's tale.

When they heard *this* heroine's tale, they'd outright worship her.

"I have a plan," I told them, grinning like an absolute fiend.

That night, after we'd changed and gone over our new plan repeatedly until our eyes nearly bled, I stalked from the baths toward our bed. Amelia, my poor sweet mate, was shocked and uncomfortable with my idea. She didn't think she was worthy or capable of being what we needed. When all we needed was for her to be herself. She'd eventually, hesitantly, agreed.

Exhausted, she'd foregone a bath and fallen straight into bed. It hit me as I gazed down at her that we needed to have a midwife see Amelia soon. It hadn't been long since she became pregnant, but I wanted to be sure she was well looked after. The only orckin who knew anything about human pregnancy was Rìgh Thorn. I'd learned at the Academy all about pregnancy and caring for a pregnant female. But Amelia was mostly human.

A difference that made worry slither into my belly. As did the thought that someone might purposefully harm her or our child during her pregnancy for power. Finding a trustworthy midwife amongst the orckin here would be a distressing task.

If we could pull this off, all of the clan would protect her, not just a few of us who loved her. Hell, even most of the orckin would come to her defense. Our bairn would be protected. Their future wouldn't be fraught with the horrors of my own childhood and life here amongst the Oc'Turin.

I slipped into bed behind my cridhe and pulled her close. She'd been crying. The pain that struck me was harsh. All I could do was murmur to her in Teanga Dubh and stroke her hair until sleep claimed her. I lay awake long after her soft snores began, like a melody that soothed the soul as old as our people, as old as life itself.

The masses had already feared me. And would fear me again. That much was a surety. We needed them to love *her*.

We needed to become the Night King and the Moon Queen from legend. The couple with a love so strong it created the cridhe bonds. Formed the royal lines and our world, our histories, with the promise of a love like no other. They decorated the walls in separate royal baths, were in countless songs and tales, and were as recognizable to all as the moons and suns overhead.

I was and would become the dark night that shadowed and veiled the world while she would be the moon that guided them all home. Two sides of the same coin in a dance as old as time.

Poetic. Magnetic. Unforgettable. Just like my cridhe. Closing my eyes, I let her soft snores lull me into sleep.

CHAPTER 18

AMELIA

Gods, I was beyond exhausted. My brain was mush, and I had the alertness and mental capacity of a sloth on Ambien. I'd gotten *maybe* four hours of sleep. Which many people could function on. I was *not* one of those people.

Rhuger's arm lay over my middle as if shielding me from some imaginary harm in his dreams. Cute. I wiggled out of his hold and went to the bathroom, my bladder grateful for the reprieve as I rubbed hard at my face.

Today was the day we would be dealing with, and convincing, the council allegedly appointed by the Oc'Turin people, that I, a lone human, granddaughter to an Oc'Dellor line thought doomed without an heir, who'd enchanted the most vicious warrior the Oc'Turin had ever known, sparked the hope of the people and the lust of any male who saw her, had mated her warrior love and conceived him an heir, all without knowing he was an exiled prince from a rival clan... was a heroine.

Personally, I thought most of that was a load of horseshit. Well, the parts about me being some sort of heroine, anyway. Some reincarnation of the Moon Queen from legend.

Rhuger had told me the legend of the Night King and the Moon Queen. The Rìgh na Oidhche and the Banrigh na Gealach. Their fated love was so strong, it had resulted in the formation of the cridhe bonds. That the Moon Queen's love for the Night King, the most powerful and formidable of warriors, who stalked the land and shrouded it in darkness, was enough that she came down to Talam from the skies. Gave up her celestial place just for his love. He, who bowed to no one, had fallen to his knees the moment he'd laid eyes on her and swore his fealty to her alone. Undone before the luminous glow of his neamhnaid love.

From that love, not only did cridhe bonds come into existence, but all royal lines stemmed from them, the neamhnaid sheen proof of lineage back to the Moon Queen herself. There had been something regarding a promise made for the benefit of all and then broken generations later, from which the an'sgudal and the dorcha'aon came into existence. Sources as to what the promise was and who broke it, evidently varied in the academic circles of Talam, but one thing *was* clear.

The story went, that one day the Moon Queen would return to help free the orckin from the tyranny and horrors of the an'sgudal and the dorcha'aon.

Their tale was so beloved by not just the Oc'Turin, but *all* orckin, that they even showcased their likeness in the royal baths. The plush curvy female I'd seen depicted in that bath had been the Moon Queen herself.

Rhuger's plan was as brilliant as it was insane. He claimed it would be the easiest route to get the people to listen if they *thought* I might be the Moon Queen returned. Rhuger had explained that we never had to actually *claim* that I was the Moon Queen, and he the Night King. All we had to do was lay out our story in such a way that they came to that very conclusion themselves.

Just as he'd realized the uncanny similarities, we'd make sure they did too.

When I'd first grimaced at the idea, he'd pointed out that, had I not come from the stars? Had I not wooed one of the most dangerous warriors ever to grace the halls of both the Oc'Turin *and* the Oc'Dellor? A male known to be an Orcling of Neit and a Duhb'Oidhche, a Black Night. Had I not freed a people from a tyrant who had sought to enslave and claim her? Did my skin not glow like the moons overhead, my royal lineage made clear? Had I not dispensed justice as a Banrigh?

I'd rolled my eyes but couldn't deny how good of a picture this all painted. Even Kholt was impressed as he ran his fingertips across his lower lip in thought. So our plan had taken a severe left turn. Now, instead of figuring out how to convince them we were right, we were going to tell them my story. Just enough, said just the right way, that those in the room would conclude what we needed them to.

Because if they believed, they would follow. If they believed, then the need to dispense *justice*, as I had, would nearly be erased. For that alone, I'd take part in this deception, though it rankled.

Because what if I couldn't follow through on what they expected of me because of this tale? What if I couldn't be the Moon Queen they needed? How was I going to live up to something like this when I was just... well, *me*?

Leaving the bathroom with those questions haunting me, I made for the bath. I needed to make myself presentable for this damned council meeting. Good thing I was pregnant, hopefully, my *pregnancy glow* would make up for the bags under my eyes.

The council meeting went far better than I expected.

They treated us with respect as we entered. Rhuger had pulled out my chair, and I'd sat. Only then did everyone else find their seat. Weird, but okay. I'd dressed in a flowing gown in a dove grey everyone insisted I looked beautiful in. A dress that, thankfully, covered most of me. Unlike the thing I'd been forced to wear for Orok. But it was flouncy and fluttery and I looked like a fat pigeon in it and no amount of flattery would change my mind.

But wearing it was to help cement the whole suggestion that I was the Moon Queen returned and Rhuger was the Night King. He'd even worn all black. It still made me cringe every time I thought about it, despite how yummy Rhuger looked. I did *not* sign up to be in some fantasy savior movie, m'kay, thanks.

Thus began the very long, yet simultaneously short story of who I was, where I came from, how I'd fallen in love with Rhuger, and how Orok had stolen me from my clan and enslaved Rhuger. How, through Rhuger and I's love, the cridhe bond had returned. From there it was all about how we planned to rule the Oc'Turin, how we wanted to save all orckin and open a way to Earth where we might find willing mates, and maybe even cridhe mates, to keep our kind from going extinct.

Each time the councilors had hemmed and hawed, Rhuger would somehow turn the conversation back to how closely we embodied their fabled king and queen. How through their wisdom and benevolence, the orckin had flourished. How we aimed to emulate their legacy and save all orckin from extinction.

The tough part came in that, even if we were to get them to agree to the reforms we wanted to put into place, how could we possibly get a Clan Meet to occur? It was notoriously difficult to get even *two* clans to meet to discuss anything. Between Rhuger's intimidation and my charm, we'd have to maneuver the Rìghs and Banrighs to agree to meet. To at least *discuss* combining resources and the possibilities that lay in securing the Geata.

The councilors debated amongst themselves, Rhuger and Kholt provided options, and discussion continued well on into the evening. We'd taken breaks for food and drink, and to use the facilities, but they were short. There were a few servants in the council room. One of them was the female who had caught my interest the previous day. The one who had offered me the towel to clean my hands. The slim female with golden eyes.

Every opportunity she had to serve me, she did. She even began standing behind my chair, ready to help at a moment's notice. It was unnerving. Kholt didn't seem disturbed by it, but rather seemed relieved. As if this female was one that he trusted enough not to poison me. It was enough to convince me to accept her self-appointment, even if it weirded me out.

I'd *really* need to get to know who she was as soon as I could. I needed to understand where she fit into this whole pattern of events that were playing out around us. Otherwise, all of this might fall apart before it ever began.

RHUGER

It was late when the councilors finally agreed to support our vision. Not all of it. They still had questions that needed answers and possibly some bribing to ensure the people didn't go up in arms over the stricter laws. Especially the one that made females legally equal to males and changed the rules regarding taking mates. Leaving the choice up to the females instead of the males. Giving them back the power that should have never been taken from them, to begin with.

It wasn't perfect, but it was a start.

They'd devoured all insinuation of Amelia being the Banrigh na

Gealach reborn. Thirsty for anything that could hold the Oc'Turin in high regard amongst the clans, what with Amelia being the *Oc'Turin Banrigh*. Easily distracted fools. Some of them were more astute, holding their opinions close to their chests. Regardless of whether the tale was true, it painted a lovely picture that the people would love. And it would make it easier to swallow all the changes that were about to occur on Talam.

We could have done all of this without the council, but *with* them as spokespersons for the people, they were more likely to sway them. With the council, the idea of Amelia being the Moon Queen would spread. She would be the figurehead for the future we'd dreamed of together, late at night after lovemaking, over the past week. And I would be her support, the night that cradled the moon, loved her, protected her.

In the end, it was all about creating a future where our people flourished, not about Amelia or me, or anyone else in particular. I'd never truly thought myself an idealist until Amelia showed me another way to see things. And I knew that as long as we did it together, there was nothing we couldn't accomplish.

CHAPTER 19

RHUGER

Once everyone had said their goodnights and began meandering from the study we'd repurposed as a meeting room, I heaved a sigh of relief. Amelia, the brave female that she was, kept her head high and spine straight even though bruises of exhaustion etched themselves under her eyes.

We followed the councilors out of the study into the hall and stood off to the side together. A unified front. Kholt paused to talk to the slim female who had personally served Amelia. Whoever she was, I'd need to speak with Kholt about her. And Amelia. After all, didn't Banrighs need ladies-in-waiting? Like Sagra had been for my mother?

But that would wait. It'd been days since I'd tangled with my mate, and the frenzy wasn't willing to let me wait any longer. My mouth watered as the wicked thought I'd had the previous day in the throne room sprung to mind.

"Come with me," I asked quietly in the hallway. The last of the councilors were leaving for their beds after our long debate.

"I'm pooped, Rhuger." She replied, a slight whine in her voice as she turned around, looking up at me. I bent down and laid a swift kiss on her temple before moving in to breathe softly into the shell of her ear. A light shiver ran over her and her scent ripened so quickly I almost lost it. Almost took her right then and there.

"This will be worth it, I promise, pearl," I murmured roughly into her ear. My heart rate already increasing just with the idea of what I was about to do with her. To her. Amelia nodded, her cheeks and ears bright red. A wicked smile she couldn't see spread across my face. "I need to hear you say it."

Her breathing hitched, and I had to reign in the urge to let out a primal, possessive growl. Needing something, any part of her in my mouth, I settled for the delicate tip of her ear. I ran my tongue up along the outer curve and she grasped my tunic, holding on as her breathing came in little pants. When I reached that delicate tip, I sucked it into my mouth, grazing my sharp teeth against it in a slight nip. A small sound escaped my pearl as I groaned at the taste of her skin, closing my eyes and imagining it was her clit in my mouth instead of her ear.

A ragged moan escaped her lips, and I clamped a hand over her luscious mouth to muffle the sound. To anyone leaving the council, it would look like I was speaking quietly to my cridhe. Kholt glanced our way momentarily, but one look from me and he headed off, too. The last of the orckin from the council rounded the far corner, and I flew into action.

Releasing her ear, I dropped my hand from her mouth to grasp her throat as I turned us, and pressed her up against the wall. *Fuck*, how her body cushioned mine as I pressed myself into all of her softness was divine. I tilted her head up so I could drown in her uisge-beatha eyes.

Amelia wrapped her arms around my waist and slid her hands up under the back of my tunic, gently raking her nails deliciously down my back. My eyes rolled in my head for a moment as I remembered how those claws could leave their mark on my flesh as she came undone in my arms.

A flush had turned her cheeks rosy, and we stared at one another for a heartbeat before our mouths crashed together in a desperate, hungry dance of teeth, tongues, and lips. My hand shifted to the back of her neck and I fisted her hair there, tilting her head back at a sharp angle, tearing her mouth from mine.

"Needy little pearl, aren't you?" I crooned into the air between us as if I wasn't just as needy for her as she was for me.

"That's funny. I'm not the one pressing the other against the wall in an open hallway." She panted, her sass making me chuckle.

"And I'm not the one grinding my sex against the other's thigh." And gods, she was. She didn't stop once I'd pointed it out either, and I could feel my kilt getting damp from the juices I longed to have on my tongue.

"You put your thigh there, not me. What do you expect me to do? It's so perfectly *placed*. But I could think of better things to have between my legs than your thigh..." Her voice turned husky, sultry, as her gaze dipped down to my mouth, mirroring my thoughts.

Growling with a grin on my face as she writhed against me, I swooped down and scooped her up into my arms. She squealed and threw her arms around my neck before setting her mouth on my throat and ear. Sucking, biting, and in all ways being a delicious distraction as I stalked toward the throne room.

"Keep that up, cridhe, and I'll fuck you right here in the middle of this hallway." I bit out as we passed a group of guards on patrol. One of them cleared his throat in surprise. But I just kept going. Unable and unwilling to stop, even if the end of time were upon us.

I needed her body against mine like I needed air in my lungs, the suns on my face, and food in my belly. Finding pleasure with her was as exhilarating as freedom and countless times more satisfying.

Finally, we made it to the doors of the throne room. I kicked them open despite their size and weight and wrangled them closed behind us. For what I was going to do to her, I didn't want any witnesses. This was for me, her Rìgh mo cridhe, and me alone.

"Need some help with that?" She asked dryly as she paused leaving marks on my neck with her damnable mouth, to watch me try to elbow shut the second half of the door over my shoulder.

"No," I grunted as the door finally heaved closed. With an irritated sigh, I started for the Throne of Fangs and what was going to be the best night of sex I'd shared with Amelia yet.

A thunderous *riiiiipppp* sound echoed in the empty throne room. I stopped immediately and Amelia and I both looked at one another wide-eyed, before looking down at where her dress was now in ribbons around her body. Her breasts, soft belly, and hips pillowed around where the shreds of her dress pulled tight against her flesh. As one, we turned to look over my shoulder to where her dress had gotten stuck between the two doors. And the dangling shreds of her dress that stretched from the doors to us.

My beautiful pearl, my cridhe, and the Banrigh of my soul outright snorted. Her snort turned into a chortle, into an unhinged cackle as she threw her head back and howled her laughter to the high stone ceilings. Kicking her little neamhnaid feet in glee. After a moment of watching her laughing so hard that tears streamed down her cheeks, I chuckled, too. Then laughed, then outright bellowed in mirth as I ripped the last of the dress off of her by continuing my trek to the throne.

"What are we even doing in here?" She whispered, trying to be quiet around her giggles. As if she hadn't just made the throne room ring with her laughter. Her words echoed against the stone walls, anyway.

216

"What's the use of being Rìgh if I can't have my Banrigh mo cridhe writhe upon my cock as I sit on the Throne of Fangs?" I asked as I halted at the base of the dais. I held her close as her body slithered down against mine until she gained her feet. Her cheeks were rosy with a blush, her soft bare body flush against me, her little neamhnaid hands splayed across my chest.

"No audience this time?" She asked coyly, looking at me from up under her lashes. I grasped her chin and tilted her head back so she couldn't look away from me.

"That was the only time I plan on taking you publicly, though you are a blasted temptation every time you move, pearl," I growled, a possessive need demanding that I clutch her to me and rut her until the only name she could remember was mine. "Unless, of course, it's something that you want... though if I had my way, no one would see your lush, perfect body but me."

"Getting caught was... exciting. But I don't think I'd care for a full audience again. The only person I want to perform for is you." She said, her eyelashes fluttering as she remembered all the ways she'd performed for me over the past week.

"Good." I nearly snarled as I released her chin and pulled my tunic off over my head. I dropped it in a heap on the floor. Then I went to unbuckle my kilt, but she'd already beat me to it, her breathing coming faster in her excitement to get me naked.

As I watched her fumble with the buckles, I reached down and slid my fingers between her thick, juicy thighs to her pussy, which was already dripping for me. Amelia gasped, her hands stilling as I stared into her uisge-beatha eyes and parted the folds of her cunt with my fingertips to slide them up and down her swollen flesh. Her head tilted back as she moaned outright, her hips twitching as she attempted to grind against my hand.

I didn't let her, instead tormenting her with soft caresses when I knew she wanted me hard against her, inside of her. Anything and everything I could give her. Oh, and how she would get it.

"Aren't you supposed to be unbuckling my kilt?" I asked calmly. A complete lie as I was trembling from restraining myself. My cock was tenting my kilt alarmingly, and I couldn't stop my hips from pressing the crown of my cock into the soft rolls of her belly through the leather. Desperate for her touch in any way I could get it.

"Ahn." was all she could murmur as she arched into my hand, her belly pressing against the hard length of my cock in a way that made my toes want to curl in my boots.

Reluctantly, I pulled my hand from the apex of her thighs with one lingering swirl around her sensitive clit. I drew my fingers from her and licked them clean, letting my long black tongue wrap around them, reminding her of what, exactly, my tongue was capable of. She moaned and clenched her thighs together.

Good. I wanted her wild with need before I impaled her tight little cunt with my cock and railed her until either the guards came running from her screams or we both collapsed into oblivion.

"Be a good lass and finish unbuckling my kilt, och?" I murmured and set her hands back on my hip.

Her hands moved urgently against the buckles, new motivation making her nearly tear the leather with her tiny claws. She released the last buckle and let go as if it burned her. It fell to the floor at our feet. Before I could move, she'd gone up on her tip-toes and thrown her arms around my neck. My arms automatically went around her waist as her soft, supple body crashed against me even as her mouth found mine.

I sunk one hand into the hair at the nape of her neck, cradling her head as I tilted it where I wanted it. Devouring her, I swallowed her panting moans just as the darkness swallows the light, hungry and desperate for more. The other hand clutched her ass and hauled her against me. My clawed fingers sank into the pillowy softness of her backside. Such a temptation that it made my fingers flex as I groaned into her little pink mouth. My cock throbbed where it was trapped between us, painting her belly in my slick.

Pulling away from her left me light-headed as my lungs fought to re-learn how to breathe air that wasn't hers. Looking down at the flushed, panting face of my cridhe, with her lips swollen with my kisses, I noticed a thin strand of saliva stretching from her mouth to mine. Flicking out my tongue, I licked it and it severed.

"I want to sit on my throne, and look at you, Banrigh mo cridhe." My voice was raw as we shared breath. "I want you to stand before me so I can bask in your loveliness. Want you to touch yourself for me like you did the day we earned these..."

My fingers released her neck to trace the cridhe marks spanning her chest. We both shivered at my touch. Amelia looked up into my eyes and nodded without hesitation. I growled and dipped my head to nuzzle her neck where my bite mark lay.

"That's my good little pearl." I breathed into her ear and she shuddered in my arms.

She reluctantly let go and I kicked off my boots before nearly stumbling up the steps of the low dais. I turned and sat down with as much regal power as I was capable of. Which, considering I was a trembling wreck for her with my cock leaking a steady stream of pre-cum, I wasn't as confident as I'd imagined. Then again, anything involving this female left me reeling and defenseless.

I leaned back on the throne, legs splayed and cock jutting proudly in the air for her as I settled in for the show. And, as with everything she did, she did not disappoint. Watching her as she moved and writhed for me, letting her fingertips trail over her generous curves, set my teeth on edge.

Fuck... sitting on the throne I'd been raised to claim, had reclaimed thanks to my cridhe, naked except for my torque, with Amelia touching herself before me in the empty throne room, was almost too much to take. My cock leaked slick in a river as I fought to keep my hands on the armrests of the Throne of Fangs. Fought not to fall to my knees before my Banrigh, my goddess, my mate, and worship her.

There'd be plenty of time for that.

And when her fingers trailed through the slick on her belly before she slipped them into her mouth, her tongue sliding over and between them as she took to the stairs, my claws sunk into the ivory of the throne. I snarled, and my cock jumped between my thighs. Before I knew it, she was before me, standing between my knees, uisge-beatha eyes boring into mine from under her lashes. She continued to touch her body for me, clutching at her hips and breasts, slipping her fingers between her thighs to gather her own desire before painting her nipples in it.

She was waiting for me to decide what I wanted next.

I couldn't decide what was more thrilling. The idea of her submitting here, kneeling at my feet, and sucking my cock. Or the idea of having her sit on my throne, as I knelt at her perfect little neamhnaid feet, to spread her wide, her calves hooked over the armrests, as I devoured her sweet cunt.

Both. I decided on both.

AMELIA

"On your knees, little pearl." Rhuger nearly snarled, his chest heaving with his breathing, his claws sunk into the armrests of the

Throne of Fangs as he pinned me with a stare so feral, I was surprised he hadn't pounced on me yet. "Kneel before your Rìgh."

Oh, fuck-a-duck... and that little lucky ducky was me.

My knees nearly gave out at the gravelly, raw, commanding tone that tore from his throat as his teeth snapped. I kept my feet, even giving him a coy little smile before I slowly got to my knees between his spread thighs.

"Be a good lass, pleasure your Rìgh, and I'll reward you." He rasped. I smiled because he didn't even have to ask. I was planning on swallowing him whole from the moment I felt his cock press against my belly through his kilt.

Kneeling at Rhuger's feet and giving him what Orok had demanded was a sharp dichotomy that somehow didn't make me feel awkward. Instead, I felt like I was giving Rhuger, the rightful Rìgh of the Oc'Turin, his due. As his mate, his cridhe, and his Banrigh.

I got a wicked little idea and leaned forward, bracing my elbows on either side of his hips on the seat of the Throne of Fangs. His cock collided with my chest, the undersides of my breasts brushing the tops of his thighs. I shuddered, eyes going wide as Rhuger hissed above me, and an echo of pleasure from him thrummed through me.

Oh, this was going to be far better for *both* of us than I'd planned.

Gently, I cupped my breasts, wrapping them around his slick cock, trapping it between them. I didn't have the biggest breasts in the world, but they were big enough for this. A creaking sound caught my attention, and I glanced to the side where his claws were nearly splintering the ivory of the throne. Hiding my smile, I slid my tits up and down the shaft of his cock. The textures of his shaft and knot felt so damned *good* against the skin of my breasts. And when his cock slid up my breastbone and over my cridhe marks?

I could feel an echo of what it felt like for him to have my soft breasts around his dick, how aroused it made him, and it made me want to do more. So I dipped my head down and suckled at the head of his cock. As I licked the deep slit that wept pre-cum for me, his taste exploded on my tongue. I whimpered as I slid my tongue under his foreskin and around his crown.

Rhuger's hips snapped up *hard* against my chest as he openly growled, the sound of it reverberating off of the stone walls. I'd discovered that if I palpated his sac and that place just behind it as I sucked him off, he couldn't control himself. His hips would buck and his moans would turn ragged and plaintive as he cradled my head between his massive hands. Guiding my mouth onto his cock just as surely as he was following my own movements. I wasn't able to do that in this position, but it seemed like a titty fuck was just as provocative for him.

His hips twitched and jerked against my chest in growing urgency. I had to clench my thighs together and cross my ankles against the deep throbbing that wracked my core as his cock shuddered against my cridhe marks. The echoing pleasure as I sucked and licked and moved my breasts along his shaft left me dripping and close to orgasm.

"*Fuck*, pearl. Och, do that thing with your- *uuuhhhhhnnnn... yes. That.*" He snarled and moaned as I slid my tongue under his foreskin once more, tickling his frenulum with the tip.

His breathing hitched in that certain way that told me he was about to come. I lifted my head and squeezed down on my breasts, tightening the space between them around his knot. Rhuger roared as he came in thick ropes that splattered over my breasts and hands in a hot rain.

CHAPTER 20[*]

RHUGER

As Amelia got to her feet before me, I watched, utterly enraptured, as she looked down at herself, where my seed decorated her neamhnaid skin like tiny pearls. She dragged her fingers over her breasts, capturing my cum, before sticking her fingers in her mouth. She sucked my seed from her fingertips and I groaned at the sight. I couldn't help it. She just gave me a wicked little smile that set my heart pounding in my chest and my knot flooding with cum once more.

"Be a good girl for me, pearl." I gasped as I looked at her from under my brows, fighting every bloody urge to take her to the ground and rut her like the beast I was. I stood, fighting my control, as grasped her shoulders and turned us, guiding her back until she sat on my throne.

Her breathing hitched, her breasts heaving with the movement, as I slowly knelt at her feet, my gaze never leaving hers. Her thighs squeezed together, and I smiled as I bent and kissed each of her knees. Slipping my hand under one, I lifted it and hooked it over an armrest, then did so with the other leg. Spreading her wide, her legs hooked over the armrests, a feast fit for a Rìgh. *This* Rìgh.

"Oh, yes." I breathed as my gaze raked her lush, pillowy form. Her breasts were taut, still covered in droplets of my seed, and her nipples pebbled from the cold air. Her belly bunched in delightfully enticing rolls I longed to kiss. And oh, how the light that filtered in set her neamhnaid skin aglow.

My moon goddess incarnate seated upon *my* throne. Upon *her* rightful altar. And here I knelt, her most devoted worshiper on his knees for no one but her.

I realized it then. I'd thought of her as the Moon Queen of legend, long before I ever imagined I'd end up back here in Oc'Turin lands. My own moon goddess, I didn't dare think to claim. Untouchable, distant, and lovely. Yet here I was, kneeling between her lusciously thick thighs as she trembled on my throne, her tousled brown waves clinging to her rounded cheeks, about to wring every cry of pleasure from her lips I could.

"Don't worry, my pearl. You'll have your own throne soon enough..." I murmured, curling my forearms around her hips. With a swift tug that left her gasping, I pulled her to the edge. Just where I wanted to keep her.

"I thought your face was my throne?" She said in that dry, teasing tone I loved, her eyes still huge in her face as her heartbeat fluttered at her throat. Trying to disguise how her desire rolled off of her in perfumed waves.

"It is... but you'll get another to sit here next to mine. Another Throne of Fangs. And then..." I shuddered at the thought as my cock twitched, leaking slick. I placed a swift kiss on the inside of her thigh, her desire coating my lips from where it dripped from her cunt. Licking my lips, her taste invaded my senses, nearly driving me mad. "I'll sit you upon your rightful throne, kneel before you, and feast upon you long after you beg me to stop. But for now... you'll have to settle for *my* throne."

Amelia whimpered as I bent my head down, eyes never leaving hers, and let my tongue elongate as far as it would go. Then I licked her in one long, luxurious stroke from ass to clit. She cried out as my tongue ran against her sensitive clit, a pearl in its own right, and I flicked it with the tip of my tongue. Chuckling darkly, I shifted, so I was comfortable, looked down at my delicious meal, and took her into my mouth.

As I slid my tongue inside of her core, her delicious, musky taste coating my throat, memories from that night when she'd drunk the luibh gaoil flickered behind my eyelids. I couldn't have possibly hoped that she was my mate, my cridhe. Yet here we were, with matching cridhe marks as I devoured her while our bairn grew inside her.

I pressed my hand down into her soft belly above her pubic bone while my thumb gently circled her clit. Amelia was jerking under me already, as hungry for release as I was to give it to her. Her panting turned into soft cries, trying to stay quiet in the gloom of the empty throne room. This made me chuckle.

The vibrations from my laugh catapulted her into her orgasm and she squealed as her thighs flew together, crushing my head between them. My laughter turned into a moan as her hips rolled and her orgasm had her clenching down around my tongue. The slight pain of it was intoxicating and made my knot feel like it was going to burst if I didn't get it inside of her *now*.

As soon as her orgasm faded enough for me to remove my tongue, I palmed my cock, stroking it, coating it in slick as I got up onto my knees from where I'd been sitting on my heels. I planted the tip of my dick against her opening and thrust into her in one hard, furious thrust. That wild beast I kept locked away inside me emerged for just a moment as I speared her upon my cock.

But she let out a husky, desperately ragged moan. Her thighs wrapped around my hips, and I couldn't hold back anymore. The beast wanted his mate. My hips snapped forward, and I rutted the very fucking soul out of her. My mind blanked to anyone and anything but my mate in my arms, my cock in her cunt. Blind to anything but how my hips cracked against her ass like thunder, her flesh shuddering and jiggling with the impact.

I slammed my arm into the throne behind her, my claws digging into the wood and carved bone, raking it until I found purchase. Curling my other arm around her thigh and back, her shapely calf up near my head, I railed her fast and hard. I sunk my face into her hair by her neck and snarled as I inhaled her scent. It drove me absolutely wild, as did her cries of pleasure.

I pumped into her furiously as deep as our bodies would allow. My knot swelled with each stroke until I almost couldn't get it inside of her. I was desperate to be as close to her as possible. As if trying to fuse our souls into one, as they should be.

After a few more thrusts, my lovely pearl screamed my name from that decadent pink mouth of hers. Despite her hungrily clenching cunt making her so much tighter, I didn't slow down. My knot popped in and out of her obscenely as she came, and it grew painfully full.

But like hell was I going to come now.

Slamming into her, I growled harshly as a dorcha'aon as my teeth grazed my mating mark. The place where I'd bitten her. I shuddered as I felt a ghost of what she did through our cridhe marks across our chests. It was a delightful side effect of the cridhe bond no one had bothered to mention. One that I thoroughly used to my advantage to pleasure my mate.

My mouth and tongue and teeth against the scars I'd left on her shoulder sent her flying into another orgasm. Mid-cry, she bit down on my shoulder where her own teeth marks were permanently displayed.

Pleasure hit me like a nocrys it was so blinding, and I roared my release. Her walls clenched down so hard, she emptied my knot in one burst, my seed filling her already-ripe womb.

I finally came back to myself, my inner beast sated for the time being, and slumped against the throne, doing my best not to crush Amelia beneath me. Releasing her leg, I laid my head against her shoulder as I tried to relearn what it was like to be contained in my body.

Her arms and legs wrapped around me, and I startled at the gesture before melting into it. Amelia's gentleness, in times like this, was something I was still adjusting to. She cradled me against her and hummed that song she sang sometimes as she stroked my shorn hair. The one about stars and being the one she adored. I floated in the moment as she hummed the tune. When she was done, I pulled back and kissed her deeply, our tongues dancing lazily for a moment, before I released her.

Groaning, I straightened and looked down between us, watching as my cock slid from her body, my knot soft. For the moment. We were still in the clutches of the frenzy, and it would take more than just this for us to be satisfied enough to return to our rooms.

A flood of our combined cum cascaded from her throbbing cunt, down the seat of the throne, to pool on the floor beneath us. I smiled at the sight. This was just as it should be.

My knot swelled again, and I moaned as I slid inside her once more. She arched her back, her little claws digging into my flesh in tiny bursts of pleasure that nearly sent me over the edge. Instead of chasing it, I pulled out of her. Both Amelia and my body were outraged at my impertinence.

Wordlessly, I stood and pulled her up onto her feet. Then I turned us and sat down upon my throne. Roughly, I grabbed her hips and spun her hard. She gasped as she attempted to catch her balance, but I'd already caught her. Bearing her weight from where I grasped her thick waist, I pulled her back and down, spearing her onto my cock.

Amelia cried out and arched her back and I hissed as I ground my hips into her juicy, plush ass. I cupped her throat with one hand and pulled her back against my chest. She whimpered and gasped as I laid kisses on her shoulder and neck. Trailing my other hand over her hip and down between her thighs.

She shuddered at my fingertips as they gently caressed her swollen, slick flesh. Amelia attempted to clench her thighs closed but I wouldn't let her, hooking her thighs over my knees so they spread her in my lap, speared upon my aching cock. An echo of when I'd sat her on my lap like this when she'd drunk the luibh gaoil and pleasured her until we'd both come. Oh, what a show we could have put on if anyone had been here to witness it.

But as it was, spreading her wide like this as I slowly rocked up into her, in a place where such a display wouldn't be acceptable, made it even more erotic and lewd. Especially as my knot popped in and out of her tight, slippery cunt with echoing *pops*. Her pussy quivered around my shaft as she threw her head back over my shoulder, her hands going to cover mine as they caressed and pinched and kneaded all the places that felt so good to her.

She'd been a good lass. Had even stroked me with her breasts as she'd suckled my cock. An experience I would love to try again later, so it was my duty to reward her. As much as my mate loved a good hard fucking, she was a sensual creature, too. Loving her senses and how they made her world come alive. So I made sure I gave her that in bed as well.

And oh, the songs she cried when I played her body like a musical instrument were extraordinary. So I told her all the filthy things I wanted to do with her, to her, on her in Teanga Dubh as I licked the mating bite, her delicately tipped ears, and her sweat as it slid down her throat. As my hands plucked and rolled her nipples until she was bucking in my arms, just to bring her back down with soft caresses to her belly. And she moaned and whimpered and cried for me, a song like no other.

And the satisfaction of knowing *I* was the only one who could ever give her pleasure like this filled a hole in me I didn't realize was there. Nurturing this aspect of her, and giving her what she craved, gave me a sense of completion I'd never had. And I reveled in it.

When I'd danced her along that line of release until she began begging me to let her come, I granted her wish. Sinking my teeth into the faint markings of my mating bite, I picked up my pace. I ran one hand down to tease her clit, the other I slid between her breasts to spread over her cridhe marks as I pinned her to my chest.

Her blood filled my mouth, and it was exquisite. Her screams of pleasure grew louder the closer she got to her climax and touching her cridhe marks ignited my very blood. I could feel her mounting pleasure as if it were my own. The overwhelming sensations and how she felt as if her soul was too big for her body had me faltering in my pace, my hips jerking fitfully as my knot strained to release inside her. I removed my bloodied mouth from her shoulder and snarled into her ear.

"Come for me, pearl."

She did.

And so did I.

AMELIA

After what felt like eons, I slowly rose from the fog of pleasure that had engulfed me after I'd shattered into a million stars in Rhuger's arms. My body was spasming, twitching with the aftershocks and tiny sparks of pleasure that tingled along my limbs. Rhuger's rough panting was the first thing I heard, followed by my own pitiful little gasping cries.

I loved it when he did this. It was equal parts ecstasy and torture to have him use my senses and how easily I could become overstimulated to rocket me to levels of pleasure I wasn't aware a person could reach. And when he included whatever special spice our cridhe marks added to the mixture, it was enough to make me forget my own name.

"How are you, cridhe?" Rhuger rasped in my ear.

"Ahmn." I managed around my dry throat as another aftershock ripple of pleasure made me shudder.

Rhuger pulled his hand away from my clit and I let out a wordless cry of outrage, pushing his hand back down where it had been. I might have been wordless and a near-delirious mess in his lap, his cock still hard inside me and my belly full of his cum, but I wasn't finished. Not yet.

"Still not sated?" He asked, and I could hear the smile in his voice. It wasn't like he was satisfied, either. I knew him too well already. With this mating frenzy, he'd need to come at least twice more before we could even consider doing anything else but fucking.

I blushed and shook my head no, trying hard to hide my burning cheeks with my hair.

"Say it for me, pearl." He demanded as he nipped my earlobe.

"More," I begged him in a hoarse whisper. He chuckled before lifting me off of his lap. Then he turned me to face him as my legs shook beneath me. Our mingled cum sluiced down the insides of my thighs as I held my arms against my chest.

"One more and then we go back to our rooms, hm?" Rhuger's voice was soothing as he grasped me by the hips and pulled me forward.

He was always so gentle with me after giving me an orgasm like that. His soft touches and slow, lazy thrusts helped my body to calm and relax and still gave me the release that my body demanded. It was still something I was getting used to, this perfect push and pull of our wants and desires. I knew it wouldn't always be like this, but fuck, I was going to try to make this last.

Rhuger then reached down and lifted one of my knees, guiding it onto one armrest. He supported me as I got my other knee up on the other one. I gazed down at him in bafflement as he ran his hands up and down my thighs with a soft smile playing on that devilish mouth of his. I grasped the back of the throne above his head, where two of the largest fangs jutted skyward, unsure of where Rhuger would take this position.

His eyes roved up and down my body and lingered at the apex of my thighs, where our cum was still dripping down the insides of my legs. With a twinkle in his silver and onyx gaze, he wrapped his forearms around my knees, resting his hands on the back of my calves as he scooted down. His legs splayed out behind me and his cock was at half-mast.

"A feast fit for a king." He grinned and pulled me forward until his mouth met my mound. "Hang on tight, pearl."

"Ah!" I cried out, hips bucking forward and spine arching as he took my dripping pussy hungrily into his mouth.

My already trembling legs failed me, but he kept me where he wanted me, supporting me by my hips and ass with his hands. I clutched and clawed at the ivory of the fangs, claws sinking deep into them. Looking down, I caught Rhuger's intense gaze as he sucked on my clit with one eyebrow arched.

Then he stuck his tongue into my core, twirling it as if trying to gather all of our cum to drink down. Head thrown back, I jerked out a cry. I heard his chuckle and the sound of him licking his lips before he sunk his fingers inside of me. He sunk three into my pussy and one, slick with our juices, he slid into my ass.

It wasn't the first time he'd done it. We'd talked about it and he'd promised me he'd take it slowly, introducing me to anal play bit by bit. And unlike my exes, he delivered, getting me used to it and building me up so that eventually, he'd be able to fuck me in the ass and I'd love it.

But for now, this was all he'd give me until I asked for more. And for now, it was plenty. I moaned at the feel of him in my pussy and in my ass as he began sliding his fingers in and out. Moving my hand down to cup the back of his shorn head, I urged him to put his mouth on me again. He must have liked what he saw in my expression as I watched him because he grinned before taking my clit back between his lips.

Rhuger sucked at my clit, *hard*, and I screamed, jerking in his arms, my hips moving away even as I pressed his head harder against me. The feeling of his fingers moving so, so slowly in and out of my cunt and ass, even as his mouth sucked hard and fast against my clit, his wicked black tongue flickering against my sensitive little nub, was too much to take.

"RHUGER!" I shrieked his name to the stone ceiling as I reeled over the edge into my orgasm. Feeling like I was free-falling even as my claws sunk deeper into the ivory. I felt a wash of my cum gush out all over my mate's hand as he slowed his pace and his tongue until it wouldn't hurt when he stopped.

I knelt there on the arms of his throne, trembling like a

newborn colt in all my curvy glory, as I relearned how to, you know, *exist*. I couldn't move because if I did, I'd collapse and probably give myself a concussion. So I just knelt there and trembled and panted.

Rhuger chuckled as he slid out from under me, between my legs, to stand. He placed a swift kiss on my temple before he pulled my claws free from the Throne of Fangs and scooped me up in his arms. Before I knew it, he'd seated me back on the throne as he bent down to snatch up his shirt and kilt before shoving his feet into his boots.

"I take it you're sated, for now, cridhe?" He asked with a devastating grin as he buckled his kilt back on.

I tapped my mouth with my fingers, then shook my fist. Indicating that, for now, I couldn't speak. Too overstimulated to get my mouth to move. Then I nodded before wrapping my arms around myself. It was cold in the throne room and my dress wasn't fit for bandages as it lay in a pathetic trail on the floor from the doors.

"Come here, then," Rhuger said softly as he strode to me with his tunic in hand. He helped me into it. As my head popped through the neck, he planted a swift, chaste kiss on my mouth. "Let's get back to our rooms and get something to eat, okay?"

I nodded with a smile, holding out my hands for him to grasp. He did and helped me to my feet. My legs still shook, but I could stand and walk. Rhuger's black tunic came down to mid-thigh on me, covering my lady bits. But it couldn't conceal the cum that decorated the insides of my thighs.

As we walked back to our rooms, we turned heads as we went. I was barely decent with the evidence of what we'd done trailing down my thighs. Rhuger held my ruined dress and slippers in one clawed hand. We held hands like high school sweethearts and couldn't keep goofy grins off of our faces. I couldn't care less what our witnesses thought. All I cared about was the male who possessed my heart as he led me through his world.

CHAPTER 21

AMELIA

The next few weeks flew by as we sent messengers to all the clans after we'd come to a consensus with the Council. While we were waiting to hear from them, we began implementing changes to the social structures in Oc'Turin. First and foremost, we changed how females were treated.

Like the Oc'Dellor, we created dormitories of a sort from an old warehouse that was easily defensible and allowed females who wanted to leave their forced mates or their families a place to live. There were to be no legal repercussions for them doing this. We didn't want to punish victims who wanted their freedom.

To show fairness, there were no repercussions against males whose mates left. Except, in the worst cases where the females were maimed or there were orcklings involved. We punished the males responsible for those deeds harshly in ways I never bothered to ask Kholt and Rhuger about. I only knew they'd come back covered in blood with harsh expressions and blank eyes.

I knew there was a deeper, darker story about why they looked that way and why they took it upon themselves to mete out this justice.

But I knew from experience that they would tell me when they were ready, or not at all. All I could do was give them hugs and tell them I was proud of them, which came as a *big* surprise to Kholt, who just blushed a vibrant green and muttered something unintelligible as he staggered off while Rhuger howled his laughter.

The first female who had taken up the offer to move into the dormitories was the slim, pale green female with golden eyes. Her name was Qweo, and she was a weaver. But not just *any* weaver.

She headed a network of females who traded in information. Because no one thought to mind what they said around females who were weaving, knitting, or sewing. It didn't take Kholt long to discover their operation, but he collaborated with them instead of reporting it to Rìgh Orok. And he wasn't the only male who had opposed Orok and the cruelties of the Oc'Turin social norms, either. Between Kholt's band and Qweo's, they'd done their best to mitigate the worst of things.

Which was why Kholt had seemed relieved that Qweo had taken it upon herself to attend to me when possible. It was still weird, but she soon proved to be invaluable. Either in helping me navigate the oftentimes treacherous waters of the court, helping me find trustworthy attendants and guards, and even showing me some of the secret passages through Cìp Carragh in case I ever needed to flee.

Qweo was known as either the Weaver or Damhan. And her mate, a cruel male named Jasyg, had stolen her from a small outlying hamlet. She was an exceptional craftsperson and Jasyg had worked her to the bone to create items for him to sell. He often brutalized her when he didn't get his way or when she refused him. Or didn't provide him with bairns.

Which she had made sure of.

It was soft-spoken Qweo who recommended an Oc'Turin midwife. A stocky female named Zelah with warm eyes and brusque hands. I hadn't realized how anxious I'd been about being pregnant until she'd sat me down in the royal infirmary and inspected me. She'd insisted Rhuger stay outside, and I was glad of it. Whenever it came to anything to do with the baby, he was like a mother hen. It would have been cute if I wasn't so cranky all the time.

And if Grandpa Thorn could stop sending me *things* every few days via messengers. At first, it was his favorite toy when he was a baby. Then it was a trunk full of soft blankets made out of something akin to wool. Then it was a full-blown cradle, which pissed Rhuger off to no end because, as he put it, *he* would build our child's cradle with his own two hands, *thank you.*

And *then* it was an entire midwife named Jhali, along with her trunks filled with tools of her trade. So now, I had *two* midwives to boss me around. Jhali had set her sights on Rhuger in the past, but upon seeing our cridhe marks, it was as if the threat of her attempting to flirt her way in between us had dissolved like mist in sunshine.

Rhuger and I shared a sigh of relief when we realized how her demeanor had changed. It left me shaken, but thankful, that the cridhe bond was so respected that even old flames snuffed themselves out. It wasn't unknown for mate bonds to be broken and re-shaped because of outside interference and persistent would-be paramours. But with the cridhe bond, we wouldn't have to worry about people trying to break us apart. We'd discussed it, and not having to worry about that left us both feeling a lot more secure.

In the end, Jhali was a lot kinder to me than I'd expected and asked me a lot of questions about the cridhe bond. Zelah was older and happily mated, but she was just as curious. I told them all that I could, as our bond was so new. But I left out the part about the echoes of pleasure that passed between us when we touched one another's cridhe marks or the mating bite marks. It seemed... too personal.

The two midwives were both very capable and had different

approaches to pregnancy. So when they bickered, I had to remind them we were all Team Baby and that we could work together. Eventually, they learned to balance their approaches, and it soon became apparent that my pregnancy was not normal by orckin standards.

My baby was growing too slowly.

Usually, orckin pregnancies lasted roughly six months. I'd originally thought Nashton to be a newborn, but he was months old and one of Jhali's patients. I had to explain to them that human pregnancies lasted nine. Thankfully, Grandpa Thorn had told Jhali about Grandma Ruth's pregnancy with my mother. How it had been short by human standards and long by orckin convention. If he hadn't told Jhali, I'd have been trying to convince *two* midwives that humans just incubated our babies longer and that they came out larger.

There was no actual way to know how long my pregnancy would be. So I had to be mindful the closer I got to the six-month mark. Just another thing for us to worry about.

Weeks passed, I was just starting to show, and we heard from most of the clan Rìghs and Banrighs. They were all curious and demanded more information before agreeing to a meeting. It was all to be expected, so they eventually agreed. Except for the Oc'Veltas. *They* demanded we come in person as living proof. After a lot of arguing, eventually we made the arduous trek to the lands of the remote island clan with Kholt and a small band of soldiers.

We'd met with an orckin named Kagan, a rare half Oc'Sentant half Oc'Veltas male with a thick brogue and a shock of red hair, who had guided us to the island through the dangerous shoals and reefs that surrounded it. We were the first outsiders in centuries to be allowed into the spire city of the Oc'Veltas. As much as the other clans felt like they were part of a fantasy RPG, the Oc'Veltas city of Tòrr Chathair was like walking into a clean, eco-harmonized, futuristic city. The small part of the city they allowed us to see was immaculate and the people friendly, if aloof. Most of them had skin the same colors as the sea around them and wore sleek, lined tunics and dresses. It would have all seemed so austere if it hadn't been for the splashes of color and the city's dedication to integrating nature amongst all the glass and metal.

Banrigh Aria Oc'Veltas turned out to be a tall, willowy older female with her hair cropped short in a bob. Her skin was the color of dark slate, and her eyes the startling white of a gull. She wore pants tucked into knee-high boots, and a slim-fitting jacket cut to showcase her narrow waist and hips.

Long story short, Banrigh Aria had finally agreed to a Clan Meet after checking that our cridhe marks were authentic and that I was, in fact, pregnant. She sent us on our way with Kagan and a full contingent of Oc'Veltas soldiers, who carried weapons resembling rifles. Evidently, we weren't welcome for a tour. Or even a night's stay.

Instead, we were escorted to the coast and dropped off at the docks of a local town. The soldiers stayed with us until we were back in Oc'Dellor territory. Afterward, we continued straight back to Clach-tholl in Oc'Turin lands. Rhuger hadn't wanted to stay away longer than was necessary. Both for my safety and the baby's, plus there was only so long we could entrust Qweo and the Steward with running our lands. The Council was assisting them both, but they hadn't earned *our* trust yet.

As soon as we returned, it was a flurry of activity as messengers were sent out and returned, dates were planned, locations were suggested and dismissed, and terms were agreed upon for the Clan Meet. In the end, we all agreed that The Craobh na Beatha was the best place to meet, as it was in the center of Talam and was where this all began and where both my world and this one would change forever.

The sky was just beginning to lighten when I opened my eyes. Groaning, I scrunched up my face and shoved it into Rhuger's chest, pulling the blankets up over my head.

"Time to wake up, pearl." Rhuger chuckled as he combed his fingers through my hair. It'd grown over the last few months and tangled easily. Rhuger's had grown out too and hung in shaggy locks over his eyes.

"Don't wanna," I mumbled, but then groaned again when I realized I had to pee. Being pregnant was wild.

With a shortened pregnancy, I was already a grumpy mess. So far, I'd passed out snoring in *multiple* strategy meetings, barfed all over a dignitary's shoes, gotten *acne* of all things, and was constantly either hangry or desperate for a restroom. *So* fucking classy.

It was a wonder I wasn't ejected from the position of Banrigh. But Rhuger didn't care, and everyone just took it as par for the course of being pregnant and also human. Jhali and Zelah were surprised when my baby seemed to go from growing too slowly to growing too damned fast. I had to remind everyone multiple times that human babies were born bigger than orckin babies.

"Do you need help?" Rhuger asked me as I sat up from our bed and glared at the sunlight streaming in through the tent flap, personally affronted by its audacity to wake me.

We'd arrived at the Craobh na Beatha the night before. The Meet was to happen this afternoon. I was already dreading it. As it was, I'd been poked and prodded by more people in the past few months than I cared to admit. I kept reminding myself that it was all for the sake of the orckin's future, our baby's future. But I swore, if *one more gotdamned hand* other than mine, the midwives, or Rhuger touched my baby bump... someone was going to lose finger bones.

"Maybe," I grumbled as I rubbed my face. I felt the bed shift, and a moment later Rhuger was standing naked before me. A glorious sight that I always appreciated, but there was too much to do today to play hooky and have a little fucky-fun. Plus, I had to PEE.

Rhuger took my hands and helped me to my feet, naked as the day I was born and boobs big enough that I couldn't see my baby bump if I looked down. Unless I parted the boobs. The cleavage fairy had skipped my house as a teen, but now was making up for it in a supremely inconvenient fashion.

But at least Rhuger was enthralled. He was always looking for an excuse to plant his face between my breasts, smothering himself in bliss. He spent countless hours playing with them whenever we were alone, especially if it got me in the mood. Sometimes I had to yank his head out of there by his short locks, telling him he couldn't suffocate and die, leaving me here to deal with all of this shit on my own. He'd just grin at me in that devastating way he had, then shove his face somewhere else until I forgot to be mad at him.

Once pee-pee business was taken care of, Rhuger buckled on his kilt, the leather obscuring that fine dump truck of an ass and how it glowed in the morning light. Yeah, baby hormones were *wild*. I was always horny, hungry, and feeling hung over.

"If you don't find something else to think about, pearl, we won't make the Meet." Rhuger's amused rumble had me looking up from his ass to where he was watching me from over his shoulder.

"Can you blame me? You're hot." I said with a shrug. His eyes snapped down to my breasts as they jiggled with the movement. "And look, you're one to talk, gumby."

A slow grin spread across that devilish mouth as he looked up at me beneath his lashes. I gulped and tried to focus. Failed. Rhuger turned around and stalked toward me in that predatory way he had, where his hips seemed to hypnotize the fuck out of me.

"You'd better stop drooling, love, or I'm going to have to really give you something to drool over." He said, bending down to snag a specialty dress pregnant and breastfeeding females wore that had convenient ties and lots of room.

"Like your cock between my breasts as I lick it?" I asked, and he paused for a moment before pulling the dress up my arms and onto my shoulders like a robe.

"Be a good lass for me, and I'll reward you later. We can see if you can keep quiet or if you'll be naughty and scream, waking the entire camp." He growled with a heavy-lidded stare as he began tying the dress onto my body. "But then, we both know I'd have to punish you."

The memories of how we'd played this game in the alcove back in Cìp Carragh hit me. My eyelashes fluttered and my breathing hitched in my chest. His cock tented his kilt and my thighs were already slick with need as I clenched them together.

I swallowed. Hard. But on saliva, not what I really wanted. He had two ways he could fill my belly, and we delighted in both.

"We'd better go," I muttered as I broke our stare first.

I knew from experience that we were heartbeats away from pouncing on one another. The frenzy was supposed to be over by now, yet we were still horny like teenagers with too many hormones in our systems. I finished the ties myself and slipped my feet into some soft shoes before striding for the tent flap and fresh air to clear my head.

Perhaps it was just the baby hormones. Perhaps it was the cridhe bond. Whichever or whatever it was, it was both delightful and an occasionally literal pain in the ass.

CHAPTER 22

AMELIA

I was excited to see Grandpa Thorn, and nervous. It was the first time I'd seen him since the day after Rhuger and I became mates and we found out I was pregnant. The first time I'd seen him since before becoming a Banrigh.

We were out in front of the Craobh na Beatha, the breeze rustling through the leaves and feathers of the winged tree. The high crystalline chiming from the boughs cleared my mind where I sat on a chair someone had procured for me.

It baffled the hell out of me we'd brought along *chairs* and *our gotdamned bed* on this little excursion. I'd expected to sleep on a cot or in a hammock and huddle around a fire on logs like with human camping. But I guess when you're royalty, and pregnant, comfortable glamping is a must. Rhuger made sure of it, the cute grumpy wall of muscle.

My cridhe stood a ways away, speaking to Kholt as they surveyed the nearby treeline. We were waiting for someone, anyone, to show up. It'd already been an hour and we were starting to grow anxious. I wasn't sure if being fashionably late was a sign of prestige or if people got waylaid on their journey here. *Everything* depended on this meeting.

So I sat in my purple pregnancy dress, edged in fine embroidery that probably cost a fortune, in shoes that felt like clouds, wrapped in one of the super soft blankets Grandpa Thorn had sent, feeling like a *very* irritated whale. Before I could grouse to Jahlia, who'd become a friend in the last few months, Rhuger and Kholt perked up. As did our small group of warriors and attendants.

It took a minute for me to finally hear what they did with my duller human hearing. A rustling and creaking, like the forest had come alive. I sat up a little straighter in my chair. Birds and critters took flight as a train of nocrys appeared around a bend in a trail leading to the trees. Leading them all, sat my Grandpa Thorn upon his massive nocrys.

I couldn't help the grin that split my face as they drew near. Grandpa Thorn looked regal and fierce in his regalia. My eyes nearly bugged out of my head when I saw that Sigg, Sharn, and Grammie Ruksala were with him. Laughing, I got to my feet and walked toward them, Rhuger following me with a grin.

"Would you look at you!" Sharn called, her white sharp teeth nearly blinding in the light of the morning suns. She dismounted her nocrys and loped toward us as Sigg helped a disgruntled Grammie Ruksala down from her saddle on the smallest nocrys of the group.

Sharn enveloped me in a hug and suddenly I was laughing and crying all at once. I gripped her to me hard and choked. *Gods* I'd forgotten how much I'd missed her and my friends from Baile Coille. It seemed like a lifetime ago.

"Aww, what are the tears for Amelia?" She asked, trying to wipe them away but more just came coming out. Until it became almost a little game if she could wipe them away fast enough.

"I missed you!" I wailed, letting her paw at my face in her haste to wipe them away.

"Och, out of the way!" Came a gruff voice and Sharn was knocked aside good-naturedly as I was enveloped by Sigg. My face slammed into his surprisingly buff chest and I started sobbing harder into the fabric of his tunic. He patted my head and chuckled. "The pregnancy getting to you then, Neamhnaid?"

"I see you're all glad to see me too, then." Came Rhuger's dry tone behind me. But it was full of amusement. Sigg let me go and I turned a blubbery face to my mate, who just beamed an indulgent smile at me.

I'd been doing this a lot recently. I'd always worn my feelings on my sleeve, hiding them was too difficult unless I donned that mask. And with everything, I didn't have it in me anymore to try. Rhuger had just been his sweet self, holding me and crooning to me when I needed it. Or getting me to laugh when I was grumpy or hangry.

"Can you blame us? She's a sight fair prettier than you are." Sigg grinned and Rhuger shoved him with a snort and a smirk.

"So *this* is what those cridhe marks look like," Sharn said, eyeballing where mine curled over my chest above the dress.

"Can you stop staring at my mate's breasts, Sharn?" Rhuger grumbled. A hint of his possessiveness coming out.

"I'm sorry! They're just..." Poor Sharn grimaced at me in a panic.

"Enormous? Yeah." I laughed. "Jhali and Zelah told me orckin females' breasts rarely get this big. It's pretty common with human women, though."

Sharn and Sigg shared a look with eyebrows raised, then glanced at Rhuger as if to confirm it. Rhuger just grinned like a rogue and pulled me in against him. Sigg shook his head like he was... well *shook* and Sharn just turned away blushing a silver so bright it was almost white against the storm grey of her skin.

"He's been enjoying them a little too much." I eyeballed Rhuger and he pretended like he had no idea what I was talking about. "When the baby comes he'll be fighting them for titty time."

"He'd better let my great-grand-bairn eat as they should." Came the deep formidable rumble of oncoming thunder that could herald only one thing. Grandpa Thorn strode up to us shaking a finger at Rhuger in a half-serious way.

"I'd never come between an Oc'Dellor and their meal," Rhuger said blank-faced.

Grandpa Thorn paused with his mouth open and I watched as the little hamster in his brain ran a thousand miles per hour. Then wiped out as my Grandpa's storm-dark skin turned silver. He shut his trap with a scowl and I laughed.

"Thinking of Grandma were you?" I asked. He'd been thinking of her more and more lately. Sending me messages asking about her, wanting to learn everything he could. He was trying not to be too hopeful that we could fix the Gaeta, but I know it burned bright in his chest like the North Star.

"Och!" Grandpa Thorn groused dismissively as he made a face at Rhuger who just grinned. They grasped forearms in greeting and I paused.

Seeing them actually *happy* to see one another made me re-evaluate. Had my grandpa always liked Rhuger? I'd been wondering if I would have to play mediator between them, but if this greeting was any indication, it seemed I wouldn't have to.

"Come here, chestnut." Grandpa Thorn muttered softly and bent down to hug me gently.

Then he surprised the hell out of me by getting down onto his arthritic knees and grasped my small baby bump in both massive hands and started to weep. Blubbering in barely understandable Taenga Dubh to the baby growing in my belly. He laid soft kisses on my belly and I looked up at Rhuger who had an understanding look on his face.

"Oh, Grandpa..." I chuckled. "It's okay."

"I know, chestnut. I just remember when Ruth was pregnant with your mom and when your mom was pregnant with you. It's a blessing like no other to get to have a third woman in my family and in my life to be pregnant." He pulled out a handkerchief and blew his nose loudly, dabbing at his eyes before tucking it away and slowly getting to his feet. "I'm just so happy I get to spoil you and your bairn too."

He swept his arm back to a *wagon* of boxes and chests. I looked at it and sighed, shaking my head in disbelief.

"Oh, Grandpa, *no*..." I lamented as I looked at my cridhe and then my grandfather.

"Grandpa, *YES!*" Grandpa Thorn laughed as he set his fists on his waist like a giant version of Peter Pan.

"You've done too much. This is too far!" I cried, about to argue with him over his *latest* shipment of gifts, when he got whacked in the side of the head with a wooden staff.

"OW!" Grandpa Thorn cried, grasping the side of his head as he turned to the side to see who had dared harm him. "Màthair!"

"Get out of my way." Grammie Ruksala groused, glaring up at her mountain of a son.

"Grammie Ruksala!" I grinned and bent to give her a hug. She chuckled and patted my cheek lovingly when we pulled away.

"I tried to stop him, girl. But he'd just go buy out the market the very next day." She said with a sigh and a wry smile. "I would have lied and said he'd doom us all by over-expenditure, but he knows when I'm lying about my sight."

"It's good to see you Fear a Chì Ruksala." Rhuger respectfully greeted her with a formal bow.

"It's good to see you, too. *Rìgh* Rhuger. Finally where you should be." Grammie Ruksala winked at him.

"I could have never been here without Amelia." He said, shaking his head.

"Precisely," she replied dryly with an eyebrow cocked, her expression telling him to keep up.

"Can you give us any wisdom on today's outcome?" Rhuger asked hesitantly.

"I can, but I won't." Grammie Ruksala snorted. "Just be yourselves and it will all work out fine."

I saw my grandfather head over toward the wagon to make sure everything got unloaded. I murmured some sort of platitude and left Grammie Ruksala and Rhuger to go speak with him. There were things still weighing on my mind from when I'd first arrived on Talam, and I needed some answers.

"Grandpa." He halted when I called. I walked up to him and looked him in the eye. "I know Rhuger wasn't on your list of suitors you'd wanted me to choose from."

"What are you talking about, chestnut?" He asked, brows furrowing. "Why wouldn't you think he'd be on that list?"

"Because he's from another clan. An exile." I stated, getting really confused.

"Och, he was that. But he's a gifted warrior, a loyal orc, a fit male, and an honorable one. I respect him highly." Grandpa Thorn cocked his head at me as if confused why I'd even ask this.

"But how you responded after I took him for my mate..." I drifted off, brow furrowed as I tried to make sense of it all. His expression cleared.

"Och... well, you'd never discussed it with me." He began as he moved his arms awkwardly, his expression contrite. "As is your right. And you've always been my little chestnut. It hit me hard that you were all grown up and making your own life choices. That you didn't need saving by your grandpa. And you made me so happy to be with child. My emotions were a teensy bit all over the place."

We were quiet for a bit. He'd approved of Rhuger, to begin with? He had tried to get me to be stubborn like I used to be before my ex-husband. I looked up at him and blinked a few times before my grandfather's hand came down onto my shoulder in a gentle pat.

"I knew the second I saw you together, I didn't have a chance of convincing you to choose another. The way you two look at each other is the same as how your grandmother and I did. As if no one else exists." He murmured, his beloved old face scrunching up as he attempted not to cry.

"Then why...?" I asked softly, a storm of emotion brewing inside me. Confusion, irritation, understanding, and exhaustion warred. Exhaustion won.

"Why did I press you to find a mate?"

"Yes."

"Because I'd hoped you'd take Rhuger as your mate quickly so his brother couldn't get his rotten claws on you." Grandpa sighed. "I respect Rhuger. I knew he would be good to you and I would never worry about your well-being. And he's proved that. If it wouldn't have caused a clan war, I would have flayed Orok myself. As it is, my precious granddaughter did it for me. I'm so proud of you, chestnut."

"Thanks, grandpa..." I murmured as the mask started slipping into place so I could process what he'd told me. The ins and the outs and the whys.

A loud humming noise permeated the skies. It sounded much like a jet engine and I whipped my head around, looking for the source. Grandpa Thorn patted my shoulder and returned to his knot of advisors. I strode toward Rhuger and Kholt met me halfway as I looked around, frowning, trying to find the source of the noise.

"There," Kholt said, pointing towards a ridge.

Without even a 'how do you do', a gotdamn *spaceship* swooped over the ridge and banked towards us.

"Is that..." I began, mouth falling open and eyes nearly bugging out of my head as Rhuger joined us.

"It is a starship," Kholt confirmed.

"I take it that this starship flies into outer space?" The calm in my voice was deceptive. Inside, I was screeching like a spider monkey.

The ship looked like something out of a Marvel movie, sleek and mobile. It was an odd grey color, something that edged more toward red than anything else. A surprising color of a people from the sea. It came in toward us, its propulsion engines shifting and moving until they were directly under the craft. Trees swayed dangerously and animals fled from it. Legs protruded, and it touched down in a glade on the other side of a copse of trees.

"Yes. The Oc'Veltas have developed it for space travel. They've rarely shared their technological advances with us." Kholt sounded bitter.

"Why not?" I asked, bewildered.

"The an'sgudal hit them the worst in the beginning. Other clans refused to send them aid, trying to focus on their own people. The

Oc'Veltas swore to not only reverse the effects of the plague but to advance our race while refusing to aid any other clan." Rhuger said, reminding me, and Kholt nodded.

"I mean..." I muttered. "I get wanting some recompense, but being that petty when *everyone* was suffering?"

"Most of our clans had fallen down to six males for every female. The Oc'Veltas dropped to ten orcs per female. Many of their females died with their orclings still growing inside them." Kholt rasped, an unreadable expression on his face that made me pause.

"But to leave the rest of your kind in the dark ages while you advance to flying spaceships? It's almost genocidal." I scowled as we eyed the starship through the trunks of the trees. It was clearly visible to us and my eyes roved over it as the engine fell to silence.

"That's the Oc'Veltas for you..." Kholt sighed, weary already as the hatch to the starship hissed and opened. Stairs descended, and the Oc'Veltas came into view. "It would truly be a miracle if you gain their support."

"I have a feeling it'll be like pulling teeth," I muttered as we returned to our section before the Craobh na Beatha. "Banrigh Aria was very austere when we met with her. She's implacable like the sea."

"Banrigh Aria heard us out when we visited the Citadel. Let's hope she's thought about our ideas and will listen to the entirety of our plan." Rhuger said. "I'm less worried about the Banrigh Aria, and more concerned with the Oc'Blyre and Oc'Sentan. Rìgh Pàdruig is very genial, so it's hard to tell what he's truly thinking. And Rìgh Frang? Well... if you're not powerful, he won't listen."

"Well, if they want a chance at human mates for their people, they'll have to listen." I groused, trying to keep my Banrigh composure instead of snarling like a feral beast.

"They'll likely demand more. Try to jockey for power amongst themselves. Possibly push us out." Rhuger muttered. "Their memory is as long as are their grudges."

"Well, we're doing this fair or not at all." I sniffed. "It's not like they know what the hell is on the other side of the Gaeta or could manage, anyway."

Rhuger grinned down at me. Seemingly proud of my stubbornness regarding how things were going to work. I was the grandchild of two notoriously stubborn folks and daughter to an attorney. If they thought I'd roll over just because I was this sweet, plump human, they were dead wrong.

CHAPTER 23

AMELIA

It was a while before the Oc'Veltas wove through the trees to greet us. I sat in my chair like a plump partridge, leaning on the excuse of being pregnant. There was some stilted silence as the self-outcast clan rejoined its siblings. I made to get up to smooth things over, but Grammie Ruksala hobbled forward and introduced herself, speaking long with Banrigh Aria, who towered over my much smaller great-grandmother. When she caught my eye, Grammie Ruksala winked before turning back to the blank-faced Banrigh before her.

Then the Oc'Sentan arrived. Nocrys drew their brightly painted wagons, full of color and fanfare. There was some other beast of burden I'd never seen before that resembled a rhino, a deer, and a cow all at once. Their Rìgh and Banrigh dismounted and came forth toward our group with a lot of laughing and smiling. It seemed Kagan, who was half Oc'Veltas half Oc'Sentan, who waved to us from his place amongst the Oc'Sentan, wasn't the only one of his clan to be so cheerful.

Last, the Oc'Blyre showed up. Instead of nocrys, they rode massive hairy beasts similar to bison, but with white shaggy fur and a spiraling single horn from their blockheads. I guess unicorns really existed. But they were far more muscular and smelly than what medieval artists depicted them as. The Oc'Blyre were the rudest of the lot. They were surly that they didn't get the prime camping spots, grumbling that there wasn't a stream closer to water their uni-yeti-bison, and crabby that our set-ups were nicer than theirs.

I got the distinct impression that the Oc'Blyre were the Debbie downers and Karens of the clans. All the camping spots were solid. There was a stream within walking distance for me, the pregnant lady. And we weren't responsible for anyone else's camping gear but our own. The Oc'Veltas were going to be a challenge for sure, but I had the feeling that the Oc'Blyre would be our biggest issue. They wanted to be better than the other clans, thought as much, and when equality was offered, they thought they were getting less than they deserved. Two ends of the same spectrum, only one took matters into their own hands to elevate themselves, and the other seemed to make it everyone else's responsibility.

It made me not like the Oc'Blyre immediately. I whispered as much to Rhuger as everyone was setting up their gear. As we were hosting, we were providing food, though other clans brought some as well to share. Lunch was made available to all, and Kholt brought over our food first.

"Why does that female get to sit and do nothing but be fussed over?" A mountain of an Oc'Blyre female groused, jutting her chin out at me as she challenged me like an idiot. She had small tusks that jutted up from her bottom lip, and with her beady eyes and foul expression, she looked like a snaggle-toothed bulldog.

"Oh, I dunno, maybe it's because *I'm the Oc'Turin Banrigh and I'm pregnant!*" I snapped, glowering and baring my teeth at her. Rhuger just chuckled and ran his fingers over my head, attempting to soothe my temper. It worked like it always did and I turned, kissing his palm.

The female squinted at me and sucked at her teeth with a sour expression before turning her head away to continue erecting a tent. I knew the Oc'Blyre didn't treat their females very well, and the jealousy was going to be a problem once they were the only clan not making their females equals. When they saw firsthand how even the Oc'Turin have changed their ways.

I wondered if we'd have to actually convince the females of the Oc'Blyre clan that they were oppressed by their males. Like women who disavowed feminism back home, even though it was for their personal benefit. Pick-me's who felt more at home with a man's boot on her neck than standing tall, proud, and free. I desperately hoped not.

There was a distinct difference between enjoying and finding fulfillment in a more 'traditional' female role and using it as a means to shit on women who didn't care for it. Same for those feminists who looked down on women who enjoyed traditional structures and femininity. When in reality, it was us against a patriarchal system that thrived on our infighting and profited off of both sides. And that *everyone* benefited from inclusive feminism. There was a lot that carried over in theory to Talam's political and societal structures but had differing nuances. Nuances I hoped I wouldn't have to navigate by instinct.

Eventually, all the clans got their camps established and the Rìghs and Banrighs sat in the circle we'd delineated. Our bodyguards stood directly behind us, but it was agreed that we would station all the soldiers and attendants in full view during our discussions, to keep subterfuge to a minimum. As everyone sat on the various chairs they'd brought, the Rìghs and Banrighs eyed one another uneasily.

I wanted to roll my eyes in frustration, but I had to remind myself that they hadn't had a clan meet like this one since the an'sgudal had hit hundreds of years ago. What mattered today was establishing communication and hopefully getting everyone to see the wisdom of our plan.

"What are all these, then?" Asked a massive Oc'Blyre named Ruairidh Oc'Roideach as he swept his arm out to encompass the boxes and trunks that had been set off to the side. He was the mate of the smaller, but more terrifying, Rìgh Frang. Frang looked like he'd as easily gut you as pick his teeth with a twig.

"Well, it *is* traditional ta send gifts ta other clans when a new Rìgh or Banrigh is crowned, aye?" Said the wiry Rìgh Pàdruig Oc'Sentan, one eyebrow cocked as he lounged next to his Banrigh, an elegant female with golden neamhnaid skin named Ealasaid. Ealasaid's eyebrows rose slightly as she looked down and away. I got the feeling she didn't much care for the Oc'Blyre and was trying not to laugh at their faux pas.

"It's also tradition to send gifts when a Banrigh is expecting." Banrigh Aria Oc'Veltas murmured as she crossed her legs where she sat on her gotdamned *hover stool*. I couldn't be mad at her, though. She'd added boxes to the staggering pile Grandpa Thorn had started.

"Precisely!" Rìgh Pàdruig exclaimed in his thick brogue, pointing to Banrigh Aria with a grin. It was then that I noticed his teeth. His canines were *incredibly* long. They even peeked out from his lips when his mouth was closed. The rest of his teeth looked almost human, and it was a little disconcerting. As if he were a saber-toothed cat in human form.

I almost opened my mouth to say 'you guys didn't have to', but shut my trap. I'd learned that saying such things, while a nice sentiment back home, was *not* done here. It was one of the rudest things you could say to someone who was giving you something. Made me feel kinda shitty about telling Rhuger I couldn't take his *house*. The more I learned about orckin culture through my classes in Clach-tholl, the more I realized how understanding and kind everyone had been to me back in Baile Coille.

Instead, I said, "Thank you all again for your lovely gifts.

They're very much appreciated."

This was met with smiles and nods from the seated Rìghs and Banrighs. Except for the Oc'Blyre who looked at one another uncomfortably. They hadn't added anything to the pile. Not that I'd expected anything from anyone, to begin with. I didn't hold it against them.

"Did ye really kill Orok with yer wee hands?" Rìgh Frang asked in a gravelly voice so deep it was almost hard to make out what he was saying.

"Och, that she did. Orok tried to get her to grovel on her knees and suck his cock before her cridhe." Kholt rasped from behind us. Everyone turned to look at him, and my grandpa looked like he was going to either throw up or throttle someone. Or both simultaneously. "She played his game, but stole his boot knife and slit him knee to groin. Severed his malehood, stabbed him in the neck, then stood and beheaded him with his own sword."

"This wee plump thing?" Rìgh Frang looked at me again, scowling even more than before.

"Rawr," I said and held up my hands in a grabby motion, extending my claws. Grandpa Thorn snorted and soon all of them were laughing.

"Orok underestimated my little chestnut from the beginning." Grandpa Thorn said as he looked around at all the gathered leaders of the clans. "She is my granddaughter. Of my blood through my marriage to a human woman named Ruth on the other side of the Geata. You all know that I was gone for decades. My brave granddaughter got the Geata to work for her, and it brought her through. Rìgh Rhuger found her, led by a dream, not unlike I was all those years ago. Not only has she brought me joy in being here, but she's also found her cridhe mate and is carrying a bairn already. Not to mention becoming a Banrigh and changing the Oc'Turin ways, which were cruel to females, toward equality. I believe we should all hear out her plan and not discredit her for her age or her human heritage."

There were nods of ascent and mutterings as the assembled leaders of the clans turned their heads and eyes to me. I swallowed hard, gripping my blanket around me, ready to speak even though all of my carefully crafted points, thoughts, and arguments scattered from my brain like a flock of birds taking flight. My heart beat faster and I felt like I was going to puke as these literal heads of small countries looked at *me*, a woman who'd fled an abusive marriage and had somehow bumbled her way through an interstellar portal with no goal in mind other than finding her grandpa, onto another planet and somehow through some near slapstick-comedy-level shenanigans became a *queen*.

Everyone seemed to have far more faith in me than I thought I deserved. I felt Rhuger tense beside me, to move in to speak, but I knew I had to do this myself. Knew I needed to stand my ground and earn my credibility. So I went to speak again, mouth open and words ready to fall from my tongue, when everything halted.

"What in te Seven Sands is that?" Cried Rìgh Pàdruig, looking up at the boughs of the Craobh na Beatha in horror.

I turned to look behind me as cries went up amongst the guests. A dorcha'aon had stepped out onto a bough-less section of one of the lower branches of the Craobh na Beatha, roughly fifty yards up in the tree. The orckin nightmare made flesh watched calmly as chaos ignited far below. It looked down at me and a heartbeat later, I recognized it as the one who had snatched me in Noc'tal Forest. The same one who had killed most of Orok's men and eaten the face of the giant orc who had hurt me.

"Dorcha'aon!" Grandpa Thorn bellowed behind me as pandemonium broke out. "Get me my bow!"

"Warriors, prepare!" Came Rìgh Frang's deep roar.

"Get the Banrighs and females to safety!" Rìgh Pàdruig shouted as the sounds of assembling soldiers and the creaking of bows being pulled back crowded the space behind me.

"WAIT!" I cried and stood, waving my arms to get everyone's attention. Bless the cleavage fairy, because evidently having a big girl with bouncing titties waving her arms around was enough to make everyone pause.

Rhuger stood tense beside me, bow in hand, but he hadn't even drawn an arrow. Sigg and Sharn were looking between us and the dorcha'aon confused as all hell with weapons drawn. And even Grandpa Thorn looked like he was a breath away from felling it himself. While our guests were in various stages of panic and preparedness.

Only Grammie Ruksala sat on her overstuffed chair and looked on in vague amusement. She'd known this would happen. Which meant if she wasn't worried, I could get them to listen.

"That is a dorcha'aon, lass. It will kill us all if we don't act now!" Rìgh Frang snapped at me.

"I know what it is!" I snapped back. "It's not going to hurt us as long as we leave it alone, *that* I can guarantee!"

"I've had enough of this!" Rìgh Frang growled, pulling an arrow from his mate's quiver, pulling back on his recurve bow, and letting his arrow fly.

But it never made its target. It was shot out of the sky by another arrow. I glanced beside me as Rhuger lowered his bow. Everyone turned to glare at him, affronted that another Rìgh would defend a beast who had killed so many. The dorcha'aon lay down on the exposed portion of the branch as if it had known the arrow would never reach it and watched us. Its tail moved lazily back and forth as it waited.

"There are things you don't know," Rhuger said calmly. "I can't say for other dorcha'aon. But this one will not harm us unless we attack first."

"An' *how* exactly would ye know that?" Asked Rìgh Pàdruig, so far the most engaged of the Rìghs and Banrighs. He cocked his eyebrow as he stared at us in open exasperation.

CHAPTER 24

RHUGER

"They know because that same dorcha'aon kidnapped my granddaughter and left her alive." Rìgh Thorn said from across the circle as he handed his bow back to one of his attendants.

"Wha' did ye say? I think I misheard ye…" Rìgh Pàdruig said low as he turned around, glaring daggers at Rìgh Thorn with his head cocked. His fangs, a signature feature of the Oc'Sentan line, flashed as his mouth formed the words.

"No, you heard me right." Rìgh Thorn said. His gaze flicked between Amelia and me, the dorcha'aon where it lounged like it didn't have a care in the world up on that branch, and Rìgh Pàdruig. Gauging, estimating the true level of threat against what we wanted to achieve here.

"Can you all explain to me what is going on here? What do you mean?" asked the Banrigh of the Oc'Veltas.

"It's best if you hear it from them." Rìgh Thorn said, nodding toward us.

I felt Amelia stiffen beside me. Felt her ready to take on the brunt and the mantle of what was going to be extremely disturbing news for the other clans. But I would not let that happen. Not only did she deserve some peace, wherever and however I could grant it, but the others were used to thinking of me as a villain.

After all, I'd slain more orckin, more of our dying kind, than the leaders of the clans combined. So what was another sin to tell them the truth of our long-held foe? Just another drop in the Muir Sgàil, the Shadow Sea that churned beyond the Citadel.

"It's a long tale. We should sit and get comfortable," I said, guiding my cridhe to her chair. Kholt, bless him, picked up her blanket that she'd flung aside in her haste to keep everyone from killing the beast. He held it out and wrapped her up in it as I took a seat beside her.

"Get comfortable…? Get comfortable! How do you expect *anyone* to get comfortable with that *thing* eyeing us like we're *dinner*?!" Cried Banrigh Ealasaid Oc'Druim, Rìgh Pàdruig's mate.

Her normally placid, elegant countenance twisted into something real, for once. Ealasaid was known for her beauty and her unflappable calm. Just a well-worn mask. It was refreshing to see this honest side of her, despite the acrid tang of her fear. Her mate hushed her, murmuring gently to her as he guided her to her seat.

"Actually, he's a male." Amelia piped up from where she was bundled up in her nest of blankets. She was often cold these days, all of her energy going toward growing our bairn, so we wanted to make sure she was warm out here in the open under the looming shade of the Craobh na Beatha.

"What?" Asked Rìgh Frang's mate, Ruairidh, his face contorted in horror. Everyone had turned to look at my cridhe who'd just finished getting comfortable. She looked around at everyone's stares with wide, innocent eyes.

"What?" she repeated. "The dorcha'aon is male."

"Lass, yer goin' ta have to explain it a little more than that." Rìgh Pàdruig huffed with a slight laugh.

"Like I said, it's a long story. And one that begins when Amelia arrived on Talam." I stated. Everyone had returned to their seats, even if they kept casting dubious glances up above our heads at our unusual guest.

Once I had everyone's attention, I began telling them what had happened. How the dorcha'aon had passed by the gàrradh Amelia's first night on Talam. That we'd alerted the guard, and there had been no other sightings until that fateful day when Amelia went flower-picking for the Mating Tournament. How she'd followed Inassa out into the wilds of Noc'tal forest.

Amelia took up the tale from there, explaining how the dorcha'aon above us had shown up, had sniffed at her, nudging her like it wanted something. Then snatched her up in its jaws by her basket and made off with her into the forest. How it had dropped her, then *changed* from a six-legged nightmare into a four-armed male who didn't look too far removed from an orckin.

How he had *spoken*. The stunned silence and nervous gazes up behind us where the dorcha'aon in question lounged was charged like a storm ready to break lightning over the world.

"And we're supposed to believe you now?" Banrigh Aria asked, not unkindly. She knew all of this already, yet she was helping us navigate the treacherous waters of our current situation.

We'd told her most of what had happened when we'd visited her at Tòrr Chathair. Banrigh Aria had been shocked at the gift of information on the dorcha'aon. But it had evidently bent her toward our causes. Though she might try to deny it, we knew she wanted this agreement as much as we did. After all, human technology differed from theirs. And perhaps, if we were lucky, and the Source smiled upon us, we'd be able to find a cure for the an'sgudal together.

"Because I saw it too," I said firmly to dispel any doubts.

"How convenient that you, her cridhe and mate, would see it too." Ruairidh scowled. Rìgh Frang cast a baleful look at his mate.

But I couldn't blame him. After all, I'd killed his previous mate in that skirmish all those years ago. The night I'd become Duhb'Oidhche. Ruairidh had held a grudge against me ever since. That I *had* a cridhe, and he didn't, only seemed to make the male more prickly than usual.

I didn't deign his comment with a response, though. Amelia must have sensed something amiss with me in that way she had, because her hand found mine and gave it a gentle squeeze. I shot her a small, thankful smile before I took on the rest of the tale.

I told them how Amelia and I had become mates and discovered she was pregnant before we faced down Orok's henchmen. That I'd fallen, to the surprise of everyone present, and how I'd awoken later tied to a tree, to see Amelia carried unconscious into a tent. Of the pandemonium that came later in the dark of night when the torches sputtered in the mist.

How the very same dorcha'aon, along with a few of his kin, had laid waste to the Oc'Turin forces. And how the dorcha'aon above us had bitten off Ergit's face for harming Amelia.

At that, a snarl, like metal on stone, ripped through the clearing, startling everyone. Warriors half-unsheathed their weapons. The Rìghs either put themselves between the dorcha'aon and their mates or went pale. Nocrys and other beasts of burden threatened to bolt from their handlers, and the remaining orckin cowered.

Even I'd jumped at the startling sound behind me, all of my will going into not reacting. Not notching an arrow and letting it fly into the beast's eye. A bead of sweat slid down my temple and I had to unclench my fists from where they rested on my knees. Trickles of blood from where my claws had punctured my palms stained my kilt. I wondered if I'd been wise to knock Rìgh Frang's arrow out of the sky or not.

"Thank you for that, by the way!" Amelia called up to the dorcha'aon with a little wave and a smile. An answering rumbled purr was his response.

I looked at her, head tilted to the side in askance at her sanity. I knew she was human and thought differently, even from her own kind, but her response had me slightly worried. Kholt had barely flinched when the dorcha'aon had snarled and now fought from laughing at his Banrigh's friendly wave at a beast that could devour us all in a matter of moments. Amelia's gaze met mine as she turned back around in her tiny nest of warmth.

"What?" she asked innocently. I cocked an eyebrow at her and gave her a droll stare. "Do you really think he'd have let me live *three times* now, avenged me against Mr. Big-bad-and-ugly, and attempted to *talk* to me if he'd actually meant me harm? He's clearly sentient, can speak Common in his... *other* form, and is obviously here as a representative of his own clan."

I blinked slowly, letting my breath out through my nose before looking over my shoulder at our tentative ally. He just swished his tail and stared down at us in great nonchalance. I could hear everyone returning to their seats.

"His own... clan?" Asked Rìgh Frang.

"Well, that's what I'm assuming." She said with a shrug as she popped a dearc ruadh from a bowl Kholt gave her, into her mouth. "I mean, why else would he be here?"

Everyone paused at that and reassessed the dorcha'aon above

us. Suddenly, the concept of his transformation, speech, and help didn't seem so far-fetched. Because wasn't it a Rìgh's duty to excel and have a fortitude and strength that would benefit his weaker clan folk? Whether it be intelligence, physical strength, cunning, economics, or any other number of specialties, each Rìgh and Banrigh here held many strengths, not just one. They put their people first through their dedication to excellence and wisdom.

Looking at Amelia, I asked myself what her strengths were. That was easy. Her compassion, wit, and the uncanny ability of hers to see right through to someone's heart. It didn't hurt that she was clever, patient, and deadly. And now that she was carrying our bairn, feisty and irresistibly sexy. Gods, I loved this female in all of her phases, like the moons that danced across our sky.

"She's right." Ruksala sniffed from where she sat next to Rìgh Thorn. No one dared argue with the tiny force of nature.

"So. We all know now that there is a lot more to the dorcha'aon and the an'sgudal than any of our histories or lore explains." Rìgh Thorn said. Everyone turned to look at him in the quiet that followed. "But that's not the main reason we are here today."

"Och, aye this Geata business." Rìgh Pàdruig said, stroking his chin. "In yer missives, ye mentioned fixing tha Geata. Of finding mates, and possibly cridhes, for our males. Why only fix this one?"

"It's the only one that has a chance of being fixed." Fear a Chì Ruksala snorted from her plush chair next to Rìgh Thorn. "The others are smashed, either on our side or Earthside. This one was the only one to be left mostly intact. And it has worked for both my son going to Earth and returning, and my great-granddaughter's arrival. Orckin and humans have traveled through this Geata unharmed. If there's a chance of fixing a Geata, it's this one."

Of all the Rìghs, only Rìgh Thorn had brought his Fear a Chì.

Not that anyone would be able to keep her from coming. There hadn't been a Fear a Chì amongst the Oc'Turin for quite some time. Orok's father had killed the last one and my brother had never seen to appoint another one. Yet another task to complete on the long list of things my brother had neglected as Rìgh.

"Not just males, but females, too." Amelia asserted. "There are too many variables and there's no way to control a cridhe match. But as there are *more* males than females, we will start with the males. It will reduce the risk to our orckin females as well until we find a method that works."

There was a round of grunting approval at this. No one wanted to risk our females if we could help it. I sat back, resting my hand behind my cridhe's back, rubbing soothing circles as she brightened at the opportunity to explain our plan. One she'd put countless hours into in order to ensure safety and consent. My pride in her nearly burst my heart in my chest.

"Our first objective is to secure and fix the Geata. Now, I know that Earthside, the Geata is complete, except for one of the crystal acorns. I found it broken in half, but the halves stuck together with my blood when it cut my finger." Amelia explained. "My grandmother was there with me when I went through, so I'm sure she's kept watch on the Geata *and* the broken acorn. So there's a good chance that I can get back."

"Why just ye?" Asked Rìgh Frang. His eyes were that icy piercing blue of ancient glaciers, the only beautiful thing about the scarred and fierce orc. He squinted at my cridhe as if weighing her words carefully instead of openly dismissing them as his mate did.

"Well, Grammie Ruksala mentioned that my blood was holding the acorn together on the other side. Until we replace the acorn, the Geata is keyed to me."

"You could just leave us all here!" Ruairidh waved his arm as he bared his teeth and tusks at Amelia. I flashed him my teeth in a warning and he grimaced at me. We both knew I'd gut him if he faced me.

"Pregnant with my cridhe on the other side, permanently? Do you *hear* yourself? No. I am going for all of you, and my cridhe is what I'm risking." Amelia bit out. I swallowed hard and clenched my fist on my knee, leaning into the pain to keep the panic at bay that threatened to make me snatch my cridhe up into my arms and run as far and as fast as I could.

It had been a sticking point when we'd spoken to Ruksala about the Geata. About if it was even possible to fix it. Ruksala wouldn't say either way what would happen. As if telling us would jinx the endeavor. And I wouldn't risk forcing the issue in case I did jinx it. Because everything I'd ever wanted and needed, was at stake.

And if Amelia couldn't fix the Geata, couldn't return? It would break me like nothing and no one else ever could.

"Tell us more," Banrigh Aria said, inclining her head, her gaze boring straight into us.

CHAPTER 25

AMELIA

We were all wound tight. The appearance of the dorcha'aon, though somehow not surprising to me, complicated matters more than necessary. It took a while to get everyone to calm down enough to sit down again and be willing to resume our discussion of the Geata. It was like there was a clock inside of my chest, ticking down the seconds. Until what, I wasn't sure, just that a sea of dread churned in my gut.

If we didn't come to an agreement soon, today, it would be too late to change the fate of the orckin. I knew that without a doubt, deep in my bones.

Banrigh Aria had prompted me to continue, so I did. I'd spent so many hours planning this discussion with Rhuger and Kholt, Grammie Ruksala, and Grandpa Thorn, that I would wake up at night rambling things I planned to say. And now here I was, laying out our plan at the feet of the leaders of all the clans like a holy tribute instead of the desperate gambit it was.

They liked the idea of slowly introducing human women to the orcs and orckin customs. We explained the layout of Grandma Ruth's farm, with copies of the map Grandpa Thorn had drawn of it as a visual aid with rudimentary plans for home sites, barracks, and other living areas for the orckin.

The humans would stay there as part of a lonely hearts matchmaking service called Lovey Dovey. Named after Grandpa Thorn's nickname for Grandma Ruth. His dove. When I'd told him that little detail, he'd broken down crying and hugged me for a long, long time. Reuniting my grandparents after so many decades apart was a driving force that kept me moving, even when it all seemed insurmountable.

The next part was tricky. Explaining that this would not be a free for all, Black Friday-style 'grab a mate'. Not just anyone would be able to go across to Earth. They would have to be trustworthy and kind. Something some clans were better about than others.

"This won't be a popular point, but one that will need to be strictly adhered to," I warned, as I took a cup of water from an attendant and drained it. "I know that there are a lot of different ways that females are treated here on Talam. And ways that are deemed acceptable for males to act toward females. But moving forward, we *all* will need to unify as one people in our laws surrounding equality and equity between males and females."

"Females have their place as we have ours." Rìgh Frang said quietly, yet firmly.

I paused and looked him dead in his gorgeous, frigid eyes. I could almost feel those threads again as I gazed at him, felt some tug and others give. But there was no way forward yet. They needed to hear it all.

"Consent is absolutely crucial for this to work. Humans are similar yet so different from orckin. If you force human females, there will be blood. And it won't be theirs." Rìgh Frang blinked at my words, and I returned my gaze to the gathering at large. "Prospective males will need to be honorable and in good standing in their clan. They will *also* have to be vouched for by the females of the community. If males don't fit *all* the criteria, then they will not be allowed to pass through the Geata to Earth."

Dead silence met my words before a discussion broke out that swiftly threatened to turn into violence. I knew it would be bad, but not this bad. The Banrighs all looked at me in a mixture of horror and awe. Even a little fear. Grammie Ruksala just grinned a proud gap-toothed smile. If we had popcorn, she would have eaten it by the fistful and watched the unfolding tableau like it was Pay-per-view.

"QUIET!" Rhuger roared from beside me, not even bothering to stand. I watched, wide-eyed and startled, as all the other leaders, their warriors, and attendants fell silent. "Are all of you so dense and blinded by your own pride to not see the wisdom in this? We've held our females, even our Banrighs, beneath our boots for far too long, and look where that has gotten us! On the brink of extinction!"

I knew Rhuger possessed some sort of otherworldly confidence and capability, but to watch the leaders of these varying, disparate clans fall silent at his words, now *that* was something. Staring at him wide-eyed, I felt tears threatening to spill over my lashes. Love and pride in him burned so bright in my chest that I thought it would burst through my ribs. And damn me if he wasn't sexy as sin.

Then I remembered I wasn't doing this all alone. I wasn't trying to convince these beings from another planet to give up their misogynistic ways all on my own. I had an amazing, intelligent, powerful, and cunning cridhe at my side. One who held the same values and the same goals. We were doing this, changing this, together. We'd never be fighting alone ever again.

But then, it hit me like an avalanche. If this went wrong and I was stuck on the other side of the Geata. I would be alone. He would be alone. I wanted to throw up with the sudden visceral understanding that rippled through me and left goosebumps in its wake.

Reaching out, I grasped his hand. His silver irises burned as his gaze met mine for half a heartbeat. And in that half a heartbeat, the universe paused. It felt like there was nothing between our souls at all. Not space, not time, not matter. Just brilliant, infinite unity. Fate had brought us together, and I'd be damned if I let it keep us apart.

"If a male isn't of good standing with the females of the clan, then he must *earn* his chance to be chosen to go to Earth." My cridhe said. "He will also need the funds necessary to build a home there, as is tradition here on Talam. Those funds will be gifted to Banrigh Ruth's farm, along with whatever the clans wish to provide. It is only fair that if we are to utilize Orc Rock Farm to find mates, we contribute."

"What if no males from a clan are vouched for?" Banrigh Ealasaid asked in the tension that followed Rhuger's declaration. All eyes swiveled to her and even Rìgh Pàdruig looked at his mate in mild surprise. But she didn't waver and kept her head held high.

"Then no males from that clan will go," Rhuger said simply. "Until they can win over their *own* females."

"This is all nonsense." Rìgh Frang waved his hand dismissively. "Once tha' Geata is fixed, how can ye stop any of us from going ta Earth?"

"We want unrestricted access to the human lands," Ruairidh demanded, folding his massive arms over his chest.

"No. Are you crazy? Having a horde of orcs who don't understand human ways and lacking subtlety running rampant and kidnapping women? Absolutely not! Do you have any understanding of exactly *how fast* our military would shut that down, take over the gate, and possibly even *invade* Talam?" I sputtered at the audacity of this giant who, I realized, was both a petulant child and passionately hated Rhuger. "Do you really think you have *any* notion of what Earth is like?"

"It does not matter." Came his dry response.

"Uh... it does if you want to fix the Geata. And, you know, *not* get captured by our government and dissected? For science?" I was getting sassy at this point. This Ruairidh was going to have to watch it. I beheaded the last guy who underestimated and devalued me.

"How barbaric." Banrigh Aria hissed, scowling.

"Well, humans fear what they don't know and would rather kill first and ask questions later. Very aggressive human men run our military mostly so, if you truly want mates for your clans, you will need to work under my rules and allow the women to come to you." I snapped. "This is going to be fair, or it isn't happening. You need *my* grandmother, *Rìgh Thorn's wife's*, permission to use *her* land and gate."

A certain quiet met my words. I had their attention now.

"Banrigh Ruth, my grandmother, has a farm with an inn on it." I said, trying to figure out a word for 'air bnb' that they'd understand. "We will change it and create a retreat for lonely single women," I explained. "The chleoc rings will be necessary for any orc who travels to Earth. That was how Rìgh Thorn hid his orckin appearance from humans when he was there. The orcs chosen from each clan will need to wear one until they find their mate."

"Not every orckin has a chleoc ring. Most are kept as heirlooms from old families." Banrigh Ealasaid said, holding up her hands as she shrugged. "We don't know how they were made, so we cannot forge more. Those magics are long since gone from Talam."

"Then we will need to pool our resources. All chleoc rings will be given to the cause and held in trust. We will ensure that they are cataloged to eventually be returned to their rightful owners." Rhuger decreed with the authority of the king he was.

I couldn't lie. It was a *huge* turn-on to watch him command such authority and power without even raising his voice or lifting a finger. The Oc'Turin people might have purposefully forgotten Rhuger's prowess and who he was always meant to be. But the other clans had not. They knew my mate, my cridhe, wasn't the kind of male you wanted to pit yourself against. Because he would win, no matter the cost to himself. I had to shift my focus back on the matter at hand, otherwise, my scent would have him carting me off to our tent instead of finishing the negotiations for the Geata.

"There's a huge chance that the humans will be scared—even if they fall in love with an orc and they reveal themselves. It is why it's imperative that I be there and that the orcs who come to Earth listen to me." I stated. "I know I am new to my orckin heritage. But that doesn't mean I'm not committed to the survival and growth of our people. I want this to succeed, more than you know, and I'll do everything I can to make it happen. But not at the expense of human lives and definitely not without the clans of Talam unified for the cause."

Again, silence reigned as they digested our words. I glanced up above us and the dorcha'aon was still there. Still watching us as we tried to win over an entire race. I wondered what he thought of our plan. And how the dorcha'aon would fit into this new world we were building. Until we could speak with them, it was a guessing game that served no one.

"Rìgh Thorn's wife runs this inn and farm. We do not trust the Oc'Dellor or the others ta hold true to their word ta be impartial." Rìgh Frang stated, his piercing gaze sweeping the circle. We knew that this would be a sticking point. The clans had been far too long at war with one another to allow for an easy alliance.

"Well, I'm a Chance. And mostly human. So why don't you take a *chance* on my idea? Really, every clan will get equal treatment and can choose their own representatives to go to Earth to find mates once we fix the Geata." I replied.

"And who is going ta enforce this? Ensure tha' all is kept fair?" Rìgh Pàdruig asked, eyes narrowing as he leaned back, looking all the world like a loose-limbed pirate.

"Ideally, there would be a group of warriors whose sole dedication is to the Geata and ensuring that the rules are enforced."

"There is too much loyalty to one's own clan for that to be a viable option." Grandpa Thorn said, shaking his head. Grammie Ruksala gave him the side eye.

"How about loyalty to the females?" I asked. Everyone went quiet.

"Explain." Banrigh Aria bit out.

"I think my cridhe should be the one to do that," I said with a shit-eating grin as I turned to beam up at Rhuger. "It *is* his idea, after all."

CHAPTER 26

RHUGER

I wasn't really expecting Amelia to pass off the explanation of the revitalization of the Iolaire'lasair to me. After all, it was about females. But her eyes sparkled with a mixture of mischief and pride and, as always, I couldn't resist the smile she gave me. Clearing my throat, I pushed away the thought of her smiles and laughter as we'd fucked last night out of my mind, and did my best to focus.

"Our tales tell of a band of elite female warriors within each clan that operated as a unit. The Iolaire'lasair. I would like to revive this tradition." My voice seemed to ripple through our guests. Some brightening, others scowling, all of them shifting with confusion.

"To risk our females in such a way?" Rìgh Thorn asked, appalled. We hadn't shared this information with him about our plan. I could count on one hand how many people knew, and all but one was present.

"Let me put this into perspective. Our females are beyond exhausted from being forced to fuck and breed. Some don't wish to be mothers. Others don't prefer men at all. In reviving this tradition, we are providing an option and opportunity that was stripped from them all this time because of the an'sgudal. Not only will they be able to have greater control over their own lives, but it will be beneficial for any female human coming through the gate to have female orcs in charge of their safety." I explained as I looked from leader to leader, Rìgh, and Banrigh alike, letting them see the veracity of my words in my gaze. "Too much is at stake to not safeguard against males who would take advantage of this situation, of the human females."

"Didn't you, though?" Ruairidh barked a laugh. "The first human to come through the gate in gods only knows how long, and you went and took advantage."

"It was entirely my choice. Always. He has always held my honor in high regard." Amelia snapped, jumping to my defense and glaring at Ruairidh like she'd gut him if he were closer. "If I'm honest, he did his damnedest to convince me he wasn't good enough. But he's my cridhe and far more worthy of me than anyone else in the entire universe. So *excuse you*."

If I had been standing, I would have staggered. No one had ever come to my defense like this. Her pride in being my mate, my equal, when others only wanted to use me and refused to see me as a person, stole my breath. None of my previous partners had ever been proud to be with me. Even Kholt had kept it quiet.

But not her, not my cridhe. She'd soar through the air like a proud and fierce iolaire'lasair, screaming our union for all to hear if she could. Instead, she held my hand in public, showed me love and affection both behind closed doors and in front of others, and defended me against anyone wishing to demean me. I was truly Source-blessed to have such a cridhe.

"Ye are taking our females away by doing this." Rìgh Pàdruig stated, laying his hand protectively on his Banrigh's shoulder. It said a lot about the male that his mate looked up at him with love and understanding on her face.

"No, we're not. The female warriors can choose what to do with their romantic lives. And there will be more human females willing to find a mate among the orckin to fill the gaps left behind by the female orcs. The Iolaire'lasair will be tasked with the highest of honors—to ensure our survival by defending the Geata and those who would pass through. They'll train in combat to keep unwanted and unapproved orcs from crossing to Earth. Plus, what male orc in his right mind would put a female orc at risk? Would hurt her?" I asked, looking to Rìgh Frang, the Oc'Blyre being the most obstinate about holding to the ways of our forebears.

"A crazed one." Rìgh Frang replied, cocking his head like a predator as his icy gaze bore into mine.

"And what do you do with a nocrys that is crazed?" I asked, glancing across the circle to where Sigg and Sharn stood behind Rìgh Thorn and Ruksala.

"We put it down." Sigg's grin was blinding. He knew what I was getting at.

"Exactly."

"Brutal, but effective. I like this plan of yours, Rìgh Rhuger." Banrigh Aria said with an approving nod. I couldn't keep the smile from quirking the corners of my mouth.

"What I want to know is who will be the one to lead the orckin on Earth?" Banrigh Ealasaid asked. It was a fair question.

"The best way to think of it is that I am the leader of my own clan. The Chance clan." Amelia began and already the gathered leaders and their clans folk bristled. "The orcs who come through will need to swear fealty to my grandmother Ruth and me while they live on Earth. Once they return to Talam, they will, *of course*, default to their clan of origin."

"You wish to turn the orckin against their own? Grab power for yourself? Treacherous female!" Ruairidh yelled, making my cridhe flinch beside me. But she didn't falter.

"NO! I don't want power. I want human women to be treated well. I want to ensure that the way forward for the orckin is as smooth as possible. And that cannot happen without fealty of some kind." She was shaking as she spoke, but her voice was steady and sure. "I'm trying to combine your ways and human ways in the most palatable way I can fathom to ensure joy and survival. As I said, any and all fealty to Banrigh Ruth and I would end as soon as the orcs return to Talam."

"What about when you come through? Will you demand more? Demand fealty still?" Rìgh Pàdruig asked, squinting at us.

"Nothing beyond that which I already can demand within orckin law. I am Banrigh of the Oc'Turin and granddaughter of Rìgh Thorn of the Oc'Dellor. I would never expect fealty from another clan. It is not my place, and it is not right." Amelia replied, straightening her spine.

"Her words make sense, they are fair. She has enough orckin in her to make sure she stands true to her words. But what of the humans?" Rìgh Frang asked. Ruairidh sputtered beside him, affronted that his mate would say that.

"Not all humans are good. Some are vile and deserve death. But they're not unlike us in that. We orckin vary and so do humans from person to person." Rìgh Thorn explained. After all, he'd lived on the other side of the Geata amongst the humans almost as long as he'd lived here on Talam. If anyone could speak on human ways, it would be him.

"I know a lot of humans are slippery assholes. But there are a lot of good people who are honestly just trying to find love and companionship somewhere, anywhere. There are many people like me…" Amelia began and swallowed hard, blinking back a sudden rush of tears. I put my hand on hers. She looked at me then, uisge-beatha eyes sparkling with unshed tears. Squeezing her hand, I silently showed her the support she needed, no matter if she shared her experience or not. The choice was hers, always.

Taking a deep breath, she returned her gaze to our guests. "All I ever wanted was to find someone to share a life with and have a family and safety. My ex-husband abused me. I never thought I'd love anyone ever again. But then, I got the Geata to work, and I found my cridhe here on Talam." Rìgh Thorn looked ready to explode in his rage over his granddaughter's mistreatment. He cast a grateful nod my way, and I returned it.

"How do you plan on drawing in willing human women like you?" Banrigh Aria asked. She'd remained cool and level-headed throughout our discussions, but that didn't mean she approved or was going to accept our terms. Calm didn't mean compliance. I knew that well enough myself.

"If marketed correctly, we will attract lonely women who, like me, truly seek what a cridhe bond can provide. It will be up to the individual orcs to woo and secure the women as mates. But there *will* need to be rules of conduct." Amelia declared.

"Like what?" Banrigh Aria prompted.

"The Oc'Dellor's treatment of female orcs is commendable and, from what Amelia and Rìgh Thorn have said, the closest to what they expect on Earth. So we will all need to adopt similar laws. The Oc'Turin have in recent months, and it has benefited us immensely already." I explained. "If an orc were to force himself on a human woman, or an orckin female, without her consent, then he would forfeit his life."

Shocked gasps and discontented muttering clamored as the clan representatives and leaders argued amongst one another.

"What if the female or woman lies!" Someone among the

attendants cried.

"A Fear a Chì will need to preside over each case to discern the truth," Ruksala said above the racket and the orckin quieted to hear her. "We are not just tellers of the future, but the past as well. It is our sacred duty to be impartial and do no harm."

"The worst punishment for such a thing is exile." Rìgh Pàdruig said. Censure was clear in his demeanor. While the Oc'Sentan were more open-minded than some of the other major and minor clans, they still held true to the old laws.

"When has that ever stopped a male? And how often was he pardoned from punishment?" Silence met my words.

AMELIA

"Well, let me tell you that as a female who has been used, death would be a mercy. Those who force a woman, a female, will *always* seek to do it again. To the same female or another, it doesn't matter. Males like that should be put down. *Anyone* who would do that to someone else, male, female, or other, should be put down. And I will do it myself." I patted Orok's blade at my side and I saw some appreciative and thoughtful expressions. "There *is* no room for such behavior if you wish the orckin to thrive and grow."

"Are there any other laws you wish to set down, granddaughter?" My grandfather's eyes were sparkling with pride, and that gave me enough emotional room to breathe. There were some grumbles after I mentioned putting down females as well as males. But I didn't give a shit. If we were aiming for equality then that meant punishments were equal just like rewards.

"While there, the chosen orcs will need to help out around the farm. It will be in exchange for room and board. And it will keep the orckin busy and allow the human females time to admire and possibly choose an orckin. There will be no guarantee of a mate. All that is being offered is a chance." I continued. "If an orckin cannot find a mate within a certain period, he will be required to return so that another orc can take his place. He will be granted another turn later. If an orc were to run off to search for a mate and not stay on the farm, he will be tracked down and cast back through the gate, his privilege at attempting to find a human mate forever revoked."

"Ye aren't giving us much opportunity, ye ken?" Rìgh Pàdruig asked with a huff of a laugh.

"It is the only opportunity your kind has at a chance with mine. Your kind is so far back in our history that you're relegated to fairy tales we tell to children to scare them. Not flesh and blood people who look completely different from humans. In order for our kinds to come together, time and space and patience must be paramount in our approach." The firmness in my voice belied the shaking of my hands that I'd shoved into my blanket. The high of releasing this plan was wearing off and I felt a shutdown coming.

"What happens when a human female discovers that we are orckin? What will keep them from becoming afraid then?" The question came from an attendant, some of the leaders scowled in his direction, but it was a question that needed to be asked, regardless of who it came from.

"That... is a really good question." Grandpa Thorn said, taking over the discussion. I tossed him a grateful smile and sunk into my blanket. Rhuger leaned over and planted a chaste kiss on my cheek, letting me know I'd done a good job. It warmed me down to my toes. "I think it's going to be a matter of exposure and knowledge that will keep them from being too afraid. Some women will not be open to it. You'll all have to be prepared for that. We're not sure how to break the news yet. We can have the ladies sign documents where they will be legally bound not to say anything. Beyond that, I'm not sure."

"We were hoping the Oc'Veltas would have the history of how such things were handled before the gates were broken." Rhuger offered, opening the discussion to Banrigh Aria.

"The human females were brought here. Kept here until they found a mate or acclimated. Most human females were provided as sacrifices by their own people." She said, shaking her head sadly.

"They *what*," I demanded, utterly appalled.

"Humans weren't as advanced as us—they thought we were gods for a long time. Then they decided we were demons for taking mates amongst them."

"Thus the war?" Rhuger asked.

"Och, yes. They broke the Geata. Claimed they were closing portals to hell." Banrigh Aria explained.

"Well, that escalated quickly..." I muttered and shared a shocked, yet unsurprised, look with my grandfather. We knew how prone to extremes humans were.

"How do you suppose we approach this now?"

"Well... a lot of women like science fiction and fantasy romance... we might be able to swing the advertising to approach them first." I offered. Everyone but Grandpa Thorn looked at me with blank stares. "Stories, they like stories that include beings like orcs."

I sighed as the others nodded and murmured their understanding. Thank goodness for that.

"What happens if there is a serious enough transgression?" Banrigh Ealasaid asked.

"Like what?" I asked.

"If a clan were to attempt to take over Clan Oc'Chance." Her words fell like stones into a bottomless ravine. The air became so thick with tension I could have slapped it and watched it jiggle like Jello. The fact that someone was already calling my little operation Clan Oc'Chance was heartening, but her question left my stomach in knots.

"If a clan were to do that, then it would spell our doom. The other clans must rally in defense of the Geata alongside the Iolaire'lasair. If it goes further than that... then the Geata will be broken for good. And our kind will die out." Rhuger rumbled.

"I will have our chosen males swear fealty ta Clan Oc'Chance while on Earth." Rìgh Pàdruig announced with a jaunty grin into the ensuing quiet. "Your words are fair and you are very wise ta think such a thing through so well. I am impressed. And you are correct, there're many ways in which we can improve how we treat our females. I believe we are lucky indeed ta have such a wise and strong female commanding this endeavor, with such a fierce Rìgh at her back."

"I am in agreement with Rìgh Pàdruig." Banrigh Aria stated and gave us a firm nod. Grandpa Thorn nodded as well. There was only one clan left to swear to this plan.

"I do not like this." Rìgh Frang said, and I was surprised. I thought we'd nearly won him over. My heart sank. If we all didn't agree then this would be the end of it all.

"What is te harm in trying? What is there ta lose compared te what we can gain?" Rìgh Pàdruig asked as he stood, exasperated at Rìgh Frang's obstinance.

"It's a fool's bargain." Rìgh Frang bit out, knowing full well that his clan's males would not measure up to the standards being laid down. Not yet anyway.

"Then call me a fool. Many of us, myself included, hope for a cridhe mate like Rìgh Rhuger has found in Banrigh Amelia. What male in his right mind would not want a chance at tha'?" Rìgh Pàdruig asked, poking Rìgh Frang further.

Everyone held their breath and looked behind him to where his Banrigh sat with a victorious smile. At least they were of the same mind about it. Marriages of alliance were common for the leaders of the clans. They weren't often as caring as the bond between Rìgh Pàdruig and Banrigh Ealasaid, though.

And then I felt it again. That shift, a path opening amongst the threads of fate that was not there before.

CHAPTER 27

AMELIA

In the end, after all the Rìghs and Banrighs argued for hours, Rìgh Frang finally agreed. No one knew when the dorcha'aon had left us, which put us all on edge. Ruairidh had been quiet and watchful of his mate while Rìgh Frang debated with the other Rìghs. Like he knew that what they had wouldn't last through this.

I'd been so dizzy and nauseous in my relief that I had to lean against Rhuger as he guided us back to our tent. We'd just dodged one hell of a bullet.

I couldn't understand why it'd felt so imperative to reach an agreement that day. It'd take months to form the Iolaire'lasair, have males chosen amongst the clans by their females, and prepare for our mini alien invasion of my grandmother's Tolkien-inspired bed-and-breakfast. But whatever had been on the cusp of breaking, had shifted instead and flowed toward the future we all desired.

"You did well, pearl. I'm so proud of you." Rhuger told me as we neared our tent. His voice rumbled in his chest, a soothing sound I could listen to forever and never tire of. I smiled up at him, and he placed a gentle kiss on my forehead. "How are you? How's our bairn?

Should I call for Zelah or Jhali?"

"I'm just tired. It took more out of me to do that than I thought it would." I murmured as he lifted the flap of our tent and ushered me inside. "I was trying not to go silent. Thank you for helping me so much, Rhuger. I love you."

"I love you too, pearl." Rhuger flashed a small smile my way, the corners of that sinful mouth of his causing small dimples to form in his cheeks. "Are you hungry?"

He sauntered over to a small table that was nearly bowing with the weight of the food that had been left for us. Female orckin had voracious appetites, in more ways than one. And Rhuger's dump truck ass was looking particularly fine at the moment.

"I'll take your scent shifting as a yes." He purred, casting a heated glance over his shoulder at me, where I'd sat down on the edge of our bed. He was piling a plate full of our favorites and popped a dearc ruadh into his mouth as he prowled to me like the sexiest predator in existence.

"Can you blame me? You're so damned sexy it's hard to focus on anything else but you." I chuckled as I kicked off my shoes. "Now that I don't have our presentation taking up residence in my brain, no distractions left, all I can think about is you and getting some sleep."

"Well, I can help with all three." He grinned, swooping down to kiss my mouth before placing the plate on the bed. He tasted like the tart juice of the dearc ruadh and I couldn't help but lick my lips.

Rhuger sat on the edge of the bed next to me and reached for some caraiceag, a fluffy bread, similar to a pancake that was filled with ground nuts and honey, and a handful of dearc ruadh. Turning to me he held one of the blood-red berries up to my lips.

"Go on." He prompted gently. "You barely ate during the Clan Meet. And you'll need your strength if you want me to make you scream. It'll give the others further incentive to rally to our cause to know how pleasurable a cridhe bond can be."

His heated gaze lifted from the berry at my lips to my eyes. The silver rings of his irises thinned as his pupils blew out and his scent shifted. I'd begun to notice it, certain shifts in his scent that told me when he was aroused. Not like the visual cues weren't enough to go by, especially when his kilt tented as alarmingly as it did right then.

"Hmm," I hummed as I opened my mouth and he slid the berry inside. He went to pull away, but not before I nipped the pad of his finger.

A rough growl ripped from his throat a moment before his mouth was on mine, the dearc ruadh bursting, its juices slipping from our mouths as our teeth and lips clashed. Rhuger hauled me against him before shoving the plate of food off the bed, sending the plate clattering to the floor. Then he rolled us and I gasped as I found myself straddling his hips. Sitting up, I looked down at my cridhe as his silver and obsidian gaze raked over the curves of my body.

I was already wet and throbbing, grinding against him shamelessly as he plucked loose the ties on my dress as if he had all the time in the world. He undid the last tie and pushed the front panels of the dress back, exposing my naked body beneath it. Making a frustrated sound, I started unbuckling his kilt. Rhuger *tsk*ed me, his eyes bright silver brands as he grinned up at me from under his lashes.

"So impatient." He chuckled. "But you were a good lass, so I'll let you have what you want."

He didn't bother removing his kilt, just slid it out of the way, pressed the tip of his cock to my quivering core, and slid inside of me in one swift, hard thrust. I wailed in ecstasy as he filled me with the ribbed length of him and his swollen knot

His fingers dug into my hips and ass as he helped me ride him.

Rising up he took one of my nipples into his mouth and I cried out, my hand fumbling blindly for my clit. I rocked faster and harder, not bothering to hide my moans and wails, so focused on my cridhe and the bond between us, the mounting pleasure, that I forgot all else. Rhuger braced his feet on the mattress and began to pound into me as I rode him. My moans turned to screams as he brought me to the brink of climax and I shattered into a shuddering mess atop him. His name upon my lips was the only thing I could remember as Rhuger roared his release between my breasts.

"Oh, now look what you've done, pearl." Rhuger teased once we'd fallen back into our bodies. He sat up and changed positions to where he was pinning me face down on the mattress with my ass in the air, spread wide like a butterfly. The one position he knew would have me creaming and screaming until he decided *he* was finished. I moaned loud and low, fisting my hands in the bedding, knowing he was going to stay true to his word from that morning. Rhuger sighed dramatically. "You've gone and woken everybody. Such a naughty little pearl. Looks like I'm going to have to punish you..." His delighted grin flashed brilliantly in the dark right before his hand connected with my ass in a hard *smack*. Pleasure rippled up my spine until I cried out.

And gods, he did. He edged me and used every damned trick he'd learned to make me come undone over and over again until the suns rose over the rim of the world. Only stopping to make sure we stayed hydrated and fed. But once we had, he either planted his devilish mouth between my thighs, his hands spanning my little baby bump while he ate me out, or rutted me like he'd die if he didn't.

The next morning was a mixture of mortification for *everyone* except Rhuger, who couldn't keep the shit-eating grin off of his face. Even when Grandpa Thorn glared at him like he wasn't sure if he was furious or impressed.

My midwives, Zelah and Jhali, just looked at us and shared an exasperated sigh. Our baby wasn't in danger from having so much sex, evidently. Something about orckin seed making it so the baby grew healthy and strong. The additional orgasms fed into the female's fertility, so she didn't miscarry. But it *was* unusual for a mated pair to, uh, mate *quite* as much as we did. Like we'd drank a vat of luibh gaoil. Everyone just chalked it up to a mixture of the cridhe bond and baby hormones. Or my human heritage.

I couldn't look at anyone. My human upbringing made me blush at my own wantonness. But that didn't mean I missed the hungry looks cast my way by many of the males. And some females. They weren't looking at me, per se, but at the cridhe marks that peaked above the dress.

Those who didn't look at me like that were staring at Rhuger, who was the epitome of a fully satisfied male. Showing off his cridhe marks proudly as he kept me close, either on his lap or with his hand in mine. As he so often did after a night of passion. Which was, let's be honest, more often than not.

I couldn't help but wonder if last night had been part of his plan. To let all the Rìghs, Banrighs, and their clans folk hear for themselves how satisfying the cridhe bond was. Even if it hadn't, it sure as hell cemented the agreement we'd struck. Rìgh Frang was more committed for sure, even his mate Ruairidh, who obviously didn't want to lose Rìgh Frang, was more agreeable.

My Grandpa Thorn was more anxious and wistful when he looked at us than jealous or angry. As if he couldn't help but remember Grandma Ruth. I couldn't blame him. Gods, I hoped our plan worked. For their sake, if not the sake of orckin kind.

But it was Rìgh Pàdruig and Banrigh Ealasaid who I caught staring at us the most. It was obvious they made a great team, and there was love there, but nothing of a romantic sort. That they both wanted their cridhes more than anything and would end their own bond for it made me wonder how many more couples would break up. How many more families would change, once more orckin took the chance to find their cridhe amongst the humans?

I fervently hoped we weren't making things worse by trying to make them better.

CHAPTER 28

AMELIA

Months later, we stood at the base of the massive six-winged tree within Noc'tal Forest. Staring up, I watched as the massive wings stretched in the morning light of Talam's twin suns. The chiming sound that came from the tree sent a shiver down my spine like drinking a quad espresso.

Gods. Coffee... I nearly cried thinking about it, and then *did* cry when I realized I couldn't have any when we got back because I was *pregnant.* Not that I didn't love the little nugget that had started moving in my belly, but this mama-to-be needed a date with Uncle Cuppa Joe something *fierce.*

Patting my baby bump, the light catching on the enormous pearl and silver ring Rhuger had crafted for me as an engagement ring, I looked around the bustle and commotion around us. Not only were all the Rìghs and Banrìghs and their heirs present to honor this momentous occasion, but craftspeople from all over Talam had arrived to begin construction on a small town that would spring up around the base of the tree like a fairy ring. It would be a waystation and a place for the Iolaire'lasair to live and train.

Rìgh Pàdruig had been the one to suggest we build it and had even provided some of the Oc'Sentan home wagons for people to live in. At least until they could build barracks, each of the Rìghs and Banrighs had chipped in on this venture. Providing supplies like sand for glass, stone, wood, food, sunstones for forging and light, and tools. And also spearheading projects.

Rìgh Pàdruig headed the construction of the yet-unnamed town. Rìgh Frang and Ruairidh provided sunstones and smiths to forge anything the town needed. Banrigh Aria got Banrigh Ealasaid's help in designing vertical gardens, similar to what we saw at the Citadel, and turning the surrounding glades and groves into fields and food forests with edible plants from all over Talam.

It was surreal to think that just a handful of months ago, I'd fled my ex-husband and stumbled through the Geata, nearly right into the arms of my cridhe. So much had happened since then. It felt like a lifetime ago.

And here I was, cridhe bound, pregnant, and ready to return to Earth to help others find what I had. Suddenly, the reality that I might be leaving all of this behind permanently, leaving *Rhuger* behind, hit me *hard*. I had to swallow past the lump in my throat and blink back an onslaught of tears, or else I'd lose courage.

"Are you ready?" Sharn asked from behind me. I turned and gave her a nervous smile.

"About as ready as I'll ever be," I replied with a shrug. "I really hope this works."

"We all do." She said quietly.

Everyone who was planning to go Earthside had gathered together with their belongings, weapons, and tributes. There was a group of Iolaire'lasair that were to go to Earth as well. To protect that side of the gate as well as this one. Sharn had done an amazing job as

Captain of the Iolaire'lasair and I was immensely proud of her. She'd won her place in a tournament that had been held weeks prior. All the females who wanted to have a place amongst the Iolaire'lasair had competed.

Sharn had been the one to win.

Little surprise there, given she'd had *both* Rhuger and Uther training her. I'd been happy with Uther visiting us because that meant I got some quality baby time with little Nashton. Who was growing rapidly and no longer needed a sling. Instead, he was toddling around and getting into all sorts of baby mischief.

Now Sharn was the Captain and had taken her role seriously. Working tirelessly to train up the Iolaire'lasair and to plan for any and every possibility that they would face. Her brilliance as a tactician quickly gained her respect, even amongst the brutal Oc'Blyre warriors.

Fully outfitted in armor that Conn, the Oc'Dellor's Master Smith, had devised, Sharn was a vision. The lovely swooping lines of it and the weapons the Iolaire'lasair carried were reminiscent of the daggers he'd forged for me. Wickedly sharp and shaped like feathers. Rendering all the females who wore it into the firebirds they were named after.

"I'm going to go scout the cave," Sharn said as Rhuger approached us. Rhuger gave her a nod and Sharn turned on her heel, spear in hand, and stepped within the cave nestled amongst the Croabh na Beatha's roots.

"She really doesn't need to do that, does she?" I asked my cridhe, looking up at his beloved face.

"Yes, and no. Regardless, it gives her practice in her role and puts her mind at ease." Rhuger said, eyes going soft. "Amelia, I... I wish you didn't have to do this. I wish I could at least go with you."

"I know, gumby." I whispered and held a hand up to his cheek.

He closed his eyes and leaned into my hand with a pained sigh.

We'd already said our goodbyes earlier that morning. Rough and tender and blistering with need. Our cridhe marks pulsed in time as we came down from the highs of our pleasure and cried together. Because there was the very real possibility that I might not get the Geata to work once I made it to Earth. That I might be stuck on the other side with Grandma Ruth. The two of us separated across the universe once more.

"It's empty," we heard Sharn call out from the interior of the cave nestled amongst the massive roots of the Croabh na Beatha. Rhuger stepped forward toward the mouth of the cave.

"Och, we'll start bringing everyone in now," Rhuger announced before heading back out. He strode toward me with that loose swagger I loved so much and held out his hand. I took it and he tucked his arm around my shoulder as we walked toward the Geata and the start of something wondrous.

"Oof!" my voice echoed within the cave as I tripped over my own feet. Couldn't even blame a rock or root as the floor was smooth-packed earth.

"Careful, pearl." Rhuger admonished as we came around the corner. He had his arm protectively around my waist, his broad hand splayed against my baby bump.

"I'm fine!" I groused up at Rhuger, feeling about as graceful as a gazelle drunk on champagne. Sharn's grin was like a beacon in the gloom of the cave as she watched us approach.

"He's allowed to be protective of you," she teased.

"He can be protective without making me feel incapable!" I whined, and Sharn chuckled at my expense. I didn't have to look at my cridhe to know he was failing at keeping a straight face. No matter how ornery I got, he just thought I was adorable. Even called me a nocrys cub, hissing at anything and everything or crying and needing a cuddle. "Honestly, Sharn, I don't know how you put up with him all these years!"

"With great annoyance," came her wry reply and Rhuger's expression turned into a scowl then. Evidently, Sharn's attitude wasn't as charming to him as mine.

"Are you doing okay? Today's gotta be nerve-wracking for you." I whispered as we passed her. She gave me a tight nod, and it didn't fool me. Sharn had worked her ass off to become the Captain of the Iolaire'lasair. But she still felt like she didn't deserve it. So she worked twice as hard as anyone else would have.

Rhuger held me against him as we took the stairs to the Geata. I could hear the others shuffling in behind us, eager to bear witness to the Geata working, and to claim their own futures. But each step was like wading through molasses. Time kept slowing down the closer we got to the Geata. Yet, I blinked, and suddenly we were before it on the top step.

My heart thundered in my chest, a panicked bird desperate to flee. To find refuge. I felt like throwing up as my whole world narrowed to that pink crystal acorn. Once I touched it, I knew the Geata would open and I would be sucked through to Earth. I knew that red thread I'd seen when I'd first entered it would trail behind me, linking me to Rhuger. But the panic that it wouldn't survive the return trip was like ice in my veins.

I gave Rhuger's hand a squeeze with a reassurance I didn't have. His lips met my temple before he stepped back and let me go. It would have hurt less had I been stabbed in the heart.

But I wasn't raised by a feisty grandmother and determined mother for nothing. The only time I'd feared in my life had been living under my ex-husband's thumb. I'd feared very little since. And I knew that I couldn't leave room for fear now. Or else all would fail.

"Well, here goes nothing," I said with a lightness I didn't feel as I stood next to Sharn. I offered her a small smile and raised my hand to touch the middle crystal, the pink one. The cave was silent, none of us daring to breathe. A moment passed, then two, and frustrated sighs slipped from those nearby.

Then suddenly the magnificent rings carved behind the depiction of the Craobh na Beatha shuddered and ground into motion. Elation and horror warred within me as I fought to breathe. Fought to think and remain present.

"It's working!" someone called from behind me. But my gaze was locked on the Geata blooming before me, my attention riveted on my cridhe behind me and that red thread I could suddenly feel that connected us.

The door carved within the giant archway on the Geata split in half and slid away. Bright white light and rainbows poured through, bathing us all in celestial radiance. No thread led from me through the Geata. I'd already found my destiny, and here I was, gambling it all on a whisper of hope.

Without conscious thought, I took one step into the tunnel. I couldn't help but glance at Rhuger with all the love I had in me. He was openly weeping, and I felt my own echoing tears slide down my face.

Something grabbed my shoulder and between one heartbeat and the next, the Geata sucked me through. And it felt like my heart got wrenched out of my chest with it. I flew through the tunnel of light and rainbow, unable to breathe, as I hurtled through this intergalactic portal. Tears slid from my eyes to be swept away into the chiming, rushing beams of light and color.

I only hoped that what gods could hear me would be kind. Would let me fix the Geata and see my cridhe once more. Because I already felt so empty without him. That red thread stretched so thin it threatened to snap as I spanned the universe in heartbeats instead of light years.

A dark wall appeared ahead of me, the other end of the Geata that lay within the sea cave at Orc Rock Farm. I only hoped it was low tide. Between one blink and the next, I fell through. Something jerked me as I fell and all I could see was leather as I fell to Earth. Whoever it was had cushioned my fall as we met the wet sand with a *thud*.

I wanted to weep, and I had to swallow a keening sound as I hauled myself up off of the person who had cushioned my fall and probably saved my baby. Because I knew in my gut that it wasn't Rhuger. They groaned, and I blinked as I registered who it was.

"Gods, Sharn!" She cried as I rolled off of her. She struggled to draw in the salty sea air, my weight having knocked the wind out of her. "How did you get through?"

She groaned, muttering before she could finally draw a breath. I waited until she could breathe easily. The chleoc ring had worked. Sharn looked like an absolutely stunning human woman. Tall and lithe, with raven black hair, honey-colored skin, and the deepest blue eyes I'd ever seen. She was sure as shit going to have her choice of girlfriends.

Sharn sat up and looked at me, a puzzled expression on her face. "I'm not sure. I saw a red thread and knew I needed to come with you. So I grabbed your shoulder."

"Red thread, huh?" I asked absently as we looked around. The sea cave looked just as I'd left it. And I pondered what it meant that I hadn't been the only one to see that red thread. What it meant that hers led her to Earth. Perhaps it was an indicator of a cridhe bond. But I had to stop thinking about the cridhe bond or I would break. "Well, this definitely looks like the sea cave on Earth."

Sharn stood up in one lithe, fluid motion and held her hand out to me. Grasping it, I got clumsily to my feet. After dusting off some wet sand, I looked back up at the Geata and nearly ran up the short flight of stairs to the intricately carved stone wall. My heartbeat fluttered and my lip trembled, but I fought to keep it together. It wouldn't do for a Banrigh to come apart at the seams in front of a Captain of the Guard. Even if that Captain was her best friend.

I could hear Sharn following me. Her presence gave me more hope and courage than I could ever repay. Hesitantly, I pulled out the pouch with the crystal acorns. Grammie Ruksala had given them to me, explaining that they were the seeds from the Craobh na Beatha. Once a new seed was planted in the Geata, it would come alive again and work as it should. She'd given me more than one, just in case.

Glancing up at my best friend, I took a shaky breath and removed the broken acorn. A strange hum that I hadn't realized was there ceased, and the Geata went completely silent. Gone cold and dead like some lifeless thing.

Sharn reached out her hand to take the halves of the broken crystal acorn from me. She paused and blinked in utter bafflement. "Amelia..." she rasped, and I offered her a small smile.

"Looks like the chleoc ring still works its magic. You look human." I said as Sharn felt her own body for the changes that made her appear human. Her bewilderment as she saw me as a human nearly made me chuckle despite the gaping hole in my chest. "We'll talk about it in a minute. I want to get the gate working before Rhuger and Grandpa have a collective aneurysm."

"A what?" She asked breathlessly.

But I ignored her. More focused on bringing my cridhe to me than breathing. I opened the pouch with steadier hands than I felt, and drew out an acorn. It was the size of an apricot and glinted clean, bright white and rainbow in the shafts of afternoon sun that filtered in from the holes above.

It had survived the trip intact. So, with bated breath, I pushed the seed of the Craobh na Beatha into the empty divot. It slid in perfectly with an audible *click*.

A few moments passed, and nothing happened. I felt the facade I was wearing begin to crack and crumble with each second that ticked away. I was going to lose him. Lose the only person in the entire universe that understood me so effortlessly. Who made me a better person. I'd doomed us both to lifetimes of aching loneliness. I'd—

Then the points of light around the carved doorway lit up, scattering rainbows across the sea cave in a riot of sparkles. The carved rings ground into motion as the door opened back onto the tunnel of light. Sharn pulled me aside to safety, but not before I saw my red thread stretching out toward my cridhe.

I couldn't take my eyes off it. I couldn't breathe past my aching ribs. Couldn't hear or see anything else. Not until my Rhuger was here with me. Not until I was whole again.

"Amelia," Sharn murmured, elbowing me back to the present. "Someone's here."

CHAPTER 29

AMELIA

I turned, wanting to scream and rage at whoever had dared to interrupt my vigil as I waited beyond hope for my cridhe to be returned to me. But then froze. It was Grandma Ruth, disheveled and panting and on the verge of tears. I took a big breath past the ache in my heart and started laughing and crying.

"Grandma!" I cried and bustled over to her where she stood staring at me as if I'd disappear if she blinked. "Grandma, I'm back!"

"And *pregnant*! What the hell happened to you over there, sweetness?" She asked, her voice shaking with confusion and choked emotion. She clutched me to her like she'd drown if she didn't. "Who is this?"

"There's *so much* to explain, but this is Sharn. She's orckin and my best friend." I said as a chiming sound echoed behind us. Relief flooded my system. Grandma Ruth's confusion was adorable. "But there's more. I've got a surprise for you..."

Heartbeats later, Rhuger and Grandpa Thorn stepped out of the tunnel of light. I could *feel it* and I nearly broke down sobbing in relief.

Sharn moved away from us, going to take up a position nearby where she could watch over everyone. I stepped back, out of the way, so my grandmother could see who had just come through the Geata.

"*Thorn...*" Grandma Ruth breathed as she looked past me. Her eyes were wide and unbelieving, her breathing fitful, as tears tumbled over her lashes in twin waterfalls down her weathered cheeks. "*THORN!*" Her voice broke on his name as she stumbled and fell to her knees in the wet sand.

I turned, looking behind me to where my grandfather had just stepped out from the Geata. He looked ridiculous in his fancy outfit and hairdo. He'd been so worried about what she'd thought of how he looked now. But he'd forgotten that he'd washed ashore in a shredded shirt, leather kilt, and boots all those years ago. He'd been an orckin, not a man, but she'd fallen for him anyway, accepted him regardless. She'd never cared what he looked like. She'd only ever cared about who he was as a person.

"*Ruth...*" Grandpa Thorn whispered her name like a prayer he'd kept reciting in his heart every day he'd lived without her. A broken sob escaped my grandmother's throat. That was all it took. My grandfather rushed to her, landing in front of her, scattering damp sand as he scooped her up into his burly arms.

Grandma threw her arms around his shoulders and began bawling. He cradled her head against his shoulder and murmured to her in Teanga Dhubh as he always did to soothe her. Seeing them together like this after decades apart... It was almost as if no time had passed at all.

"I'm so sorry, my dove. I'm here." Grandpa Thorn said thickly, choking on his emotions. Rhuger, having passed through with my grandfather, stood behind me and wrapped me in his arms, laying kisses on the top of my head. Both of us were finally able to relax now that we were together again.

If such a short time apart made me feel so anxious and incomplete, I couldn't fathom what it had been like for my grandparents. Because now that I knew what it meant to be a cridhe pair, I knew that's what they had together. Marks or no marks.

"Don't you *dare* 'my dove' me, you old goat!" She shouted, her green-rimmed glasses askew on her face as she shoved back from my grandfather's chest *hard*. Her voice shook as she glared daggers at him, and for once, he looked a little afraid.

Yep, no time at all.

"You *left me behind!*" Grandma Ruth's face scrunched up, a sob escaping her again as she started beating her fists against his chest. Her voice echoed in the vast sea cave before traveling out over the ocean.

Everyone went silent, even the last of our party who had just come through the gate behind us as the drama unfolded. The pain in her voice was unbearable to hear. Decades' worth of it, summed up in four words.

To Grandpa Thorn's credit, he looked utterly devastated. Reaching up, he caught her tear-stained face in his massive hands, cupping her cheeks and tilting her head up so she had to look at him. She did, but her bottom lip trembled and she looked all the world like an abandoned little girl as he brushed her tears away with his thumbs.

"Ruth I..." Grandpa began but words failed him.

"Oh, I bet you had yourself a whole *slew* of females once you got back! Didn't need *me*, did you?!" She spat, trying to pull away. As if seeing him with such love in his eyes was more than she could stand. Was more painful for all the years he hadn't.

"No."

"What do you mean, *no*?!" She was incredulous, pissed,

affronted. Suddenly desperate to get out of his grasp. But he'd wrangled my grandmother for enough years to know that sometimes she fled rather than face her feelings. So he held on and didn't let her go.

"There has been no one, Ruth." His gaze bored into hers and she finally calmed enough to listen. "I rejected all offers, because... Because there *isn't* anyone else for me but you. There was no one right for me before I met you. And after we met... No one could ever come close to how perfect we are together, my dove. How could I possibly look at another when you are all that I crave?"

"The peaks and the valleys..." Grandma Ruth whispered, leaning her forehead against his with a defeated sigh. He nodded, and they sat like that for a few moments. An understanding settled between them over a phrase I'd never heard them use before.

"Amelia told me you never..." Grandpa Thorn swallowed hard, unable to finish his question.

"Not even once." She looked into his eyes. "Believe it or not, a 7-foot tall orc prince from another galaxy, that arrived here by some magic Bifrost tree shenanigans, who built me my dream farm, is the father of my kid, and makes me come my brains out... is a tough act to follow."

Grandpa Thorn barked a rough laugh even as his face contorted in pain. As if he'd always wondered if she'd found happiness without him. Had started over without him. Because she was human and didn't have the cridhe bond to bind her to him, as it had obviously bound him to her.

"The only regret I have in this life..." Grandpa Thorn murmured, tears slipping from his copper and onyx eyes as he stared at the woman he'd always cherished, even from across the universe. "...is not making sure I held your hand in mine when I entered the Geata."

Grandma Ruth threw her arms around his neck and nearly

tackled him to the ground with the ferocity of her kiss. Grandpa Thorn adjusted his grip and held her so tight it was like he was trying to press their souls back together. Their kiss soon became uncomfortably passionate and then my grandma outright *moaned* and, though I loved that journey for her, that was a little too much for me.

"Ugh, Grandma!" I made a face, attempting to fake being grossed out to break the tension.

I mean, I was more worried they'd start fucking right there than grossed out. There were a lot of alien orcs gathered around behind us, watching on in curiosity as my very human grandmother tackled a giant Rìgh to the wet sand. And I somehow didn't think she wanted half of Talam as witnesses to their, um, *reunion*. Grandma Ruth pushed away from Grandpa Thorn, who looked at her starving and dazed.

"*WHAT*?! That's some attitude coming from my granddaughter, who got herself *knocked up* on another planet!" She looked at me in exasperation.

"Fair." I shrugged and smiled at the two of them. Rhuger shifted his hands to cup my growing baby bump. Mollified, Grandma looked back down her nose at Grandpa.

"I guess I'll keep you." She muttered, and Grandpa Thorn grinned wolfishly.

"Good, because I've got a lot to make up for. And it's been far too long since I've heard you scream my name." Grandma Ruth went beet red in the face as Grandpa Thorn scooped her up in his arms and stalked off toward the entrance of the sea cave. Before he turned the sharp bend in the cave's tunnel, he called over his shoulder, "Take your time setting up in the barn! And don't come to the house until sunset!"

"EWWWWW!!!" I cried after them between my cupped hands. Their laughter filtered back out into the cavern, and I grinned. Looking up at my cridhe and the warm smile that lit his perfect face, I was beyond grateful that I had him here with me. "Shall we get started?"

"After you, Banrigh mo cridhe." He murmured and placed a swift, chaste kiss on my lips.

We knew that if we kissed like we wanted, full and lingering and passionate, we wouldn't be leaving the cave for a long, long time. Being separated, though only for a short time, had left us both shaken. And horny. I could smell the shift in him, feel the possessiveness in his hands where they clutched me to him.

But we had so much work to do until we could assuage the fear that had hung over us ever since we'd first concocted this wild plan of ours to bring the orckin and the humans together.

Oh, we were going to fuck later all right. And suddenly I couldn't get the image of Rhuger pinning me to the floor of one of the hobbit holes and railing the hell out of me out of my head. I was going to spoil the hell out of this orc with all the love I planned on giving him. From this breath to my last.

CHAPTER 30*

AMELIA

After being on Talam for so long, being back on Earth made it all feel like a fever dream. Except for the fact, my soon-to-be *husband* was out digging post holes with the others to replace Grandma Ruth's rickety fences. I smiled to myself as I pulled over another box that I'd stashed in my rental car when I'd arrived on Orc Rock Farm months ago. Grandma Ruth had brought everything inside and returned the car for me, bless her, and I was on light duty around the farm. What with being so pregnant it was a wonder I could walk at all.

As I was going through some of my stuff from the box, I started coming across photos of my ex-husband and me. My gut twisted, and I shook my head as I yanked over the paper shredder. I threw down with big cunt energy and shredded them like old CVS receipts. Those were memories I'd like to not revisit ever again.

I had a new life, new future, new love—my one genuine match in all the universe. I would never look back again. And I'd be a good past self to my future self and get rid of the gotdamn evidence. Let the memories slowly wither and die in the blazing light of my future without triggering objects to stumble over and rain on my parade.

Watching the face of my ex-husband slide into the shredder, I felt a sense of peace wash over me. The divorce had been finalized. I'd signed the paperwork the day we'd gotten back from Talam as they'd been waiting for me. The marital property was divided and my cats were running around Orc Rock Farm as if they'd always lived there. Terrorizing the pygmy goats and chickens and keeping the rodent population under control.

We'd been back for a few months now. The orckin had brought a chest of tiny neamhnaid pearls and gold as a gift to Grandma Ruth and as a thank you for allowing the orckin to stay and try to find their cridhes. Grandma Ruth was no dummy, though she stuttered like an old engine when they'd set the chest at her feet in the farmhouse and opened the lid. She'd accepted the gift with complete bafflement.

As she'd promised all those years ago, she called the number on that weirdly heavy card given to her by the FBI agent who'd helped her back when Grandpa Thorn had first arrived on Earth. Less than 24 hours later, a tall, slim, distinguished gentleman in horn-rimmed glasses and a suit had knocked on the farmhouse door, newly painted haint-blue thanks to the orckin. They'd *insisted* on working on the farm, updating it, and fixing things to earn their keep. Again, my grandma wasn't a dummy and let them have at it.

He introduced himself as Agent Forrest when I'd opened the door.

"And here I thought you'd croaked. What are you still doing working for the FBI? Shouldn't you be in retirement by now?" Grandma Ruth had said when she'd come to the door with Grandpa Thorn not far behind.

"Good to see you too, Mrs. Dellor. I came out of retirement just for you." He had replied with wry humor.

The three of them had gone into the library and shut the door, which surprised me, as most of our discussions had been open. A few hours later they'd come out and Agent Forrest had nodded respectfully before leaving as quietly as he'd appeared. And it was as if the calm eddies of his leaving had summoned a tempest of change.

An appraiser had arrived to look at the pearls and gold given to my grandma. They then transferred their above-market evaluation price over to her account. Grandma Ruth had checked her bank app on her phone and deadass fainted.

Then a gentleman at a driveway specialty place had arrived with a metric shit-ton of gravel and a notice from the FBI to re-gravel the drive. Grandma had waved the guy on to do what he'd come to do as I'd looked at her like she was short a few marbles. But as I said, she was no dummy and wasn't about to look a gift horse in the mouth.

Once the driveway had been replaced, Grandma Ruth had announced at dinner out at the Green Dragon outdoor dining area, that the orcs here could start building cottages. Not the little hobbit holes used for the bed-and-breakfast, but full-blown cottages they could live in, and if they found their cridhes, stay in.

She pulled Rhuger and me into her plan one night when she'd called us into the library with Grandpa Thorn.

"We're going to create our own mini town and matchmaking service." Grandma Ruth had announced once we were all seated on the tufted leather sofa, The Notorious B.I.G. presiding over the council from the painting over the fireplace. Grandma loved her gangster rap.

"We're *what*, now?" I asked. We'd planned most of this, but Grandma Ruth had been against it at first. Worried that it would shatter her dream farm and what family time she could have with us.

"We're going to create our own little orckin settlement here on Orc Rock Farm. The money from the sale of the pearls and gold is more than enough to fund it. Thorn explained how orckin males make homes of their own for their mates." She explained. "An official one, as Clan Oc'Chance. It will keep them all busy as we try to figure out the ins and outs of the matchmaking service you guys suggested. Plus, Agent Forrest is on board with the concept and will come over regularly to see how things are going."

"That's a solid plan, Banrigh Ruth," Rhuger said as he stared into the flames. "We will need to further fix up the property and repurpose the barn as a barracks."

So far, the males and Iolaire'lasair had strung up hammocks in the barn to sleep in, taking turns using the showers in the farmhouse and the small communal bathroom for the hobbit holes. It was a functioning setup, but not sustainable long-term.

"Perfect! Well, we'll need to make a call to the town to get the permits. Hopefully that Tolkien fan is still approving them and is not retired. Maybe we can bribe them with more free stays. And you, dear husband, are going to need to call over to the Sherrif's department to talk to Sanchez to see if his family still runs that supply place." Grandma Ruth said, looking up at my grandfather's bemused expression.

"That's an easy task. He'll shit bricks when he hears my voice." Grandpa Thorn replied with a chuckle. He'd been best friends with Sherrif Sanchez and the retired Sherrif Brighton before he'd left. They knew him for who and what he was and accepted him all the same.

With that, we began the process of gaining permits, blueprints, supplies, and contractors for what the orcs weren't able to do. Like electrical. Gosh, having them see what a vacuum cleaner could do was hilarity incarnate. All modern appliances had been a shock to their system, especially the TV. They'd picked the damned flatscreen up off the wall and were looking for the people in the movie we were watching *inside the walls*, knocking on the plaster and asking for them to speak so they could rescue them.

I hadn't forgotten what Sharn had mentioned when she'd come through the Geata with me. She could see the red threads of fate and who they attached to when they went through the Geata. Or were near it. And I had a sneaking suspicion she'd seen her own.

So when she'd suddenly blurted out a request to build a cottage, Grandma Ruth and I had shared one look and agreed. Sharn had been baffled and went beet red in the face. What she was asking, I knew from my studies at Clach-tholl and my days in Baile Coille, that it wasn't something females did. Request to build a home. That was something the male orckin did to prepare for, impress, and secure a female mate. To prove that he was worthy of being a partner and father.

None of the males argued with her right to do so, which *did* surprise me. They accepted her as one of their own and a few had even offered to help her with the normal assisted tasks of beam raising and digging. I'd cried more than once over how wonderful the males were being about Sharn's Tog Taigh, or her orckin urge to build a home. In orckin lore, it was often an indicator of an orckin finding, or about to find, their cridhe.

Rhuger assured me that in the eyes of the males, Sharn had more than earned her right to build a home and find a mate, she'd also attained permission from the Oc'Chance clan leaders-Grandma Ruth and I- and possessed that deep-seated urge to build a home. Something that evidently couldn't be denied once inspired in the orckin.

It was why acts of service to the clan were so important. To weed out those with the true Tog Taigh and those who weren't dedicated. Only an orckin truly in the clutches of the Tog Taigh would put themselves through so much just to build a home for a mate that they *might* win. Though with the lapse of cridhe pairs, the acts of service to the clan were lowered to encourage folk to find a mate and start a family, even if they weren't cridhe.

But *now*. With Rhuger and I as cridhe, and even Grandma Ruth and Grandpa Thorn declared cridhe after they'd made a brief trip to Talam and their marks had appeared on their chests, the old bars of excellence were raised once more. Cridhe mates were officially back and humans were the key to bringing it back fully.

What was going to be tricky, and *highly* risky, was how to introduce humans to orckin, and orckin to humans, without it all exploding in our faces. Which is where Agent Forrest came in. It was all still a work in progress, but progress was being made. He had protocols on top of protocols to the point where my eyes bled. Evidently, this integration had been planned to the nth degree by the government *just in case*.

Lifting the now empty cardboard box, I waddled my way toward the front door to take it out to the recycling bin. My mind was full, thoughts and ideas and concepts tumbling around in my head like rocks in a dryer. Hoping that something would stick and I'd be able to see a path forward through all of this like I had that day in the throne room after beheading Orok. So I didn't hear the vehicle as it crunched its way down the fresh gravel drive. Didn't register the vehicle getting thrown into park as I opened the recycling bin and ripped the tape off of the bottom of the box so I could take it apart and stuff it into the already overflowing bin.

"Hello, Amelia." A voice I thought I'd left far behind me called. I froze.

I turned my head, the Pacific winds whipping my wavy brown hair around my face, obscuring the driveway. Almost like saying 'No, sis, don't look back.'

But I looked back. A slender man, just a few inches taller than me, closed the door to a big, black, shiny pickup truck. He wore a worn baseball cap for a team I couldn't care less about, cargo shorts, and a brewery t-shirt. His beard and fingers were stained a rusty orange from the sheer volume of nicotine he insisted on inhaling on the regular.

My ex-husband looked just the same as he did the day I left him.

CHAPTER 31*

AMELIA

It felt like ice was oozing into my veins, like my chest was freezing and cracking even as my heart beat so fast and light I thought I'd pass out if I couldn't control it. Flashes of the past flew behind my eyelids each time I blinked and fear—cold, slick, slippery fear—began worming its way into my limbs.

"Adam," I replied automatically. A cold, dead bite to my words. I knew my PTSD was acting up. I knew he legally shouldn't have been here. That he had no right to hunt me down. How he'd found me, I had no clue.

"Took a while to find you." He said, coming to a stop a ways from me, his voice accusatory.

"That was kind of the point, Adam," I said flatly. His face screwed up. He did not like this. "What are you doing here?"

"I came to see how you were doing. Figured I'd come to get you and bring you home." He shrugged his shoulders.

"And I would come back with you because...?" I asked.

"You're my wife."

"Ex-wife, Adam. We're divorced. The paperwork was finalized. Legally, you're not even supposed to be anywhere near me," I said, voice as sharp as steel. How I managed to keep any semblance of composure was a blasted miracle. Because inside I was one mouse fart from falling apart, from having the worst meltdown of my life.

"It was a mistake. I'm not sure what happened, but if you'd just come home, we can figure this out." He said, taking a step forward and reaching out a hand.

"You know what happened," I whispered, as I stepped back instinctively.

"Amelia I— " The door to the side of my grandmother's house banged open and Rhuger's words died in his mouth as he took in my defensive stance and the ex-cinder block who'd tried to drown me in misery.

Rhuger's presence changed immediately from loose and open to predatory. His gait had that smooth, elegant swagger to it that tigers had as he prowled toward me. His gaze was riveted on Adam, fierce and intent. And the fool had the audacity to take a step closer to me as if staking his claim.

"I wouldn't do that if I were you." Rhuger rumbled, low and smooth. His tone was almost sensual, like that of a lover or the one who was about to end you. Seeing that Rhuger, whilst looking human, was still a giant, ripped, shirtless man in a kilt, I wondered absently which way my ex-husband would take Rhuger's tone.

"Who the hell do you think you are?" Adam asked, trying his best to look intimidating and... well... failing. The verdict was still out on how Adam, a cis het white guy, would take Rhuger's tone, accent, and appearance.

"I'm Amelia's husband."

The Pacific winds paused as the world around us held its breath. We were about to have ourselves another little game of power play. Only this time, there was *no* doubt who the victor would be. Rhuger wasn't technically my husband *yet,* but stating that he was—and he *was,* in all the ways that mattered—acted like a shield between my abuser and me. As he'd already shielded me in so many countless ways. The love I had for him bloomed in my chest, so bright and warm, scattering the shadows of the pall my ex-husband cast. It triggered my baby hormones, and I simultaneously wanted to cry and push Rhuger down and ride him right then and there.

Adam scoffed at Rhuger in disbelief. Turned to look at me, noted my raised eyebrows as I shut the lid to the recycling bin, and frowned. He looked between us a few times before rallying himself.

"You have got to be kidding." Adam bit out.

"Why on Earth would I kid about something as precious and holy as that?" Rhuger asked in that dark tone again. Bless my cridhe for saying *Earth* instead of *Talam.* Adam shivered, and I got the answer to my question.

My mind blanked as all the puzzle pieces that had been before me, that had confounded me and confused me about my ex-husband over the years, one by one, clicked together. The entire picture came sharply into focus so fast it hurt. Hurt in a visceral way that would have had me screaming had I not spent years with Adam forcing me to quiet. I felt that mask slip into place. Another shield that had kept me safe even as that tiny, vicious part of me roared.

Rhuger scented the change in me and closed the last bit of distance between us. He gently grasped my chin and raised my face to meet his. I could swear lightning flickered in his storm-grey eyes. So different with the white sclera, his irises darker, but still they were the eyes of the male I loved.

Calm slid through me like quicksilver as I breathed in the scent of my cridhe. That sinful pomegranate, leather, and spice. I was not alone. I'd never be alone again. And I wouldn't be facing Adam by myself. I had the most amazing male at my side who protected both my heart and my body. Adam could not touch me.

He could not touch me.

Grammie Ruksala's small prophecy came back to me then. Like a small stone dropping into water, sinking down. Sinking into my bones.

He could not hurt me.

Rhuger wouldn't let him.

And neither would I.

Something snapped inside of me. Some chain that had held down that shadow part of me, the vicious part that had whispered strength and comfort during the dark nights of my soul when I was in Adam's clutches, when things were at their worst, broke. The chains fell away, and the shadow unfurled. Igniting in my breast with a bestial war cry as blazing wings burned away the frigid fear.

"Because *I'm* her husband!" Adam barked, and I flinched despite myself. Rhuger slid his gaze indolently to my ex-husband and *tsk*ed at him. He was about to say something when I spoke.

"You really think..." I began, the words falling from my lips like melted slag as I turned to stare wide-eyed at the man who'd spent so many years breaking me down. "That I would give up Rhuger for *you*?"

A tic worked in Adam's jaw as his tobacco-stained hands clenched into fists at his sides. I knew this expression well. One of distaste and irritation, bordering on anger, that would result in small cruel punishments stacked one on top of the other until I suffocated. Or perhaps another big one that would ruin me.

But my months on Talam had strengthened me far beyond what I thought was possible. I'd faced alien monsters, enormous felines, carnivorous giant mollusks, battle-hardened orckin, and one cruel despot that mirrored my ex-husband in more ways than I could have ever imagined.

So when I stared into the eyes of the man who had haunted me long before I ever left him behind, all of those memories just... fell away. The darkness of the memories he'd chained me with burned to ash. Those things had happened to me, and they were awful, but I was far beyond their reach now. Far beyond *his* reach.

As the ichor of all of those cruelties that had stained my heart and soul and body all these years, slid down the proverbial drain, all that was left was the sheer ridiculousness of this whole situation. Which slapped me upside the head so hard I felt my marbles rattle.

Because next to my glorious cridhe, my ex-husband looked like a malformed muppet.

Yes, that's right. I just called this grown-ass man a malformed, ratty-ass, pilling, looked like he crawled out of Oscar the Grouch's trash can, sticky like he got used as a fleshlight passed around at a frat party, deep-throated an ashtray at a tobacco convention, shoulda been sucking on a brewer's nutsack, unraveling at the seams, couldn't find the clit if there was a billboard *MUPPET*.

Next to the ex-muppet my tall, regal, fist-bitingly hot, hung like a horse, muscles for days, devil may care, badass, randy, flirty, thicker than a snicker, panty-ripper romance cover model, warrior *king* who treated me like a goddess, teddy bear of a mate who fucked me like he'd die if he didn't, stood like a pillar of secure, emotionally intelligent masculinity.

This wad of used play-doh thought I'd go back to *him*? What a joke!

I couldn't help it. I cackled. Then slapped a hand over my mouth as I shook, bending double in my mirth. Gasping for breath, I looked up at my mate, who looked alarmed, scared, and amused all at once, and flicked my finger between him and the ex-muppet.

"He-he thinks he's better than you." I wheezed. "Thinks I'll go back to him."

"You're mine." Rhuger drawled, a slow, lazy smile curling his luscious mouth. His simple possessiveness was like a warm blanket.

"I know!" I tried catching my breath and ended up laughing all over again. "He thinks... He thinks I'd willingly go back to him after having all of this!" I Vanna White motioned at all seven feet plus of perfection that was my mate. Rhuger preened and puffed out his chest a little at the praise, the adorable dork.

I could literally hear Adam's teeth grinding in the background. But for the first time? I wasn't afraid at all.

Rhuger, understanding that I was now okay, calmly stepped behind me and wrapped his arms around my waist. He bent his head to nuzzle against the exposed skin of my shoulder. While I chuckled and fanned my face, attempting to get my mirth under control, he rumbled contentedly against my neck like a purring nocrys.

"What a fucking *simp*." Adam spat in disgust, looking at Rhuger. Attempting, in his small dick energy way, to tear down my mate. My laughter died as my lip curled in disgust.

"What's a simp?" Rhuger mumbled, sounding slightly drunk off of my scent. He'd been too preoccupied to note Adam's tone.

"A man who's considered submissive by other men because he pays a woman too much attention." I supplied, rolling my eyes. Rhuger just laughed, the sound of it like pure velvet against my skin. His large, warm hands slid down my sides and spanned my baby bump. Adam went stock still at the sight.

"Och. What kind of man refuses to pay attention to his woman and denies her what she craves?" Rhuger snorted and I could feel his lips trailing open-mouthed kisses along my shoulder and neck, likely to piss off Adam. But my baby hormones were all over the place right now. Rhuger was making me incredibly horny, and I was supremely irritated that Adam refused to fuck off somewhere away from me so I could drag my cridhe off and mount him.

"You're pregnant," Adam said in a monotone.

I was. *Thanks*, Captain Obvious. I *never* would have known.

I was currently around six months pregnant and had a few more months to go. Grandma Ruth's pregnancy with my mother Esther had only been eight months instead of the usual human nine. We weren't sure where I'd fall between the various time periods given my partial orckin heritage, so we were all currently on baby alert. Ready to dash to the hospital the moment the little womb nugget decided to come out.

Thankfully, Agent Forrest had gotten me an OBGYN who didn't ask too many questions. She was a lovely Latina woman named Alma Montes who used a wheelchair. She was quick-witted, gentle, and completely dedicated to her patients. I knew my pregnancy was in excellent hands the moment I'd met her. When I looked into her rich brown eyes, I could feel that thread, a strong one, that was passed down her line from mother to daughter. She had a gift for healing, for helping people bring their babies into the world. This knowing had shaken me somewhat, and I started to wonder if I had inherited some of Grammie Ruksala's sight.

"You're just realizing this now? How unobservant." Rhuger's voice was dark and spoke not only of the hours spent making our baby, but also of how he'd make Adam hurt if I let him. A bright flush stained Adam's cheeks as he stood there flustered.

I mean, I couldn't blame him. Rhuger's voice was sexy as fuck.

If I was completely honest, I'd fallen in love with Rhuger the first time he'd opened his mouth and said, "What's a lovely pearl like you doing in a dump like this?" all those months ago when he'd found me in the cave beneath the Craobh na Beatha.

"Yes, I'm pregnant, Adam. What of it?" I asked, suddenly tired and irritated and just itching to kick him in the balls. I wasn't sure if it was my time on Talam, becoming Banrigh, or being pregnant that made me so fiesty instead of demure, but I couldn't be bothered to care anymore.

I'd already cared more than enough.

"What if it's *mine*, Amelia? You can't keep me from my own child!" Adam roared. I flinched, my body remembering the trauma even though my mind and heart were at peace.

"It's not yours. It's mine." Rhuger grinned like the predator he was and held me tighter. Letting me know he saw and understood and was here for me. "Your weak seed never took, did it?"

Adam looked like he was about ready to boil over. His face went from pale to puce, and his eyes bulged in his head. "So you jumped the first dick you came across, you slut?"

"Well, when that dick is *his* dick, then hell yes," I replied, trying not to laugh again. This encounter was a doozy, making my emotions run around like a toddler high on sugar, waving sparklers in the air. I was gonna take a *good* long nap when this was over. Once Rhuger gave me a good railing, of course. This shit was *exhausting*.

Staring at the man I'd once called husband, I sighed heavily and rolled up my proverbial sleeves. It was time to get this all over with. I had a mate to fuck, a growing baby to feed, and a nap to take. All were things far more worthy of my time than this shit show.

"Rhuger is the father, no one else. I'm not going to take any more of your controlling shit, Adam. You *raped* me. You *abused* me.

You were a shit lover and an even worse partner. I *left* you." I took a commanding step forward, pulling gently from Rhuger's loving arms, head held high, and for once? Adam was the one who took a step back. "If you come here again. If you come to any of my friends or family again. I will *ruin* you."

"You're *threatening* me, you bitch?!" Adam screamed, the cords and tendons in his neck standing out as tobacco-tainted spittle filled the air between us.

"It's no threat. It's a promise. Now, get off my land." I growled, and he jumped at the sound, shocked.

Just then, the orcs—looking all the world like a band of himbos and herbos about to do a charity calendar photo shoot—came out from the trees, behind the house, and even from the hills towards the ocean. Almost as if I'd summed them like magic. Kagan actually snuck up behind Adam on cat-like feet and when he walked around him, his face was mere inches away in a fierce scowl, making Adam startle. Looking all the world like a very tall Tormund Giantsbane with his wild eyes and fiery auburn hair.

"What, you've got yourself a little harem here, you whore?" Adam spat, then let out a dark, evil bark. Building me up to be such a villain in his own twisted head. "Fucking all of them? How the hell are you even supposed to *guess* who the bastard in your belly belongs to?"

"Talk about my granddaughter like that again, and I'll rip your head from your body with my bare hands." Growled my Grandpa Thorn, who had just stomped out the side door like Paul Bunyan, cracking his knuckles.

Rhuger came to stand beside me, eyes alight and a feral grin on his face, his fingers twining with mine, facing down Adam with me as a unified front. I knew if I even *looked* at my cridhe, and granted him permission, he'd take his time ending Adam. And then add what was left of him as decoration on the Traitor Tree back in Baile Coille as he'd promised. Adam finally had the good sense to look around him and realize he was out-manned—in far more ways than one—fifteen to one. And each male towered over him by at least a foot. Even most of the females did too.

"I thought you said your grandfather was dead." Adam snapped, eyes flicking between the band of orcs who were grinning, flexing, and generally showing off to intimidate the ex-muppet.

"Surprise!" was all I said, throwing my arms wide.

CHAPTER 32*

AMELIA

Adam stood there staring at me for a good minute before he spoke. "Marrying you was the worst mistake of my life. You got sick and then you did jack shit to get better. All you did was cry and complain. You would freak out over *nothing* while I took care of everything and *paid* for everything. Hell, you barely brought in any money with your little *art career*. And then? *And then you ruined me in the divorce!*"

And there it was.

I had gotten sick. It wasn't something I talked about because I'd always been so healthy. I'd gotten so anxiety riddled, so depressed, so panicky, that I had made myself sick. I hadn't realized until later that I was autistic and that what I was experiencing was normal when put under so much stress and mental abuse. That the exhaustion and the physical pain came from what I was surviving.

Talam had breathed new life into me. Without the constant oppression, with the allowance to be fully myself and be accepted for it. All of that had allowed the stunted tree of my being to start growing and blooming again.

"I got sick, and *I took care of myself* while you ignored me. Your phone, your TV, hell, even the *lawn* was more important than me!" I bit out, taking another step forward. And then another. "You never really saw me as a person. Just as a means to an end. You made this pretty little script you wanted me to play a part in. Only allowing me value if I brought in money, if I behaved how you wanted me to. And when I didn't fit, didn't do as you wanted, you punished me for it."

"Who would want to spend their time with *you* when you had it so *easy* and you just decided to be *lazy*? How do you think it felt for me to have a wife who couldn't work and couldn't even be a *housewife*, right? You were an EMBARRASSMENT!" He roared.

I took another step forward and tilted my head back as I laughed. The rough bark of it as the chuckles fell from my mouth sounded right out of a villain origin story. If this was mine, I was content with that.

"I'm not a *Build-A-Bitch*, I'm a person, you *expired coupon*. You got off on me being helpless. On being sick and under your thumb. You pinned me right where you wanted me and tried shoving my infinite being into a finite space, into a box *you* created." I took another step forward as I slipped my hands into my cardigan pockets. Easily finding what I needed. "You wanted me to be the vast, dark expanse of space so that *you* could shine like a bright star. So that people would look at you and think so highly of you for having such a sad, sick, helpless wife that you *took care of*. And the divorce may have been your ruin, but it was just payment for you laying your hands on me, for *forcing* yourself on me."

I stopped a foot from him where he'd bumped into the front of his truck, and stared deep into the eyes that I once adored. Let him stare into mine and see that I had looked so long into the dark of my own soul that I saw the darkness blink back. Had found strength in it and made friends with it. He may have shredded my wings, but he forgot I still had talons. And a cridhe who would catch me if I faltered and fell.

"Come near me again and I'll skin your shaft and use your sac as a coin purse," I whispered, remembering Grammie Ruksala's threat to Rhuger when she'd made him my bodyguard. I pulled the pruning knife from my cardigan pocket that I'd been using to open boxes. With a deft flick of my wrist, I flipped the pruning knife in my palm and pressed the tip of the knife into his... well... *tip*.

"You wouldn't dare..." Adam swallowed, breaking out into a cold sweat.

I tilted my head back and laughed, deep and heartless. I let everything fall away from my face except the deadly certainty that I could, and would, follow through on my threat. The smile that then split my face wasn't exactly sane. *Definitely* villain origin story material.

"You keep talking shit about my unborn child, my husband, and my kin, and I'll show you *real* pain. I'll cut you three ways. Long, deep, and continuous. If you're lucky, I'll just boil your teeth and not leave you with meat mops for hands." I twisted the knife, and he hissed, panic lighting his features. "You've always thought me weak, yet these hips will birth untold generations, so it would be a simple thing to crush your skull between my thighs."

"You're a monster." He whispered as a bead of sweat dripped down from under his faded baseball cap along his temple.

"And you made me this way," I replied. A few moments passed before I rolled my eyes, yanked the knife away, and turned on my heel. "Take out the trash, will you, guys?"

I waved over my shoulder and the surrounding orcs grinned as one before stalking toward my ex-husband. Rhuger took me in his arms and kissed me deeply before grinning like a madman over my shoulder and gripping my ass hard with both hands. Obviously showing Adam I was his. I blushed at his claiming me despite myself.

Adam was shouting something behind me. I turned in Rhuger's arms and his hands shifted to gently curve around my baby bump, their favorite place to rest when we stood together like this. Kagan was standing on top of a hog-tied Adam while my grandfather, the only orc with any driving experience, got behind the wheel of Adam's truck. The others were shouting and jeering as they hauled a shrilly hollering Adam onto the hood of the truck like a hunting trophy. Adam kept shooting me death glares before Kagan snatched his face and yanked it to meet his.

"If ye don't shut yer yap and stop lookin' at the lady, I'll be cuttin' out yer eyes and tongue, och?" Kagan grinned. Adam shut the fuck up—the first smart thing he'd done in years.

"We'll be back soon, my little chestnut. Gonna go leave him in the woods for a mountain lion to find him." Grandpa's grin was wicked as Adam outright *pissed* himself all over the hood of his own truck.

"Och, what weak prey you had for a husband." Rhuger growled into my ear.

I froze as Grandpa backed up down the long driveway. The orcs either piled into the bed of the pickup, whooping and hollering, or followed the truck on foot.

"I could have snapped him in half." I whispered. It was true, I was stronger and trained to fight. If Adam had come at me directly, it wouldn't have been a contest. When Rhuger grunted his agreement, I continued. "He killed me in inches, over years. I didn't know what he'd done to me until it was too late. I'd trusted him not to harm me like that. All I could think of was surviving."

I could feel Rhuger's gaze boring into me. Unable to look at him, I just kept looking forward as the orcs disappeared around a bend in the drive. His arms came up to wrap around my chest as he waited quietly for me to continue.

"It was... almost like every one of my foremothers whispered to me at once. Telling me that if I didn't move, it wouldn't hurt so bad. That if I didn't fight, maybe... maybe he'd let me live."

The words slipped from my lips and were carried away on the breeze. A deep truth that resonated back through time to every woman of my line who had survived, just as I had. Who had continued and had children and, hopefully, lived a good life. Now it was my turn. And I planned on making them all proud.

"There's nothing dishonorable about surviving, pearl. The only one shame and dishonor should fall on is him." I looked up at him with glassy eyes. "You are brave to survive. It takes strength and bravery and will to endure what you did. To keep your head while so afraid and in pain. I do not think any less of you for what you've endured. I am proud of you."

I nodded, tears slipping free. He wiped them away with his thumbs. Leaning up, I gave him a soft kiss. His hand wrapped up to cup my cheek and I melted against him, his strength cradling my softness. When our lips parted, a thought struck me.

"Didn't you once claim you'd hunt Adam down and take him back to Baile Coille to face orckin justice?" I asked, looking up at my cridhe.

"Och, I did." He smiled down at me and laid a brief kiss on my forehead. "But you're a Banrigh in your own right. You faced him with incredible valor and you won. You proved to him, to us, and, most importantly, to yourself that he's so far beneath you, that he isn't worth the effort."

I couldn't help the tears that threatened to spill over my lashes as he gently tucked some wisps of my sea breeze-tousled hair behind my rounded human ear. He looked at me with so much tenderness it hurt. The stark difference between the man I'd left behind and the orckin cridhe I'd found across the universe was incomparable.

How was he just so damned perfect? How did he always know what I needed? My heart felt like it was spilling over as tears finally slid down my cheeks again.

"I am so incredibly proud of you, my pearl." He whispered as he brushed away my tears. "I know it wasn't easy... I *do* wish I could kill him, though," Rhuger said with a dramatic sigh. "I'd make sure he was *well looked after* before that, *I promise*."

"As we've discussed, things like that are illegal here." I chuckled.

"So you've said." He said with dry distaste before looking down at me from the corner of his eye. "If you ever change your mind... we could always drag him back to Talam and—"

"Is that piece of shit gone?" My Grandmother Ruth's voice came out from the kitchen door.

"Yes, Banrigh Ruth," Rhuger called over his shoulder.

"Just Ruth or Grandma, you weirdo. How many times do I have to tell you?" Grandma Ruth stomped out of the kitchen with a bloody butcher knife and my brows rose. She saw my expression and huffed in exasperation. "What? I'm making roast chicken for over twenty people, Eley. Granted, I'd have used it on that prick of an ex-husband of yours if the guys hadn't dragged him off."

"Prick?" Rhuger asked, looking between Grandma and me. Grandma's grin was wicked as she held up her free hand and wiggled her arthritic pinky at him.

"Tiny penis." She hissed.

Rhuger tipped his head back and roared his laughter.

"Did I hear someone say roast chicken?" Called a voice, we all turned to see Sharn swagger back down the gravel drive, a hoe over one shoulder, looking all the world like a ranch hand in her jeans, white t-shirt, boots, and cowboy hat.

"I'm makin' roast chicken to celebrate y'all takin' out the trash!" Grandma Ruth hollered and Sharn whooped—pumping a fist in the air.

"What happened? Why aren't you with them?" Rhuger asked his friend as she drew close.

"Rìgh Thorn asked me to come back and let you know they're going to run Adam to the authorities as he's here illegally. Said something about a 'restraining order'?" She asked, looking at me.

"It's a legal document provided by the government stating that the person who gets the restraining order against them cannot contact or be within a certain distance from the person who requested it," I explained. "It helps. Especially in cases like mine."

"I see." Sharn's lovely face grew thoughtful. "What will happen to him?"

"At worst, they'll send him to jail for a while."

"Not a harsh enough punishment," Sharn said, eyes hard.

"No, but if Grandpa drops him off to the Sherriff, they'll be aware and will be on alert to help protect me," I said. "Not the most effective thing ever, but it's something."

"Well, Amelia, you don't have to worry about him with us around. Oc'Chance protects its own." She declared with a cheeky grin. I couldn't help but smile back as I leaned into Rhuger's embrace, feeling safe, loved, and accepted amongst these spicy Scottish-sounding space orcs who'd so quickly become my family.

EPILOGUE

AMELIA

Later that evening, Rhuger and I had just crawled into bed after he helped me take a shower. Even doing something as mundane as washing my own feet and coochie had become something I couldn't manage. And he'd *enthusiastically* helped. Ensuring I was clean *everywhere* and enjoying how I twitched and my breasts leaked for him as I came. He'd needed to help me wobble to our bed

"So, cridhe, what was it you said to that gaiseadh that made him look like he was going to piss his pants?" Rhuger grinned down at me, his expressive eyebrows and lidded eyes sparking with mischief.

"What?" I asked, dazzled. My cridhe was just as stunning as a human as he was an orckin. I hadn't adjusted to this same yet different flavor of sexy so it still caught me off guard fairly often.

"After you mentioned boiling his teeth? Not sure what that meant."

"Oh, it's not important," I said quickly before thinking back. I didn't really need to tell him about *that* torture method I'd devised in my head over the years. "I told him 'These hips will birth untold generations. It would be a simple thing to crush your skull between my thighs.'"

"Och! Yes..." His look became hungry as he skimmed his hands down against my hips, skimming my baby bump. It still threw me for a loop that he found me attractive when I felt like a whale. "Do you think you could crush my skull between your thighs?"

His voice was deep, rumbling, and velvet all at once. Heat pooled in my core so fast my pussy clenched at nothing. I swallowed, thighs squeezing together and his hungry look turned predatory as he caught my scent.

"Pretty sure we've tested this theory. A *lot*. And that's why I'm pregnant. Not to mention you're pretty hard-headed." I told him a little breathlessly.

"Och, well maybe I'm not making my mate orgasm hard enough. If I die, I would choose it to be by a good skull-crushing for making my mate come so hard with my tongue." He took the opportunity to lick his sharp teeth with his wicked black tongue.

"You mean *when* you die." I laughed, trying hard not to completely lose all sense at the memory of what those teeth and lips and tongue could do to a girl. To *me*.

"If I were to die *before* you. I plan on waiting until we're both old and grey. I'll wait until you go first and once you breathe your last, I'll breathe mine." He said it so easily like it was the simplest thing in the world.

"What?" I croaked, tears flooding my vision.

"I want to go after you, so you're never alone." He told me, wiping the tears from my eyes.

"Cheeky blighter," I whispered, and he chuckled as his lips met mine.

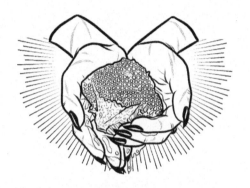

Turn the page for an excerpt from:

SHARN'S HONEYBEE

ORC MATCHED 2.0

Coming 2023!

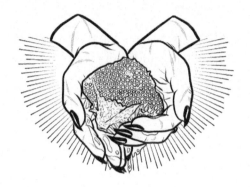

SHARN

My eyes adjusted to the dim light within the cave at the base of the Craobh na Beatha. The enormous tree that sat on the border of the Oc'Turin and Oc'Dellor lands. It dwarfed every tree in Noc'Tal Forest. Clouds snagged on the uppermost boughs as its six white wings fluttered and stretched in the light of Talam's twin suns.

Nestled within the Craobh na Beatha's roots, shafts of buttery afternoon sunlight pierced through holes overhead, spilling onto the hard-packed earthen floor of the cave and the carved gate along the back wall. The Geata depicted the Craobh na Beatha in minute detail. Seventeen points of light glinted along the carving that spread from the ceiling and floor. One of them glowed pink.

This was a holy place. One I'd rarely been in. And one that always made me nervous.

"It's empty," I called over my shoulder as I grasped my spear tightly in my fist.

"Och, we'll start bringing everyone in now," Rhuger announced before heading back out.

So much had changed in such a short time. My friend Rhuger was now Rìgh, or king, of the Oc'Turin. Amelia, the strange human with orckin ancestry who'd come through the Geata, was his cridhe, his soul-bound partner. His Banrìgh. His queen.

Amelia had brought much change and hope to our people. The orckin had been slowly dying out from plague, monsters, and war. Now, all five clans were working together because of her and the hope of finding our own cridhe mates amongst the humans.

"Oof!" Amelia's voice echoed within the cave.

"Careful, pearl." Rhuger admonished as they came around the corner. He had his arm protectively around her, his broad hand curving around her waist and baby bump. Her cridhe marks, twin to those spanning Rhuger's chest, showed above the neckline of her tunic.

"I'm fine!" She groused at her mate and I smiled.

"He's allowed to be protective of you," I called.

"He can be protective without making me feel incapable!" She snarked, and I laughed. Amelia was a wonderful person. It was an honor to call her my friend. "Honestly, Sharn, I don't know how you put up with him all these years!"

"With great annoyance," I said dryly. Rhuger scowled at me and I flashed him a grin.

"Are you doing okay? Today's gotta be nerve-wracking for you." Amelia whispered as they passed, and I gave her a small nod.

Today was a test of sorts. I was the first captain of the Iolaire'lasair, a band of all-female warriors, in centuries. They had chosen me via a tournament to lead the group of females picked from all clans. Our mission was to protect the Geata and those who would pass through it. And it was my duty to protect the clan leaders as we attempted to fix the Geata.

Rìgh Thorn of the Oc'Dellor, Amelia's grandfather, came in next. He was nervous as a green youth and kept rubbing his palms against his tunic. His human mate, Banrigh Ruth, was on the other side of the Geata. He hadn't seen her in over twenty cycles. I hoped for his sake, for all of our sakes, that this would work.

Behind him came the rest of the group. A few members of the Iolaire'lasair, and a group of three males from each clan, totaling fifteen. Each chosen by the females of their clans for their excellent treatment of them. A requirement Amelia had established, stating that if the females declared them unfit, the human females would definitely dismiss them. It had been a sore point amongst the males. Which was why I was here.

The warriors with me looked at me for direction. I pointed to four of them and motioned toward the mouth of the cave. They split off and the remaining warriors stayed within the cavern, spaced out with their eyes open and their weapons at the ready.

I mounted the stairs, spear in hand, and inspected the Geata while everyone readied themselves. It was a beautiful thing, carved to look like the Craobh na Beatha in exquisite detail. All the clear crystal acorns, the seeds of the tree, glinted in the sunlight that filtered in above. All except one. The middle crystal along the seam of the door that was fashioned into the trunk of the Craobh na Beatha carving. That one held a pinkish-red hue.

Amelia had explained her blood had held the two halves of the crystal on Earth together as she went through. The Oc'Veltas had postulated that she'd be the only one to get back through the Geata, as it was now tied to her very blood. She'd have to go through alone. A fact that had *not* sat well with Rhuger or Rìgh Thorn.

But Amelia was fearless. Turning, I looked at my friend as she kissed her cridhe, whispering to him as he fought the trembling in his hands. Desperately afraid he'd lose her like Rìgh Thorn had lost Ruth.

That she'd make it through the gate, but he'd couldn't follow. Doomed to live his life on Talam without her or their bairn growing in her belly.

Stepping away from her cridhe with purpose and determination, she waddled toward me and climbed the steps. Her bairn was growing quickly, far faster than orckin females carried, and the little one was large enough for concern. Per Amelia and Rìgh Thorn, she was two-thirds of the way through her pregnancy. They'd assured us all that the medical care Amelia would receive Earthside was comparable to the medical advancements the Oc'Veltas had finally started sharing with the other clans.

One of the many cunning additions to Amelia and Rhuger's terms with the clans who wished to take part in finding a mate Earthside. The concept was simple. We were many clans, yes, but we were also one people, fighting to survive. So all the best of each clan was combined and shared.

So far, it had been both a blessing and a curse as clans squabbled over resources and the changes to their ways of life. But in the end, things had smoothed out and every female on Talam breathed a collective sigh of relief.

The burden of keeping our kind from dying out was not our burden alone anymore.

"Well, here goes nothing," Amelia said when she stood next to me. She offered me a small smile and raised her hand to touch the middle crystal, the pink one. The cave was silent, none of us daring to breathe. A moment passed, then two, and frustrated sighs slipped from those nearby.

Then suddenly the magnificent rings carved behind the depiction of the Craobh na Beatha shuddered and ground into motion.

"It's working!" someone called. But my focus was solely on the Geata and Amelia, ready to snatch her back at the first hint of threat.

The door carved within the giant archway on the Geata split in half and slid away. Bright white light and rainbows poured through, bathing us all in celestial radiance. I saw something red pull taut and glanced down. A red thread wound down from my heart to my left hand and out into the tunnel of light that stood before us.

The red thread of destiny. Of fate. And my destiny lay on the other side of the Geata. My breath hitched in my lungs.

Amelia took one step into the tunnel, and I knew I had to go with her. I had to make it through. So I reached out and grabbed her shoulder. A tight pull in my belly yanked me forward into the light with Amelia.

We flew through the tunnel of light and rainbow. It throbbed with the tinkling of bells, the beating of great wings, and the sound of wind through trees. I couldn't draw breath with the force of how fast we hurtled through this pulsing vein of the Source itself.

A dark wall appeared ahead of us in the tunnel. An end. Between one blink and the next, we tumbled through it. I yanked Amelia back, and I turned with her in my arms as we fell to the ground. My shoulders and back met wet sand as Amelia landed atop me. I groaned, unable to draw breath. Amelia pulled back and looked down. Her face changed into one of shock.

"Gods, Sharn!" She cried as she rolled off of me. I wheezed, desperately trying to get air in my lungs. My friend was a lush, plump female, and she was pregnant. I was glad I cushioned her fall with my willowy frame, but I would have been more glad for some air. "How did you get through?"

I groaned some unintelligible nonsense and finally drew in one long, rasping breath. Once I could breathe, I sat up and looked at Amelia. "I'm not sure. I saw a red thread and knew I needed to come with you. So I grabbed your shoulder."

"Red thread, huh?" Amelia asked absently as we looked around. The Geata was there, just as it had been in the cave on Talam. But this one was made of stone, the wet, sandy floor slippery with kelp and smelling strongly of brine. "Well, this definitely looks like the sea cave on Earth."

I stood and held out my hand for Amelia. She grasped it in hers and I helped her stand. She looked back up at the Geata and went up the short flight of stairs. I followed her, spear in hand, hope a rising tide in my chest.

Could we actually do this? Get the Geata to work for more than just Amelia?

I watched as she pulled out the pouch with the crystal acorns that were the seeds from the Craobh na Beatha. The same crystals that shone in the divots within the identical carving to the one on Talam. Only the pink crystal on Talam was in one piece, this one was cleaved in half.

Amelia glanced up at me, took a breath, and removed the broken acorn. I reached out a hand to take the halves from her. A hand that was now a honey-gold color instead of my silver-grey skin.

"Amelia..." I rasped, and she smiled up at me.

"Looks like the chleoc ring still works its magic. You look human." I glanced at her in utter panic and realized she looked different, too. Her ears were rounded and her skin no longer held that pearl grey luster. "We'll talk about it in a minute. I want to get the gate working before Rhuger and Grandpa have a collective aneurysm."

"A what?" I asked a little breathlessly. But she ignored me and opened the pouch in her fist. She drew out an acorn and studied it. Deeming it whole, she then gently slid it into the empty divot.

A few moments passed, and nothing happened. Then the points of light around the carved doorway lit up, scattering rainbows across the sea cave. The carved rings ground into motion as the door opened back onto the tunnel of light. I pulled Amelia aside. But not before I'd seen two red threads. One attached to Amelia, and one that faded out past the gate.

I turned to see where the second red thread led here on Earth and paused. A human woman stood there, panting, with wild eyes. She had silver grey hair tied up in a knot on the top of her head and looked an awful lot like Amelia, despite the weathered wrinkles on her face.

"Amelia." I murmured and elbowed her. "Someone's here."

Amelia turned and looked where I was staring at the female. She took a big breath and started laughing and crying.

"Grandma!" she cried and bustled over to the human female who still stood staring at Amelia as if she'd disappear. "Grandma, I'm back!"

"And *pregnant*! What the hell happened to you over there, sweetness?" The woman, who I realized must be Banrigh Ruth, clutched Amelia to her like she'd drown if she didn't. "Who is this?"

"There's *so much* to explain, but this is Sharn. She's orckin and my best friend." A chiming sounded behind us as Amelia said, "But there's more. I've got a surprise for you..."

Heartbeats later, Rhuger and Rìgh Thorn stepped out of the tunnel of light. I stepped back, out of the way, so I could watch as things played out.

"*Thorn*..." Banrigh Ruth breathed as she looked at where Rìgh Thorn had just exited the Geata. Her eyes went wide, and she had a hard time finding her breath as tears tumbled over her lashes. "*THORN!*" Her voice broke on his name as she collapsed onto the wet sand.

"*Ruth*..." Rìgh Thorn whispered his mate's name like a broken prayer. A wretched sob escaped Banrigh Ruth's throat. Rìgh Thorn rushed to her. He landed in front of his mate on his knees and pulled her into his massive arms.

Banrigh Ruth threw her arms around his neck and wailed like her heart was breaking. Or mending. Watching them hold one another tight, crying, and letting the years apart fall away from them was beautiful. And painful.

Because it was a cridhe bond they shared. That red thread had stopped at Banrigh Ruth's hand and disappeared once Rìgh Thorn had stepped through the Geata. Amelia and Rhuger weren't the first orckin to find their cridhe. It had been Rìgh Thorn and Ruth, his human mate.

Swallowing hard, I quietly stalked to the mouth of the cave as they had their well-earned reunion. There was too much inside my head and heart to stand around and watch. So instead, I picked my way along the dark tunnel that led out onto a sandy beach. Ocean wind blew my hair out of my face as my boots met sand. Waves crashed along the shore in a slate blue-green.

Looking up, there was only *one* sun hanging in the sky, small and bright. Fog slipped by overhead and the world dimmed. Strange birds called to one another. Some were white and grey with orange feet. These had high calls and fought over what they found on the beach. The others were all black, large, and imposing as they sat in a tree that grew out of the side of the nearby cliff face. A trail switchbacked along the cliff from the beach to the top where Orc Rock Farm must be.

Nothing dangerous seemed to be in the nearby vicinity and I breathed a heavy sigh of relief, setting the butt of my spear in the sand. Amelia had told me the farm was peaceful, with only a few people who lived or worked on it. Regardless, I'd mentally planned out every likely scenario.

Glancing down, I looked at my body, my skin, and my clawless hands. Where my skin had once been a lovely light storm grey color, now it was the color of watered-down uisge-beatha. Like the honey our notoriously difficult seillean produced when they pollinated our fields. My hair was still inky black, but I knew my eyes would be different and it unsettled me. How would they look with all the black around my irises being white instead?

And beyond my physical changes with the chleoc ring on my finger, I felt heavier in my body, and a riot had begun in my chest like a massive storm. I only came here as captain of the Iolaire'lasair. As a guard and leader to help establish this opportunity for my kind. If the red thread between Amelia and Rhuger, Rìgh Thorn and Banrigh Ruth meant they were cridhe...

Did seeing my thread mean that my cridhe, the one person in all the universe who was the other part of my soul, was here on Earth?

Heart racing and my ribs feeling like they were about to splinter, I stared out at sea, at the rolling waves as they overlaid one another on their way to shore. Then the one question I dreaded swelled in my mind. I swallowed hard and grit my teeth against the pain.

Would my cridhe be male?

Or would my cridhe defy all the odds, the will of the gods, and every tradition my people held dear regarding cridhe, and truly be what I craved with every fiber of my being? Softness and warmth wrapped up in the nurturing form of a lusciously plump goddess?

Would she be female, like me?

The flicker of hope in my chest guttered in the winds of fate, but held true.

AFTERWORD

A FEW WORDS ON CHAPTERS 30-32...

Rhuger's Pearl & Rhuger's Cridhe have not just been a love letter to Connor but also a love letter to that part of me that got me through the last few years. Through zero dark thirty, when you delve into your own soul and come back alive. I somehow got myself out of an abusive situation that would have led to this story never being written had I stayed. Because I would have found another way out.

The last few chapters took *months* to write, and it took me precisely that long to figure out why. At first, I wasn't healed enough to do it without breaking. Then I procrastinated like a little shit and couldn't figure out why I had such a hangup. When I decided to finish Chapter 32 first and work backward, it hit me in the face like a rotten salmon. It was because, in writing Amelia facing her abuser, that would mean I had to face mine, too.

I don't know if I'll ever be comfortable with how the final chapters turned out. But then again, I shouldn't have to be, should I? NO ONE should have to feel like they need to be comfortable with something like that. Should never *have* to forgive someone for that.

If you're in a similar situation, I fervently hope you get the help that you need, and a pathway out as *safely* as you can. Do not forget to look back as you heal to see how far you've really come. It's farther than you think.

If you've survived, I see you. I hope this book was as cathartic for you to read as it was for me to write. The cyclical nature of healing means we face the trauma over and over until the wound becomes a scab which becomes a scar. Until we've put enough good memories between now and then that it doesn't sting quite so bad.

I love you. You can do this. Keep going.

WHAT THOSE WORKING CLOSELY WITH ME ON THIS BOOK HAD TO SAY WHEN I LET THEM KNOW CHAPTERS 30-32 WERE DONE...

"But Carlotta you need to pause... pause... You just wrote this chapter. And it was so hard to write you couldn't figure out why it was so hard to write. So, like, think about that. It's very true. It's a really good wrap-up. And it feels like you can set the book free. Just like you freed yourself."

- Jenifer Wood *Editor*

"And yes, Carlotta, Jen is absolutely right. You're setting the story free, and therefore setting yourself free. And I'm so fucking proud of you."

- Jersey Konlyn *Main Beta Reader*

"My pride in you only increases, you are pushing yourself so hard, and you have pushed yourself out of your comfort zone. You are amazing. I'm proud of you. The path to recovery is shrouded in anger and pain. You have gone so far, and are still pushing on, you are a warrior. You're a badass. Just so you know."

- Connor *Lover and Muse*

INDEX &
PRONUNCIATION GUIDE

Online Pronunciation Guide With Audio:

https://www.authorcarlottahughes.com/orc-matched-pronounciation-guide.html

ALL VOICE CLIPS SOURCED WITH PERMISSION FROM
https://learngaelic.scot/

Please note that not all words have a pronunciation guide or a link to the audio. These words are pronounced phonetically and are the creation of the author.

EVERYDAY WORDS

NAMING:

Cridhe (p. Cridheachan): [/krʲi.ə/] Heart; the title of an orckin's soulbound partner and mate

Daonna: [/dɯːNə/] Human

Fògradh: [/fɔːgrəy/] Exile

Gaiseadh: [/gaʃəy/] Blight

Taobh A'Muigh: [/tɯːv/ /ə'muj/] Outsider; usually what someone is called if they are not part of a clan

Neamhnaid: [/Nʲãũnɪdʲ/] Pearl; often a nickname for a princess or female of royal blood or someone with a pearly sheen to their skin

Duhb'Oidhche: [/ duh/ /ɐ̃çə/] Black Night; a rare night that is both moonless and starless, the dark all-encompassing. A nickname given to the Orclings of Neit, the god of war.

FAMILY:

Màthair: [/maːhərʲ/] Mother

Athair: [/ahərʲ/] Father

Piuthar: [/pju.ər/] Sister

Bràthair: [/braːhɪrʲ/] Brother

ROYALTY NAMING:

Rìgh: [/Riː/] King

Banrigh: [/bãũNRɪ/] Queen

Leanabh Rìgh: [/Lʲɛnəv/ /Riː/] Prince

Leanabh Banrigh: [/Lʲɛnəv/ /bãũNRɪ/] Princess

Fear a Chì (p. Feadhainn a Chì): [/fɛr/ /ə'/ /hee/] Spiritual leader of each clan. They are conduits to the Source and are often caretakers of the orphaned orclings; often female

ROYAL ITEMS:

Seud Iteach: [/ʃiad/ /ihdʲəx/] A feathered ornament that Leanabh Rìgh wear in their hair

Seud Neamhnaid: [/ʃiad/ /Nʲãũnɪdʲ/] A pearl ornament Leanabh Banrigh wear in their hair

SPIRITUAL PLACES:

Craobh na Beatha: [/krɯːv/ /nə/ /bɛhə/] Tree of Life

Gàrradh: [/gaːRəɣ/] A circle of trees interwoven like a protective cage with a fire pit and resting places for weary travelers; a holdover from when Talam was first created

Geata: [/gʲɛhdə/] gate, the carved gate within the Craobh na Beatha and the sea cave at Orc Rock Farm

Neach-gleidhidh: [/Nʲɛx/ /gleː/] Sentinel, one of the giant beings that look as if they're made of stone. It is an ancient tale regarding the birth of Talam and how if ever a time came when the planet would be ruined by the orckin, the Sentinels would come alive and wipe the planet clean to start again

SPIRITUAL ITEMS:

Chleoc: [/klɔːxgə/] An ancient type of ring that cloaks the appearance of orcs to look more human-like, a common item left over from the ages past when humans and orcs traveled to one another's lands

Clach Grèine: [/kLax/ /'ɹɾʲeːnʲə/] sunstones; stones that absorb the heat of the sun during the day and expel the heat at night

Frith-rathad: [/frʲi/ /Ra.ad/] Path; often regarding one's life path or destiny

Tog Taigh: [/tog/ /tʁj/] The building of a house for the express purpose of impressing a potential mate. The urge to build a home for a mate is strong amongst males, but can also occur amongst females, though this is rare. This urge and creation of a home is something revered amongst the orckin as a rite of passage and often has to be earned by acts of service within the clan.

LEGENDARY PEOPLE:

Banrigh na Gealach: [/baũNRɪ/ /na/ /gʲaLəx/] The Moon Queen who fell in love with the Night King. She gave up her celestial position and came to Talam to be with him. He fell to her knees, love-struck and she was the only one he ever bowed to. Their love spawned the cridhe bond and began a new age of prosperity for the orckin.

Rìgh na Oidhche: [/Riː/ /na/ / ɤçə/] The Night King who fell in love with the Moon Queen who came down from the stars out of love for him. He fell to his knees and swore fealty to her alone. Their love spawned the cridhe bond and began a new age of prosperity for the orckin.

LANGUAGE:

Common: English

Teanga Dhubh: [/tʲɛŋgə/ /ɣuh/] Black tongue, the primary orckin language

HEALTH & WELLNESS:

An'sgudal: [/əN(ʲ)/ /sgudəL/] The wasting illness that strikes the orckin, predominately affecting females and orclings; accompanied by the Dorcha'aon, it is unknown how they are connected

ANIMALS:

Buabhall: [/buə.əL/] A fluffy, bison-looking creature that wanders the plains within Oc'Turin territory

Cnuimh: [/krũĩv/] Worm

Cuileagan: [/kulagan/] Flies

Dorcha'aon: [/dɔrɔxə/ /ũ:n/] An apex predator with six legs, six glowing eyes, and a maw filled with sharp teeth; they come with the an'sgudal and eat the males and their nocrys

Eun'bogha-froise: [/ian/ /bo.ə'frɔʃə/] A large bird whose plumage is the colors of the rainbow; they like to fly amongst rainbows after a storm

Iolaire'lasair: [/juLɪrʲə/ /Lasɪrʲ/] Fire eagle or phoenix

Moileasgan: [pronounced similarly to mollusk] Enormous mollusk that is carnivorous and will lie under the sand in wait then snap closed around their prey; neamhnaid are found within the Moileasgan

Nocrys: Large felines which act as steeds and guardians to the orckin; they have black or dark grey fur and scales and choose their rider

Fuar Nocrys: [/fuər/] Nocrys that are found in the snowy mountain ranges of the Oc'Blyre; they are white and grey to blend in with their surroundings

Seillean: [/ʃeLʲan/] Bees specific to Talam. They are notoriously difficult to hive as they often will have two queen bees per swarm

FOOD:

Luibh Gaoil: [/Lɯiv/ /gɯ:L/] Whiskey spiked with an herb that triggers a state similar to the cridhe frenzy

Uisge-beatha: [/ɯʃgʲə'bɛhə/] very strong whiskey distilled by the orckin

Fìon-math: [/fiən/ /ma/] A floral wine that's lighter on the palate than uisge-beatha

Cofaidh: [/kɔfɪ/] A drink similar to coffee

Dearc Ruadh: [/dʲɛrxg/ /Ruəɣ/] An edible red berry the size of a cherry that grows on a bush with black leaves; has a tart taste similar to cherries

Tiùbar: [/tʲuːbər/] Edible tubers with a mushroom-like stalk that looks like a dildo. All parts are edible but need to be roasted

A'crathadh Cnòthan: [/ə/ /krahəɣ/ /krɔ̃ː.ən/] Nuts from the tree with the waving noodle-like spikes on the trunk; the nutmeat tastes like pumpkin seeds and peanuts

Aran: [/aran/] Bread

Càise: [/kaːʃə/] Similar to cheese, it's made from the hardened sap of a tree

Fighe Inntinn Bog: [/fi.ə/ /ĩːNʲdʲɪNʲ/ /bog/] Similar to marijuana but a lot stronger

Caraiceag: [/karɪgʲag/] Pancake-like food stuffed with nuts and honey

PLANTS:

Folach Vines: [/fɔLəx/] Long trailing vines that are found growing over the entrances to Baile Coille within the Fàinne Sleagh. They have broad, spear-like leaves and their flowers bloom on the underside of the leaves. The flowers have a pleasant odor and the pollen has properties connected to the dorcha'aon.

ITEMS:

Concrait: [pronounced similarly to concrete] A building material similar to concrete

LOCATIONS & CLANS:

EARTH:

Earth: The planet where Amelia is from

Orc Rock Farm: A dilapidated farm that Ruth buys and transforms, with Thorn's help, into a Tolkien-inspired bed-and-breakfast based on Hobbiton

TALAM:

A planet with three moons that orbits twin stars in a solar system across the universe from Earth. There are many continents, but none have been explored outside of the primary continent in which the orckin reside.

Talam: The planet on which the orcs live, also the continent on which they reside

Muir Sgàil: [/murʲ/ /sga:l/] The Shadow Sea, is a large body of water that is a host to all kinds of monster-like creatures that make sailing across it impossible

OC'DELLOR:

A clan of orckin who reside in the forested lands of Talam. They tend to have grey coloring to help them blend in with the shadows, teeth similar to a wolf's, and live in tree homes built into the giant trees.

Leader: *Rìgh Thorn Oc'Dellor & Banrigh Ruth Dellor*

Baile Coille: [/balə/ /kɤLʲə/] The forest city of the Oc'Dellor

Daingneach: [/daiŋʲgʲNʲəx/] The fortress where the Oc'Dellor rulers live

Eun'bogha-froise Market: [/ian/ /bo.ə ˈfrɔʃə/] A large winding market lined with vendor stalls and colored brightly like a rainbow.

Craobh Bean Glic: [/krɯːv/ /bɛn/ /gliçgʲ/] The wise woman tree where the Fear a Chì and the orphaned orclings live

Craobh Brathaidh: [/krɯːv/ /brahəɣ/] The traitor tree where traitors are hung for their crimes; is located next to the fortress Daingneach

Fàinne Sleagh: [/faːNʲə/ /ʃlɤɣ/] The stone ring of the caldera that juts up through the trees surrounding Baile Coille as a natural fortification

Noc'tal Forest: The wide forest surrounding Fàinne Sleagh that borders Oc'Sentan and Oc'Turin lands

OC'TURIN:

A clan of orckin who reside in the steppes and rolling hills of Talam. Their coloring leans more towards greens and browns to blend in with the grasses and stones of the steppes. Their teeth have large, sharp canines and flat molars. They live primarily in stone homes with living roofs, blending into the environment. They are often considered the harshest of the orckin as their training is brutal and starts early and they are rigid in their views of females.

Leader: *Rìgh Orok Oc'Verna & Banrigh Sagra Oc'Byrne*(**PREVIOUSLY:** *Rìgh Orok Oc'Verna & Banrigh Sagra Oc'Byrne)*

Clach-tholl: [/kLax/ /tɔuL/] The stone capital city of the Oc'Turin built into the sides of a gorge over a river.

Cìp Carragh: [/kʲiːhb/ /kaʀəɣ/] The stone keep where the Oc'Turin rulers live; there are many caves dug into the hard rock of the steppes that are connected to it

Feurach Clachach: [/fiarəx/ /kLaxəx/] The name of the steppes and stone grasslands of the Oc'Turin that borders the Oc'Dellor and Oc'Blyre lands

Carrachan Neach-gleidhidh: [/kaʀəxan/ /Nʲɛx/ /gleː/] A Sentinel surrounded by a unique ring of standing stones; cairns are erected for the dead here in a spiral pattern

OC'VELTAS:

A reclusive clan of orckin who reside in the isles on the eastern coast of Talam. Their coloring leans more towards blues and sea greens to blend in with the waters that they often swim in. Their teeth are narrow and sharp. They live primarily in The Citadel in homes made of stone and glass. They have isolated themselves for generations and have technologies far beyond the other clans.

Leader: *Banrigh Aria Oc'Veltas*

Tòrr Chathair: [/tɔːʀ/ /kahɪrʲ/] Oc'Veltas city, also often called The Citadel

Geodha Corranach: [/gʲɔ.ə/ /kɔʀanəx/] The crooked coves, channels, and islands that are scattered between The Citadel and the mainland

OC'SENTAN:

A clan of migrating orckin who reside in the jungles and desert of northern Talam. Their coloring leans more towards dun and orange colors to blend in with the rock and sand. Their teeth are the most human-like with prominent canines. They are the most difficult of the clans to track down as they migrate with their mobile homes following the rains. They are excellent trackers and hunters.

Leader: *Rìgh Pàdruig Oc'Sentan & Banrigh Ealasaid Oc'Druim*

Fras Raonach: [/fras/ /Rɯːnəx/] The rain wilds are a mix between plains and desert, the monsoon rains come seasonally and replenish the wildlife

Òrdha Beinn-sheilg: [/ɔːrɣa/ /beiNʲ //] The jungle in which the Oc'Sentant do most of their hunting and gathering with lots of wild edible plants

Fàsach Coinnich: [/faːsəx/ /kɤNʲɪç/] The circular plain within the jungle where the caravans meet up each triple moon cycle to trade

OC'BLYRE:

A clan of giant orckin who reside in caves carved into the mountains in the south of Talam. Their coloring ranges from brows to greys to whites to fit in with their cold, rocky climate. Their teeth are sharp with tusks and can reach over eight feet tall. They are well adapted to the cold and mine the mountains for ore and sunstones.

Leader: *Rìgh Frang Oc'Blyre & Ruairidh Oc'Roideach*

Niomhair Abhainn-deighe: [/Nʲivɛrʲ/ /a.ɪNʲ/ /dʲejə/] A giant glacier that snakes like a river through the mountains

Neulach Callaid Bheann: [/NʲiəLəx/ /kaLadʲ/ /bjauN/] The mountain range along the south of Talam with peaks so high they're obscured in the clouds

Creagan Speur: [/krʲegʲan/ /sbiər/] A cliff city carved into a mountainside where the Oc'Blyre live

CONTENT AWARENESS*

I have sought to be thorough in identifying potential triggers, both explicit and mentioned, including kinks and mental health awareness. This is for the comfortability of readers who are sensitive to triggering content and because I believe in the informed consent of my readers. If you find any mentions of triggering content that I have not included, email me at *authorcarlottahughes@gmail.com* so I can address it within reason.

*Please note that chapter titles marked with an * mean there are explicit scenes. I've included mentions of triggering content below, though they are not specially marked in the chapter titles. Some triggers are generalized throughout the book and aren't specifically identified in the chapter breakdowns (i.e. misogyny). I do not write rape scenes. However, characters have that as part of their backstory and there are questionable consent moments (immediately stopped, addressed, and resolved).*

List of General Triggers: Misogyny, Extinction, Gaslighting, Societally Expected Pregnancy, DV Survivorship

List of Explicit Triggers: General Violence & Assault, Beheading, Abduction, Pregnancy, Head Trauma, Autistic Shutdown, Torture, Mutilation of Hands/Feet, Dismembered Arm, Concussion, Eye Injury,

Neck Grip, Bruising

List of Mentioned Triggers: Mentioned Sexual Assault, Mentioned Neurodivergent Conformity, Mentioned Mental & Emotional Abuse, Descriptions of Corpses, Descriptions of Wounds, Mention of Attempted Incest, Descriptions of Torture, Mention of Death by Beheading

List of Kinks: Praise, Knotting, Pleasure Dom, Breeding, Exhibitionism, Primal, Bloodplay, Marking, Tandem Masturbation, Masochism, Overstimulation, Back Clawing

List of Mental Health Awareness: PTSD, Anxiety, Depression, Panic Attacks, IED, Autism, Emotional Release, Autistic/Neurodivergent Shutdown, Autistic/Neurodivergent Meltdown, Dissociation

Chapter 01*: Pregnancy

Chapter 02*: General Violence, Dismembered Arm, Beheading, Eye Injury, Head Trauma

Chapter 03*: Head Trauma, Concussion, Neck Grip, General Violence, Dismembered Arm

Chapter 04*: Dissociation, Descriptions of Corpses, Bruising

Chapter 05*: Descriptions of wounds: broken nose, bloodied feet, split lip, swollen eye, deep lash marks, bound and chaffed wrists, bruising

Chapter 06*: Dissociation, Forced Voyerism, General Violence, Sexual Violence, mention of SA, Explicit Misogyny, Description of wounds: chaffed wrists, bruising

Chapter 07*: Descriptions of torture, wounds and bruising, Dissociation, General Violence, Gore, Beheading, Exhibitionism, Voyerism, IED

Chapter 08*: General Violence, Beheading, Gore, Bruising, Exhibitionism, IED, Mention of Attempted Incest (M/M)

Chapter 30*: Confronting Abuser

Chapter 31*: Confronting Abuser, PTSD, Flashbacks, mention of SA, mention of abuse, Gaslighting

Chapter 32*: Confronting Abuser, PTSD, mention of SA, Gaslighting, mention of chronic illness, mention of abuse, mention of restraining order, threats of removing manhood and eyeballs

Epilogue:

Excerpt From Sharn's Honeybee: Orc Matched 2.0:

Afterword: Mention of trauma, mention of SA, mention of depression, mention of suicidal ideation, mention of abuse

ACKNOWLEDGMENTS

A huge thank you to YOU for reading my book! I hope you've enjoyed Amelia and Rhuger's story! But it won't end here... you'll see them again.

I have to give a *major* shout-out to my fellow Trash Cats, podcasting buddies from *Smut Tea Stories Podcast*, writing comrades, and overall besties Jenifer Wood and Jersey Konlyn. You guys kept me sane, kept me going, and bribed me into completing *Rhuger's Pearl* and *Rhuger's Cridhe*, the 'orc bible', with coffee and flowers.

Connor, no amount of thanks will ever be enough to express my appreciation and gratitude for you. You've gone MIA and all I can do is wait for my Righ mo Cridhe to come home. No matter what, I'm incredibly proud of you and all that you've overcome in your life. You've brought color back into my world when all I could see was an endless grey. To me, you are the embodiment of every perfect, beautiful, poignant moment I've ever experienced, condensed into a giant grumpy bean, a hardass, and a wolf who's really a puppy on the inside. I see you, and I am not afraid.

I'd like to thank my writing group, The Degenerate Syndicate: Maddie Syn, Chloe Parker, Brianna Everly, Krista Luna, Ursa Dax, Sara

Ivy Hill, Ami Wright, L.A. Holloway, Jinx Layne, Victoria Aveline, Anne Riland, Kimberly Lemming, Luna Wolff, & Matilda Vega. Thanks for the encouragement, help, alien peen jokes, and for letting me live-stream drawing alien peen during our hangouts. We do it for the science.

And to my fellow authors whose support has meant everything: S.E. Wendel, M. Bonneau, Bevin Shea, Miranda Sapphire, Mary Warren, Mita Merak, Trish Heinrich, Tiffany Roberts, Wren K. Morris, Lark Green, Flora Quincy, Jenn Howlett, Catrina Bell, Luna Wolff, and so many more!

ABOUT THE AUTHOR

Carlotta Hughes is a giant orc-like lady living with her four cats and an enormous book collection. She wrote a creation story with a polar bear at age five and has been writing ever since. When not reading or writing, she's often exploring, hyper-fixating on a new creative outlet, and generally being a bubbly goblin hermit. She loves snacks, being warm, weapons, and snuggles.

Carlotta writes thorny, corny, horny stories with sassy one-liners, alt-human love interests, sexually frustrated characters, lots of simping, and guaranteed HEA. Her stories explore the spectrum of humanity, including disabilities, gender, sexuality, kinks, and survivorship. You know, for science.

- Website: https://www.authorcarlottahughes.com/
- Amazon: https://www.amazon.com/Carlotta-Hughes/e/B09P9S6JVH
- TikTok: @authorcarlottahughes
- Instagram: @authorcarlottahughes

ALSO BY...

ORC MATCHED SERIES

0.5 THORN'S DOVE (2022)

1.0 RHUGER'S PEARL (2023)

1.5 RHUGER'S CRIDHE (2023)

2.0 SHARN'S HONEYBEE (Coming 2023)

2.5 RHUGER'S TINSEL (Coming 2023)

3.0 SIGG'S KITTEN (Coming 2023)

Made in the USA
Coppell, TX
16 September 2023

21651988R00203